Anonymous

The Arena

Anonymous

The Arena

ISBN/EAN: 9783337404338

Printed in Europe, USA, Canada, Australia, Japan

Cover: Foto ©Andreas Hilbeck / pixelio.de

More available books at **www.hansebooks.com**

No. 36

A Common-Sense Remedy.

In the matter of curatives what you want is something that will do its work while you continue to do yours — a remedy that will give you no inconvenience nor interfere with your business. Such a remedy is ALLCOCK'S POROUS PLASTERS. These plasters are not an experiment; they have been in use for over thirty years, and their value has been attested by the highest medical authorities, as well as by voluntary testimonials from those who have used them.

ALLCOCK'S POROUS PLASTERS are purely vegetable and absolutely harmless. They require no change of diet and are not affected by wet or cold. Their action does not interfere with labor or business; you can toil and yet be cured while hard at work. They are so pure that the youngest, the oldest, the most delicate person of either sex can use them with great benefit.

Beware of imitations, and do not be deceived by misrepresentation. Ask for ALLCOCK'S, and let no solicitation or explanation induce you to accept a substitute.

WANTED, TO CORRESPOND

WITH some philanthropic person of means, looking to the development of a project in aid of and for the benefit of suffering humanity. I have written an Industrial-Financial Drama, dedicated to our Social-Industrial Victims, which I desire to place on the stage, with a view of raising funds to in a degree relieve the temporary evil conditions of these victims. The play can be staged in thirty days, but I am not financially able to do it, hence my desire to correspond and negotiate with some party who may be. I have a plan fully matured by which I believe it possible to realize from $500 to $1,500 per night, and make it immediately available. My design is to raise a sort of an emergency fund to relieve worthy cases temporarily, still to leave it open to people to aid any fund for which they may have a preference. I desire that the entire proceeds of the play shall go to some relief funds after the running expenses of presentation are deducted, although there would be no objection to a sinking fund to repay the advance made to get the play on the boards and to form a fund against contingencies; but in a general way it should not be made a personal money-making scheme. Any one willing to take hold of this project, which may be of such vast relief to our social victims, and having the money, will receive my plans in detail by addressing

S. G. HOWE, Detroit, Mich.

Beautiful Japan Proofs.

A limited number of Japan Proofs of Kingsley's Original Wood Engravings can be had by sending the order to the address of the artist as given below. The following is only a partial list of subjects:

1. **CROWN OF NEW ENGLAND. Original. Price, $20.**

   This is Mr. Kingsley's latest work. "It is a scene in the White Mountains, in the northern part of New England, where Maine and New Hampshire join their boundaries with Canada, and where, on an elevated plateau, many different water courses take their rise. From this Crown of New England, tributaries lead northwest and northeast to the great St. Lawrence; eastward the rivers of Maine wind their tortuous channels to the Atlantic; while the beautiful Connecticut, starting from the uttermost point of the Granite State, takes a straight southern course through the heart of New England to Long Island Sound."

2. **NEW ENGLAND ELMS. Original. Price, $15.**

   This is one of the most beautiful Proofs in the collection.

3. **SILENCE. Price, $15.**

   After William Bliss Baker. This is considered by many to be Mr. Kingsley's finest work.

4. **THE OLD WELL. Price, $15.**

   After J. Francis Murphy.

5. **HISTORIC GROUND IN THE CONNECTICUT VALLEY. Original. Price, $10.**

   This interesting Proof shows the site of an Indian battle-ground in Hadley, Mass., in 1675; it commemorates that vague but beautiful legend of the sudden and mysterious appearance of General Goffe at the head of the citizens, and by whose skill and prowess the Indians were defeated.

6. **MIDSUMMER. Price, $15.**

   After Daubigny. A most beautiful Proof.

7. **LATE SUMMER. Original. Price, $10.**

8. **A JOURNEY NORTHWARD. Original. Price, $10.**

9. **BOHEMIANS. Price, $5.**

10. **BLOODY BROOK. Price, $5.**

11. **FIRST ENGRAVING FROM NATURE. Price, $5.**

All these Proofs are printed on Japan paper properly mounted, and are signed by the Artist. They will be sent by mail or express upon receipt of the price. Address all orders to

ELBRIDGE KINGSLEY,

HADLEY. MASS.

COPLEY SQUARE SERIES.

I. Bond-Holders and Bread-Winners.

By S. S. KING, Esq., Kansas City, Kansas.

The most powerful book of the year. Its argument is irresistible. You should read it.

President L. L. Polk, National F. A. and I. U., says: "It should be placed in the hands of every voter of this country."

Price, post-paid, 25 cents.   Per hundred, $12.50.

II. Money, Land, and Transportation.

CONTENTS.

1. A NEW DECLARATION OF RIGHTS. *Hamlin Garland.*
2. THE FARMER, INVESTOR, AND THE RAILWAY. *C. Wood Davis.*
3. THE INDEPENDENT PARTY AND MONEY AT COST. *R. B. Hassell.*

Price, single copy, 25 cents.   Per hundred, $10.

III. Industrial Freedom. The Triple Demand of Labor.

CONTENTS.

1. THE MONEY QUESTION. *Hon. John Davis.*
2. THE SUB-TREASURY PLAN. *C. C. Post.*
3. THE RAILROAD PROBLEM. { *C. Wood Davis.* { *Ex-Gov. Lionel A. Sheldon.*

Price, single copy, 25 cents.   Per hundred, $10.

IV. ESAU; or, The Banker's Victim.

"ESAU" is the title of a new book by Dr. T. A. BLAND. It is a political novel of purpose and power. As a romance it is fascinating: as a history of a mortgage it is tragic, and as an exposé of the financial policy of the old parties it is clear and forcible. It is a timely and valuable campaign book.

Price, single copy, 25 cents.   Per hundred, $12.50.

V. The People's Cause.

CONTENTS.

1. THE THREEFOLD CONTENTION OF INDUSTRY.
   Gen. J. B. Weaver, Presidential Nominee of People's Party.
2. THE NEGRO QUESTION IN THE SOUTH.
   Hon. Thos. E. Watson, M. C. from Georgia.
3. THE MENACE OF PLUTOCRACY. *B. O. Flower, Editor of The Arena.*
4. THE COMMUNISM OF CAPITAL. *Hon. John Davis, M. C. from Kansas.*
5. THE PENDING PRESIDENTIAL CAMPAIGN. *Hon. J. H. Kyle, State Senator from South Dakota, Thomas E. Watson, M. C. from Georgia.*

Price, 25 cents a copy.   Per hundred, $10.

ix

LIBRARY OF THE WORLD'S BEST BOOKS

EMBRACING

Masterpieces of the World's Greatest Thinkers.

On the following pages we give a brief description of a choice collection of the world's best books. Each volume is handsomely bound in dark brown cloth, stamped in gold, with gilt top. They are bound for libraries. The type is large and clear, the paper excellent, and everything in the general make-up handsome. The price of each volume is $1.00, post-paid, but all orders should be sent direct to us.

Part I. Standard Works for Thinkers.

JOHN RUSKIN.

Ruskin's Crown of Wild Olive, and Sesame and Lilies.

The Crown of Wild Olive, and Sesame and Lilies. By JOHN RUSKIN, LL. D. Portrait.

Under the first of these fanciful titles are presented three lectures on Work, Traffic, and War, and under the second, one lecture upon Reading and Books and another upon the Education and Social Condition of Women. They all show the pronounced characteristics of their author, wild and extravagant in thought and diction, but marked by intense power, suggestive and original, and often keenly logical. Although his province is primarily and peculiarly Art, Ruskin here appears as a thinker impelled by sympathies of extraordinary power to reflect on the general condition, social and religious, of mankind. In this capacity he is probably the foremost writer of the day on practical sociology or economic ethics. As a great and fearless leader of thought, and antagonistic to many features of our social order, he is naturally the object of much violent criticism, but is warmly admired and loved by a great part of the reading world, and coming ages will accord him his due. He has told the world new truth, and the world will grow up to his majestic stature. — *Robert Thorne.*

The Origin of Species, by Means of Natural Selection, or the Preservation of a Favored Race in the Struggle for Life.

By CHARLES DARWIN.

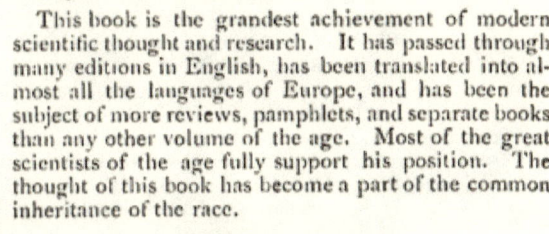

This book is the grandest achievement of modern scientific thought and research. It has passed through many editions in English, has been translated into almost all the languages of Europe, and has been the subject of more reviews, pamphlets, and separate books than any other volume of the age. Most of the great scientists of the age fully support his position. The thought of this book has become a part of the common inheritance of the race.

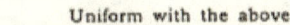

Uniform with the above,

The Descent of Man.

By CHARLES DARWIN, with Portrait.

CHARLES DARWIN.

Since the publication of the " Origin of Species " by the same author, no book of science has excited a keener or more widespread interest than the " Descent of Man." On its appearance it aroused at once a storm of mingled wrath, wonder, and admiration. In elegance of style, charm of manner, and deep knowledge of natural history, it stands almost without a rival among scientific works. In the " Origin of Species " the doctrine of *organic evolution* by means of *natural selection* was set forth and illustrated in the general way. In this volume we have the author's own first application of the general theory to a given case, namely, man himself. *Sexual selection* is here brought forward more prominently, and *natural selection* is presented as adequate means of the evolution of not only man's natural organism, but also his moral faculties, his emotional susceptibilities, his instincts and his intelligence from rudimentary forms. Clearly it is impossible to overestimate the magnitude of the issue. Later investigation may confirm the older belief that man's intellect and moral sense are and ever must be inscrutable from the point of view offered by natural history; still much of Mr. Darwin's work must stand for all times. He had long held the *derivative theory*, before he convinced himself of *natural selection* as the *mode*. Finally his vast accumulation of facts not only established this special principle, but also furnished the strongest evidence ever presented of the general doctrine of descent. — *R. T. Horne.*

Essays.

By RALPH WALDO EMERSON.

The terse, epigrammatic force, the intense life and singular beauty of Emerson's writings demonstrate that he has something to say and knows how to say it. He has much practical acuteness, and his observations on society, manners, and character evince great sagacity and insight and a familiar acquaintance with the homely phases of life. He is the truest and noblest exponent of the American spirit and citizenship, and the deep impression he has made upon his age bespeaks for him an enduring fame. He exercised a great power over men; he brought them wide comfort, and to him more than any man of his time belongs the glory of having taught them that life was worth the living.

RALPH WALDO EMERSON.

Standard Works for Thinkers — Continued.

First Principles.
By HERBERT SPENCER.

Mr. Spencer, rising to a sublime scope of thought, has presented to the world the conception of a universal system of philosophy, the explanation of the universe in its physical, mental, and moral aspects, by the operation of a single law ; the persistence of force under multiform transformations. Mr. M. S. Lilly says : "I regard him with much admiration, sincere respect, and lively gratitude. I admire the fertility and subtlety of his intellect and his singular power of generalization. I respect the heroic courage and faith."

HERBERT SPENCER.

Uniform with the above.

Data of Ethics.
By HERBERT SPENCER, with Portrait.

Herbert Spencer is the foremost name in the philosophic literature of the world. He is the Shakespeare of science. He has a grander grasp of knowledge and more perfect conscious correspondence with the external universe than any other human being who ever looked wonderingly out into the starry depths ; and his few errors flow from an over anxiety to exert his splendid power of making beautiful generalizations. Plato and Spencer are brothers. Plato would have done what Spencer has, had he lived in the nineteenth century.— *From "The World's Best Books," by Frank Parsons.*

A Thousand Miles Up the Nile.
By AMELIA B. EDWARDS.

The volume contains a little history, many interesting facts, much practical suggestion, abundant humor and charm, and also numerous illustrations of Egyptian discoveries and remains. Miss Edwards' description of Cairo, of the Nile voyage in a dahabeeyah, of the ancient city of Thebes, of the passage of the cataract, of the sacred island of Philea, in short, of the fascination of Egyptian travel, is like "apples of gold in pictures of silver." Rarely does a book contain instruction in such large measure as this one.

AMELIA B. EDWARDS.

Bryce's Holy Roman Empire.

The Holy Roman Empire. By JAMES BRYCE, D. C. L. Portrait.

The "Holy Roman Empire" is a work of great learning, and is universally conceded to show a high degree of historical power. This continued existence of the Roman Empire through the middle ages is, as Freeman remarks, the key to a correct understanding of the whole period. Giving, as it does, a clear portrayal of the mutual relations of Rome and Germany during these centuries, of that singular connection which received the name of Holy Roman Empire, but of which Voltaire said, that it was neither holy nor

JAMES BRYCE, D. C. L.

Standard Works for Thinkers — Continued.

Roman nor empire, the book may ever be the beginning of any systematic study of German history. — *Robert Thorne.*

The object of his treatise is not so much to give a narrative history of the countries included in the Romano-Germanic Empire, as to describe the Holy Empire itself, as an institution or system, the wonderful offspring of a body of beliefs and traditions, which have almost wholly passed away from the world. — *Author's Preface.*

Bacon's Essays. The Essays of Counsels Civil and Moral of Francis Bacon.

Including also his Apophthegms, Elegant Sentences, and Wisdom of the Ancients. With an introduction by HENRY MORLEY, LL. D., Professor of English Literature at University College, London. Portrait.

Bacon's "Essays" take a high place among the greatest books that have ever been written in English, or in any language. With the single exception

FRANCIS BACON.

of the "Essays" of Montaigne there are no writings of the essay kind that compare with Bacon's in fame, popularity, or intrinsic worth. They contain the condensed wisdom gathered during the whole long lifetime of one of the mightiest minds of modern times. They are the life counsels of a man who was familiar with its every path ; a man who knew what it was to bear the burdens of debt and disgrace, as well as to live in luxury and power, conscious that he was acknowledged to be the greatest man of his age. There were originally only ten "essays" published in 1597, but Bacon kept them by him, day after day and year after year adding, altering, and improving, until in 1612 an edition of thirty-eight essays appeared, and in 1625 the present complete number of fifty-eight. In the essay upon "Studies" he says: "Some books are to be tasted, others to be swallowed, and some few to be chewed and digested." His own belongs to the last-named class. I have read and re-read these wonderful pages, many of them for the hundredth time, and always with a new delight. The book stands on my desk by the side of Shakespeare, Irving, and Emerson, within my easy reach ; and its very nearness while I work is an inspiration and a pleasure. — *Frank Parsons.*

Smiles' Self-Help.

Self-Help, with Illustrations of Character, Conduct, and Perseverance. By SAMUEL SMILES. Portrait.

SAMUEL SMILES.

"Self-Help" is pre-eminently one of the world's best books; best, in that it shows most forcibly how all that is best in the world, in civilization, has been achieved ; in that it holds up to men and urges upon them the means of making the best out of themselves and obtaining the highest success, the truest enjoyment out of all conditions of life. Through the medium of these familiar talks with young men, Mr. Smiles impresses the truth that all nations have been

Send all orders direct to Arena Publishing Co., Boston, Mass.

xiii

Standard Works for Thinkers — Continued.

made what they are by the thinking and working of many generations of men, that patient and persevering laborers in all ranks have contributed toward the grand result, one generation building upon another's labors, and carrying them forward to still higher stages. In his illustrations of what each can in a greater or less degree do for himself and for the world, he cites the life history of such benefactors of humanity as Stephenson, Watt, Heathcote, Arkwright, Turner, Pallissy, Jacquard, and countless others, who, by dint of persevering application and energy, raised themselves from the humblest ranks of industry to eminent positions of usefulness and influence. With convincing force, he proves by logic and example, that energy, integrity, and perseverance are now, and in all ages have been, the essential elements of success. He inculcates the principles of self-help, self-respect, and self-reliance, and the indomitable power of *will*, the homely and rugged qualities which have enabled our American ancestors to make America what it is to-day.

SIR EDWARD SHEPHERD CREASY.

Creasy's Fifteen Decisive Battles of the World.

The Fifteen Decisive Battles of the World, from Marathon to Waterloo. By E. S. CREASY, M. A., Professor of Ancient and Modern History in University College, London; late Fellow of King's College, Cambridge. Portrait.

This famous book was written by Sir Edward Shepherd Creasy, an Englishman, born in 1812, the author of several historical works, the best of them being the "Fifteen Decisive Battles."

The author is a wonderful word-painter. So vivid are his descriptions that one feels as though he were present at the scene himself listening to the counsels of the generals, hearing the tread of marching columns, watching the gleaming spears and bayonets, armies of infantry, charging cavalry, breach, rally, and retreat, deafened with the roar of batteries, saddened by the death of friends, and flushed with triumph; and at last the reader lays the book away exhausted with the rush of feeling through his heart. — *Frank Parsons.*

Meditations of the Emperor Marcus Aurelius Antoninus.

The Meditations of the Emperor Marcus Aurelius Antoninus. Translated by GEORGE LONG, M. A., with a biographical sketch and a view of the philosophy of Antoninus by the translator. Including also an essay on Marcus Aurelius by CANON FARRAR. Portrait.

"The noblest book of antiquity" is Canon Farrar's estimate of the "Meditations of Marcus Aurelius;" and his regard is shared by thousands who have been made better and truer men by the ennobling influence of the great soul and lofty character of this pagan emperor. Marcus Aurelius Antoninus became the head of the vast empire of Rome in A. D. 161, succeeding his adoptive father, Antoninus Pius. He stands forth

MARCUS AURELIUS ANTONINUS.

Send all orders direct to Arena Publishing Co., Boston, Mass.

xiv

Standard Works for Thinkers — Continued.

as one of the majestic figures of the world's history, the despot of the civilized world, a successful general and conqueror, a man among men, and yet a magnanimous, just, and conscientious ruler, a rigid, upright, and consistent moralist in a period of the greatest luxury, corruption, and immorality. He was a stoic philosopher, but as Tenneman says, "he imparted to it a character of gentleness and benevolence by making it subordinate to a love of mankind allied to religion."— *Robert Thorne.*

Proctor's Other Worlds Than Ours.

Other Worlds Than Ours. The plurality of worlds studied under the light of recent scientific researches. By RICHARD A. PROCTOR. With an introductory note by FRANK PARSONS. Portrait.

This book had from the first a very extraordinary success. It appeared in 1870, and at once attracted the attention of the scientific world and of all who were interested in knowing what the telescope and the spectroscope have revealed to the tireless gaze of science. The volume is written in a most charming style. Like Huxley and Tyndall, Mr. Proctor sees the poetry of his subject, and knows how to bring the largest truths within the comprehension of a child, and make the deepest researches as interesting to the general reader as a novel. What the earth teaches us, what we learn from the sun, Mars a miniature earth, Jupiter the giant of our system, the nature of nebulæ, the constitution and shape of the universe, the probability that other worlds are inhabited — such are his themes, and he brings to their discussion all the knowledge of one of the profoundest mathematicians and astonomers of this age and all the power of a poet on the perception and expression of beauty. — *Frank Parsons.*

Guizot's History of Civilization in Europe.

The History of Civilization in Europe. By FRANÇOIS PIERRE GUILLAUME GUIZOT. Translated by WILLIAM HAZLITT, with a biographical sketch of the author. Portrait.

As a man and a man of letters, a historian and a statesman, M. Guizot is among the most illustrious of his nation and age. This volume, the most famous of all his works, comprises a course of lectures delivered while he occupied the chair of History in the Sarbonne in 1828. They made a profound impression at that time, and indeed marked an epoch in the history of education, raising the reputation of their author at once to the highest point of fame, and placing him among the best writers of France and of Europe. They are not a description of events, but an embodiment of conclusions which rest on the solid basis of most thorough research, and a presentation of the processes by which these conclusions have been reached. — *Taken largely from "A Manual of Historical Literature," by Charles Kendall Adams.*

Carlyle's Past and Present.

Past and Present. By THOMAS CARLYLE, with an Introductory Note by ROBERT THORNE, M. A. Portrait.

Carlyle is without question the most prominent Englishman of letters of this century. In this volume he presents an impassioned and exaggerated contrast between England as it was in the twelfth century, and the England of to-day, taking for his hero-text the character of Samson, the Abbot of St.

Standard Works for Thinkers — Concluded.

Edmundsbury, in Suffolk, and lauding the days of paternal and despotic government, while all things modern, men and institutions, society and politics, with the unreality and insincerity which pervades them, he denounces in terms of violent and unmeasured invective. We are all become utilitarians or sceptics: " There is no longer any God for us." . . . " Man has lost 'the *soul* out of him ; " and this lack of *soul* is the " plague spot, the universal social gangrene, threatening all things with frightful death." His is a strong voice, calling men from the sordid cares of daily life and warning or exhorting them to higher efforts; seeking to dissuade them from the hollowness of metaphysical speculation on the one hand and the growing materialism of the present day on the other. His bidding is to do the allotted work of life silently and bravely, and there is probably no person who has not gained strength by the reading of his strong and earnest writings. — *Robert Thorne.*

THOMAS CARLYLE.

Part II. Standard Works of Fiction.
Uniform with Standard Works for Thinkers. Price per volume, $1.00.

Thackeray's Vanity Fair.

Vanity Fair, A Novel Without a Hero. By WILLIAM MAKEPEACE THACKERAY. Portrait.

" Vanity Fair," the first of Thackeray's chief works, is called " A Novel without a Hero." It is possessed, however, of two heroines — Rebecca Sharp, the impersonation of intellect without heart, and Amelia Sedley, who has heart without intellect. " Becky Sharp" is, without doubt, the ablest creation of modern fiction. The selfish, prudent, brave little woman, who, without lend or helper, wins her way, claims the reader's interest, and very artistic is the set-off WILLIAM M. THACKERAY which the silly, yet most lovable Amelia presents to the character of Rebecca. As a whole, the book is full of quiet sarcasm and severe rebuke. It is replete with humor and morality, and rivets attention to the end by the vivid reality of all the persons and scenes. This work alone might bear out the charge of cynicism against Thackeray ; but a careful reading will perceive the kindly heart that is beating under the bitterest sentence and the most caustic irony. In his delineation of the character and genius of Fielding, Thackeray has drawn his own. He had the same hatred of all meanness, cant, and knavery, the same large sympathy, relish of life, thoughtful humor, keen insight, delicate irony and wit. — *Taken largely from " A Manual of English Literature," by T. B. Shaw.*

The Personal History of David Copperfield.
BY CHARLES DICKENS.

" David Copperfield" is a novel full of tenderness and purity of feeling, and in it Dickens presents to the full that comprehensiveness of sympathy which springs from a sense of brotherhood with all mankind. When old

Send all orders direct to Arena Publishing Co., Boston, Mass.

xvi

Standard Works of Fiction — Continued.

Peggotty sets off, stick in hand, to tramp over France, Germany, and, if needs be, Italy, to find his niece, misguided "Little Emily," the tears start, and we stand amazed, not knowing that there was so much pity in our hearts.

The Old Curiosity Shop.
By CHARLES DICKENS.

The "Old Curiosity Shop" abounds with vivid descriptions of human life and character, and the reader's attention is held until the very end. Of all of Dickens' works there is none which appeals more strongly to our heart than this story of childish abnegation and devotion.

The Posthumous Papers of the Pickwick Club.
By CHARLES DICKENS.

The "Pickwick Papers" chronicle the travels and adventures of the immortal Mr. Pickwick and his fellow-members of the Pickwick Club, and the varied pictures of life through which we follow the kind old bachelor, his three friends, and his attached servant, the inimitable Sam Weller, are of absorbing interest.

CHARLES DICKENS.

The Life and Adventures of Nicholas Nickleby.
By CHARLES DICKENS.

Nicholas, the hero of the tale, is, upon the whole, so manly, so honest, and so lovable, that we overlook his faults, and sympathize with him in his misfortunes, and rejoice with him in his successes.

Uarda, A Romance of Ancient Egypt.
By GEORGE EBERS.

Dr. Ebers, probably the first Egyptologist living, has given us in a series of dramatic romances a vivid and most interesting portrayal of the social life and manners, the learning and art, the philosophy and religion of the ancients. Amid all the tempest of passion and expectation incidental to such a tale, the novelist evolves a charming story of love and constancy rising superior to class prejudices, and of the sweet amenities of social ties and family affection.

GEORGE EBERS.

Westward Ho! or, The Voyages and Adventures of Sir Amyas Leigh, Knight.
By CHARLES KINGSLEY.

"Westward Ho!" is one of the most vigorous, powerful, and fascinating of novels. It is strong and graphic in its portraiture, intense and dramatic in its diversified coloring. The story is one of thrilling adventures on land and sea. With equal felicity the author brings before our imagination the wildly beautiful scenery of Devon, terrific sea fights, and the tropical beauty of South American forests. The nervous and effective style, the skillful

Send all orders direct to Arena Publishing Co., Boston, Mass.

xvii

Standard Works of Fiction — Continued.

blending of the manifold portraits into one comprehensive picture, are among the merits which have made this Kingsley's greatest work.

Hypatia.

Of all modern novels probably no one has been more widely read than this. It is historical in its nature, the scene being laid in Alexandria in the early centuries of the Christian church, and it is a most brilliant delineation of Christianity in conflict with rude Gothic paganism and the expiring philosophy of Greece. Hypatia, the heroine of the story, a daughter of a

famous mathematician and astronomer named Theon, was born in that city about A. D. 370. She went to Athens and studied under the Neo-Platonist, Plutarch, and on her return, opening a school of Neo-Platonic philosophy, her talents, beauty, eloquence, and modesty gained for her great fame and influence. Her lecture-room was thronged, and she was consulted by the most eminent men in the city; but as a pagan and a philosopher she provoked the bitter hostility of Cyril, the Bishop of Alexandria, and eventually met her death at the hands of the Christians. Amid the widespread corruptions of Alexandria, she lived as spotless as a vestal; and if her teaching was not one that could lay a strong hand on the vices of heathen-

CHARLES KINGSLEY.

ism, and arrest their course, it was at least sufficient not only to preserve herself from pollution, but also to inspire her with a love of beauty, truth, and goodness, that was Christian in its spirit and earnestness, if heathen in its form and limitations. The plot is well developed, the characters are vigorously drawn, and the scenes and incidents show great dramatic power, while the language and word-painting are exquisite. The book holds throughout, with a firm grasp, our sympathy and interest, Kingsley being one of the very few who have succeeded in throwing a strong human interest into a historical novel. — *Robert Thorne.*

Romola.　　　　By GEORGE ELIOT.

George Eliot is admitted by thoughtful persons to have been endowed with one of the greatest minds of this century. "Romola," which is one of her earlier works, is also one of the most popular. The movement is so rapid, and the situations are so dramatic, that the interest never flags; but the effect of unity is gained by the careful mingling of many elements. The most careless reader will be struck by the wealth of historical knowledge and the power and vividness with which the Florentine life of the time is depicted, by the interest of the story itself and by the beauty of the language.

GEORGE ELIOT.

Adam Bede.　　　　By GEORGE ELIOT.

"Adam Bede" is a novel of great strength. It abounds in thrilling and dramatic situations and in subtle delineations of strongly marked and powerfully contrasted characters. The ease with which George Eliot rivets attention, and the tact she possesses in reaching the heartstrings of her readers, is as wonderful as it is certain and powerful.

Send all orders direct to Arena Publishing Co., Boston, Mass.

xviii

Standard Works of Fiction — Continued.

The Mill on the Floss. By George Eliot.

"The Mill on the Floss" commends itself strongly to the reader by its fine analyses of the motives, its vivid force in description, and its quality as a work of literary art.

Scott's Ivanhoe.

Sir Walter Scott.

Ivanhoe. A romance. By Sir Walter Scott, Bart. Reprinted from the author's edition. Unaltered and unabridged. Portrait.

Ivanhoe is one of the most famous and brilliant of all the master romances of Sir Walter Scott, who is placed by many at the head of modern novelists. The scene is laid in England in the reign of Richard I., when ancient chivalry prevailed with all its pomp and splendid ceremony. Sir Wilfred, Knight of Ivanhoe, is the favorite of the king, but has been disinherited by his father, Cedric of Rotherwood. Assuming the garb of a pilgrim, he goes to his father's castle and meets there Rowena, his father's ward, and falls in love with her. He next appears prominently at the grand tourney, as the "Desdichado" or Disinherited Knight, and he prevails over all combatants. Through the intercession of the king he is reconciled to his father, and finally marries Rowena. Rebecca, the beautiful Jewess who appears in the story, gentle yet high-spirited, is said to have been Scott's favorite character. The breadth and power of Scott's style and his charm as a story-teller are too well known to need comment, and in this volume we have him at his best.—*Robert Thorne.*

De Quincey's Confessions of An English Opium-Eater.

De Quincey.

Confessions of An English Opium-Eater, and Selected Essays. By Thomas De Quincey. Edited with notes by David Masson, Professor of English Literature in the University of Edinburgh. Portrait.

Irving's Sketch-Book.

Washington Irving.

The Sketch-Book of Geoffrey Crayon, Gent. By Washington Irving. With an introductory note by Frank Parsons. Portrait.

The book is refined, poetical, and picturesque, full of quaint humor, exquisite feeling, and a thorough knowledge of human nature. Robert Collyer tells us that to the "Sketch-Book" was largely due his early thirst for good reading, which laid the foundation of his success ; and probably it would be difficult to find a person who is familiar with its pages who does not cherish it as one of his most valued possessions.

Send all orders direct to Arena Publishing Co., Boston, Mass.

xix

Standard Works of Fiction — Concluded.

"The Spectre Bridegroom;" "The Broken Heart;" "The Legend of Sleepy Hollow;" "The Christmas Dinner;" "Rip Van Winkle;" "The Art of Book-Making;" and "The Country Church," are among the most charming pieces of fancy and picturesque word-painting to be found in any language. The book is an expression of the man, and daily converse with it cannot fail to give us something of the beauty, sweetness, and nobility of his nature. — *Frank Parsons.*

Collins' Moonstone.

WILKIE COLLINS.

The Moonstone. A Novel. By WILKIE COLLINS. Portrait.

Next to Charles Reade, Wilkie Collins must be acknowledged to command the largest audience in the English novel-reading world. In the art of constructing a story he has no living superior. In the delineation of character, or in the use of a story for the development of social theories, or for the redress of a wrong against humanity or civilization, others may equal if not surpass him, but in his own dominion he stands alone, without a rival. Like the generality of his romances, the interest of "The Moonstone" depends chiefly upon the development of a plot whose systematic intricacies pique the curiosity until the last moment, and upon the concealment of a mystery which baffles and defies solution until it shall have contributed to no end of cross purposes and caused a prodigious amount of incertitude and wretchedness. At the storming of the city of Seringapatam by the English troops in 1799 a diamond of fabulous size, and which for centuries had been owned and held in veneration by its possessors, the moon worshippers, is stolen by an English officer and taken with him to England. Its subsequent history, until it is regained by the Indians, furnishes Mr. Collins with the material from which to form a story which not alone fascinates us by its dramatic situations, but also thrills us with cunning detective enterprises, and surprises us with novel methods of committing crime. It must not be supposed, however, that in this, the best of Mr. Collins' romances, the love story is not present, for, incidental to the tales of robbery and murder, the author evolves a charming story of love and conspiracy, wherein vice is ultimately punished and virtue most nobly rewarded. In "The Moonstone" Mr. Collins exhibits to a remarkable degree the power of constructing a story whose close it will defy an expert to tell and which will hold the reader's attention to the very end. — *Frederic Mynon Cooper.*

SOME VALUABLE CLOTH-BOUND BOOKS.

We have purchased the entire cloth-bound edition of the following four works from

BENJ. TUCKER.

MY UNCLE BENJAMIN.

A humorous, satirical, and philosophical novel. By CLAUDE TILLIER. Translated from the French by Benj. R. Tucker. With a sketch of the author's life and works by Ludwig Pfau. This work, though it has enjoyed the honor of three translations into German, has never before been translated into English. It is one of the most delightfully witty works ever written. Almost every sentence excites a laugh. It is thoroughly realistic, but not at all repulsive. Its satirical treatment of humanity's foibles and its jovial but profound philosophy have won its author the title of "the modern Rabelais." My Uncle Benjamin riddles with the shafts of his good-natured ridicule the shams of theology, law, medicine, commerce, war, marriage, and society generally. 312 pages.

THE RAG-PICKER OF PARIS.

By FELIX PYAT. Translated from the French by Benj. R. Tucker. A novel unequalled in its combination of dramatic power, picturesque intensity, crisp dialogue, panoramic effect, radical tendency, and bold handling of social questions. Probably the most vivid picture of the misery of poverty, the extravagance of wealth, the sympathy and forbearance of the poor and despised, the cruelty and aggressiveness of the aristocratic and respectable, the blind greed of the middle classes, the hollowness of charity, the cunning and hypocrisy of the priesthood, the tyranny and corruption of authority, the crushing power of privilege, and, finally, of the redeeming beauty of the ideal of liberty and equality that the century has produced. 325 pages.

QUINTESSENCE OF IBSENISM.

In this work Mr. G. Bernard Shaw has given one of the best studies ever printed of the great Scandinavian poet, prophet, and philosopher. Some idea of the value of the work will be gained by noticing the following subjects reviewed and discussed by Mr. Shaw:—

The Two Pioneers, Ideals and Idealists, The Womanly Woman, The Plays, Brand, Peer Gynt, Emperor and Galilean, The League of Youth, Pillars of Society, A Doll's House, Ghosts, An Enemy of the People, The Wild Duck, Bosmersholm, The Lady from the Sea, Hedda Gabler, The Moral of the Plays.

RUSSIAN TRAITS AND TERRORS.

The collective signature employed by several contributors to the "Fortnightly Review."

By E. B. LANIN. This work out-Kennans Kennan in its description of the atrocities practiced by the Russian government, and includes an ode written by Swinburne inciting to the assassination of the Czar. All the assertions in the work are sustained by the most convincing documentary proofs. The interest which it will excite may be judged by the following

TABLE OF CONTENTS:

I. Lying.—II. Fatalism.—III. Sloth.—IV. Dishonesty.—V. Russian Prisons: The Simple Truth.—VI. Russia: An Ode.—VII. Sexual Morality in Russia.—VIII. The Jews in Russia.—IX. Russian Finance: The Racking of the Peasantry.—X. The Russian Censure.

The price of any one of the above volumes is $1.00, but we will send all four for $3.00 to any one ordering them during the next thirty days.

ARENA PUBLISHING COMPANY.

Just Out.

A Brilliant Realistic Novel by the Author of
"Is this Your Son, My Lord?

Pray You Sir Whose Daughter?

HELEN H. GARDNER

GERTRUDE FOSTER

ETTA BURTON

FRANCES KING

ARENA Publishing Co.

PRICE, PAPER, 50 CENTS; CLOTH, $1.00.
ADDRESS ALL ORDERS
ARENA PUBLISHING CO., Copley Sq., Boston, Mass.

HIS beautiful book has just been issued from THE ARENA press. It is the direct result of the most wonderful and successful expedition ever undertaken by a woman anywhere in the world. It contains nearly 500 pages and almost 400 illustrations, reproductions of photographs taken by this intrepid woman in the course of her long journey.

This sumptuous volume contains the first and most accurate information in regard to the lives of the natives of Africa that has ever been published.

NOLI ME TANGERE

SWEET
GRASS
NECKLACE.

HER
STAFF.

SULTAN MERIALI.

Leaving her delightful home in London and bidding good by to family and friends, the author, in the early part of 1891, went to Zanzibar, and there organized and equipped her splendid caravan and

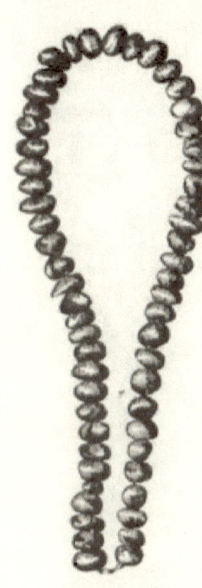

personally led it into the wilds of Africa. She visited in the course of her travels thirty-two different tribes, some of whom had never before seen a white face. In consequence of her superb outfit M. French-Sheldon travelled like a queen, and brought back from the Dark Continent the largest collection of curios, implements of war, and the marvellous products of the native metal workers, ever shown outside of Africa.

The story of this wonderful march is told in graphic style, and the book is a valuable addition to African literature.

Appreciating the value of independent action, Mrs. Sheldon wisely decided not to go to

DOWA BEAD
NECKLACE.

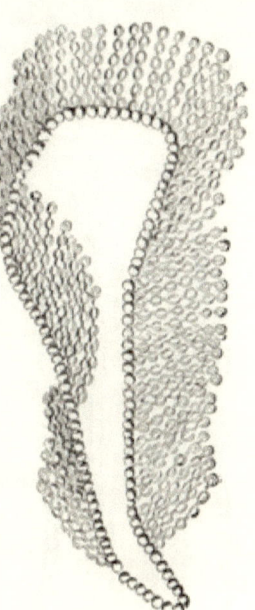

CHAIN GIRDLE.

FOM POMBE CUPS.

Africa as the representative of any society, or under the patronage of any government. She relied wholly upon her own resources, and paid her own bills from her own private purse; the whole cost amounting to nearly $50,000. This brave American woman, carrying the American flag at the head of her caravan, was received by the various Sultans with every mark of friendship and respect. Many powerful tribes vowed open allegiance to the "White Queen," as they called her, receiving her as an honored guest. Within a month the same natives were engaged in a hand-to-hand conflict with some of the German troops when they attempted to force a passage

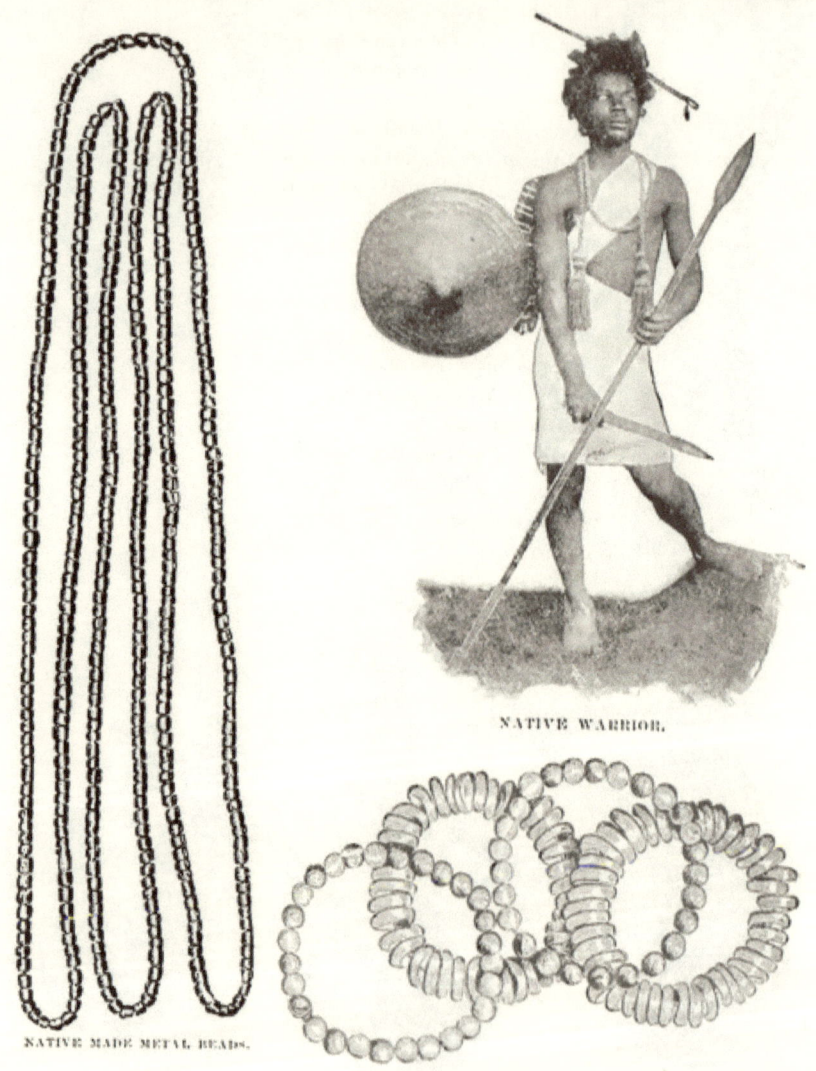

NATIVE WARRIOR.

NATIVE MADE METAL BEADS.

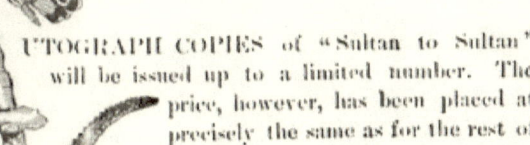

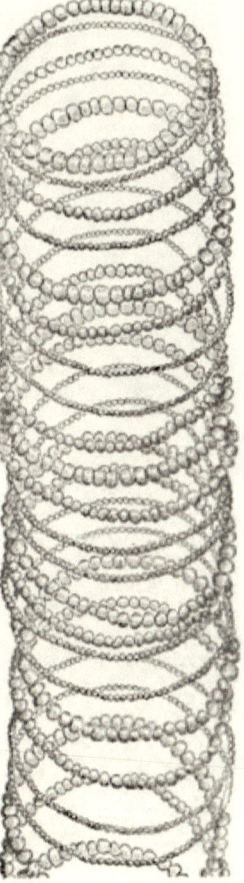

UTOGRAPH COPIES of "Sultan to Sultan" will be issued up to a limited number. The price, however, has been placed at precisely the same as for the rest of the edition, viz., $5.00. In order to secure an autograph copy, the price must be remitted to the publishers direct.

The book is handsomely printed on coated paper and is bound in a rich African red, silk-finished cloth, stamped in gold on the back and side. It is without exception the most valuable and most beautiful holiday book of the year. It contains besides the most accurate accounts of the habits, customs, and inner life of the natives of East Africa that has ever been published in the world. The author emphasizes the good rather than the bad qualities of the natives, for she went bearing emblems of peace, and saw them at their best.

Upon her return from her successful journey, M. French-Sheldon was greeted with the warmest applause by the press of two continents. Her work was a

RESS notices of the most complimentary character have been showered upon M. French-Sheldon from all parts of the world. Her enterprise, her courage, her fair and friendly attitude toward the natives, and most of all her independence in paying the whole cost of the expedition herself, have been praised to the skies.

PRESS NOTICES.

BOSTON TRAVELLER.

First Woman Explorer of East Africa

Never before in the history of the world have the opportunities for women been so great and varied as at the present time. Among the wonderful women of the present day is the African explorer, Mrs. May French-Sheldon, the wife of a London banker. Both husband and wife are Americans. Mrs. French-Sheldon is a woman of charming personality, culture and refinement. When Mrs. French-Sheldon appeared before the army of the Sultans, or natives of distinction, she made a grand toilet and wore a court gown of white silk, covered with silver gauze, a jewelled sword, belt and dagger. The gown was covered with stage jewels, which she presented to the natives, also large quantities of rings. Her costume was made by Worth, especially for the expedition. She has appeared in it over twenty times, and it is as beautiful as when first worn. Her palanquin was of wicker work, circular in form, a foot and a half wide and five feet long. It was covered with green awning and gilt fringe, and lined with yellow silk. It was fitted up with little lockers, containing bedding and scientific instruments. She bore all the expenses of the journey, and spent quite a little fortune.

LONDON TIMES.

The Richest and Rarest Exhibit.

Last night's meeting of the Anthropological Institute was one of unusual interest. After Mrs. French-Sheldon and her lecture -- the most attractive feature of the evening — was the very fine exhibition of objects which she has been able to bring back from Africa. It was admitted that this was the richest and rarest exhibition ever held in connection with the society. Mrs. French-Sheldon was able to win the confidence of the

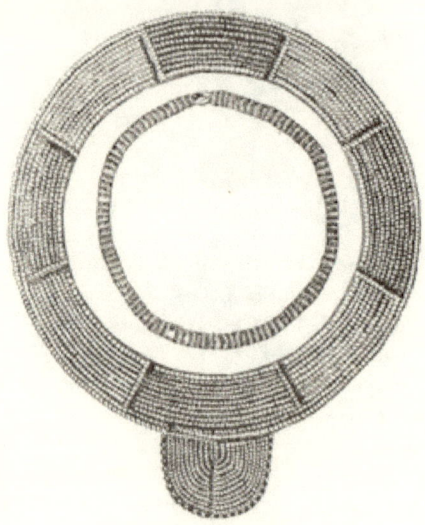

TEVATA NECKLACE.

natives in a way no male traveller can ever hope to do, and in this way succeeded in obtaining information of great interest and novelty, and securing objects which had never been seen out of Africa before.

NEW YORK WORLD.

While in the Dark Continent Mrs. French-Sheldon, the African explorer, had two moving adventures by flood. Once her porters let her fall into a cataract, and she was carried thirty or forty feet down stream; then, as this performance lacked finish, they let her fall on the rocks, so that she sustained serious injury.

CHILDREN IN AFRICA.

In an interview with the *Washington Star*, Mrs. M. French-Sheldon, the distinguished African traveller, says: "The people were not savages to me. I had no white person with me; nobody but one hundred and thirty-eight black men and half as many black women. In all that two thousand miles of exploration I never received one insult nor saw one indecent action. Never but once insubordination. At the foot of Mount Kilimanjaro eight of

my guard refused to obey my orders to move on. I had to force my authority.

Stanley has told us very little about the women and children of Africa, of love, family life, marriage, manners, fun, games. Africa under the equator is the children's paradise. In all these months, among the children every day, I never saw a child struck, and I heard a child cry only twice while in the Dark Continent. Up to the age of six or eight the children go as naked as they were born; after that they wear a small piece of cloth or leather, and are little men and women learning to be bread-winners. The young ones early begin to learn — learn to work: the girls to sew in their rude way, and the boys to swim and run, and to use the bow and arrow expertly. There is a definite division of labor between the sexes: the men kill game, do the fighting, make the weapons (fundas), and fabricate the women's ornaments; while the women work the gardens and plantations, tend the herds, and build the dracean hedge. The married woman dresses simply in some animal's skin drawn around her shoulder, the unmarried woman in a fig-leaf apron. Girls are often married at ten; at fifteen they are old maids.

HARPER'S WEEKLY.
A Woman of Charming Personality.

Mrs. M. French-Sheldon, who is now in this country, enjoys the reputation of having led a caravan through a wild and savage portion of East Africa. She is a woman of charming personality, and an American by birth.

She headed an expedition that started from Zanzibar with one hundred and thirty-eight black men as escorts and carriers. She began her trip into the interior from Mombasa and penetrated as far as Kilimanjaro, covering in all nine hundred and ninety miles, and walking at the head of the little band nearly all of the way. The savages of the region received her with wonder and respect, and as a woman she was enabled to study the home conditions and customs of the natives, a privilege hitherto denied to travellers.

WESTERN MORNING NEWS.
A Palpable Hit.

Once again a lady has made the most palpable hit in the geographical section (of the British Association). This year the palm is carried off by Mrs. M. French-Sheldon, a dauntless explorer, who yesterday at Cardiff deeply interested a large audience by a graphic account of her recent adventures and hair-breadth escapes in the wilds of Africa.

THE LONDON TIMES.

The excitement on the appearance of Mrs. M. French-Sheldon was strong enough to fill the hall when this adventurous lady appeared to tell the story of her journey to Kilimanjaro. Her address contained enough to show that she had seen a good deal more of the inside life of the natives than has fallen to the lot of male travellers.

BRITISH ASSOCIATION, CARDIFF.

Sir Francis de Winton congratulated Mrs. Sheldon (after her lecture, extending over one hour) upon her discovery of the true native character, and her patience in dealing with it; but he could not advise other women to emulate her in adventuring into the interior of Africa.

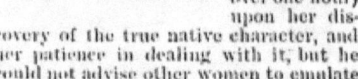

NATIVE WATER-CARRIER.

BOND-HOLDERS AND BREAD-WINNERS.

BY S. S. KING, KANSAS CITY, KANSAS.

A PORTRAYAL OF SOME POLITICAL CRIMES COMMITTED IN THE NAME OF LIBERTY.

Facts and Figures from the Eleventh Census, with Maps and Illustrations.— Massachusetts Enabled to Accumulate More Wealth than 9 Great Western and Southern States!—Pennsylvania More than 12!—New York More than 15!—Agriculture and Labor Robbed.—It is less than two weeks since the First Copy left the Press.—Read what they say:

SENATOR W. A. PEFFER: You have done a good work in your little book "Bond-Holders and Bread-Winners." It is the best presentation of the subject ever made.

CONGRESSMAN JOHN G. OTIS: This little book ought to be in the hands of every voter in the United States. To my mind it is the best hand-book published for the campaign of 1892.

CONGRESSMAN JOHN DAVIS: It is the best general campaign document I have seen, and you deserve the red-hot thanks of every friend of humanity for your most truthful and timely exposition of the present facts and conditions as they exist in this country.

CONGRESSMAN WM. BAKER: It's a perfect little gem. It ought to be in the hands of every loyal citizen of this country.

CONGRESSMAN O. M. KEM (Nebraska): After careful perusal, I unhesitatingly pronounce it a grand little work, and ought to be in the hands of every American citizen.

PRESIDENT L. L. POLK: It should be placed in the hands of every voter of this country. In no work that I have seen have the unjust and ruinous effects of class legislation been so forcibly and faithfully depicted.

PRESIDENT L. LEONARD (of Missouri): Without injustice to any of the many most excellent presentations of the subject, I regard this the most thorough, concise, and orderly exhibit of the present politico-economic condition of the country I have yet read. It is absolute, positive demonstration. I most heartily commend your book to all candid and earnest seekers after the truth.

ALLIANCE ECHO (Kansas City, Mo.): We have read it, and unhesitatingly pronounce it a gem.

C. C. POST, the great leader and author (Georgia): It is a valuable addition to the reform literature of the day The showing of who wins and eats the bread of the people is clear and lucid. The work is unusually readable.

HON. C. H. J. TAYLOR, the great negro orator and editor: The profound lawyer and thinker, S. S. King, has given the world a most interesting and what will prove a highly useful book called "Bond-Holders and Bread-Winners." All the people should read Mr. King's book.

SINGLE COPIES, 25 CENTS.

Address all orders,

ARENA PUBLISHING CO., BOSTON, MASS.

The Rise of the

Swiss Republic.

By W. D. McCRACKAN, A. M.

With Large Colored Map and Full-Page Portrait of the Author.

W. D. McCRACKAN, A. M.

THE ARENA PUBLISHING COMPANY take great pleasure in announcing that they have just issued a brilliant history of the Swiss Republic, which deals in a popular yet scholarly manner with this ideal republic, which is attracting the attention of thoughtful Americans as is no other foreign nation in the world to-day. The author has devoted five years of careful study to this work. A large portion of this time has been spent in Switzerland, and every important locality has been visited and studied that a clear and intelligent idea of the events described might be presented. The archives of the little republic have yielded much information little known even to the continental reader. This work is scholarly, yet written in a popular style, and will be a delight alike to the student and general reader. It is also of special value to thoughtful Americans, as it contains comparative chapters where the two republics are contrasted.

SPECIAL FEATURES.

AMONG the special features of this volume are chapters on the recent experimental innovations made by the Swiss Republic, the revised Constitution of Switzerland (1874), a general reference index to works by Swiss authorities, and a handsomely colored map of Switzerland.

It contains over four hundred pages, printed from new and handsome type on a fine quality of heavy paper. The margins are wide, and the volume is richly bound in cloth.

PRICE, POST-PAID, $3.00.

Address all orders, ARENA PUBLISHING COMPANY, Copley Square, Boston, Mass.

Just Out! • •
A POWERFUL NOVEL OF THE MODERN WEST.
By Hamlin Garland,
Author of "Main-Travelled Roads," "Jason Edwards," "A Member of the Third House," "Little Norsk," etc.

A SPOIL OF OFFICE

By

Hamlin Garland

ARENA PUBLISHING COMPANY,
Copley Square, Boston, Mass.

—— 350 PAGES. ——

Price, Paper, 50 cents; Cloth, $1.00; Library, $1.50.

ARENA PUBLISHING CO., Copley Square, Boston, Mass.

The Dream Child.

By FLORENCE HUNTLEY.

A Beautiful Theosophical Story.

THIS story will charm all readers. It is written in a most fascinating manner and is quite out of the ordinary line of fiction; indeed, many readers will be convinced that this strange, weird, and in many respects original story is far more than a story. It is one of the finest presentations of the central ideas of Theosophy ever published.

Price, paper, 50 cents; cloth, $1.00.

Arena Publishing Company,

Boston, Mass.

JUST OUT.

A BOOK THAT IS BOUND
TO CREATE A GENUINE
SENSATION. . . .

Dr. MAX NORDAU

*Writes enthusiastically of the "splendid form
and noble morality" of this unique work.* .

Who Lies?

An interrogation.

Blum - Alexander.

Boston

Arena Publishing Co.

Price, post-paid, ... 50c.

For Sale by the Trade.

LAWYERS' DIRECTORY.

Each member of the following list of attorneys has been recommended as thoroughly reliable and of good standing in his profession.

ALABAMA.

BIRMINGHAM. John D. Watson, 201½ Second Ave.
BRIDGEPORT. Nelson MacReynolds.
HUNTSVILLE. David D. Shelby, 3½ Bank Row.
JASPER. E. W. Coleman.
MOBILE. Gaylord B. & Francis B. Clark, Jr., 17 No. Royal St.
MONTGOMERY. Wm. S. Thorington (City Attorney).
WETUMPKA. W. P. Gaddis.

ARIZONA.

ST JOHNS. Albert F. Banta.
TOMBSTONE. James Reilly.
WILLCOX. G. W. Baker.

ARKANSAS.

DE WITT. E. L. Johnson.
FORREST CITY. Norton & Prewett.
FORT SMITH. J. B. McDonough.
HARRISON. Crump & Watkins.
HOT SPRINGS. Charles D. Greaves, Attorney and Abstracter of Land Titles.
LAVACA. Neal & Rhea.
LITTLE ROCK. Samuel R. Allen.
MARIANNA. C. A. Otey.
NEWPORT. John W. & Jos. M. Stayton.
PINE BLUFF. White & Stephens.

CALIFORNIA.

ALAMEDA. Edward K. Taylor, Artesian Block.
FRESNO. Geo. E. Church, Rooms 4, 5, and 6, First National Bank Building.
HANFORD. Benjamin C. Mickle.
LOS ANGELES. Henry C. Dillon.
" " J. Marion Brooks.
RIVERSIDE. Wm. J. McIntyre (City Attorney).
SAN DIEGO. Sam F. Smith, cor. 5th and F Sts.
SAN FRANCISCO. E. A. Belcher, 234 Montgomery St.
" " W. H. H. Hart, 230 Montgomery St.
" " W. R. Daingerfield, 508 California St.
" " F. M. Husted, 528 California St.
SANTA ANA. Ray Billingsley.
SAN JOSE. J. H. Campbell.

COLORADO.

DENVER. Norris & Howard, Ernest & Cramner Bldg.
MONTROSE. Goudy & Sherman.
OURAY. Robt. H. Wilson; Mines and Mining Law a specialty.
" John Kinkaid.

CONNECTICUT.

HARTFORD. Lewis Sperry, 345 Main St.
" Sidney E. Clarke.
NAUGATUCK. Henry C. Baldwin.
NEW HAVEN. Charles Kleiner, Room 23, Exchange Building, Cor. Church and Chapel Sts.
STAMFORD. James H. Olmstead, 14 Town Hall Bldg.
WILLIMANTIC. John L. Hunter.

DELAWARE.

DOVER. Fulton & Van Dyke.

DISTRICT OF COLUMBIA.

WASHINGTON. Ferdinand Schmidt, 511 Seventh St., N. W. Titles examined.

FLORIDA.

ARCADIA. Nelson MacReynolds.
BARTOW. J. W. Brady.
TAMPA. Sparkman & Sparkman.
" Macfarlane & Pettingill.
" Wall & Knight.

GEORGIA.

ATLANTA. E. A. Angier.

IDAHO.

BLACKFOOT. John T. Morgan.
BOISE CITY. J. Brumback.
" Richard Z. Johnson.
KETCHUM. Wm. Hyndman.
LEWISTON. Jas. W. Reid.
MONTPELIER. { Robert S. Spence.
PARIS. {
" Hart & Sons.

ILLINOIS.

CARROLLTON. Withers & Rainey.
CHAMPAIGN. J. L. Ray.
CHICAGO. Kate Kane, 116 East Monroe St.
" Norris Sprigg, 218 La Salle St., Room 617.

CHICAGO. Thornton & Chancellor.
" Ashcraft & Gordon, First Nat. Bak. Bldg
" Ball & Barrett, 78 La Salle St., Room H.
" Cratty Bros., Tacoma Building.
" Thos. J. Holmes, Room 54, 94 La Salle St.
" Smith's Collection Agency, 80 Metropolitan. Block.
DANVILLE. D. D. Evans.
EFFINGHAM. Sylvester F. Gilmore.
" Henry B. Kepley.
ELGIN. Edw. C. Lovell, Rooms 7 to 10, De Bois Bldg.
GALESBURG. Z. Cooley, 232 Cedar St.
GENESEO. Dunham & Foster.
JACKSONVILLE. John A. Bellatti, 224 South Main St.
JOLIET. C. B. Garnsey, 329 Jefferson St.
KANKAKEE. C. A. Lake.
KEWANEE. Chas. K. Ladd.
LITCHFIELD. McWilliams & Son.
MT. VERNON. Chas. H. Patton.
OTTAWA. Rector C. Hitt.
" Silas H. Strawn.
PEORIA. Rice & Rice, 311 Main St.
PONTIAC. A. C. Ball.
RANTOUL. Thomas J. Roth.
SPRINGFIELD. R. L. McGuire, 123 West Side Square.
" Sanders & Bowers, Over Fst. Nat. Bak.
TOLEDO. W. S. Everhart.
VIENNA. P. T. Chapman.
VIRGINIA. J. N. Gridley.
WINCHESTER. J. M. Riggs.

INDIANA.

BLUFFTON. Levi Mock.
BOONVILLE. Handy & Armstrong.
CRAWFORDSVILLE. Thos. F. Davidson.
EVANSVILLE. J. S. & C. Buchanan, Rooms 1 and 2, Business Men Block.
FRANKFORT. Joseph C. Suit.
FORT WAYNE. James E. Graham & Son, Room 26, Bank Block.
GOSHEN. John H. Baker.
INDIANAPOLIS. Chas. E. Barrett.
" Josh. E. Florea, 29½ No. Penn. St.
" Mitchell & Mitchell, Room 22, Vance Block.
JASPER. Fraylor & Hunter.
LA PORTE. C. H. Truesdell.
" Frank E. Osborn.
LEBANON. Charles M. Zion.
MONTICELLO. Guthrie & Bushnell.
PLYMOUTH. R. B. Oglesbee, 113 Michigan St.
PRINCETON. Land & Gamble.
SOUTH BEND. Dunbar & Dunbar, No. 3 Odd Fellows Block.
SPENCER. Inman H. Fowler.
UNION CITY. Theo. Shockney.
VALPARAISO. A. D. Bartholomew.
WINAMAC. Nye & Nye.
WINCHESTER. Watson & Watson.

INDIAN TERRITORY.

MUSKOGEE. Shepard & Shepard.

IOWA.

ANAMOSA. Sheean & McCarn.
" C. N. Brown.
ATLANTIC. Willard & Willard.
" L. L. Delano.
CEDAR RAPIDS. Cooper and Crissman, Rooms 1 and 2, Oriel Block.
" " Rickel & Crocker.
CHARLES CITY. T. A. Hand.
CLINTON. Robert R. Baldwin.
DANBURY. J. H. & E. R. Ostrom.
DES MOINES. J. R. Harcroft.
DUBUQUE. T. J. Paisley, Cor. 7th and Main Sts.
MARSHALLTOWN. J. L. Carney, 2d Floor Court House.
MISSOURI VALLEY. J. S. Dewell.
MORNING SUN. Fred. Courts, Jr.
MT. AYR. M. L. Bevis.
OSAGE. Eaton & Clyde.
OSKALOOSA. G. C. Morgan.
SIDNEY. Joseph Murphy.
SIOUX CITY. T. P. Murphy.
WEBSTER CITY. Wesley Martin.

KANSAS.

ANTHONY. J. P. Grove.

FALL RIVER, J. C. McDoulet.
GARDEN CITY, Brown, Bierer & Cotteral.
GREAT BEND, Clarke & Russell.
HARPER, Sam. S. Sisson.
KANSAS CITY, Clogston, Hamilton, Fuller & Cubbison, Husted Building.
LARNED, H. C. Johns, Wilson Block.
McPHERSON, Frank O. Johnson, 111 North Main St.
NESS CITY, C. J. Bells.
OBERLIN, S. M. McElroy.
OSBORNE, E. F. Robinson.
OSKALOOSA, Marshall Gephart.
OSWEGO, Case & Glasse.
SCOTT CITY, L. V. Craveres.
STOCKTON, W. B. Ham.
TOPEKA, Douthitt, Jones & Mason, Bank of Topeka Building.
WICHITA, Sankey & Campbell, corner Douglas and Market Sts.

KENTUCKY.
BARBOURVILLE, James D. Black.
HENDERSON, Montgomery Merritt.
LOUISVILLE, Rowan Buchanan, 418 Centre St.
MORGANFIELD, H. D. Allen.
MT. STERLING, Wood & Day.
" O'Rear & Bigstaff, Maysville St.
PADUCAH, Thomas E. Moss.

LOUISIANA.
COLFAX, GRANT PARISH, Andrew Thorpe.
HOUMA, L. F. Suthon.
MONROE, Franklin Garrett, cor. Wood and St. John Sts.
NATCHITOCHES, D. C. Scarborough.
NEW ORLEANS, Harry H. Hall, 133 Common St.
" " Moise & Cahn, 21 Commercial Pl.
ST. JOSEPH, TENSAS PARISH, Clinton & Garrett.

MAINE.
PORTLAND, Strout, Gage & Strout, 52 Exchange St.
" Clarence Hale, 39 Exchange St.

MARYLAND.
ANNAPOLIS, James M. Munroe.
BEL AIR, Septimus Davis.
HAGERSTOWN, Frank W. Mish.
ROCKVILLE, Anderson & Bouic.

MASSACHUSETTS.
ATHOL, George W. Horr.
BOSTON, Walter L. Church, 9 Franklin St.
" Southard & Baker, 27 School St.
GREAT BARRINGTON, O. C. Bidwell.
NEWBURYPORT, Charles C. Dame, 59½ State St.
PEABODY, Chas. E. Hoag.
PITTSFIELD, E. M. Wood, 9 Bank Row.
ROCKLAND, Geo. W. Kelley.
SALEM, William H. Gove, Post Office Building.
SPRINGFIELD, Edward H. Lathrop, Room 18, Fuller Block.
WORCESTER, Rice, King & Rice, 6 P. O. Block.

MICHIGAN.
COLDWATER, John S. Evans.
EAST SAGINAW, Herbert A. Forrest.
GRAND RAPIDS, Clark H. Gleason, 53 Pearl St.
HASTINGS, James A. Sweezey.
KALAMAZOO, Wm. Shakespeare, 130 W. Main St.
MUSKEGON, F. A. Nims.
SAND BEACH, Chas. L. Hall.
SAULT STE. MARIE, Jno. A. Colwell.

MINNESOTA.
BLUE EARTH CITY, Geo. W. Buswell.
DULUTH, T. J. Mitchell, Furgusson Block.
" R. R. Briggs, 501 to 503 Chamber of Commerce.
" Alfred Jaques.
JACKSON, T. J. Knox.
MINNEAPOLIS, James O. Pierce, 21 4th St., So.
ST. PAUL, Ewing & Ewing, 716 Pioneer Press Bldg.
" William Foulke.

MISSISSIPPI.
BATESVILLE, L. L. Pearson.
BROOKHAVEN, R. H. Thompson.
CANTON, F. B. Pratt.
FRIARS POINT, D. A. Scott.
GREENWOOD, Jas. K. Vardaman.
JACKSON, Frank Johnston.
MERIDIAN, Cochran & Bozeman, formerly R. F. Cochran.
" McIntosh & Williams.
ROSEDALE, Chas. Scott.

MISSOURI.
APPLETON CITY, W. W. Chapel.

BETHANY, J. C. Wilson.
KANSAS CITY, Brown, Chapman & Brown, 424 Main St.
LOCKWOOD, W. S. Wheeler.
PARIS, Temple B. Robinson.
ST. LOUIS, Henry C. Withers, 711 Odd Fellows Bldg. Illinois Business.
" Chas. Claflin Allen, Laclede Building.
" Seneca N. Taylor, Rooms 408 and 410 American Central Building, Locust and Broadway.

MONTANA.
BOZEMAN, Luce & Luce.
HELENA, Massena Bullard, Room 8, Gold Block, Main St.

NEBRASKA.
ARAPAHOE, J. A. Dudgeon.
KEARNEY, John E. Decker.
NORTH PLATTE, William Neville.
OMAHA, Sanders & Macfarland.
PLATTSMOUTH, H. D. Travis.
YORK, George B. France.

NEVADA.
VIRGINIA CITY, W. E. F. Deal.

NEW HAMPSHIRE.
EXETER, Charles H. Knight, Ranlet's Block.
GREAT FALLS, Wm. F. Russell.
LANCASTER, Ossian Ray.
PETERBOROUGH, R. B. Hatch.

NEW JERSEY.
BELVIDERE, John H. Dahlke.
CAMDEN, Herbert A. Drake, 127 Market St.
NEW BRUNSWICK, James H. Van Cleef, 391 George St.

NEW MEXICO.
ALBUQUERQUE, Bernard S. Rodey.
LAS VEGAS, A. A. Jones.

NEW YORK.
ELMIRA, Denton & McDowell, 335 E. Water St.
ELLENVILLE, John G. Gray.
FULTON, C. H. David.
ITHACA, David M. Dean.
MALONE, J. C. Saunders.
MIDDLETOWN, Charles G. Dill, 3 South St.
NEWBURGH, John M. Gardner.
NEW YORK CITY, Theodore R. Shear, Drexel Bldg., corner Wall and Broad Sts.
PORT JERVIS, Wilton Bennett, St. John's Block.
POUGHKEEPSIE, John H. Millard, 52 Market St.
PLATTSBURG, Jay K. Smith.
SYRACUSE, Smith, Kellogg & Wells.
THERESA, D. Bearup.
WHITEHALL, O. F. & R. R. Davis.

NORTH CAROLINA.
LOUISBURG, F. S. Spruill.

NORTH DAKOTA.
FARGO, B. F. Spalding, 1 Broadway.
VALLEY CITY, Frank J. Young.

OHIO.
ATHENS, Sleeper & Sayre, Newton Bldg., Main St.
BATAVIA, A. T. Cowen (Late Common Pleas Judge).
CANAL DOVER, John A. Hostetler.
CHILLICOTHE, J. B. McLaughlin.
CLARION, Reed & Wilson.
CLEVELAND, Harvey Keeler, 236 Superior St.
" John O. Winship, Room 10, Blackstone Building.
" W. E. Ambler, 263 The Arcade.
CINCINNATI, Wm. Hook, N. E. corner Walnut and Canal Sts.
" Orris P. Cobb, S. E. corner Main and 9th Sts.
" Pogue, Pottenger & Pogue, United Bank Bldg.
FINDLAY, W. H. McElwaine, 325 So. Main St.
GALION, J. W. Coulter.
LIMA, Josiah Pillars.
MANSFIELD, Donnell & Marriott, 43½ No. Main St.
PAULDING, Seiders & Seiders.
TIFFIN, Lutes & Lutes.
WILKES BARRE, W. L. Raeder.

OREGON.
PORTLAND, Woodward & Woodward, Abington Building.
SALEM, Seth R. Hammer.

PENNSYLVANIA.
CLARION, Reed & Wilson.
NEW BLOOMFIELD, W. N. Seibert.
NEWCASTLE, E. T. Kurtz, 81 Pittsburg St.

PITTSBURG. Marshall Brown, 157 Fourth Ave.
SCRANTON. Edward Miles, 225 Washington Ave.
SHAMOKIN. Addison G. Marr.
TAMAQUA. J. O. Ulrich.
TITUSVILLE. Geo. A. Chase, Chase & Stewart Block.
WARREN. Wm. M. Lindsay.
WILKES BARRE. W. I. Raeder.
WILLIAMSPORT. T. M. B. Hicks, Cor. Fourth and Williams Sts.

SOUTH CAROLINA.
DARLINGTON. E. Keith Dargan.

SOUTH DAKOTA.
ABERDEEN. Chas. N. Harris.
" H. H. Potter.
PIERRE. D. F. Sweetland, Law and Real Estate.
" Coe I. Crawford.
RAPID CITY Edmund Smith.
SIOUX FALLS. U. S. G. Cherry, Com'l and Divorce Law.
" Bailey & Stoddard, Metropolitan Block.
" J. M. Donovan, Com'l and Divorce Law

TENNESSEE.
CHATTANOOGA. Clark & Brown.
NASHVILLE. Sumner A. Wilson, Room 20, Vanderbilt Building.

TEXAS.
ALBANY. A. A. Clarke.
AUSTIN. Z. T. Fulmore.
CAMERON. Henderson & Streetman.
" W. T. Hefley.
CLARKESVILLE. H. B. Wright.
CLEBURNE. S. C. Padelford.
COLORADO. Ball & Burney.
FORT WORTH. Oliver S. Kennedy.
" " Newton H. Lassiter.
LA GRANGE. R. H. Phelps, Masonic Building.
LAREDO. Nicholson, Dodd & Mulally.
LONGVIEW. Edward O. Griffin.
PEARSALL. R. W. Hudson.
MASON. Holmes & Bierschwale.
SAN ANTONIO. Cassius K. Breneman.
WACO. Edward A. Marshall, *Land Lawyer and Notary Public.*

UTAH.
SALT LAKE CITY. Maurice M. Kaighm, Rooms 4, 5, & 6, Old Tribune Building.
SALT LAKE CITY. Shepard, Cherry & Shepard.

VIRGINIA.
CHARLOTTESVILLE. Micajah Woods.

HILLSVILLE. D. W. Bolen.
LAWRENCEVILLE. N. S. Turnbull.
LEXINGTON. Letcher & Letcher.
LYNCHBURG. J. E. Edmunds, 807 Main St.
PEARISBURG. J. D. Johnston.
PORTSMOUTH. Wm. H. Stewart, " Land Specialty."
STAUNTON. Braxton & Braxton.
TAZEWELL COURT HOUSE. A. J. & S. D. May.

WASHINGTON.
SEATTLE. Edwin A. Latty, Haller Bldg.
TACOMA. Frank T. Reid & Frank A. Smalley.
WALLA WALLA. Thos. H. Brents.

VIRGINIA.
LAWRENCEVILLE. H. S. Turnbull.

WEST VIRGINIA.
CHARLESTON. Brown & Jackson.
PARKERSBURG. J. G. McCluer.

WISCONSIN.
BARRON. Fred B. Kinsley.
CLINTONVILLE. G. T. Thorn.
DARLINGTON. Orton & Osborn.
GREEN BAY. Wigman & Martin.
LA CROSSE. E. C. Higbee, Rooms 3 & 4, 305 Main St.
MILWAUKEE. Winkler, Flanders, Smith, Bottum & Vilas, 37 Mitchell Building.
NEILLSVILLE. O'Neill & Marsh.
OSHKOSH. Charles W. Felker.
" Hooper & Hooper, Room 9, Algoma Building.
RACINE. John T. Wentworth.
STOUGHTON. Luse & Wait.
SUPERIOR. D. E. Roberts.
" Carl C. Pope.
" E. R. Manwaring.
WEST SUPERIOR. J. R. Bane.
" Reed, Grace & Rock, Rooms 9 to 14, First National Bank.
WHITEWATER. T. D. Weeks.

CANADA.

QUEBEC.
MONTREAL. Burroughs & Burroughs, Nos. 613 and 614 New York Life Building, Place d'Armes Sq.

ONTARIO.
PEMBROKE. James H. Burritt.

PHYSICIANS' DIRECTORY.

Each member of the following list of physicians has been recommended as thoroughly reliable and of good standing in his profession.

ALABAMA.
GADSDEN. E. T. Camp, M. D., 428½ Broad St.

CONNECTICUT.
BRIDGEPORT. S. J. Damon, 59 Harriet Street.
" J. D. S. & Elizabeth G. Smith, M. D., Broad and Gilbert Streets.

DISTRICT OF COLUMBIA.
WASHINGTON. Irving C. Rosse, 1701 H. St., N. W.

FLORIDA.
MICANOPY. L. Montgomery, M. D.

INDIANA.
INDIANAPOLIS. C. T. Bedford, M. D., 290 Massachusetts Ave.

MASSACHUSETTS.
BOSTON. J. P. Chamberlain, M. D., 6 James St.
" M. White Tilton, M. D., Hotel Oxford, Huntington Avenue, Electricity and Diseases of women.
FRANKLIN. J. Cushing Gallison, M. D.
ORANGE. Walter M. Wright, M. D., 37 West Main Street.

MICHIGAN.
GRAND RAPIDS. W. H. Ross, M. D., Room 45, Widdicomb Block.

NEW YORK.
HORNELLSVILLE. John S. Jamison, M. D., 8 Center Street.

OHIO.
AKRON. Kent O. Foltz, M. D., 181 So. Howard St.
LORAIN. Frank Ernest Stoaks, M. D.

PENNSYLVANIA.
LEBANON. D. P. Gerberich, M. D.
PITTSBURG. Frederick Gaertner, M. D.

RHODE ISLAND.
BRISTOL. Gertrude Gooding, M. D.

TENNESSEE.
NASHVILLE. Henry Sheffield, M. D., 141 No. Vine St.

ELECTRICAL APPLIANCES. Address, the Thomas Battery Co., Cardington, O.

EDUCATIONAL INSTITUTIONS.

The Claverack College and Hudson River Institute

Will open its 38th year September 14, 1891. For catalogues, address REV. A H. FLACK, A. M., President, Claverack, N. Y.

NEW JERSEY, BERGEN POINT.
School for Young Ladies.

Location on Salt Water, eight miles from New York.
A. E. SLOAN, M. A.,   LEPHA N. CLARKE, B. A.,
Principal.   Lady Principal.

Christian Science Theological Seminary.

EMMA CURTIS HOPKINS, President.
Office 415, Chicago Auditorium.
Send for catalogue to E. MARTIN, Secretary.

Mt. Auburn Institute.

French and English Home School for Young Ladies. H. THANE MILLER, President, Cincinnati.

College for Young Ladies, Nashville, Tennessee.

Three buildings, 30 officers; 400 pupils; Vanderbilt Privileges; Music, Art. Literature, Kindergarten; Complete Gymnasium; Health Unsurpassed. Send for Catalogue.
REV. GEO. W F. PRICE, D. D., President.

Baldwin Seminary, 20, 24, & 26 Summit Ave., St. Paul, Minn.

A select boarding and day school. Fall term begins Sept. 14. Superior advantages. Healthful location. Certificate admits to Wellesley and other colleges. Address
CLINTON J BACKUS, M. A., Principal.

The Baltimore Medical College

Preliminary Fall Course begins September 1, 1892. Regular Winter Course begins October 1, 1892. Excellent teaching facilities, capacious hospital, large clinics. Send for catalogue, and address
DAVID STREETT, M. D., Dean,
405 N. Exeter St., Baltimore, Md.

TENNESSEE, Brownsville.
Brownsville Female College

Claims to stand, as to the substantials of higher education, in the front rank of American female colleges. Cheap; superb fare; twelve instructors; five degrees; every step for solidity; exactly same advantages offered as in male colleges; increase in patronage under present administration of three years nearly 200 per cent; mild winters.
Pres. T. H. SMITH, A. M.
(Alumnus of University of Va.)

School of Expression. Vocal and literary training. Opens October 6, S. S. CURRY, Ph. D., 154 Beacon St., Boston, Mass.

Harvard University. Summer Courses, Voice and Expression, 5 weeks July 15 Address S. S. CURRY, 154 Beacon St., Boston, Mass.

Province of Expression. Broadest survey of the whole subject.— Herald. School of Expression, 154 Beacon St., Boston, Mass.

The Grammar School, Berthier en haut P. D., Canada.

A thorough school with all comforts of home. French Conversation. Preparation for commercial life or universities. The number being limited (about thirty) and there being four teachers, each pupil is assured of a large amount of individual attention. Boys can enter at any time.
MAX LIEBICH, Principal.

Educate for business at Watertown Commercial College

And School of Shorthand, Typewriting, and Telegraphy. *Shorthand successfully taught by mail.* Send for free trial course. Large illustrated catalogue for stamp.
H. L. WINSLOW, President.
Watertown, S. D.

Mt. Carroll Seminary, Carroll Co., Ill.,

Gives tuition and use of books, *free*, to one student from each county, who meets certain requirements. *"OREAD," free*, gives particulars—send for it. No earnest, faithful student of marked ability, though small means, need fail to secure a Normal, Collegiate, Art, or Music education.

Illinois, Rockford.

Rockford Seminary for young women; 43d year. Full college and preparatory courses, superior advantages for Music, Painting, and Drawing. All departments in charge of Specialists. New Science building. Best advantages for scientific study and investigation. Four well-equipped laboratories — Biological and Botanical, Physical, Chemical, and Mineralogical. Special inducements for teachers who wish to take advanced work. Resident physician, fine gymnasium (40 x 80 ft.), Sargent system. Delicate girls show marked gain in strength while pursuing regular course of study. A new cottage offers students opportunity to reduce expenses to lowest rates. Catalogue gives full particulars as to entrance examinations. Correspondence invited. Lock Box 19.
SARAH F. ANDERSON, Principal.

NEW YORK, BROOKLYN, 160 JORALEMON ST.
Miss Katherine L. Maltby, B. A.,

Formerly principal of the Nassau Institute, will open her spacious and inviting residence, 160 Joralemon Street, Brooklyn, September 24, 1891, for the reception of Young Ladies who desire to spend a winter in the city in the enjoyment of its Art or Musical advantages; for students who will attend the sessions of day schools in Brooklyn; or for pupils who wish special instruction under her charge. Address for circular.
Third Year.   MISS MALTBY, Principal.

MICHIGAN, ANN ARBOR.
School of Chemistry and Pharmacy

In the University of Michigan. Training for service as an analytical or manufacturing chemist. The register of Alumni, with the professional occupation of each, furnished on application.

The St. Louis Hygienic College

OF PHYSICIANS AND SURGEONS will begin its Sixth Annual Course of Instruction Thursday, September 29, 1892. Men and women are admitted. This is the *only Hygienic College* in existence. It has a full three years' course, embracing all the branches taught in other medical colleges; also Hygeio-Therapy, Sanitary Engineering, and Physical Culture. Address for announcement,   S. W. DODDS, M. D., Dean,
2826 Washington Ave.
St. Louis, Mo.

Harned Academy, Plainfield, N J.

A select boarding school for twenty boys. Pleasant home. Thorough instruction. Send for circular.
EDWARD N. HARNED, Principal.

xlii

THE ARENA ELITE HOTEL DIRECTORY.

Christian Science Theological Seminary.

EMMA CURTIS HOPKINS, President.

•

Full course of instruction in Esoteric Christianity,
whose vitality is now entering thousands of lives.

Office, 115 Chicago Auditorium.   Send for Catalogue.

E. MARTIN, Secretary.

xliv

STANHOPE BUGGY.

The above cut accurately represents our

Latest Pattern Stanhope Buggy,

trimmed with a handsome green English woolfin cloth, full Victoria leather top, wings on top; best English mail lamp. Top arranged with Victoria joints, so as to lay perfectly flat when tipped down (cut of same shown later in this magazine). The body panels painted a beautiful Quaker green, with all mouldings and medallions a jet black; a fine gold stripe at edge of body, with all mouldings, etc., blocked out in same. Gear on wheels, etc., painted a dark olive green, with a wide, heavy black stripe edged with a double fine gold stripe.

This vehicle is a marvel of beauty and elegance, and well worth a grand effort to possess.

From time to time we shall show other cuts of our most desirable vehicles, all of which will be of the latest design and most approved construction.

We are manufacturers and dealers in the best grades only. We occupy more floor space than any other house in New England. We always have on hand a number of good second-hand Coaches, Landaus, Broughams, Coupes, Rockaways, Carryalls, and Buggies of all descriptions.

S. A. STEWART & KIMBALL BROS. CO.,
110 TO 116 SUDBURY ST., BOSTON.

This stylish and costly buggy, the price of which is $400, will be given **ABSOLUTELY FREE** for a certain number of annual subscriptions to The Arena.

For particulars send two-cent stamp and get our special premium offer.

ARENA PUBLISHING CO.,
COPLEY SQUARE, BOSTON, MASS.

EMERSON

FINEST TONE, BEST WORK AND MATERIAL.

PRICES MODERATE AND TERMS REASONABLE. **ESTABLISHED IN 1849.** # PIANOS.

60,000 Made and in Use.   Every Instrument Fully Warranted.

The Emerson Upright Pianos especially have obtained a remarkable success during the past few years, and have invariably received a high award wherever exhibited. In all the essential qualities of a **FIRST-CLASS INSTRUMENT** they are second to no pianos manufactured in the country.

EMERSON PIANO CO.,
WAREROOMS: 174 Tremont St., Boston, Mass.   92 Fifth Avenue, New York.

This splendid Emerson Upright Piano given absolutely FREE for subscriptions to The Arena.

Send two-cent stamp for particulars and special premium list.

ARENA PUBLISHING CO.,
COPLEY SQUARE, BOSTON, MASS.

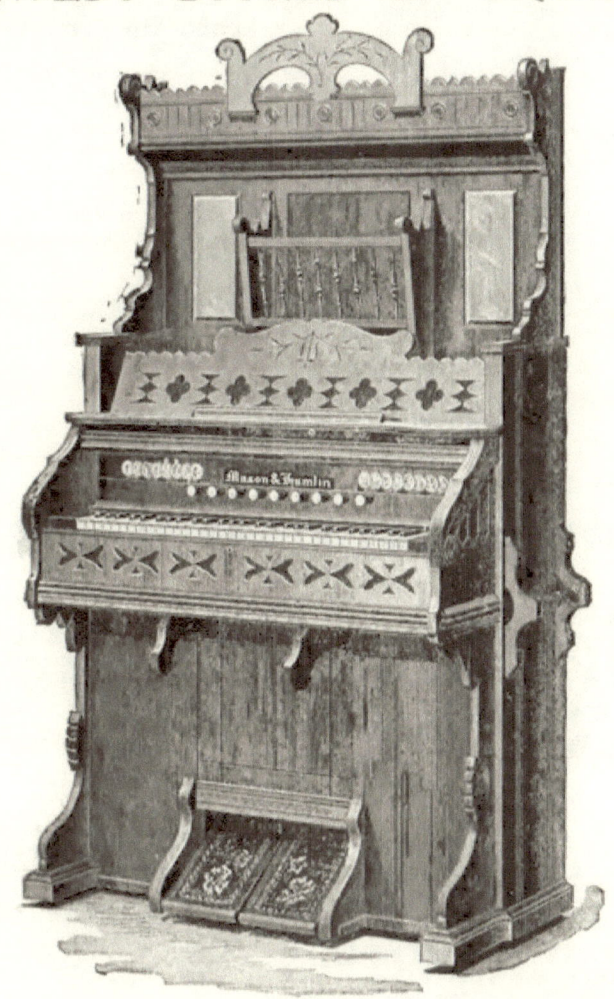

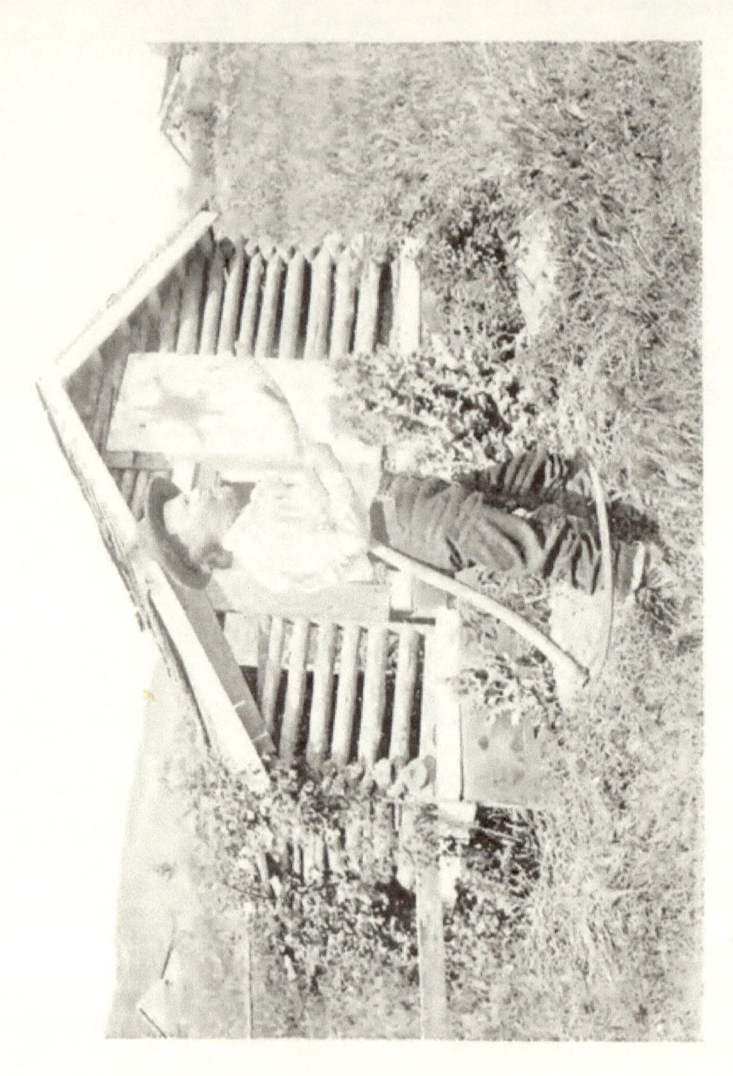

Lange Nirlan; at home. Aug 15.52.

THE ARENA.

No. XXXVI.

NOVEMBER, 1892.

LORD SALISBURY'S AFGHAN POLICY.

BY THOMAS P. HUGHES, D. D.

THREE days before Sir Bartle Frere died, at his home in Wimbleton, he expressed a wish to see me. It appeared that this distinguished statesman was desirous to ascertain the views of those acquainted with the frontier of British India regarding that Afghan policy with which his name had been so closely associated. Sir Bartle was a consistently religious man; and inasmuch as his Afghan policy had brought about two wars, together with the massacre of the British Embassy at Cabul, he seemed anxious to know whether so much war and bloodshed could have been averted.

At that time I was regarded as an authority on everything affecting the Afghan people. I had been government examiner in the Afghan language, I had known the late Shere Ali Khan very intimately, I had resided among the Afghans for twenty years, had travelled through the length and breadth of the frontier, and I had associated with many leading Afghan chieftains on the most friendly and intimate terms; and Sir Bartle clearly recognized my right to have an opinion on this great political question, which was at that time exciting much acrimonious feeling.

It was an interesting circumstance that the late Mr. Forster, Mr. Gladstone's secretary for Ireland, was visiting the dying man at that time, and I found that Mr. Forster's views on the Afghan question were completely in harmony with those of his dying friend.

I told Sir Bartle I honestly believed that a collision with the ameer was inevitable, and that history must vindicate "Lord Salisbury's Afghan Policy." What I said seemed to

comfort the dying hours of the Anglo-Indian statesman, and
I am glad of an opportunity of contributing to the pages of
THE ARENA my views regarding this Afghan question.

Sir Bartle Frere had been for many years the chief com-
missioner (or governor) of the province of Scinde, and had
during that time adopted a line of Afghan policy diametri-
cally opposed to that of Sir John Lawrence when governor
of the neighboring province of the Punjab. Sir Bartle was
selected by the queen to accompany the Prince of Wales on
his visit to India in the winter of 1875-76, and he was the
trusted adviser of Mr. Disraeli, when he, as prime minister,
first inaugurated a change of policy with regard to the ameer
of Cabul from what had been known in India as the
"masterly inactivity" of Lord Lawrence.

The acrimony of feeling to which I have referred was created by the extreme sensitiveness of Lord Lawrence regarding his Afghan policy, and upon which his biographer, Mr.
Bosworth Smith, seems to have staked the reputation of his
hero.

India is the nursery of administrators but not of statesmen,
and Sir Bartle Frere stood out almost alone as the one member of the Indian Civil Service who was prepared to indorse
the views of the Conservative government regarding the
Afghan question.

I write of "Lord Salisbury's Afghan policy"; but in
truth it was the great Semetic statesman, Mr. Disraeli, who
discovered that Constantinople is not on the way to India,
but that Egypt is! and probably Cyprus! that it is easier
to fight Russia on the confines of India than to invade the
Crimea or blockade the Baltic. Consequently it needed the
foresight of a statesman rather than the shortsightedness of
the mere politician to discern that in the negotiations with
Shere Ali in January 1877 the British government was
simply fighting Russia under the guise of a treacherous
Afghan. Even when the crash did come, the British government had accomplished its purpose with comparatively
small losses and with a result which, under different auspices, could only have been achieved by a long, tedious, and
expensive European war.

Many English people thought the Afghan war unnecessary
and even cruel; but I have never met with an Afghan who
did not fully realize that British domination in Afghanistan

is a most vital question, affecting the very existence of British rule in India.

Of course the whole thing was muddled. The British never do enter upon an enterprise which is not "muddled" at first. It was pre-eminently so with Lord Salisbury's Afghan policy.

The change of policy was inaugurated by a political conference, the first meeting of which took place in my library in Peshawar on Jan. 30, 1877. Those who participated in that conference are dead. Sir Lewis Pelly, Dr. H. W. Bellew, Sayyid Noor Muhammad and his Persian secretary (whose name I do not now remember) are dead. Lord Lytton, Sir Louis Cavagnari, Mr. Jenkyns, Ameer Shere Ali Khan, not to speak of many others who also took an active part in those negotiations, have all passed over to the "great majority."

Lord Salisbury was singularly unfortunate in the selection of his men. Lord Lytton as viceroy was pre-eminently unfit to control that large body of intelligent and courageous men who constitute the Civil Service of India. The poetic viceroy was an object of ridicule and distrust among the officers of the government from the very day he entered Government House at Calcutta, and history is never likely to change its verdict as to the weakness of his Indian administration.

Poor Sir Lewis Pelly was an over-estimated man. As "Gun-boat Pelly" he had frightened the Persians at Bushire, but he was powerless to intimidate the Afghans at Cabul. He had absolutely no knowledge of frontier questions.

The selection of Sir Louis Cavagnari, as the first embassy to the city of Cabul, was still more unfortunate. As a magistrate on the frontier he was known as a vain, ambitious, irascible, overbearing young man. The massacre of Cavagnari, with his aides-de-camps Jenkyns, Hamilton, and Kelly, took no one by surprise. There is not the least doubt that it was Cavagnari's ungovernable temper which brought about the calamity by firing the first shot.

Even the selection of my dear lamented friend Dr. H. W. Bellew was unfortunate. For although beloved by the Afghans, he was known among them as a strenuous advocate of the annexation of their country to India.

Sir Lewis Pelly, with his gun-boat fame, and Dr. Bellew,

the avowed advocate of annexation, were not likely to give to the Peshawar Conference the aspect of peace and conciliation.

When the author of "Lucile" wrote to Shere Ali "You are a mere earthen pot between two cast-iron vessels, floating on the current of time, and you will be crushed by the inevitable," it is no wonder that Ameer Shere Ali, who had been a man of war from his youth, and never friendly to the British, should place himself on the defensive and call in the assistance of Russia.

The Cabul Envoy Sayyid Noor Muhammad was a personal friend of mine; I had known him for some five years; I was with him when he died at Peshawar during the time of the conference; and I do not hesitate to affirm that throughout the whole of the negotiations of the Peshawar Conference the Cabul envoy was under the impression that Lord Lytton intended to annex Afghanistan. Time has now shown the Afghans that such was not the intention of the British government; and I should think that, ere this, Ameer Abdur Rahman Khan must be convinced of England's sincerity.

The great difficulty in the way of the change of policy was the strong prejudice against it by those whose duty it was to have supported Lord Lytton, no matter to what extent they mistrusted the man. Lord Lawrence's masterly inactivity had failed, and Lord Salisbury, as secretary of state for India, was determined to act vigorously with regard to the Afghan ameer. The petty jealousies which existed among the Anglo-Indian officials at this time seemed to me, as a disinterested spectator, perfectly amazing. I then saw, what the history of the British nation has so often proved, that the peace of an empire can be sacrificed by officials of microscopic proportions. They were small men who stood in the way of Lord Lytton's policy, but they very nearly defeated the purposes of the government in India, to the great delight of the Grand Old Man at home.

Lord Salisbury's new policy was first initiated in March 1869, when Lord Mayo received Ameer Shere Ali Khan at Umballa. From Peshawar to Umballa the ameer's progress was one grand regal pageant. The Imperial *durbar* of Lord Mayo on that occasion has been well described as "an oriental edition of the Cloth of Gold." But to a wild, rough, warlike son of the desert like Shere Ali, the Barakzai, such a pageant of royalty meant nothing. He enjoyed the dancing of English ladies. He criticised and admired what he called "the almost indecent garb" of the Scotch Highlanders. He sipped the cherry brandy of the foreigner with delight. He appreciated, as he could not fail to do, the manly presence of the viceroy. But what did it all mean?

Lord Mayo was a Tory viceroy serving a Liberal administration. His voice was the voice of Salisbury, but his hands were the hands of Gladstone. Shere Ali Khan returned to Peshawar, a disappointed man, as I can testify from my personal intercourse with the ameer at that time. He felt he had been deceived. And when the ameer's envoy visited Lord Northbrook at Simla in 1875, we have it on the authority of the parliamentary Blue Book, that "he stated implicitly that his master had now a deep-rooted distrust of the good faith and sincerity of the British government."

The political situation in September 1892 is precisely that of March 1869 unless twenty-three years of experience have taught Mr. Gladstone a lesson. A Tory viceroy is now serving a Liberal prime minister. But a quarter of a century has wrought a marvellous change in the feelings and opinions of British officers in India. There is probably not a civil servant in India who does not understand the importance of the position of the ameer of Cabul with reference to the future of India, and they have been so indoctrinated with the firm and vigorous policy of Lord Salisbury that they will probably take unkindly to the shifting and scuttling-out methods of the Liberal leader.

The present political situation is perilous in the extreme. Any want of determination to place Afghanistan beyond the reach of Russian intrigue may cost England her Indian Empire. When Shere Ali Khan was dethroned because he received the Russian embassy and rejected the British, an old Khyberee who witnessed the fall of Ali Musjid and the British advance into Afghanistan, said to me, "I now see that England is not afraid of Russia." And there are three hundred millions of people more or less, many of them belonging to the most warlike races of the world, who with that old Khyberee have their eyes turned in the direction of Cabul and the Russians.

No secrecy is needed. There need be no state secrets.

England does not want the ameer's country, but she must have his alliance. If Abdur Rahman is tricky and untrue, the British can at any moment march an army to Cabul or Candahar with the fullest assurance of victory. Whilst Afghanistan is a difficult country to hold, it is easy to invade. The march of General Pollock in 1842 proved this. So have more recent campaigns. The Bolun and the Khyber Passes are, thanks to Lord Salisbury's Afghan policy, under British protection. There are good roads both to Cabul and Candahar, and every square mile of the country has been carefully surveyed.

The selection of Ameer Abdur Rahman was a political venture. He had for some years been the guest of the Russian government, but he became ameer of Cabul with British gold and British bayonets. He can be dethroned within a month, and the ex-Ameer Yakoob Khan, now a guest of the British, could reign in his stead. Yakoob Khan has always been friendly to England, for the massacre of the embassy during his rule was, I maintain, the fault of the embassy itself.

The ameer of Cabul is no longer a personality. He represents an idea — the domination of the British power in the East.

Russia may extend her frontier to Pekin or Canton, and it would not cause a ripple among the three hundred millions who acknowledge British rule in India ; but Russian ascendancy in Herat, Candahar, or Cabul would be an immense weakening of England's prestige among the warlike races of India.

England already possesses a portion of Afghanistan. The Peshawar valley is part and parcel of Afghan territory, inhabited by Afghans of the purest stock, speaking the Afghan tongue. During the mutiny of 1857 it was Lord Lawrence's policy to " retire modestly " from Peshawar, and no negotiations are ever entered into with the ameers of Afghanistan without some attempt being made on their part to secure the Afghan occupation of the Peshawar valley, as a basis for a friendly treaty.

Lord Salisbury's vigorous policy has completely obliterated the faintest hope of such a possibility, and the British possession of the Khyber Pass is a clear intimation to Russia that if she is determined to fight for supremacy in the east, the struggle will probably take place in the valley of Peshawar, the historic battle-ground of centuries.

Occasional difficulties at Merv, or in the Pamirs, or at Punjdeh, or in the Black Mountain, are only incidents which are among the inevitable environments of the Afghans. The Afghans resemble the Irish in many respects: they are never quite satisfied unless they are dragging their coat-tails round in a spirit of defiance. In dealing with such a people it is absolutely necessary to be truthful, straightforward, and firm.

Unfortunately the ameers of Cabul know nothing of the Britisher in his traditional character as John Bull. Englishmen speak and write of Russian duplicity and intrigue, and arrogate to their own nation the moral quality of straightforwardness; but the ameer of Cabul can see no difference whatever between the two nations as regards the ethical development of their respective characters in diplomatic affairs.

Why should he? Russia, he knows, never did profess much in the direction of probity and honesty; and experience has taught him that, in the midst of a great deal of political cant, the most treacherous designs can be consummated, even by the "straightforward Englishman." It is impossible to get an English diplomat to see these things from an Afghan standpoint; hence the difficulty. The ameer of Cabul reasons very much in this way: The peaceful commercial mission of Sir Alexander Burns in 1832 ended in the invasion of Afghanistan, and the dethronement of Ameer Dost Muhammad in 1837; the Umballa conference of 1869, with its assurance of friendly help, ended in the Seistan arbitration which robbed the Afghans of a province; the Peshawar conference of 1877 brought about the dethronement of two ameers and the prosecution of two Afghan wars.

Now, should there be any change at the present time consequent on the transfer of power from Lord Salisbury to Mr. Gladstone, it will only add to the Afghan's conviction that British statesmen at Simla and Peshawar can lie and deceive just as vigorously as the Russians of Samarkand and Tashkend.

It is positively unjust to assert that the Afghan cannot keep a treaty. The only straightforward and John Bull transaction which has ever been enacted between Great Britain and Cabul was the treaty of "perpetual peace and friend-

ship" which was established and signed and sealed by Ameer
Dost Muhammad and Lord Dalhousie on the first day of May
1855. Dost Muhammad stuck to this treaty like a man.
As a friend to the British he expelled the Persians from
Herat, and two years afterwards he held back his own people
from invading India during the troubles of the mutiny.

The only hope for the settlement of this great question
is the continuance of that policy of " masterly determination " which has characterized the British treatment of the
ameer during the last six years. The construction of a railway to Candahar and to Cabul, both of which were contem-
plated by Lord Lytton, would do more to a peaceful settlement of the turbulent Afghan than any other step which
could be suggested. If the British government intends to
keep its hold on Afghanistan, it must develop the resources
of the country, otherwise it will become depopulated. I find
from English newspapers, published in India, that the population of the country is rapidly decreasing; naturally so,
when the Afghan finds that he has only to settle in India to
live in peace and develop his material resources.

I believe in the Afghan; his treachery has passed into a
proverb; but during twenty years of my life I have slept in
his dwelling, dined in his guest house, and trusted my life
to his protection; and I honestly believe, notwithstanding
much which may be said to the contrary, that the Afghan
can be trusted and can be true.

The " unspeakable Turk " has jeopardized the peace of
Europe for centuries; and it seems probable that unless a firm
and determined attitude is maintained by England, the uncontrollable Afghan will jeopardize the peace of Asia in the
same way. But there is this great difference—that while the
Turk belongs to an expiring race, the Afghan is as strong
and vigorous in his physique and individuality as he
was in the days when his forefathers conquered Northern
India. In dealing with the Afghans the British are dealing with a nation of men as well as with a nation possessing
inherent powers of development. Lord Beaconsfield, as an
Oriental, realized the possibilities of the Asiatic; and when
he sent regiments of Afghans, Sikhs, and Goorkhas to the
island of Malta, it was as a hint to Russia that the fighting
power of India, under the command of British officers, is
simply inexhaustible.

THE NEW EDUCATION AND ITS PRACTICAL APPLICATION.

BY PROFESSOR JOS. RODES BUCHANAN.

IN asserting the claims of "full-orbed education," I deemed it sufficient to refer to its triumphant success in developing the nobler elements of humanity and repressing all vicious tendencies in the state reform school of Ohio, under Mr. G. W. Howe, at Lancaster, in the famous school of Fellenberg, at Hofwyl, and in the Rauhen Haus, near Hamburg, under Mr. Wichern. As the triumphant success of the full-orbed ethical method in three different countries, amply authenticated, ought to be conclusive with every candid thinker, I need not refer to other examples before answering the question of all practical philanthropists, What is the full-orbed ethical method, and how does it differ from that of our common schools, in many of which the unrestrained turbulence, mischief, obscenity, and juvenile rowdyism that abound make a moral malaria from which faithful parents should withhold their children, at least until they are old enough to withstand it.

What a signal contrast our common schools offer to the three institutions just mentioned! and as it is in our own country, I refer especially to the school at Lancaster, O., in which, although the pupils were all the convicts of the courts of the state, there was an ideal condition never perhaps seen in our public common schools, — no quarrels or fights, no profane or obscene language, no wanton mischief, no disrespect to teachers, no cutting or defacing furniture, but at all times a steady, industrious, and gentlemanly deportment which made them acceptable to the people of the neighborhood, and a steady progress in maturing and confirming by habit the moral nature, which generally in less than three years enabled the authorities to give them a friendly dismission or graduation, as truly prepared to lead a correct life. The report of 1873 says: "We receive bad boys, and see them greatly benefited; idle boys, and see them become industrious; vicious and revengeful boys, and see them become mild and teachable; profane and evil-speaking boys, soon to find that no evil communications proceed out of their mouths."

If so much can be done with prison convicts, what may not be done with the uncorrupted youth of good families? Is it extravagant to affirm, with such experience before us, that a single generation grown up through full-orbed ethical education would scarcely have one criminal in a thousand, and would be almost entirely free from the frauds, the vices, the selfishness, and the domestic discord and misery that darken the picture of society to-day, and raise in many minds the question, Is life worth living? It is entirely safe to say that between two nations reared under such an education, WAR WOULD BE IMPOSSIBLE, and that which the religious teaching of ADULTS through sixty generations has not accomplished, would be accomplished in one by directing our labor to the pliant minds of youth. The deplorable failure of all accepted methods of the state, the college, and the church throughout all history to avert the progress of crime, pauperism, premature death, insanity, suicide, and the *national crime of war*, should rouse the conscience and fire the soul of every philanthropist and every good citizen who can think seriously for an hour, when the demonstration is presented that in one generation humanity can rise from the dark morass of misery and crime to the highlands of honor, health, and happiness, thus realizing the ideal toward which millions of the best and wisest of all ages have been toiling in vain; for instead of approaching it, they have but held the race feebly against moral and social degeneracy.

Great, indeed, is the change proposed, which would abolish the permanent industrial and social war of classes and individuals, now threatening to become a bloody civil war, all over the world, between capital and labor, and would absolutely forbid all international wars. These are permanent institutions as education has been conducted heretofore; and Von Moltke, while recognizing the principles of religion, strangely recognized war as a permanent international institution which all must be educated to understand and to meet. "War," said he, "is an element in the order of the world ordained by God. Without war, the world would stagnate and lose itself in materialism!"

Felony is born and bred into the life of nations. To murder and rob a hundred thousand people in an adjoining territory against whom we have no serious accusation is the premeditated crime for which the millions of Europe are thoroughly educated to-day, without a protest from the church or the college. Thus educated one nation may devastate another with as little excuse or justification as a horde of pirates or the Thugs of India (which has often happened); and when the horrid carnage has ended and the calmer reflection of peace arrives, neither clergymen nor philosophers nor historians generally use any moral standard in their judgment of crimes in which they see but military power and glory. The conscience that could make *remorse* for such crimes does not exist, national remorse being an unknown condition,* and the malaria of our false education plants in every nationality the slowly developing poison which eventuates in the fever of war.

War and all the other curses of our social system (poverty, crime, and pestilence) are as distinctly involved in our educational system as the oak in the acorn, and, indeed, much more distinctly; for in the elaborate scholasticism of Germany, the duel is the very crown and flower of its ethical principles, and in all educational institutions war is the gigantic picture on which the young are made to gaze in admiration, and grow enthusiastic over its most magnificent criminals, whose pugnacity they imitate upon each other, making hazing, such as disgraces West Point, and fierce struggles in the field a regular feature of college life.

In proposing a revolutionary system to eradicate the evils of the past and present, and differentiate coming generations from all their predecessors, as widely as the noble St. Bernard dog is differentiated from the black wolf, we propose nothing beyond the well-known possible variations of nature; for even the wild wolf has been domesticated into an agreeable and faithful companion for man, and the fragrant, luscious apple has been developed from the wild and worthless crab, and many a desperate criminal has been converted by religious influence into an exemplary leader in every duty. Indeed, this revolution of the moral nature is a common incident of the reformatory schools in which the true ethical education

---

* Did Victor Hugo or any eminent Frenchman ever express any regret for the assault of France on Germany under Louis Napoleon?

ELEPHANT.

HIPPOPOTAMUS.

ST. BERNARD DOG.

HYENA.

DOVE.

GOLDEN EAGLE.

EXPLANATORY NOTE ON ILLUSTRATIONS.

The fact that the status of any animal is determined by the development of its nervous system is familiar to all biologists, but the fact that the brain is chiefly the seat of psychic functions has operated as an overshadowing terror to prevent its proper study by the medical profession, which refuses to recognize the soul as the comprehensive vitality of man, or to tolerate its recognition and study as a proper subject of science, or even to extend either courtesy or justice to those who have successfully prosecuted its study.

Self-limited thus by a rigid materialism to the physical aspects of life, it is no

has been realized; and in individuals of the impressible tem-
perament I have been demonstrating since 1841 that such a
temporary change can be effected in one minute, and even
the medical colleges have learned that this can be accomplished with individuals liable to the suggestive control to
which has been given the name of hypnotism. To develop
the moral nature into exemplary control of the man is not a
more difficult task than to increase the circumference of the
chest and the arms, which every teacher of gymnastics would
readily undertake to do; but, alas, why is muscular development so well understood and practiced, while moral development, which is worth more than all the rest of education, is
but accidentally or incidentally thought of, all the way from
the primary school to the university; and if it were not a
divergence from our theme, I might show in some departments of education a positive damage to the moral nature.

In the development of ANTHROPOLOGY, which I have been
demonstrating half a century (with unanimous acceptance
wherever presented), it is shown that the evolution of the
higher nature of man is closely associated with that superior
region of the brain which distinguishes all docile domesticated animals from the fierce and untamable carnivora of the
forest — that region of the brain which (unlike the cerebel-
lum, pons, crura, thalami, quadrigemina, and striata) is not in

wonder that biologists of the now dominant school have been so extremely blind to the
development and functions of the brain, and have failed to observe the contrasted
functions and effects of the superior and inferior portions of the brain — the superior
being devoted to the higher functions of life and the inferior to the animal nature and
lower passions.

And yet this contrast of development and function is conspicuously marked throughout the vertebrata, — from man and the orang throughout the carnivora and herbivora
down to the poisonous serpents on land and the poisonous, horrible-looking fishes at
the bottom of the Pacific Ocean. If the whole animal kingdom were arrayed before us
in contrasted groups, every intelligent schoolboy would observe the comparatively
amiable, docile, and educable character of animals in which the brain (and consequently the outline of the head) rises in rounded fulness above the eyes, in contrast
with the fierce, dangerous, and uncontrollable nature of those in which the low, flat
head, broad at its junction with the neck, shows the predominance of the basilar half
of the brain.

To illustrate this I have selected a few familiar animals whose character is so well
known as not to need a full biographic contrast of their natures. The "half-reasoning"
and useful elephant contrasts with the dull and useless hippopotamus, and the fierce
lion with the lovely gazelle, whose tender eyes are compared with those of the loveliest
woman. If the gazelle is flattered in the outline it was not by design, for the outline
was taken from Buffon. The tiger that makes prey of the feeble Hindu contrasts with
the reindeer, the most valuable of all man's kindly servants. A noble St. Bernard dog,
so manlike in intelligence and kindness, contrasts with the hyena. The dove, with
voice of love and gentleness, contrasts with the golden eagle (our carnivorous national
emblem), and would make a more striking contrast with the harpy eagle, the most
ferocious of birds. The lovely and affectionate seal, whose skin in death adorns the
loveliness of woman, contrasts with the reptile crocodile.

That such contrasts, running through the whole animal kingdom (as I may hereafter
illustrate), should have been entirely overlooked by naturalists, studying with microscopic care the forms of bones, feathers, scales and viscera, reminds us of the fact that
a fly may crawl over an engraving, perceiving every line and dot, with no conception of

GAZELLE.

LION.

REINDEER.

TIGER.

SEAL.

CROCODILE.

the picture. Such has been the myopic way of studying the universe, which is still fashionable.

These illustrations may help to enforce the truth that the elevation and redemption of man depend upon the cultivation of the higher regions of his psychic nature, which are unitized with the higher regions of his brain, and thereby made more intelligible and more accessible. If the same care and intelligence which have been given to the development of the horse were given to the development and culture of man, our evolution would be very rapid. But at present the horse is in advance of the man in normal development, and many a bird and quadruped has more of the gentler elements than the cruelly carnivorous man, who slays it in wantonness.

close association with animal life and action, but separated from it by the ventricles, has a controlling and moderating power over animalism, and gives a home to the higher nature, its removal by the knife leaving the animal with but physiological existence, void of idea, emotion, or impulse.

The development of this region of the brain and its associate faculties offers no greater difficulty than the familiar development of any muscular region of the body. The simple law of development is that exercise in a normal manner produces circulation of blood, growth, and ultimately permanent organic power.

The exercise of any emotion or faculty increases its power and the facility of bringing it into play, as well as its spontaneous and irrepressible activity as a ruling element of the constitution. Hence, judicious cultivation for noble purposes changes the character permanently to a higher type, as certainly as continued intoxication debases it.

How, then, should the school begin and carry on this cultivation of the nobler nature? The first requisite is that the teacher should be of the nobler type of humanity, with the dignity and firmness that compel the pupil's respect and obedience, and the amiability that compels the pupil's love. If the pupil neither respects nor loves the teacher, he is governed only by force, and learns to hate and to cheat the teacher, or, in other words, is continually under a debasing influence. That amiability and patient kindness with the young are more common with women than men, indicates that they should take the lead in teaching, reinforced by the greater force and authority of male teachers.

All teaching should be pleasant and attractive to the pupil. I have often said that *no child should be sent to school*, for all schools should be made so interesting and attractive, that to be excluded would be a punishment — to be admitted a delight. This does not imply the coddling of the pupil in luxurious indolence, but the most energetic intellectual activity, into which he would enter with the same delight as in his athletic sports. Whatever is done with pleasure is done with vigor and freedom from fatigue, and with increasing power, as whatever is uninteresting and disagreeable, depresses, exhausts, and debilitates. How great an amount of brain power, health, and happiness has been destroyed by systems of teaching which fail to interest the pupil, and produce weariness, discouragement, and disgust, ending in permanent aversion to books, and suggesting the theory published by Dr. Clark, a learned Harvard professor, that education was too fatiguing and depressing a process for the delicate constitution of woman. The truth of this might be admitted in reference to *false systems* of education, for they have been destructive to the health of young men, and throughout this century have been making the college youth of Germany myopic. But experience has shown that women endure collegiate training at least as well as men, and that rational collegiate training improves the health. An institution that does not improve the health of its pupils, should not be tolerated.*

But every natural healthy child is a self-educator, with a curiosity that is eager to become acquainted with everything, and will follow with delight the teacher who gives him interesting and valuable knowledge of things that he can understand. He is curious concerning all things, and eager to learn, with cyclopediac variety, all that the world contains, so far as he can understand it, by seeing, by handling, and by hearing explanations and descriptions. He is in a new world to him, and there is a limitless amount of knowledge that is as attractive as a good book of travels or a well-written novel. The skilful teacher can give a fascinating interest to

*Professor Bragdon of Lasell Seminary **is authority for** these facts: **Since** the opening of the seminary in September, **up to** date, forty-two young women have gained nine **pounds** and over; three, fourteen each; two, sixteen; one, nineteen, one, twenty; one, twenty-two; and the record breaker has gained twenty-three pounds in a little over four months. The feather weight of them all weighs eighty-one pounds, the heaviest plump, one hundred and sixty-seven, and they are the healthiest set of girls in New England. So much for calisthenics, athletics, physiology, and hygiene in the curriculum of higher education. — *Boston Post.*

What a signal **contrast to** this is the cramming, life-exhausting system which still survives in spite of common sense, which was so pathetically illustrated in the death of Grace Walton, on whose death record her physician placed this sentence : "Due to the Boston school system of cramming, — too much study and brain work." Legitimate and symmetrical brain work builds up the constitution, but the false text-book system destroys it. Others have condemned it more forcibly than myself. The Rev Dr Collyer of New York, in a Sunday discourse, said: "I do not hesitate for a moment to say that there are children who will flock to their schools as to a prison, and to their tasks as to a sore bondage, and they cannot tell you why; but the chances are that the reasons are very simple if we would only take pains to look for them. They are not equal to the tasks that are laid on them, and so they are slowly breaking down, or burning up year by year, and will die in the end from overwork — though we may call it a fever — or live only half a life, while the other half has gone into their learning. Or that which they have to learn in the machines we call schools may answer in no sense to their nature or their liking, any more than if you should try to turn a duckling into a nightingale, or to train a lamb to bear heavy burdens. They revolt at their tasks, poor things, and we fret and scold, while all the time it is the revolt of nature and of God's grace hidden in their life."

But all this folly is doomed to extinction. The admirable physical culture practiced by Dr. Sargent at Harvard and at fifty other schools, of which we recently had a beautiful exhibition in Kansas City, with two thousand pupils of both sexes, in a public park, displaying their proficiency in physical exercise, marks a new era, in which I would desire merely the addition of musical and ethical culture in combination, which adds so much to the perfection of physical life and development.

his instruction when it is given orally. The young should not be confined to text-books which fatigue and devitalize, but should learn chiefly from the voice, which inspires and conveys the spiritual energy of the teacher.* Adults can profit by text-books, but they prefer to learn from the voice of the lecturer, at a tenfold greater expense. Children are far less capable of learning from text-books; yet it is upon children that this burden is placed, compelling a physical stagnation, restraint, and silence, from which oral teaching is free. Such stillness or restraint is ten times as injurious to the young as to the mature adult.

A proper school is a scene of active life and enjoyment, far more attractive to the pupil than anything he can find at home or in the street. The teacher who cannot appreciate this and does not strive for it, is not qualified for his profession. Colonel Higginson having advocated the pleasurable view, was opposed by a teacher who maintained that arithmetic could not be made pleasant, to which Louisa P. Hopkins replied: "The little classes I have taught rose before my vision again, all alive with pleasurable excitement as they stood at the board with their work in long division. Ethel and Bessie, Hetty, Teddy, and Madge, all the seven, eight, or ten year olds, fairly dancing with eager enthusiasm to complete the work with the greatest possible accuracy and rapidity. The effort on my part was to keep them cool enough to work as efficiently as they could, so that they should not become excited to the point of bewilderment. I have invariably seen a high degree of enjoyment associated with the learning and practice of long division." From my own experience fifty-eight years ago, I can say, there is no subject which a competent teacher cannot make attractive and interesting to his pupils. But our cold-blooded scholastic system has so deadened the sympathies that, until very recently, it was difficult to find books adapted to the young, the authors being deficient in sympathy. Indeed, a considerable portion of our literature has been blighted by scholasticism into a dry and dreary character, and the defect is still greater in Germany.

---

* These ideas are not unfamiliar to the *best* teachers, who differ very widely from the monotonous pedagogue. Superintendent Harrington of New Bedford, speaking of teaching history, said: "I would throw away the text-books altogether *as such*, and take the subject wholly out of the list of text-book studies. I would let no formal examinations lie in wait for it. The teachers should be free from every trammel,—free to make the instruction so *delightful and winning* as it may be within their ability to accomplish."

Incessant activity is the nature of youth and the source of all growth and development. The function of the teacher is to see that this activity is normal and complete — that it brings into play for cultivation and growth every faculty and organ which we desire to see fully developed and strong in the mature man, to make an admirable character. Early culture will do it — will determine his adult life; and there is a still more potent, because still earlier, culture, which precedes the school, and is still more neglected or mismanaged — the embryonic culture of gestation, and the prior culture of the parent. But beginning in youth, with all the defects from parentage, I maintain that a true education can revolutionize the character and redeem it from all serious defects, if the youth can be completely surrounded and controlled by the educational system; and this has been so thoroughly demonstrated by experience, that I assume it as unquestionable.

All faculties can be cultivated into a marvellous power which would *a priori* seem impossible, and human nature may be carried to every conceivable extreme, physically and morally. The South American Guacho can gallop on horseback all day, and live upon jerked beef and water, with a hardy health unknown to Europeans. The Esquimaux in the Arctic zone can flourish and enjoy life in an atmosphere fifty or sixty degrees below zero, and occupy snow houses which never have a fire, while the Hindu enjoys a temperature of one hundred and twenty to one hundred and thirty degrees, and the African can live in a climate which in a few months is fatal to the Caucasian race. Equally variable are the moral and social sentiments. Some barbarous tribes are natural thieves, but travellers ascribe to Norwegians an honesty almost incredible to our Anglo-Saxon race. The extreme amiability and courtesy of the Japanese have many contrasts in barbarian brutality. The social sentiments are educated into the utmost extremes, from the ultra monogamy, which admits no divorce, to polygamy and polyandry; and from the rigorous Puritanic ideas of marriage to the easy freedom of Vienna, where the majority of the women live without marriage; from the fanaticism of Mohammedans, who think the woman that exposes her face a detestable criminal, to the Eden-like simplicity of Japan, where the sexes bathe together in public without embarrassment or any thought of impropriety; from the honorable position of woman in ancient Egypt to her debased condition in India, and her condition of ignorance and virtual slavery in modern civilization, from which this century is lifting her.

Whatever faculties are incessantly cultivated through life must become the dominant elements of the character. Our selfish civilized society cultivates the elements that develop into robbery, murder, drunkenness, and suicide. By cultivating in the opposite direction, we may rear a race of happy men and women that would shun alcohol with loathing, and would rather be slain than commit murder.

The affective nature of man has been signally neglected, as if the intellectual alone were worthy of cultivation, the intellect being at the same time restrained by dogma and authority, enfeebled by the uninteresting and unprofitable, deprived of its normal support in the moral energies, and distorted and made lame by hereditary prejudices and falsehoods of the past, firmly enforced by miseducated teachers.

The *vital energy of the soul*, which invigorates and inspires the intellect, has been excluded from educational culture, and almost excluded from the English language, for we have not the words to express it in our degenerate form of speech. *Moral* has degenerated into an expression of conventional rules and perfunctory compliance; *emotional* has degenerated into a conception of excitement tending toward hysteria; *spiritual* into something unearthly; *psychic* into far-fetched subtlety; and *virtue* into highly respectable propriety. If these words could be restored to their proper vital and dignified meaning, they might be used to describe the normally strong, just, benevolent, lovely, happy, and heroic elements of character without which man is not fit to live, but without the culture of which colleges have been content to send him forth, often to failure and dishonor, after cramming his memory with the knowledge and opinions of some prior period,* never giving him the most advanced thought of the

---

* Colleges have always been behind the times—a drag on the wheels of progress. This I know to be terrifically true of medical colleges, by personal experience in the last forty-six years. It was true in the Roman empire, for even after the establishment of Christianity and down to the capture of Constantinople, the text-books were still the same as in the time of Plutarch. The colleges of Europe five hundred years ago were monastic institutions with monks for their teachers and Aristotle for their master. They inculcated a contempt for women. It was only because Max Muller was wanted at Oxford that the rule forbidding the marriage of Oxford fellows was abolished, as Muller had a wife. That woman was carefully excluded from colleges, is a sufficient proof of their lax ethical condition; and until recently, there was scarcely a masculine medical college fit for a respectable woman to enter. I had the

times, nor any impulse to seek it, nor any training preparing him for either moral or financial and industrial eminence. Pardon this digression; but the dreary and disastrous failures of education, as it has been — failure to save the individual and the nation — stand out as a terrible reality when we look over the past and contemplate the present. The enfeebled intelligence and enfeebled conscience of the nations is not even aware of its shortcomings, but boasts of its enlightenment like a Chinese mandarin. But what is the enlightenment worth which cannot or will not lift a nation above the level of widespread crime, pauperism, and dangerous discontent and discord among classes? If we do not realize our defects by comparison with a just ethical standard, we may perhaps realize them by comparison with a nation inferior to ours in many advantages to which we are, in our self-righteousness, sending missionaries.

When the Japanese ambassador to England was asked, a few years since, what he thought of European society, he replied: " One great drawback to it is the *entire absence of the sense of brotherhood*, which the strain and competition of modern business had produced. In Japan the members of a family are all bound together by the closest social ties. When I am in Tokio, there is no man of my native village, no matter how poor, how mean, or how destitute he may be, that could not have the utmost confidence in coming to me for assistance. *Nor could I refuse it to him.* There in the Japanese capital, with a population of one million five hundred thousand, there are only eight or nine hundred persons who depend upon the state for their support; that is, who correspond to your paupers." When will Americans be educated up to the Japanese standard of brotherhood — the universal brotherhood which they profess on Sunday in their churches, but have never imbibed in their education, and therefore know it not!

On this subject we may receive a fine lesson from Sir Walter Scott, who said, in reply to an extravagant eulogy of mere literary accomplishments, " God help us, what a poor world this would be if that were the true doctrine! I

pleasure, at Cincinnati in 1847, of opening the door of a medical college for the first time to women. Professor Dimon said, some years since, that the American college is little better than a copy of the English college, made when the English was in its worst state, one of its worst features being the slavish reproduction of this monastic feature, the exclusion of women. But a great change has begun within the last fifteen years, and possibly they may cease to cherish and prolong the horrid orthography of the English language, which has no excuse to prolong its barbarous and costly existence.

have read books enough, and observed and conversed with enough of eminent and splendidly cultured minds too in my time; but I assure you, I have heard higher sentiments from the lips of poor, uneducated men and women, when exerting the spirit of severe yet gentle heroism under difficulties and afflictions, or speaking their simple thoughts as to circumstances in the lot of friends and neighbors, than I ever yet met with out of the Bible. We shall never learn to respect our real calling and destiny until we have taught ourselves to consider everything as moonshine compared with the *education of the heart.*"

And yet this educational problem, so befogged and involved, is as simple in principle as the training of a pugilist, which, being on the level of the animal nature, is so well understood. The principle is the same — thorough action and culture. As the pugilist gives every muscle prolonged, agreeable, and vigorous action every day, so should the teacher give prolonged, agreeable, and vigorous action to every faculty of the soul, and especially to the higher and stronger faculties, which sustain and vitalize the others, and which occupy the greater portion of the brain lying above the lateral ventricles. The regions of the brain in which vivisectors have been unable to find anything in their wholesale torturing slaughter of horses, dogs, rabbits, birds, fishes, and guinea pigs, because they were looking for physical effects, and not for soul powers, are the regions of the faculties for which they were not looking, the manifestations of which require to be studied in man by the methods which I have been demonstrating for half a century; the results being confirmed instead of contradicted by the imperfect experiments on animals. These results show that whenever the circulation and consequent vitality of the superior and upper posterior region of the brain rises above its common level, the character rises correspondingly in dignity, power, and virtue; and even in animals, the survey of the entire animal kingdom demonstrates what naturalists have so uniformly overlooked, that the higher development of this region, which any one can see at a glance, elevates the animal nearer to humanity, and qualifies it for the friendly companionship of man, as we see in the St. Bernard and shepherd's dog, the Shetland pony, the reindeer, the gazelle, the sheep, the camel, the elephant, the seal, the pigeons, doves, singing birds, and poultry,

when we compare them with the lion, tiger, hyena, polar
bear, hippopotamus, crocodile, harpy eagle, hawks, and
poisonous serpents.

The normal culture of man develops the whole physical
constitution, and especially its nobler portion above the dia-
phragm (as explained by Sarcognomy) and the entire brain,
giving especial attention to that nobler portion of the brain
in which man excels all animals, and which constitutes his
superiority — a region which the most ambitious achievements of science have so effectually ignored, and which,
before the present century, was not even anatomically understood.   The culture and growth of this region is the development of that which places man at the head of the animal
kingdom, and qualifies him for illimitable progress. This
culture is simply the culture of the noblest elements of his
nature by their incessant exercise.

How are the vital elements of the soul to be cultivated?
I would not say emotional or virtuous or psychic or moral,
for these words have lost their proper meaning in vulgar
usage. They are to be cultivated by the immediate and
constant performance of every duty, until by habit and
growth such action becomes habitual and as unchangeable as
our congenital nature.

The first and fundamental duty of life is the industrial,
the duty of careful and effective self-support, that we may not
beg or rob or burden any one, and may be able to help
others — to be a benefactor, and not a burden. This duty
was utterly scorned by the old style of education, — from the
time of Plato, we might almost say to the present time, — producing a lofty scorn of labor. Such a system of education is rotten to the core. It demoralizes the entire commu-
nity, separates it into hostile classes, and devotes human life
to the greedy pursuit and the ostentatious squandering of
money, to live above the faithful and simple life of honorable
industry, without even training the money hunter to the
proper and skilful pursuit of wealth, thus preparing him for
all the cunning and corrupt methods of an unscrupulous
plutocratic society and the domineering insolence of those
who have been taught to scorn the honest laborer. Pardon
again; I cannot avoid referring to the evil, when presenting
the remedy for that half-developed and morbid civilization,
which throughout this century has been, in both Europe

and America, increasing its number of criminals and lunatics, and which, in this republic in time of peace, has a record in 1891 of five thousand nine hundred and six murders — many of them the unfortunate victims of debased and drunken husbands — crimes which speak trumpet-tongued against the system of education that has made them possible. The brain of the nation is reeling under our false system of education, which hastens instead of resisting the downfall of the intellectual and moral powers; for under this system our insane have more than doubled in thirty years. The ratio of the insane to the population, which was one to one thousand four hundred and sixty-eight in 1850, rose in 1880 to one in six hundred and fifty-six, and is still rising rapidly both in America and Europe. I hold our system of education responsible, for a true system would avert this degeneracy, *which seems to accompany education;* for the least educated nations have the least insanity. Insanity has been increasing in Italy, and in the best educated regions (as around the University of Bologna) it is five times as abundant as in the least educated regions (such as Naples and Sardinia.) Among the uneducated their religion remains as a conservative power, while it is undeniable that the soulless and godless system of modern education is diminishing religion by increasing the freedom of criticism, *diminishing religious sentiment,* and subjecting everything to the materialistic methods of physical science. Religion is everywhere on the down grade, and it will require all the power of the NEW EDUCATION to restore the religious sentiments to their normal supremacy. As our emancipated negroes increase in education and diminish their rude religious zeal and faith, they will increase their contributions to the insane asylum, as they are also increasing their contributions to the graveyard.

That the old tyrannical system of education has been an active factor in the deterioration of the brain, is shown by experience in the treatment of insanity first introduced by Pinel. The only satisfactory mode of treating it has been by the removal of restraint. Industry and self-support constitute, not only the most powerful tonic for the mind, but are themselves the most essential virtue, — the basic virtue of all virtues, without which all pretended sentimental and conceited virtues, having no backbone, fall limp and worthless to the earth. Its practice cannot be begun too soon. More fortunate than the fashionable city lad is the farmer's boy, who learns to be useful as soon as he can run about, and never thinks of lounging idly, leaving the burdens of his home upon his father, his mother, or his sisters.

ALL EDUCATION, therefore, if it is to develop the honest, manly virtues, must be *industrial from the beginning.** "Nothing to do," said Carlyle, "is worse than nothing to eat." It starves the manly energies, and millions of American children are growing up puny and inefficient compared to what they should be. The youth should realize from infancy the duty that rests upon him and his comrades, and realize that he is *never free from responsibility*, whether it be in taking care of younger brothers or assisting his parents in household duties. There may be something irksome in this at home; but at school he will feel only emulation and enthusiasm in showing that he can handle tools and manufacture useful things as well as his comrades, guided by his own judgment, or show his skill in horticulture. Rivalry is a powerful stimulant, and industrial rivalry may have something of the charm of baseball, which is nothing but rivalry.

Industrial competition, intermingled with frequent playground sport, will give intense life and energy to the school, developing manliness, industry, and self-reliance, closeness of critical observation and independence of thought, which may be turned into the channel of original invention by throwing the pupil on his own resources.

---

* There is no exception to this on account of sex. In the Normal College of New York City, industrial training of women according to the Swedish method called *Slöjd*, which is so eminently successful in Sweden, is considered a great success, and women handle skilfully the saw, the plane, the knife, and other tools of carpentry, in the carpenter's work which they are prepared to teach. Everything is done with skill, neatness, and despatch, and the impression sometimes rises in the visitor's mind, "Won't they make jewels of wives?" But of course woman's industry is not confined to carpentry.

THE WEST IN LITERATURE.

BY HAMLIN GARLAND.

A QUESTION of American literature now being so rancorously fought over will not be settled by a few men as critics, but by the mass of Americans as readers. The public is the final arbiter with regard to any literature or any art. That is to say, by the taste of the public all art and literature is finally judged. Taste is, moreover, not stationary. Demand changes, and as it changes it will inexorably subtend correlative changes in writing and in painting; and yet, inexorable as are the laws of taste, something may be done by dispassionate discussion in arriving at an understanding of the points at issue.

At some danger of being misunderstood, I should like to present briefly the principles which I conceive to underlie distinctive American art. The history of American literature is the history of provincialism slowly becoming less all-pervasive — the history of the slow development of a distinctive utterance.

By provincialism I mean dependence upon a mother country for models of art production. This is the sense in which Taine or Véron would use the word. The "provincialism" which is slightingly applied to work like Cable's novels or Riley's poems is not provincialism, but the beginning of an indigenous literature.

"The true makers of national literature," writes Posnet in his "Comparative Literature," "are the actions and thoughts of the nation itself. The place of these can never be taken by the sympathies of a cultured class too wide to be national, or those of a central academy too refined to be provincial. Provincialism is no ban in a truly national literature."

Using the word "provincialism," therefore, from the point of view of the central academy, we have had too little of it. Using it in its broader sense of dependence upon a mother country, we have had too much of it. The question of whether we are to have a distinctive literature or not, resolves itself, in my mind, after some years of special study, to this conclusion: we will have a distinctive literature, or none of any sort worth mentioning.

The open sea fronts only in one direction. We must utter something new, something distinctively modern and American, or there will be no excuse for utterance at all. There has been too much truth in the English sneer that American poets and artists have been mere shadows or doubles successively of Pope, of Scott, of Byron, of Wordsworth, and of Tennyson. Our leading poets have reflected the American spirit fairly well, but that spirit has been provincial. It has grown each generation less timid, and since the war the national feeling has had immense widening as well as deepening. Intellectual independence has been slowly won.

The whole point can be specifically illustrated in the West. That is to say, the general terms which could be applied to the whole country up to the time of the civil war can be applied specifically to the middle West to-day. As a Western man, I think I can speak freely, without being charged with undue prejudice toward the states I name.

The West is as provincial in art as it is assertive of Americanism in politics. The books it reads are predominantly the novels of Scott, Dickens, Thackeray, or the colorless "domestic" novels of Mrs. Holmes, Mrs. Southworth, Augusta Evans, May Agnes Fleming, and the rest. I have made studies of bookstores and libraries in many towns in proof of this. These typical books, of course, form the middle class of reading. Below this class of readers come those who consume some millions of tons of dime novels, "*Fireside Companions*," and the "Buckskin Sam" type of romance.

The outlook would be hopeless, did we not know that in every town there is a small group of people, growing larger each year, who read the "*Century*," "*Harper's*," THE ARENA, the "*Forum*," and who enjoy Howells, Cable, Miss Wilkins, and other distinctively American writers. They know what they like — and get it. The other class of readers know what they like — and they get "Danger Dick" and "Old Sleuth," or Ouida or Mrs. Holmes.

It is the great intelligent middle class of America, curiously enough, who are most distinctly provincial. With them the verdict of the world is all-important. Their education has been just sufficient to make them distrustful of their own judgment. They are largely the product of our schools. They have been taught to believe that Shakespeare ended the drama, that Scott has closed the novel, that the English language is the greatest in the world, and that all other literatures are curious, but not at all to be ranked in power and humanity with the English literature.

I speak advisedly of these things, because I have been through the instruction which is well-nigh universal. This class is the largest class in America, and makes up the great body of shoal-bred Westerners. They sustain all the tenets of the conservative and romantic schools in which they have been instructed.

This instruction is well meaning, but it is benumbing to the faculties. It is essentially hopeless. It blinds the eyes of youth to the power and beauty of life and literature around him. It worships the past, despises the present, and fears the future. It says mournfully, "Our great men are going. Who will take their places?" It is profoundly pessimistic, because it sees literary ideals changing. It has not yet seen that metamorphosis is the law of all living things. It teaches the student " to measure the petty writers of the present over against the heroic shades of the past." It has not yet risen to the perception that the question for America to settle is not whether it can produce something greater than the past, but whether it shall produce something different from the past. Our task is not to imitate but to create.

Instruction of this kind inevitably deflects the natural bent of the young writer or discourages attempt altogether. It is the opposite of education; that is, it represses, rather than leads out the distinctive individuality of the student. These conservative ideas affect the newspapers, and their literary columns are too often full of the same gloomy comment. They are timidly negative when not partisanly conservative. The American youth is continually called upon to take Addison or Scott or Dickens or Shakespeare as a model. Such instruction leads naturally to the creation of blank verse tragedies on Columbus and Washington — a class of work which seems to the radical the crowning absurdity of misplaced effort.

Thus the Western youth is turned away from the very material which he could best handle, which he knows most about, and which he really loves most — material which would make him individual, and fill him with hope and energy. He turns away from the marvellous changes which border-life subtends in its mighty rush towards civilization. He does not see the wealth of material which lies at his hand, in the mixture of races going on with inconceivable celerity everywhere in America, but with especial pictur-esqueness in the West. If he sees it, he has not the courage to write of it.

If, here and there, one has reached some such perception, he voices it timidly, with a humorous apologetic look in his eye.

The whole matter appears to me to be a question of the individuality. I feel that Véron has stated this truth better than any other man. In his assault upon the central acad-emy he says, in substance, "Education should not conven-tionalize, should not mass together; it should individualize." The Western youth, like the average school-bred American, lacks the courage of his real conviction. He lacks the cour-age to honestly investigate his surroundings, and then stand by his judgment. Both as reader and writer, he dreads the Eastern comment. His standards of comparison are wrong. He is forced into writing to please somebody else, which is fatal to high art. To perceive the force of all this, and the real hopelessness of instruction according to conventional models, we have only to observe how little that is distinctive has been produced by the great Western middle states — say Wisconsin, Illinois, and Iowa. Of what does its writing consist? A multitude of little newspapers, first ·of all full of local news, and larger newspapers that are political organs, with some little attention to literature on their in-side pages. Their judgments are mainly conservative, but here and there in their news columns one finds sketches of life so vivid one wonders why writers so true and imagina-tive are not recognized and encouraged. The mass of short stories in these papers, however, are absolutely colorless, where they are not pirated exotics. In all that they call "literature" these papers are without "local color." In their unconscious moments they are fine and true.

And yet for forty years an infinite drama has been going on in those wide spaces of the West — a drama that is as thrilling, as full of heart and hope and battle, as any that ever surrounded any man — a life that was unlike any ever seen on the earth, and which should have produced its characteristic literature, its native art chronicle.

As for myself, I am appalled at the majesty, the immensity, the infinite drama, of the life that goes on around me. Themes are crying out to be written. Take, for example, the history of the lumbering district of the northern lakes, a picturesque and peculiar life, that through a period of thirty years has been continually changing in all but a few of its essential features; and yet this life has had only superficial representation in the sketches of the tourist or reporter; its inner heart has not been uttered. The subtle changes of thought and of life that have come to the camps since before the war have thus far been unrecorded.

Then there is the mixture of races; the coming in of the German, the Scandinavian; the marked yet subtle changes in their character. Then there is the building of railroads, with all their trickery and false promises and worthless bonds; the rise of millionnaires; the deepening of social contrasts. In short, there is a great heterogeneous, shifting, brave population, a land teeming with unrecorded and infinite drama. It is only to the superficial observer that this country seems colorless and dull; to the veritist it is full of burning interest, greatest possibilities. I instance these localities because I know something special about them; but the same words apply to Pennsylvania, Ohio, or Kentucky. And yet how few writers of national reputation this eventful century-long march of civilization has produced!

We have had the figures, the dates, the bare history, the dime-novel statement of pioneer life, but how few real novels! how few accurate studies of speech and life! There it lies, ready to be put into the novel and the drama, and upon canvas; and it must be done by those born into it. Joaquin Miller has given us lines of splendid poetry touching this life, and Edward Eggleston, Joseph Kirkland, Opie Read, Octave Thanet, Miss Foote, E. W. Howe have dealt more or less faithfully with certain phases of it; but mainly the mighty West, with its swarming millions, remains undelineated in the novel, the drama, and the poem.

While it is true that this failure has been due to the hard environment, to lack of contrast, and to the lack of a market, not a little of it is due to conservative instruction — instruction which destroys the pupil's real individuality. This instruction, as I am able to testify, educates the young writer out of sympathy with his own land and time, into a sham sympathy with other lands and times. It has taught the young writer to take for a model some classic, some "great state," when it should have been at pains to lead out his own individuality, teaching him to accept no model save life, no master save truth.

To perceive the hopelessness of absolutism in literature, you have but to stop a moment to think. Admit that there are perfect models to which must be referred all subsequent writing, and we are committed to a barren round of hopeless imitations. The young writer is disheartened or drawn off into imitations, and ruined for any real expression. This way of looking at literature produced our Barlows and Caltons and Hillhouses, with their "colossi of cotton batting," and it produces blank verse dramas to-day. It is no wonder that conservatism shakes its head gloomily when Lowell dies.

But the relativists in art are full of hope. They see that life is the model, or rather that each man stands accountable to himself first, and to the perceived fact of life second. Life is always changing, and literature changes with it. It never decays; it changes. Poetry — that is to say *impassioned personal outlook on life* — is in no more danger of extinction to-day than in the days of Edmund Spenser. The American novel will continue to grow in truth to American life without regard to the form and spirit of the novel or drama of the past. Consciously or unconsciously the point of view of the modern writer is that of the veritist or truth stater.

But the question is forced on the young writer, even when he is well disposed toward dealing with indigenous material, Will it pay? Is there a market for me? Let me answer by pointing out that almost every novelist who has risen out of the mass of story writers in America represents some special local life or some special social phase.

Cable stands for the Creole South; Miss Murfree speaks for the mountaineer life in Tennessee; Joel Harris represents the new study of the negro; Miss Wilkins voices the thought of certain old New England towns; Mr. Howells represents truthful treatment of the cities of Boston and New York; Joseph Kirkland has dealt with early Illinois life in " Zury"; Harold Frederick has written two powerful stories of interior New York life, and so on through a list of equally brave and equally fine artists. I think it may be said, therefore, that success in indigenous lines is every year becoming more certain. You will not find your market in the West yet, but the great magazines of the country are every year gaining in Americanism.

This truthful study of Western life, or of any life, involves the study of dialect, or, more properly, the actual speech of the common people. The actual thought of the people cannot be set forth without dealing in dialect, which reflects — if it be true — the peculiarity of thought which always underlies true dialect. For those people who think dialect a low and detestable thing, I have nothing to say. To me it is an interesting, graphic, and necessary medium of expression. Nothing is of greater interest to me than the study of the direct dramatic, unconventional speech of the average man or woman. Swift, humorous, full of vital energy, it embodies in itself all that is most distinctive and powerful in American life to-day.

The study of the West must, therefore, include not one dialect, but twenty. Indeed, veritism in the novel means that each character shall have his individual accent, as he has his individual thought. Thus one of the characteristic phases of the novel in the West must be the careful delineation of German and Scandinavian manners, customs, and dialect, in all the changes which they are undergoing from generation to generation. This dialect, with its great humorous possibilities, is just beginning to be treated truthfully here and there by newspaper men, as the Irish dialect is just getting truthfully written in the East.

That this Americanism, this truth to local conditions, is the certain road to success for young Western writers, is evident already in the success of James Whitcomb Riley, Opie Read, Joseph Kirkland, Octave Thanet, James Lane Allen, and others who have written of Western people. We are certain soon to have a group of Western novelists (Will they be women?) to represent the West, as Mrs. Cooke, Miss Wilkins, and Miss Jewett represent New England. But they must be born of the soil. They must be products of the environment. They must stand among the people, not above them, and then they can be true, and being true they will certainly succeed.

This conservatism extends itself to the magazines of the West, which reflect but very faintly, incompletely, and half-heartedly the local life. The early success of the " *Overland Monthly*" was due to its local color. It is a painful fact that there is no magazine in the West that offers any encouragement to true Western art. If I were starting a magazine in the West, I should aim to develop the art resources of my locality. I should fill it with local color — not by means of dry chronicles of native industries, or histories of local celebrities or various townships, but by calling forth the art expression of the young writers of the section. It cannot be but that there are undeveloped young writers in every leading city of the West — men and women full of fresh and native energy, needing only encouragement and direction to become powerful writers of short stories. I am in receipt of scores of letters from such young people.

Art, after all, is an individual thing. A man must first be true to himself. The advice I give to my pupils who are ambitious to write is the essence of veritism: "Write of those things of which you know most, and for which you care most. By so doing you will be true to yourself, true to your locality, and true to your time." And that is the word I would like to speak to the young writers of the West to whom I may never be able to appeal by word of mouth.

I am a Western man; my hopes and ambitions for the West arise from absolute knowledge of the possibilities. I want to see her prairies, her river-banks and coules, her matchless skies, put upon canvas. I want to see her young writers writing better books, her young artists painting pictures that are true to the life they live and the life they know. I want to see the West supporting her own painters and musicians and novelists; and to that end I want to state my earnest belief, which I have carefully matched with the facts of literary history, that to take a place in the long line of poets and artists in the English language, the Western writer must, above all other things, be true to himself and to his time. To imitate is fatal.

PSYCHICAL RESEARCH — STATUS AND THEORIES.

BY M. J. SAVAGE.

I HAVE now given my readers a large number of facts. But facts are worth little unless one knows what to do with them. Aristotle was in possession of certain facts, and from them he argued that the earth was a sphere; but for hundreds of years after his time the wise men of the world came to quite other conclusions. This was either because they were not wise enough to comprehend their significance, or, as was more commonly the case, because they were dominated by some bias that led them to adopt a contrary theory. It is this latter thing that stands more in the way of truth than does ignorance itself. In religion, in politics, in political economy, in all directions there are facts enough; but the majority of people are prepossessed by theories which hinder their seeing the real meaning of the facts.

I shall then have rendered a very incomplete service to those who have taken note of my facts if I stop with these. It remains for me therefore to indicate the present status of psychical inquiry, and to point out what seems to me the significance of my facts. I do not claim to be so wise here that my conclusions will be free of all error, but without immodesty I can claim one thing: I am not dominated by any theory, and am under no bias to come to any particular conclusion. Indeed, I have reached a point in my thinking where I find it hard to comprehend how any sane man should even wish to discover anything but the truth. I know there are such people, because they have told me that they were content with their present beliefs, and even though they were wrong, they did not want to find it out. But I do not wish to be even pleasantly fooled. I wish to know the truth and adjust myself to it.

I cannot, indeed, agree with those who say that, if there be no other life, this present life is not worth having. For —

— When I look upon the laughing face
Of children, or on woman's gentle grace;
Or when I grasp a true friend by the hand,
And feel a bond I partly understand;
When mountains thrill me, or when by the sea
The plaintive waves rehearse their mystery;
Or when I watch the moon with strange delight
Treading her pathway 'mid the stars at night;
Or when the one I love, with kisses prest,
I clasp with bliss unspoken to my breast; —
So strange, so deep, so wondrous, life appears,
I have no words, but only happy tears.
I cannot think it all shall end in naught;
That the abyss shall be the grave of thought;
That e'er oblivion's shoreless sea shall roll
O'er love and wonder and the lifeless soul.
But e'en though this the end, I cannot say
I'm sorry I have seen the light of day.
So wondrous seems this life I live to me,
Whate'er the end, *to-day I have and see;*
To-day I think and hope : and so for this, —
If this be all, — for just so much of bliss,
Bliss blended through with pain, I bless the Power
That holds me up to gaze *one wondrous hour !*

If, then, this is all, I want to know it and make the most
of it. If it is only the beginning, I want to know that, and
lay out my life on a scale proportioned to the magnificence
of its possibilities. And I can conceive of no knowledge
that for one moment matches this in importance.

Before treating the present standing of psychical inquiry,
it is needful to note certain preceding conditions of human
thought out of which present conditions have been evolved.
In the pre-critical and unscientific ages, the belief in continued existence and some sort of intercourse between spirits
and mortals was practically universal. In the general ignorance of natural laws, people were not troubled by questions
of possible or impossible. All forces and happenings were
interpreted in terms of will or caprice ; and the supernatural
presented no difficulty because there was, in their minds, no
natural order. There being no standards of probability,
what to-day is meant by proof was not only not demanded,
it was not even understood. The journey of Odysseus to
Hades was as believable as was the voyage of the latest
Phœnician navigator. The appearance of spirits, messages
from the invisible world, and celestial or demoniac interfer-
ences with human affairs were a part of all religions and

of daily life. The Bibles of all peoples and all ancient literatures are abundant witnesses to these facts. If any one wishes to come in personal contact with this condition of the human mind, he need not go further than to the devout Catholic servants of his own household.

As children now are afraid of the dark, the lonely, the mysterious, so it was natural that in the childhood of the world men should be afraid of the invisible. They were in terror at the thought of the possible return of even their most intimate friends. The gods themselves were not regarded as over kind, and their wrath must be placated or their favor purchased by gifts. Perhaps, therefore, it is not strange that these feelings linger still. Most people to-day, like Madame de Staël, are afraid of ghosts even though they do not believe in them; and there are few who are brave enough to spend a night alone in the room with the body of the one they have loved best in all the world. This state of mind makes it exceedingly difficult for people to treat these psychical investigations in a rational way. Among those who believe that "the dead" are still alive, there is a general impression that the fact of death has produced some marvellous and magical change so that they are real human folks no longer. The imagination is full of either angels or devils, so that they are troubled with all sorts of theories as to what is fitting or becoming, instead of being ready to note facts first and then see what they mean afterwards.

But as one of the results of modern science, there has been, in the minds of the learned, a violent reaction against the superstitions or over-beliefs of the past. This is entirely healthy, provided science itself does not become a superstition. But a scientific theory may become as serious a barrier against the acceptance of a new truth as vulgar prejudice itself. Witness the scientific authority of Newton as it blinds the eyes of the learned to the truth of Young's theory of light, or note the attitude of Agassiz in the matter of evolution. Professor Huxley has written, with all his power of sarcasm, against modern spiritualism. And yet Professor Wallace, at least his peer in scientific eminence, told me that he had repeatedly tried to get Huxley to join him in investigating these matters, and he would not. To the mind of the ultra-scientist all these stories of the childhood world are so childish that they are to be rejected in the lump, without being accorded even the dignity of an investigation. I agree with this scientific reaction to the extent of holding that they are all to be put aside and labelled "Not proved"; that is, the basis on which they rest, whether in Bibles or out of Bibles, is inadequate, and does not in any case amount to demonstration. But it is going away beyond any truly scientific warrant to say that none of them may be true. And if, in the modern world, any similar stories should be scientifically established as true, then it would be fully in accord with the scientific method to reconsider all or any one of these traditional stories, and estimate the degree of probability in its favor.

Curiously various and contradictory have been the positions of different classes of thinkers and of those who do not think in the modern world. One class has held that all these things were childish and superstitious, and that only ignorant or flighty people could take any stock in them. Members of this class smile wisely, not to say superciliously, when any of these matters are mentioned. It is this attitude of the "unco" wise (for there is an "unco" wise as well as an "unco guid") which led a philosopher, known in two hemispheres, to say to me: "Well, Savage, suppose we become convinced that these things are true, it will only be *a couple more cranks.*" Then there are the ordinary Protestant Christians, who accept such stories as are told in the Bible, and reject all others, whether ancient or modern. Of course this is a matter of religious "faith," not reason. Again, there are the Catholics, who believe not only the stories told in the Bible, but all such as are indorsed by the Church, either in mediæval or modern times. Once more, there are the Swedenborgians, who accept the stories of their founder. They also believe in the possibility of spirit intercourse to-day, but hold it unwise if not dangerous. Then there are men like the late Professor Austin Phelps of Andover, who "know" that spirits do interfere with human affairs, but believe that they are always evil spirits. Perhaps it is consistent with that theology which he represented, to believe that God will permit devils to overrun the earth, but forbid the good spirits to make their presence known. Such, then, are some of the points of view from which these matters have been regarded up to the time when they began to be approached in a rational and scientific manner.

It is doubtless due to the experiments of Mesmer in France, and the Rochester rappings that the era of scientific psychical research has at last been reached. I do not at all mean to say that the former were the cause, in the ordinary sense of the word, of the latter. I only mean that mesmerism and spiritualism, with their allied phenomena, resulted at last in such a widespread and popular interest in the problems involved as to lead certain people to feel that the question was worthy of serious attention and ought not longer to be postponed. The attitude of Professor Henry Sidgwick of Cambridge, England, the great writer on ethics, indicates what I mean. In his first address as president of the English Society for Psychical Research, he declared it to be "a scandal" that a matter of so great importance, and involving the life interests of so many people, was not scientifically investigated and settled; and the first time that so significant a thing ever occurred, Professor Oliver Lodge of Liverpool, in his address as president of the Physical and Mathematical Section of the British Association for the Advancement of Science, only last year, took similar ground, and challenged the attention and interest of the leading scientific men of Great Britain.

Men had come to feel, in view of the fact that so many thousands uncritically accepted the claims of spiritualism on the one hand, and so many were hungry for a belief that their reasons forbade, on the other, that the truth, if possible, ought to be known. They saw that either thousands of people were deluded, and that it was worth while to help them out of their delusion, or that something was true which might comfort and help other thousands who stood helpless and hopeless in the presence of "the great mystery." It was out of such convictions that the movement for psychical research was born.

Every little while still, some presumably wise, scientific man sneers at the whole thing, and treats the search as though it were on a level with the "Hunting of the Snark." A certain class of newspapers also treat it as though it were fair game for the jester's column, classing the "spook" and the sea serpent as equally legitimate prey for the limp-minded humorist of the "silly season." It will not therefore be time thrown away if we spend a little in considering as to whether psychical research is really a rational scientific inquiry.

There are two great universe theories, some variety of one or other of which we all hold. One is the materialistic theory, which teaches that in some way life is the outcome of matter, the product of organization. It is generally supposed to be the necessary consequence of this theory that the conscious life of the individual ceases with the death of the visible body. I have not been quite able to see why, however, for there may be an invisible body; and if matter is able to produce a conscious, thinking person, who is wise enough to say that this same matter may not be able to continue the life in some invisible form? For it seems to me that Thomas Paine did not at all exceed the bounds of reason when he said, "It appears more probable to me that I shall continue to exist hereafter, than that I should have existence, as I now have, before that existence began."

But whatever may be the truth of this, the old, crude theories of materialism are antiquated, and "dead matter" is philosophically and scientifically unknown. The only materialists to-day are a few belated survivals, fossils of a bygone period of human thought. Even Clifford, before he died, was talking of "mind-stuff" as connected with matter. Haeckel, the nearest to a materialist of any great living thinker, must have his "atom-souls" in order to account for facts. Schopenhauer must have his "world-will," and Hartmann his "Unconscious" with a capital U. Huxley, though the inventor of the term "Agnostic," declares that sooner than accept the old materialism he could adopt the ultra-idealism of Bishop Berkeley. And Herbert Spencer, easily prince of them all, says that the one thing we know, more certainly than we know any isolated or individual fact, is the existence of the one Eternal Energy back of all phenomena, and of which all phenomena are only partial manifestations.

Materialism, then, is dead, and spiritualism (of course I am using the term philosophically now) is taking its place. This theory puts life back of form, and makes it the cause, and not the product, of organization. This does not teach that man has a soul. That sort of talk belongs to the old theology:—

> "A charge to keep I have,
> A God to glorify;
> A never-dying soul to save,
> And fit it for the sky."

If man is thought of as "having" a soul which he may "lose," it is but a step to thinking of him as a being independent of his soul, and as getting along without it. This theory rather teaches that man *is* a soul, and *has* a body; and on that theory, it is purely a rational question as to whether he may not be able to get along without the present and visible body.

And here we need to note to what an extent we are the fools of our eyes and ears. It is common to imagine that we can see all that is, if only it is near enough to us, and that we can hear all "sounds" that are not too far away. As matter of fact, it is only the very smallest part of the real world of things about us that we are able either to see or hear. Vibrations that reach a certain number in a second produce an effect on the eye which, when transmitted to the brain is, in some way, quite incomprehensible to us, transformed into vision. When these vibrations pass a certain other number in rapidity, then they lose the power to produce the sense of seeing. It is then only within very narrow limits that we see; while on both sides of these limits there is a practical infinity that to us is invisible, though no whit less real than that which we speak of as seeing. And all the while it isn't the eye, nor the brain, nor any visible thing that sees even the commonest object; it is the I, the self, the soul only that ever sees. A precisely similar thing is true of hearing.

It is not science, but only shallow sciolism that assumes that our present senses are a measure of the universe. Men like Professor Crookes and Nicola Tesla are already on the eve of physical discoveries that promise to reveal to us forms and conditions of matter quite unlike those with which we are already familiar. For anything at present known to the contrary, the soul or the self may emerge from the experience we call death with a body as real and much more completely alive than the present visible body, and which shall yet be invisible, inaudible, and intangible to our ordinary senses. Indeed "spirit photography," whether true or not, is not at all absurd or scientifically impossible in the nature of things. The sensitized plate can "see" better than the ordinary human eye, for it can photograph an "invisible" star. It may then photograph an invisible "spiritual body," provided any such body really exists.

As to the possible existence of a "spiritual" world in the neighborhood of the earth, I need only quote Young, who lived not long after Newton, and who is the famous scientist who discovered and demonstrated the present universally accepted theory of light. Jevons, in his "Principles of Science" (Third edition, Macmillan & Company, 1879), page 516, says, "We cannot deny even the strange suggestion of Young, that there may be independent worlds, some possibly existing in different parts of space, but others perhaps pervading each other, unseen and unknown in the same space." It is not scientific wisdom, then, but only scientific ignorance or prejudice that supposes that the student engaged in the work of psychical research need apologize to science. There is nothing which his work pre-supposes that in any way whatever contradicts any established principle or verified conclusion of science.

In the light of these facts, and considering the character and the learning of those engaged in the work, it is time that the silly attitude toward it were given up. The time is passing away when such a remark as the following should be possible. The Reverend J. G. Wood was a clergyman of the Church of England, and a world-famous naturalist. As the result of years of careful investigation, he became a firm believer in the "spirit" world, and in communication between that world and this. Some years ago he was in Boston, giving a course of lectures before the Lowell Institute. In conversation with him at that time, he spoke freely of his experiences, and told me stories as wonderful as any I have ever heard. He said: "I do not talk about these things with everybody. I used to think anybody who had anything to do with them was a fool, and " — he added with a look that told of frequent contact with the "unco" wise — "*I do not enjoy being called a fool.*" It is time, I say, that this sort of thing were gone by. The wise man whose whole stock in trade on this subject is an ignorance only less than his prejudice, will soon learn that it is not entirely scientific to "know all about" a matter about which he really knows nothing at all.

This, then, is a subject as fairly open to scientific investigation as is the germ-theory of disease, or the present condition of the planet Mars. It is purely a question of fact and evidence.

I had begun a careful study of these questions when as yet there was no English Society for Psychical Research. Before touching on the work that has been done, and the theories propounded since that organization, I wish to say a few things concerning my own personal attitude. I do this, not because I imagine that my own motives and actions are of any public importance in themselves; but in one way they may be of a good deal of importance to those who may be interested in the work I have done, and the conclusions I have reached in the matter of psychical study. If, in the case of the so-called exact sciences, — like the work of observation in astronomy, — the "personal equation" has to be taken account of, much more is it necessary in studies like these, where experience, power of exact observation, motive, and purpose may either practically assure or vitiate results. Since then I have ventured to lay before the public so large a number of cases, my readers have a right to know so much of my personal attitude and methods as will help them to estimate the value of these cases.

My evangelical training had prepared me to look upon all these things with suspicion. I believed the whole business to be either fraud or delusion or "nerves." I do not think I traced it to the devil, as so many others did, but I felt sure that it had "better be let alone." I felt towards it as all the "respectable" people of Jerusalem and Corinth and Rome felt towards Christianity — that at best it was "a pestilent superstition." On the basis of "invincible ignorance," I once delivered a scathing lecture against it, and perhaps wondered a little that certain obstinate people still continued to believe in it after I was done.

But about seventeen years ago, a year or so after coming to Boston, the father of one of my parishioners died. Soon after she came to me, saying she had been with a friend to consult a "medium." As she thought, certain very striking things had been told her, and she wished my counsel and advice. Then it came to me with a shock that I had no business to offer advice on a subject concerning which my entire stock of preparation consisted of a bundle of prejudices. Then I began to reflect that this one parishioner was not alone in wanting advice on this subject; and I said to myself, whether this be truth or delusion, it is equally important that I know about it so as to be the competent adviser of those who come to me for direction. I should have felt ashamed to have had no opinion on the Old Testament theophanies or the New Testament stories of spirit appearances or demoniacal possessions. Why should I pride myself on my ignorance of matters of far more practical importance to my people? As a part of my equipment for the ministry, then, I said to myself, I must study these things until I have at least an intelligent opinion. Such, then, were the circumstances and motives that led to my prolonged investigation.

Since then I have improved every available opportunity to study these things. I have had no prurient curiosity as to any other possible world, neither have I made it my chief object to see if I could get into communication with personal friends. I have studied these phenomena, first, as bearing on the nature and powers of the mind, as here embodied, and then with a view to finding out if any proof could be obtained that personal, conscious existence survives the experience we call death. For only a superficial knowledge of the drift of popular opinion is needed to show that if the belief in a future life is to continue as a life-motive among men, it must be based on something more recent and authentic than a shifting ecclesiastical tradition two thousand years old. The Catholic church is wise enough to see this. And the attitude of the Protestant church is a curiously inconsistent one, particularly when one remembers that the "facts" on which it relies are of precisely a similar kind to the modern ones it contemptuously rejects.

In my studies I have sought faithfully to follow the scientific method, which I regard as the only method of knowledge. By careful observation and rigid experiment I have tried, first, to be sure that I have discovered a fact. Of this fact I have made a record at the time. I have paid no attention to results apparently obtained in the dark, or in circumstances where I could not be certain as to what was taking place. I have not said that all these were fraud, but I have never given them weight as evidence. I have made a study of sleight of hand, and am quite aware of all the possibilities of trickery. But to imitate an occurrence, under other conditions, is not to duplicate a fact. The larger number of those occurrences which have actually influenced my belief have taken place in the presence of long-tried personal friends, and not with professional "mediums" at all.

When at last I have been sure of a fact, I have stretched and strained all known methods and theories in the attempt to explain it without resorting to any supposed "spiritual" agency. I say "spiritual" and not supernatural, for I do not believe in any supernatural. In my conception of the universe whatever is, is natural. If "spirits" exist, their invisibility does not make them supernatural any more than the atom of science is to be regarded as supernatural for a similar reason. And when at last I discovered facts which I am utterly unable to explain without supposing the presence and agency of invisible intelligences, even then I have not positively taken that step. For the present, at least, I only wait. The facts will keep; and if the wisdom of the world is able to discover any other explanation, I am quite ready to accept it. Stronger than my desire to conquer death is my desire not to be fooled, or to be the means, ever so honestly, of leading astray any who might put their trust in my conclusions; but I have discovered facts which I cannot explain, and they *seem* to point directly to the conclusion that the self does not die, and that it is, in certain conditions, able to communicate with those still in the flesh. It may be proper to add here that the leading man in the English Society for Psychical Research, Mr. F. W. H. Myers, has published the fact that, as the result of his investigations, he has become convinced of "continued personal existence and of at least occasional communication." The secretary of the American Branch of the English Society, Mr. Richard Hodgson, LL. D., has given to the world a similar conviction.

It is time now for me to indicate certain results which I regard as well established. There will be no room here for detail. For illustration, and for cases other than those I have already given, the reader is referred to reports and books published by the English Society. What, then, are some of the results?

1. Mesmerism, under its new name of hypnotism, is now recognized by all competent investigators. Not only this, but it is being resorted to in the treatment of disease by the best physicians of France, Germany, England, and America. It is found that it can be used in surgical operations as an anæsthetic, in place of ether. In the hypnotic state many strange phenomena sometimes appear, such as the dual per-

sonality, clairvoyance and clairaudience, that lead the student into other departments of psychical research.

2. Clairvoyance and clairaudience are well established. This means that, in certain conditions, people can see without their eyes and hear without their ears. Facts like these do not take one "out of the body," but they do suggest, with somewhat startling force, the query as to whether the mind is necessarily so dependent on our ordinary senses as is commonly supposed.

3. Next comes telepathy, or mind reading. It is found that communication of thoughts, feelings, and even events in detail, is possible between minds separated by distances ranging from a few feet to thousands of miles. It is suggested that the explanation may be found in the theory of ethereal vibrations set up by the activity of the brain particles whose motion accompanies all thought and feeling, but in any case the facts are none the less wonderful.

4. Next come what are ordinarily classed together as "mediumistic phenomena." The most important of these are psychometry, "vision" of "spirit" forms, claimed communications, by means of rappings, table movements, automatic writing, independent writing, trance speaking, etc. With them also ought to be noted what are generally called physical phenomena, though in most cases, since they are intelligibly directed, the use of the word "physical," without this qualification, might be misleading. These physical phenomena include such facts as the movement of material objects by other than the ordinary muscular force, the making objects heavier or lighter when tested by the scales, the playing on musical instruments by some invisible power, etc. I pass by the question of "materialization," because I have never seen any under such conditions as rendered fraud impossible. I do not feel called on to say that all I have ever seen was fraudulent; I only say that it might have been. Consequently, I cannot treat it as evidence of anything beyond the possible ingenuity of the professionals.

Now all of these referred to (with the exception of independent writing and materialization) I know to be genuine. I do not at all mean by this that I know that the "spiritualistic" interpretation of them is the true one. I mean only that they are genuine phenomena; that they have occurred; that they are not tricks or the result of fraud. I am not saying (for I must be very explicit here) that imitations of them may not be given by fraudulent "mediums" or by the prestidigitator; but that they are genuine phenomena, in many cases, I have proved over and over again. I ought to say a special word here in regard to slate writing. I put this one side, because I know it can be done in many ways as a trick. More than once have I detected a trick as being palmed off on me for genuine; but it is only fair to say that I have had experiences of this sort when I could not discover any trick, and in conditions where it seemed impossible. I leave it out of present account only because I do not feel justified in saying I know, as I do feel justified in saying in regard to most of the others.

But a thousand experiences of these kinds may occur, and yet find a possible explanation without crossing the borders of the possible "spirit" world. Psychometry, visions, voices, table movements, automatic writing, trance speaking — all these may be accounted for by some unusual activity of the mind as embodied. They may throw great and new light on the powers and possibilities of the mind here, and yet not lead us to the land of "spirits."

But — and here is the crucial point to be noted — by any one of these means a communication may be made that *cannot* be accounted for as the result of the mental activity of any one of the persons visibly present. Was the statement made such as was known, or *might ever* have been known, by any of the (visible) persons present? In that case, the cautious and conscientious investigator will feel compelled to hunt for an explanation on this side of the border. For since mind reading is a known cause, he will resort to that as long as he can, and only go further when absolutely compelled to do so. But if none of the people (visibly) present ever knew or ever could have known the communicated fact, then what?

It seems to me that the Rubicon, whether ever crossed or not, is here. This, therefore, calls for clear discussion by itself; but one other point, not yet sufficiently noted, needs to be disposed of first. When enumerating some of the phenomena called "mediumistic," I referred to the movement of material objects in a way not to be explained by muscular force, and to musical instruments played on by some invisible power. Is there any way to account for these

without supposing the presence and agency of some invisible
intelligence? I frankly confess I do not know of any; and
here let me refer to the opinion of Dr. Elliott Coues. For
years he was connected with the Smithsonian Institution in
Washington; and a professor there is a personal friend of
mine. He is, if not a materialist, an out and out agnostic.
I asked him one day as to the scientific standing of Professor
Coues, leaving out of account what he regarded as his "vagaries" in connection with psychical matters. He replied that
he was "one of the ablest and most brilliant scientific men
in Europe or America." Professor Coues then has said — I
quote from memory — "All material objects are under the
power of gravity. If, then, any particle of matter, though
no larger than a pin's head, be moved in such a way as not
to be explained by purely physical forces, this fact marks the
boundary line between the material and the spiritual, between force and will."

But now for a brief consideration of the most important
psychical cases with which I am acquainted. More than
once I have been told by a psychic (and in the most important cases of all the psychic was not a professional) certain
things that neither the psychic nor myself knew, had known,
or (in the nature of the case) could by any possibility ever
have known. These communications claimed to come from
an old-time and intimate friend who had "died" within
three months. The facts were matters which mutually concerned us, and which she would have been likely to have
spoken of if it were possible. There was an air of naturalness
and verisimilitude about the whole experience, though some
parts of it were so "personal" as to render it impossible to
publish the whole case, and so make it as forcible to others
as it was to me.

Now, will somebody tell me what I am to do with facts
like these? In one or two cases the facts communicated to
me concerned happenings, mental conditions, and spiritual
suffering in another state, two hundred miles away. I wish
to note briefly the ordinary attempts at explanation and see
if they appear to be adequate.

1. Guess-work; coincidence; it happened so. This might
be true of one case, however extraordinary; but when you
are dealing with several cases, the theory of guess-work or
coincidence becomes more wonderful than the original fact.

2. Clairvoyance. But my friend, the non-professional psychic, has no clairvoyant power; and, besides, clairvoyant power does not ordinarily reach so far, nor does it deal with mental and moral states and sufferings.

3. Telepathy. But this is based on sympathy between the two persons concerned, and deals with something in which they are mutually interested. But my friend, the psychic, not only was no friend of the parties concerned; she did not even know that any such persons were in existence.

4. As a last resort, it has been suggested that we are surrounded by, or immersed in, a sort of universal mind which is a reservoir containing all knowledge; and that, in some mysterious way, the psychic unconsciously taps this reservoir, and so astonishes herself and others with facts, the origin of which is untraceable and unknown. But this seems to me explanation with a vengeance! The good old lady, after reading "Bunyan's Pilgrim's Progress" with "Scott's Explanatory Notes," said she understood *everything except the notes*. So in this case, it seems to me we might conceivably *explain everything except the explanation*. No, I must wait still longer. Unless my friend was there telling me these things, I confess I do not know how to account for them.

Here, then, for the present, I pause. Do these facts only widen and enlarge our thoughts concerning the range of our present life? Or do they lift a corner of the curtain, and let us catch a whisper, or a glimpse of a face, and so assure us that "death" is only an experience of life, and not its end? I hope the latter. And I believe the present investigation will not cease until all intelligent people shall have the means in their hands for a scientific and satisfactory decision.

IN THE TRIBUNAL OF LITERARY CRITICISM.

BACON *VS.* SHAKESPEARE.

BY EDWIN REED.

PART II. A BRIEF FOR THE DEFENDANT.

The title of William Shakespeare, the actor, to the authorship of the plays and poems popularly attributed to him, rests on two foundations, to wit:—

I. Contemporaneous testimony.
II. The unique character of the works.

I. The testimony of his contemporaries, though not, it must be admitted, direct or positive, is yet without a flaw. For a period of more than twenty-five years during which time these great productions were coming out, on the stage and in print, William Shakespeare stood before the world their undisputed author. We listen in vain for the slightest whisper of any other name connected with them. This unanimity of sentiment was as absolute before 1598, while the published plays were anonymous, as it was after that date, when the title-pages almost invariably bore what purported to be the author's name. Even Shakespeare's death in 1616 had no effect on his literary tenure. Old plays newly enlarged, new plays never before heard of, some of them ranking among his best, continued to come from the press, still ascribed to him. Nature seems to have suspended her laws and given fresh harvests without seed. Two of his fellow-actors collected and published all his works, as a labor of love, in one large volume in 1623, making no suggestion, and eliciting none from the public, of any incongruity in the alleged authorship. From first to last no rival claimant dared to lift his head. One envious writer, and one only, throughout the whole career of the dramatist, intimated a doubt concerning him. That one was Greene, author of the famous posthumous squib of 1592, for which his editor, however, made an ample public apology three months later.

Other circumstances also conspired to invite suspicion, not to say, literary theft. Shakespeare was an actor and, therefore, of low repute. He was also business manager of two theatres, the owner of stage properties, including, of course, authors' manuscripts. Of his own early plays six successive editions appeared anonymously. A mob of printers and publishers put them on the market. They had their "first nights" in The Theatre, the Curtain, the Rose, the Blackfriars, the Globe, at Gray's Inn, and before the Court.

At the same time they brought the author money and reputation. They crowded the play-houses. Francis Meres, in 1598, ranked Shakespeare with the greatest authors of antiquity, declaring that, were the Muses to speak English, they would speak with his tongue.

Here, then, are two sets of facts which require mutual adjustment. Briefly stated, they are as follows : —

1. A series of dramatic works, the production of which covers a period, in one of the most intellectual ages of the world, of a quarter of a century; popular, even more than now, with all classes of theatre-going people ; giving its reputed author wealth and fame ; striking every chord of the human heart with a directness, force, and melody never equalled ; published at first without a name, then with one, the two syllables of which were often separated with a hyphen ; entered at Stationers' Hall always by, and in behalf of, others ; and continuing to appear with fresh and perfectly characteristic additions for thirteen years after the reputed author's retirement from London, and for seven years after his death.

2. The uniform, unquestioned ascription of the authorship, on the part of his contemporaries, to William Shakespeare, the actor.

Between these two statements there is but one possible connecting link. The genius of William Shakespeare, the man, must have been so commanding, his figure in the circle of his friends and associates so conspicuous, his personality, as stamped upon his works, so unmistakable, that neither his own indifference to literary reputation, nor the curiosity, envy, and malice of others could throw the slightest doubt on his title while he was living, or put it in question for two hundred and thirty-two years after his death. That is to say, circumstances strongly invited suspicion; no suspicion existed; consequently, there was no cause for suspicion. The very weakness of the environment becomes an element of strength. The greater the pressure on the capstone of an arch, the firmer the arch itself.

Fortunately, however, we are not altogether limited to negative testimony. Three of Shakespeare's personal friends are ready to take the witness' stand in his behalf. We first call

JOHN HEMINGE AND HENRY CONDELL.

These persons have each three claims on our confidence. They were fellow-actors with Shakespeare on the stage; they were beneficiaries under his will; and they edited the first collective edition of his works. In the dedication of the folio of 1623 to the Earls of Pembroke and Montgomery, they use the following words: —

" Since your L. L. have been pleased to think these trifles something heretofore, and have prosecuted both them and their author, living, with so much favor, we hope that (they outliving him, and he not having the fate, common with some, to be the executor of his own writings) you will use the like indulgence toward them you have done unto their parent. . . . We have but collected them, and done an office to the dead, to procure his orphans guardians; without ambition either of self-profit or fame; only to keep the memory of so worthy a friend and fellow alive, as was our Shakespeare, by humble offer of his plays to your most noble patronage. . . . We most humbly consecrate to your H. H. these remains of your servant Shakespeare; that what delight is in them may be ever your L. L., the reputation his, and the faults ours, if any be committed, by a pair so careful to show their gratitude to the living and the dead, as is

" Your Lordships' most bounden,
" JOHN HEMINGE,
" HENRY CONDELL."

They repeat the same statement in the preface, as follows: —

" It had been a thing, we confess, worthy to be wished, that the author himself had lived to set forth and oversee his own writings; but since it hath been ordained otherwise, and he by death departed from that right, we pray you do not envy his friends the office of their care and pain to collect and publish them."

In defence of the sincerity of these utterances, we have only to add that Shakespeare, at his death seven years before, had left these old friends, as a token of his affection, one hundred and fifty dollars (present value) " to buy them rings."

We next call

BEN JONSON.

When counsel can do nothing with a piece of sworn testimony in court, the rule is, *abuse the witness.* Jonson has not escaped the penalty due him under this practice. To be sure, he made contradictory statements regarding the ease with which the plays were written, a discrepance not very extraordinary, considering the number and variety of these works and the different circumstances under which they were produced. It is in tradition that one of them was forthcoming on demand in two weeks. On another, we are quite sure we detect marks of the hammer, if we cannot hear the ring of the anvil and see the fires of genius in which it was forged.

Jonson's testimony, delivered in 1637, just before his death, is as follows : —

"I remember the players have often mentioned it as an honor to Shakespeare that in his writing, whatsoever he penned, he never blotted out a line. My answer hath been, Would he had blotted a thousand, which they thought a malevolent speech. I had not told posterity this, but for their ignorance, who choose that circumstance to commend their friend by wherein he most faulted, and to justify mine own candor ; for I loved the man, and do honor his memory (on this side idolatry), as much as any. He was, indeed, honest, and of an open and free nature ; had an excellent fantasy ; brave notions and gentle expressions, wherein he flowed with that facility that sometimes it was necessary he should be stopped. *Sufflaminandus erat,* as Augustus said of Haterius. His wit was in his own power ; would the rule of it had been so too ! Many times he fell into those things, could not escape laughter ; as when he said in the person of Cæsar, — one speaking to him, 'Cæsar, thou dost me wrong,' he replied,— 'Cæsar never did wrong but in a just cause,' and the like, which were ridiculous. But he redeemed his vices with his virtues. There was ever more in him to be praised than to be pardoned."

Here is the statement of a man standing on the brink of the grave. It was left in manuscript when he died, and published, as he distinctly avows it was written, for the benefit of posterity. All the friends of his youth, his compeers, his rivals, Bacon and Shakespeare among them, had long since passed away. Whatever might have been his temptations in the past, he had now no conceivable motive to perpetuate a fraud.

Lastly, we summon

THE WHOLE POPULATION OF STRATFORD, EN MASSE.

Under the bust in the old church at Stratford, placed there within seven years after Shakespeare's death, we read the following inscription : —

INDICIO PYLIUM, GENIO SOCRATEM, ARTE MARONEM.*

This is the voice of his native town, uttered in tones that have reverberated through three centuries.

II. The unique character of the works.

We assume at the outset that between 1564 and 1616 there was living but one Shakespeare. In all the ages before and since, the world has not produced another. It is as certain that the plays we call Shakespeare's were substantially the product of one mind as it is that the planets of our solar system, with all their differences, rolled from the hand of one maker.

We shall not undertake to define what it is in the writings of Shakespeare which distinguishes them from all others. No one can describe the odor of the violet, yet no one mistakes it. The problem of style is like an axiom of mathematics, a matter in the last analysis of intuition. In 1795, a young man in London pretended to have discovered in a lot of old manuscripts a new Shakespearean play which he called *Vortigern*. The critics were divided on the question of its genuineness; and it was not until it had been produced amid great excitement at the Drury Lane Theatre and been howled down by the "gods" that the imposture was admitted.

The plaintiff in this action is Francis Bacon. Of all the contemporaries of William Shakespeare, the one selected to bear off his honors was a prose writer. Bacon's published works (Spedding's edition) comprise fourteen bulky volumes, on a vast variety of subjects, but without a line of undoubtedly original verse. In the specimens that are given

---

*In wisdom, a Nestor; in genius, a Socrates; in art, a Virgil.

we vainly search for a spark of that celestial fire which emblazons almost every page of Shakespeare.

We do, indeed, find there six of the Psalms of David translated metrically, a little work which its author made haste to publish to the world, and which he deemed worthy of a formal dedication to George Herbert. To us it establishes one proposition incontrovertibly, viz.:

Bacon was not averse to being known as a poet.

It goes far, also, to establish another :—

Bacon was not a poet.

We give two or three specimen stanzas, as follows :—

> " When we sat, all sad and desolate,
>   By Babylon upon the river's side,
> Eased from the tasks which in our captive state
>   We were enforced daily to abide,
>   Our harps we had brought with us to the field,
>   Some solace to our heavy souls to yield.

> " But soon we found we failed of our account;
>   For when our minds some freedom did obtain,
> Straightway the memory of Zion Mount
>   Did cause afresh our wounds to bleed again;
>   So that, with present griefs and future fears,
>   Our eyes burst forth into a stream of tears.

> " As for our harps, since sorrow struck them dumb,
>   We hanged them on the willow trees were near;
> Yet did our cruel masters to us come,
>   Asking of us some Hebrew songs to hear;
>   Taunting us rather in our misery,
>   Than much delighting in our melody."
>
>   *Psalm* cxxxvii.

> " O Lord, thy providence sufficeth all;
> Thy goodness, not restrained, but general
> Over thy creatures; the whole earth doth flow
> With thy great largeness poured forth here below.
> Nor is it earth alone exalts thy name,
> But seas and streams likewise do spread the same.
> The rolling seas unto the lot doth fall
> Of beasts innumerable, great and small;
> There do the stately ships plough up the floods,
> The greater navies look like walking woods.
> The fishes there far voyages do make,
> To divers shores their journey they do take;
> There hast thou set the great Leviathan,
> That makes the seas to seethe like boiling pan."
>
>   *Psalm* civ.

Let us try, also, the "deadly parallel" : —

PSALM CIV.

AUTHORIZED VERSION.	BACON'S VERSION.
14. He causeth the grass to grow for the cattle, and the herb for the service of man; that he may bring forth food out of the earth.	14. Causing the earth put forth the grass for beasts, And garden herbs, served at the greatest feasts, And bread that is all viands firmament, And gives a firm and solid nourishment;
15. And wine that maketh glad the heart of man, and oil to make his face to shine, and bread which strengtheneth man's heart.	15. And wine, man's spirit for to re-create, And oil, his face for to exhilarate.
16. The trees of the Lord are full of sap; the cedars of Lebanon, which he hath planted.	16. The sappy cedars, tall, like stately towers, High-flying birds do harbor in their bowers.
17. Where the birds make their nests; as for the stork, the fir trees are her house.	17. The holy storks, that are the travellers, Choose for to dwell and build within the firs.
18. The high hills are a refuge for the wild goats, and the rocks for the conies.	18. The climbing goats hang on steep mountain's side; The digging conies in the rocks do bide.
19. He appointed the moon for seasons; the sun knoweth his going down.	19. The moon, so constant in inconstancy, Doth rule the monthly seasons orderly; The sun, eye of the world, doth know his race, And when to show and when to hide his face.
20. Thou makest darkness, and it is night, wherein all the beasts of the forests do creep forth.	20. Thou makest darkness, that it may be night, When as the savage beasts that fly the light, (As conscious of man's hatred) leave their den, And range abroad, secured from sight of men.
21. The young lions roar after their prey, and seek their meat from God.	21. Then do the forests ring of lions roaring, That ask their meat of God, their strength restoring.
22. The sun ariseth, they gather themselves together, and lay them down in their dens.	22. But when the day appears, they back do fly, And in their dens again do lurking lie.

Candor compels us to say that apologies for this work based on ill health and old age, are not pertinent. The philosopher had reached the age of sixty-three, a time of life when, in the ordinary course of nature, the almond tree may flourish, but the grasshopper has not become a burden. Milton wrote "Paradise Regained" (which he regarded as his greatest work) at the same age. Cervantes was sixty-eight when the second part of "Don Quixote" appeared, and

Goethe eighty-two when he completed the " Faust." Indeed, this version of the Psalms was made by Bacon in 1624, one year only after the first folio edition of the plays was published, and not more than three after " Timon of Athens " and " Henry VIII.," as we are told, had been written or recast by him. Furthermore, Bacon's habits of composition preclude the idea of his having sent anything immature from his pen to the press. Is it, then, within the range of credibility that he concealed his authorship of " King Lear," * while parading before the public in his own name such stuff as this?

It will be hardly necessary to examine at length the two or three other poems which have been attributed by various persons and for various reasons, more or less satisfactory, to Lord Bacon; for, even if genuine, they cannot raise the standard of his poetic abilities much above that fixed by his translation of the Psalms. One of them, however, has the distinction of being cited approvingly by Spedding. It is as follows : —

> " The man of life upright, whose guiltless heart is free
> From all dishonest deeds and thoughts of vanity;
> The man whose silent days in harmless joys are spent,
> Whom hopes cannot delude, nor fortune discontent;
> That man needs neither towers nor armor for defence,
> Nor secret vaults to fly from thunder's violence;
> He only can behold with unaffrighted eyes
> The horrors of the deep and terrors of the skies.
> Thus scorning all the care that Fate or Fortune brings,
> He makes the heaven his book, his wisdom heavenly things;
> Good thoughts his only friends, his life a well-spent age,
> The earth his sober inn, a quiet pilgrimage."

At the risk of being prosecuted by some society on the charge of cruelty to a poetic shade, we place, in juxtaposition with the above, the following brief extracts from Shakespeare :

> " Night's candles are burnt out, and jocund day
> Stands tiptoe on the misty mountain tops."

> " Age cannot wither her, nor custom stale
> Her infinite variety."

> " A combination and a form, indeed,
> Where every god did seem to set his seal,
> To give the world assurance of a man."

> " Let the candied tongue lick absurd pomp,
> And crook the pregnant hinges of the knee
> Where thrift may follow fawning."

---

* " The most wondrous work of human genius."— *Richard Grant White.*

" My way of life
Is fallen into the sear, the yellow leaf;
And that which should accompany old age,
As honor, love, obedience, troops of friends,
I must not look to have; but in their stead,
Curses, not loud but deep, mouth-honor, breath,
Which the poor heart would fain deny, and dare not."

" His life was gentle; and the elements
So mixed in him that Nature might stand up
And say to all the world, ' This was a man.' "

" The rude sea grew civil at her song,
And certain stars shot madly from their spheres,
To hear the sea-maid's music."

" What! shall one of us,
That struck the foremost man of all this world
But for supporting robbers, shall we now
Contaminate our fingers with base bribes,
And sell the mighty space of our large honors,
For so much trash as may be grasped thus ?
I had rather be a dog, and bay the moon,
Than such a Roman."

Clearly the plaintiff, so far as his own poetic compositions are concerned, has no standing in court.

The main attack, however, comes from the point of Bacon's prose. The lambent flame that plays along the lines and around the periods in his philosophical works leaped, we are told, into lightning flashes when he wrote the dramas. This view of the matter places us at a disadvantage. We have no means of identifying the two manifestations, not even by the familiar expedient of flying a kite. One cannot deny a theoretical possibility. We are as helpless before it as we would be in the presence of an armed highwayman at night carrying a bull's-eye: we see a portentous shadow, but nothing more.

Our dealings are not with possibilities. That kind of discussion we have left behind us with the schoolmen. Whether or not an angel can pass from one point in space to another point in space without passing through the intermediate space, may be an open question, but we are very sure that Francis Bacon had not the power to do so. The road from prose to poetry is a shining one ; few have trodden it, but their footprints remain forever.

Our only resource is to compare prose with prose. The materials at hand for this purpose are abundant; for besides the voluminous works of Bacon on one side, we have no inconsiderable part of the plays on the other. "The Merry Wives of Windsor" is almost wholly a prose composition. Trusting again to examples, the only solid ground for our feet, we quote the following: —

From Bacon : —

"The stage is more beholding to love than the life of man. For as to the stage, love is ever matter of comedies, and now and then of tragedies; but in life it doth much mischief, sometimes like a siren, sometimes like a fury. You may observe that, amongst all the great and worthy persons (whereof the memory remaineth, either ancient or recent) there is not one that hath been transported to the mad degree of love; which shows that great spirits and great business do keep out this weak passion. You must except, nevertheless, Marcus Antonius, the half-partner of the empire of Rome, and Appius Claudius, the decemvir and law-giver; whereof the former was indeed a voluptuous man and inordinate; but the latter was an austere and wise man; and, therefore, it seems (though rarely) that love can find entrance, not only into an open heart, but also into a heart well fortified, if watch be not well kept. . . . There is in man's nature a secret inclination and motion towards love of others, which, if it be not spent upon some one or a few, doth naturally spread itself towards many, and maketh men become humane and charitable, as it is seen sometimes in friars. Nuptial love maketh mankind; friendly love perfecteth it; but wanton love corrupteth and embaseth it."

Essay on Love.

From Shakespeare : —

"Romans, countrymen, and lovers! hear me for my cause, and be silent that you may hear. Believe me for mine honor, and have respect to mine honor, that you may believe. Censure me in your wisdom, and awake your senses that you may the better judge. If there be any in this assembly, any dear friend of Cæsar's, to him I say, that Brutus' love to Cæsar was no less than his. If, then, that friend demand why Brutus rose against Cæsar, this is my answer: Not that I loved Cæsar less, but that I loved Rome more. Had you rather Cæsar were living and die all slaves, than that Cæsar were dead, to live all freemen? As Cæsar loved me, I weep for him; as he was fortunate, I rejoice at it; as he was valiant, I honor him; but as he was ambitious, I slew him. There are tears for his love; joy for his fortune; honor for his valor; and death for his ambition. Who is here so base, that would be a bondman? If any, speak; for him have I offended. Who is here so rude, that would not be a Roman? If any, speak; for him have I offended. Who is here so vile, that will not love his country? If any, speak; for him have I offended. I pause for a reply." *Julius Cæsar, III. 2.*

"This goodly frame, the earth, seems to me a sterile promontory; this most excellent canopy, the air, look you, this brave o'er-hanging firmament, this majestical roof fretted with golden fire, why, it appears no other thing to me than a foul and pestilent congregation of vapors. What a piece of work is a man! how noble in reason! how infinite in faculty! in form and moving, how express and admirable! in action how like an angel! in apprehension how like a god!"

Hamlet, II. 2.

No one can say authoritatively that the above-quoted passages may not have come, all of them, from the same pen. The exigencies of dialogue count for something in an estimate of style. And yet the unlikeness of type is apparent at a glance. Bacon is always reminding us of that printer of his essays who cut them up into inch pieces with commas. The sentences move along as though they were on parade and keeping step. They never forget themselves, never tumble over one another in a wild rush to a goal. The philosopher must have been conscious of this sin of formality, for he expressed a wonder that the stars had not been set in the heavens according to some rule.

But Shakespeare! What a contrast! As much above rules as the hero of Austerlitz! As free from formality as a shower of aerolites! Indeed, we can hardly think of him but as one of the forces of nature, untamable, universal, absolute.

OBJECTIONS CONSIDERED.

I. Shakespeare made no personal impress on the political or social life of his time, having been, so far as we know, a stranger to every man of prominence, outside of theatrical circles, among his contemporaries.

He was professionally an actor and, therefore, little better than a social outcast. In common with all others of his class, he was obliged to pursue his calling under the protection of some one in authority, or, in other words, to be a nobleman's "player"; otherwise, he was liable to be arrested as a vagabond, to be publicly whipped, and to have his right ear bored with a hot iron, not less (as prescribed by law under Elizabeth) than one inch thick. It is evident that no genius, however exalted, could have broken down a barrier laid as deep as this in the prejudices of society.

II. Shakespeare's handwriting indicates a man without cultivation and even without natural refinement.

Theories based on a problematical sympathy between mental and bodily powers must always yield to ascertained facts.

It is undeniable that Shakespeare stood at the head of one of the most exacting professions of civil life. His success in it, considering the circumstances of his origin and the intellectual vigor of the times, was simply phenomenal. We hardly have acquired a clearer apprehension of the native strength of his character, if he had written his signature in the sky over our heads.

III. The manuscripts of the plays have disappeared, a circumstance perfectly natural if Bacon were the secret author, but on any other supposition, mysterious.

The editors of the first folio had in their possession, as they claim, the author's " true original copies." They even mention certain peculiarities in the handwriting as characteristic of Shakespeare. This is the last we know of the manuscripts; evidently, they met their end, then and there, that their souls might become immortal in type. The habits of printers at this day make it certain that the laws of mortality apply to literary remains. Had the poet been living, or had his family possessed any interest, financial or otherwise, in the undertaking, the result might have been different. In either of these contingencies, the precious documents, however disfigured, might now be ruling us from their urn.

IV. From official records and from tradition alike, we must infer that Shakespeare was low-bred and vulgar, utterly devoid of intellectual ideals.

The following is a summary of the known facts in Shakespeare's life : —

1564, April 26.	Baptized at Stratford-on-Avon.
1582, Nov. 28.	Licensed to marry Anne Hathaway.
1583, May 26.	His daughter, Susanna, baptized.
1585, Feb. 2.	Hamnet and Judith, twins, baptized.
1592.	In London. Satirized by Greene.
1593.	Dedicates the poem, " Venus and Adonis," to the Earl of Southampton.
1594.	Dedicates the poem, "Rape of Lucrece," to the same.
1596, Aug. 11.	His son, Hamnet, buried at Stratford.
1597.	Purchases New Place in Stratford.
1598, Feb. 4.	Returned on the rolls of the town as the holder (during a famine) of ten quarters of corn.
"	His name, as author, printed for the first time on the title-page of a play (" Love's Labor's Lost ").

1600.	Sues John Clayton for £7 and obtains verdict.
1602.	Buys two parcels of land and a cottage in Stratford.
1603.	Appointed one of "His Majesty's servants" for theatrical performances.
1604.	Sues Philip Rogers at Stratford for £1 15s. 10d. for malt delivered, including 2s. loaned.
1605.	Purchases a moiety of the tithes of Stratford, Old Stratford, Bishopton and Welcombe.
1607, June 5.	His daughter, Susanna, marries Dr. John Hall at Stratford.
1608.	Sues John Addenbroke of Stratford, obtaining judgment for £6, together with £1 4s. costs. Addenbroke not being found, sues his bondsman, Hornby.
"	Present, as sponsor, at baptism of son of Henry Walker, in Stratford.
1613, March. 10.	Purchases a house in London.
" " 11.	Mortgages the same for £60.
1614, Oct. 28.	Guaranteed by William Replingham against loss by enclosure of commons at Welcombe.
" Nov. 16.	Comes to London.
" " 17.	Explains to Thomas Greene how far the enclosure at Welcombe will extend.
1616, Feb. 10.	His daughter, Judith, marries Thomas Quiney.
" March 25.	Makes his will.
" April 23.	His death.

The foregoing is a mere skeleton, but it is all that has survived the decay of three centuries. The Shakespeare of the biographers is not our Shakespeare. We prefer his dry bones to the rounded, almost living and breathing, form which they have constructed for us out of the tissues of conjecture and scandal. Aubrey and Davenant, *et id omne genus*, we dismiss peremptorily. They are beneath our contempt. The witticism to which one of these men owes his unenviable fame is as old as the pyramids; crawling out of the ooze of the Nile, it has made its slimy track for thousands of years through the world's literature.

Confining ourselves to the facts, we find but two that seem to be out of harmony with our conception of Shakespeare's character. They are as follows: —

1. His withdrawal from London, and consequent abandonment of intellectual pursuits, in middle life.

The exact date of his retirement is unknown. He was in London in 1613, for he purchased a house in Blackfriars in the spring of that year. He visited the city, also, a year later. It is evident that, wherever he was, he continued literary work, for the press did not exhaust his manuscript accumulations of this period till seven years after his death.

2. His frequent litigation in the collection of debts.

We have no knowledge of the circumstances under which he invoked the law on these occasions. Legal processes may not be adapted to show the "quality of mercy," but we have no reason to believe that in this case they were inconsistent with justice. Certainly, Shakespeare will not suffer on this account by comparison with the plaintiff in this action, who, living far beyond his means, was unjust to others, and (as the sequel gave terrible proof) unjust to himself.

V. The plays exhibit, on the part of the author, an intimate and thorough knowledge of classical literature, such as Shakespeare, uneducated, could not have possessed.

It is a gratuitous assumption that because Shakespeare was not matriculated at Oxford or Cambridge, therefore he was uneducated. Education is a training of the mental faculties. It has nothing to do, except as means to an end, with the acquisition of knowledge. Indeed, the less it concerns itself, while in process, with the acquisition of knowledge *per se*, the better. We must temper our tools before we put them to practical use. A goddess of song must spend years in the practice of elementary sounds, before she can wing her flight into the highest regions of melody. The pressure of what is claimed to be acquired knowledge in a university tends to unfit a young man for a life of reform, or, indeed, for any original work. Bacon saw the danger, and abandoned Cambridge at the age of sixteen, an act that made it possible for him to write the "Novum Organum." Had Shakespeare been a senior wrangler, the world would to-day be without a "Hamlet."

We may be sure that, previously to his arrival in London, the poet had learned, in the fields and woods and in intercourse with his fellow-beings, all that was necessary for vigorous and sustained exercise of his intellectual faculties. He came as a child of Nature, with heart and brain charged to the full with its richest impulses, for he had been dwelling in

> "the light of setting suns,
> And the round ocean, and the living air,
> And the blue sky, and in the heart of man."

Is it incredible, is it even extraordinary, that to such a

one, in the early maturity of his wonderful powers, and fresh from the study of that great Book the living pages of which are outspread before us all, the conquest of a few foreign languages, and of the literature contained in them, should have been an easy and congenial task?

Here, then, is our Shakespeare. A man born, where nearly all the benefactors of the human race have been born, in a cottage; descended from a line of husbandmen to whom the soil they tilled gave a silent strength; educated in a school where the mind unfolds as naturally as a flower; brought into contact with the world's literature at a time of life when curiosity and ambition have their keenest edge; a man beloved for the gentleness of his spirit, and revered for his genius. Surely, in the presence of such a character, we are impressed with a new sense of the dignity of our common nature, and feel a fresh consecration for the duties that lie before us.

ASIATIC CHOLERA, WITH SOME PRACTICAL SUGGESTIONS.

BY HENRY SHEFFIELD, M. D.

This disease is propagated from its own specific germ, and becomes epidemic only when it finds a suitable atmosphere for its development. It can be communicated from the dejections of one suffering with the disease, but the contagion is less violent than diphtheria and other diseases.

The germ of cholera is not sown broadcast over the earth nor in isolated spots, but, when epidemic, travels forward by its immutable laws. It advances from place to place by developing its own germ, in a well-marked choleraic stream which can be definitely traced. Epidemic cholera does not always follow the same route, but selects its own course in and through that atmosphere which furnishes the best condition for its rapid propagation; it marches onward across oceans, seas, and continents.

Surgeon-General Cornish has stated authoritatively that "Epidemic cholera follows the same laws in India as in any other country, and is epidemic only in certain limited parts. . . . The present epidemic crossed the Caspian Sea (where it could have been contracted) and spread among the population of Asiatic Russia; . . . that in India, with ample military aid at hand, *quarantine and sanitary conditions have been tried again and again unsuccessfully.*" This statement is undoubtedly true; for cholera germs float in the air, and there only where they can find suitable conditions for their propagation.

The Gulf Stream is a body of water flowing rapidly through another body of water which is comparatively motionless. A choleraic stream of germs flows through the air in a similar way. This choleraic stream cannot be mapped out on the ocean, but can be on land. It is well known that vessels have left the continent with every passenger on board in perfect health; in a few days they ran into this unseen choleraic stream of germs, when a score or more would succumb to the disease in a few hours. As soon as that vessel left that choleraic stream, the passengers ceased to contract the disease, began to recover, and all who survived were landed in health.

Its development and progress are similar to yellow fever, which propagates its own specific germ as it advances. A few hundred years since a stream of yellow fever germs crossed the Gulf of Mexico (where susceptible persons could have contracted the disease) and soon entered New Orleans. From thence it took an unusual route; it came north; its daily advancement was noted until it reached Memphis. The condition of the air north of that city was unsuited to the propagation of its germ; therefore, it could not go farther. At that time many persons whose systems were impregnated with its poisonous germs, came to Nashville. The air at this point was of sufficient purity to prevent the propagation of those germs and to protect those who came in immediate contact with the diseased refugees, all of whom recovered. Those persons who lived a few hundred feet from the stream of yellow fever germs on its way north towards Memphis, were exempt from the disease.

Those persons who live a few hundred feet from a choleraic stream of germs are also exempt from the disease, unless in a condition peculiarly receptive to those germs.

The present condition of the air in Nashville (and nearly every other city in the United States of America) is so pure that if the germs of cholera were introduced here it could not become epidemic; only a few susceptible persons could contract the disease. When cholera becomes epidemic in any locality, its germs displace or destroy the life-sustaining powers of the air,— the oxygen and ozone,— and every person becomes enfeebled and exhausted. At that time the digestive organs become quite powerless, therefore indifferently perform their normal functions. It seems that the lacteals become inert and cease to take up the chyle and transfer it into the viscera, thence into the blood vessels. This life-sustaining product then remains in the intestine, flows onward combining with its other contents, and then becomes corrupt matter. To use powerful astringents for the purpose of retaining this putrid mass within this perfectly natural sewer of the body is dangerous and destructive. If these putrid contents of the bowels could be medicinally or mechanically confined therein, its acridity would soon perforate their walls and escape into the abdomen.

The fountain must be pure or the stream cannot be, and a dam built across its mouth cannot make it pure.

The liver is a large gland within the body, and its secretions are absolutely essential to the formation of chyme from wholesome food. Now, during an attack of cholera, food cannot be taken into the stomach, at which time there are no secretions required of the liver to aid in digestion. The healthy liver is easily moved to active secretions by small doses of *calomel*. During an attack of cholera it will require exceedingly large doses of calomel to excite the enfeebled, weary liver to increased activity. The secretions of the liver are taken out of the blood, and it will soon become exhausted if not resupplied by the blood-making organs, and they cannot furnish it even in small quantities. In that condition, to torture the feeble liver with calomel, is dangerous in the extreme.

Now if it requires four ounces of blood for the liver to secrete one drachm of bile, it would be far more safe to take that quantity of blood from the arm than to greatly overtax the weary liver. The liver and digestive organs could then retain their own vitality, and sooner be able to resume again their normal functions.

The great sympathetic nerve (which is semi-sensitive) controls the action of the abdominal viscera. This nerve is irritated by acrid substances which traverse the intestines, and by its reflex action will produce convulsions, cramps, and vomiting. *Opium* and its congeners, in appreciable doses, will produce insensibility of the brain, paralysis of the cerebro spinal and great sympathetic nerves, and suspend every function of the entire body. It therefore should never be taken during an attack of cholera — except by suicides. It will not always bring death to them, but produce a comatose condition during which they have been buried.

Remedies that are positively known to be curative in cholera, become inert and useless to a patient who has been dosed with opium and who will succumb to the disease before those remedies can produce an impression.

Alcoholic drinks, astringent and pungent concoctions will diminish or destroy the normal secretions of the alimentary canal, and create inflammation, which is as fatal as cholera.

Iced drinks, ice cream, and sherbet must not be used during an epidemic.

Ham, sausage, boiled cabbage, milk, cheese, nuts, pickles, salads, honey, molasses, pastry, canned fish, oysters, and lobsters must not be eaten.

There is a want of appetite during an epidemic of cholera, and to use stimulants to create a morbid one will result in distress and disaster. Only foods known to be easily digested and assimilated must be eaten. Fresh beef, sound vegetables, and ripe fruits can be eaten in moderation, but must be well masticated to furnish the much-needed saliva. The digestive organs are so enfeebled they can be overtaxed easily by wholesome food even in small quantities. **Food** should be kept on ice and outside of the infected district if possible, then cooked as soon as received.

Hot water or pure cool water **may** be drunk before meals, but not with them or immediately afterwards. Limestone **water** should be boiled, put into bottles, corked and turned down to cool. Cistern water and filtered water **of** the same temperature may be drunk in moderation, but best when the stomach is empty.

The bowels can be kept in good condition by suitable food — by taking a cup of oatmeal gruel, with a little salt, before breakfast, or an enema of hot water afterwards.

A flannel bandage worn around the body is a safeguard. Copper worn next to the skin will relieve cramps and be preventive of **cholera.** The best prophylactic known is *cuprum metalecium ;* a dose daily when living in an infected district of the sixth trituration.

The only stimulant of any value whatever to relieve depression and debility during an epidemic, is spirits of camphor. Two drops on granulated sugar is the proper way to prescribe it. If taken during the first stage of cholera, a dose every three to five minutes, it alone will cure nearly every case. It is the one and only domestic remedy of any surety or value.

Cleanliness, ventilation, good nursing, and the use of disinfectants are requisite in all diseases. During an attack of cholera all the vessels to be used for receiving the dejections of the patient should be kept ready and contain a half pint or more of water, in which have been placed a few drops of *carbolic acid.*

The clothing and bedding in contact with the patient should be disinfected, as well as the apartment afterwards.

Cholera is sudden in its attack, rapid in progress; and its treatment, to be successful, must be certain, specific, and curative — not palliative, not experimental.

Homœopathic physicians have treated it successfully wherever it has appeared all over the world, and have learned that it yields readily to our specific remedies. Our individual, our combined experience, and our statistics give us supreme confidence in our remedies; therefore we have no fears of the result of our treatment of epidemic cholera for ourselves, our friends, and our patients.

To prevent confusion, I will recommend only a few remedies. For cramps, *cuprum met;* for vomiting, *veratrune alb;* for colliquative discharges from skin and bowels, *arsenicum alb;* for consecutive fever, *baptisin;* for suppression of urine, *caunabis sati;* for delirium, *belladonna;* cuprum and belladonna in the sixth trituration, the others in the third trituration.

Tablet triturates, each containing a dose, can be obtained at a homœopathic pharmacy. They can be taken dry on the tongue or dissolved in a spoonful of pure water, used according to the urgency of the case, from six to sixty minutes apart.

Patients can rinse the mouth in hot water and take a spoonful as often as the stomach will tolerate it.

Patients should be gently rubbed with a towel, then briskly with the naked hand, and patted until warmth returns to the skin.

Bottles filled with hot water placed around the body will add to the comfort of the patient.

If the foregoing instructions are followed during an epidemic of cholera, the death rate will be far less than it was during *la grippe* and no distressing *sequelæ.*

THE VOLUME OF CURRENCY.

BY N. A. DUNNING.

THE volume of currency in circulation has become such an important factor in political discussions that a careful analysis of the subject, although repeatedly made in the past, will doubtless be of interest at the present time.

Much of the confusion and difference of opinion which now obtains in regard to this question comes from an absence of clearness, and I might say fairness, in the government reports from the Treasury. If the secretary of the Treasury would plainly declare that his monthly statements simply disclose, first, the amount of currency that has been issued from the registry of the Treasury and the mints; second, the amount of this currency held in the Treasury, and third, the amount that is outside the Treasury, he would at once place the matter in its proper light and eliminate much that is now misleading and deceptive. As it is, he assumes to give out not only the volume of circulation but the per capita circulation as well. The manifest unreliability of such statements will be apparent to all after even a partial examination of the facts. The following letter from Mr. Leech, director of the Mint, fully sustains my position, that the amount of currency which the secretary of the Treasury assumes to be in circulation is really the amount outside the Treasury, which may be in circulation among the people or may be lost, destroyed, exported, or used in the mechanical arts.

Treasury Department, Bureau of the Mint, }
Washington, D. C., Feb. 5, 1892. }

N. A. DUNNING, ESQ., No. 239 N. Capitol St., Washington, D. C.

Dear Sir: Replying to your communication of the 4th instant, as to the amount of currency in the United States, I would say that the amount of $24.70 is the per capita amount of money in circulation in the United States; *that is, outside of Treasury vaults.* I enclose herewith a statement exhibiting the same.

Very respectfully,

E. O. LEECH, *Director of the Mint.*

The tables which I shall use are taken from the reports of 1889, since later reports do not contain certain valuable data. It might be proper to add that the increase of currency since that date has hardly kept pace with increased population.

GOVERNMENT TABLES.

The treasurer of the United States, in his report for 1889, pages 10 and 11, says: " The metallic stock of the country, as estimated by the director of the Mint, and the outstanding issue of paper, as shown by the records of this office, on June 30, 1889, was as follows : —

Gold coin and bullion . . .	$680,063,505 00
Silver dollars and bullion . . .	343,947,093 00
Fractional silver coin . . .	76,601,836 00
Total coin and bullion	$1,100,612,434 00
State bank notes	201,170 00
Old demand notes	56,442 00
One and two year notes	62,955 00
Compound interest notes	185,750 00
Fractional currency, estimated	5,916,590 47
National bank notes	211,378,963 00
United States notes	346,681,016 00
Certificates of deposit, act of June 8, 1872 . .	17,195,000 00
Gold certificates	154,048,552 00
Silver certificates	262,629,746 00
Total paper currency . .	999,356,248 47
Aggregate .	$2,099,968,718 47

The following tables show the amounts of the several kinds of currency in the Treasury and in circulation June 30, 1889 : —

	In Treasury.	In Circulation.
Gold	$303,387,719 79	$376,675,785 21
Silver . . .	314,935,151 52	105,613,777 48
Old paper issues .	1,094 76	7,421,912 71
National bank notes .	4,150,537 75	207,228,425 25
United States notes .	47,296,875 54	299,384,140 40
Certificates of deposit, act of 1872 . .	240,000 00	16,955,000 00
Gold certificates . .	36,918,323 00	117,130,229 00
Silver certificates .	5,487,181 00	257,142,565 00
Total . . .	$712,416,883 36	$1,387,551,835 11

This statement of the director of the Mint appeared so misleading that the treasurer was constrained to qualify or explain it as follows. He says, page 11 : —

"From the face of the preceding statements it would appear that there was an increase both in the aggregate monetary supply and in the amount held by the people. The certificates of deposit are, however, merely representative of moneys in the Treasury; and to count them with the coin and notes to which they give title would be a duplication. If these be eliminated and the actual moneys be disposed according to ownership, the result will be as shown below : —

June 30, 1889,	Outstanding.	In Treasury.	In Circulation.
Gold . .	$680,063,505 00	$186,257,490 79	$493,806,014 21
Silver . .	420,548,929 00	57,797,586 22	362,756,542 48
Notes . .	565,482,986 47	34,493,508 05	530,989,478 42
Total	$1,666,094,420 47	$278,543,585 36	$1,387,551,835 11

This is an authoritative statement of the currency that has been made by the fiat of government either at the Mint or at the Bureau of Printing and Engraving. This amount is given at $1,666,094,420.47, which I shall use as the basis of my calculations. The difference between the method adopted by the secretary of the Treasury to ascertain the amount of currency in circulation and the one I use, is this : He takes the whole amount, $1,666,094,420.47, and deducts from it the amount in the United States Treasury, $278,543,-585.36, and assumes that the difference, $1,387,551,835.11, is in circulation among the people. I shall take the amount given as outstanding, $1,666,094,420.47, and attempt to locate it, whether in the United States Treasury, as reserves in banks, lost or destroyed, or in circulation among the people. In the Mint report for 1889, page 128, is found a detailed statement of the estimate of gold and silver coin and bullion as follows : —

GOLD.

In U. S. Treasury	$186,451,708
In national banks	152,169,400
In other banks reported	46,911,553
In private banks and among the people .	294,530,744
Total	$680,063,505

SILVER.

In U. S. Treasury	.	.	.	.	.	.	$57,458,901
In national banks	.	.	.	.	.	.	23,734,469
In other banks reported	.	.	.	.	.	.	2,118,516
In private banks and among the people	.	.	.	337,237,043

Total $420,548,929

The United States treasurer's report, page 10, furnishes a statement of paper currency.

Greenbacks outstanding	.	.	.	$346,681,016 00
National bank notes outstanding	.	.	.	211,378,963 00
Fractional currency outstanding	.	.	.	6,916,690 47
Compound notes outstanding	.	.	.	185,750 00
One and two year notes outstanding	.	.	.	62,955 00
Old demand notes outstanding	.	.	.	56,442 00
State bank notes outstanding	.	.	.	201,170 00

Total . . . $565,482,986 47

This gives a total outstanding currency of $1,666,095,-420.47. These tables contain the government estimates of the amount and kind of the currency, together with the location of the coin.

BULLION.

Before beginning a detailed examination of the items of currency, I desire to call attention to the bullion account. While the amount of gold and silver held in the United States Treasury is perhaps correct, yet on page 129 of the same report the director of the Mint states that $65,995,145 is in gold and $10,444,443 in silver bullion. This $76,-439,588 in bullion can no more be called money than so much pork or wheat. It is simply a commodity and nothing else. I shall therefore deduct this amount at the commencement of the investigation.

GOLD.

In considering the amount of gold coin it is proper to state that the original estimate, which has been the basis of all subsequent calculations, was made by Director Linderman in 1872. He placed the amount of gold coin in the country on July 1, 1873, at $135,000,000. Something over $98,-000,000 was shown by official reports to have been in the banks and public treasuries; $20,000,000 was estimated as being in circulation on the Pacific Coast, with an allowance of about $10,000,000 in banks not reporting. Since this

estimate, Directors Birchard and Kimball have made three
revisions, each of which reduced this amount.   In 1885
Director Kimball deducted $30,000,000 "as a moderate
estimate for the amount of gold consumed in the arts."   In
1886 a further reduction of $15,669,981 was made, and also
one of $4,654,714, in all $50,324,695.   On page 56 of his
report for 1889, on the production of the precious metals,
Director Leech says : —

"The elements of uncertainty in these official tables have
been : first, the actual consumption of coin in the industrial
arts, and second, the amount of coin which finds its way out
of the country without being recorded."

This uncertainty is made more apparent by the following
statement, taken from the report of Director Kimball, on the
production of gold and silver for 1888, pages 42 and 43.
He quotes from the *Commercial and Financial Chronicle* of
Feb. 9, 1889, which he vouches for as being worthy of
confidence.

"In years past we have often insisted that there must be
an error in the item, because the most industrious inquiry
failed to bring to light a very considerable portion of it.   At
present there are at least $275,000,000 of the total that
cannot be accounted for.   Since the New York banks turned
their gold into the Treasury and obtained gold certificates
for it, the government gross holdings of gold have become
large.   On Jan. 1, 1888, it held gross $324,773,677 ; it
had outstanding of gold certificates issued against it $120,-
888,448, hence its net holdings were $203,885,219, as we
give them in the above table.   Even of these certificates
afloat it is impossible to trace more than seventy-six and one-
fourth millions in all, and of the gold not in the Treasury
only about one hundred millions can be found.   So whichever method the investigator may adopt,— whether by counting the gross gold in the Treasury, with an estimate for
circulation, deducting certificates which are not in bank and
in the Treasury, or by taking the course we have pursued,—
the result reached will be the same.   As to the gold in
active circulation, whatever there is of it must be in the
Pacific States ; for in the Eastern, Western, and Southern
States not one individual in every hundred receives in ordinary business transactions a gold certificate or a gold coin
once in twelve months.   Contrast that fact with the other,

that on the 1st of January, 1889, there were 60,799,321 silver
dollars in circulation in the United States, the remainder of
the $307,000,000 being in the form of silver certificates.
Of that sixty and three-quarter million silver dollars we
venture to say that every inhabitant who during the last year
has tendered a $5 bill in payment of some small purchase
made has, nine out of ten times, had offered to him one or
more in change.   Such ubiquity in the case of sixty and
three-quarter million of silver dollars proves clearly enough
that if there was even a little gold coin passing from hand
to hand, it would often be met with.   Still, in the following
statement, locating the gold in the United States, we have
made a very liberal allowance for circulation, so that the
reader may be satisfied that the amount hoarded is under-
stated rather than overstated.

In Treasury, gold and bullion, less certificates out-standing		$203,885,219
In national banks:		
Gold	$70,825,187	
Gold certificates	75,334,420	
Gold clearing-house certificates .	7,399,000	
		153,558,607
In state banks, etc.		
Gold . .	$27,015,951	
Gold certificates	937,710	
		27,953,661
In actual circulation, gold and silver certificates .		40,000,000
Total in sight and estimated in circulation . .		425,397,487
Total in country		704,608,169
Total hoarded Jan. 1, 1889 . .		$279,210,682

"In the above it will be seen that we allot $40,000,000 to
circulation, and yet even with that deducted there are still
left $279,210,682 unaccounted for.

"From these facts the conclusion is unavoidable that either
there are to-day at least $279,000,000 in gold hoarded by the
people of the United States, or else that the government
mint figures are extremely erroneous."

This is a frank admission that more than $279,000,000 of
gold coin cannot be accounted for.   It admits that it is not
in the Treasury or the banks, and is not seen in circulation
among the people.   Besides this the director of the Mint
acknowledges, on page 128, that the amount given as held
by banks other than national, aggregating $46,911,653, is

simply an estimate. In view of all this, I consider it justifiable to make a large deduction from the amount of gold estimated as being in circulation.

SILVER.

The amount of silver in the country is estimated at $333,-502,650 in standard dollars and $76,601,836 in subsidiary coin, or a total of $410,104,406 in silver coin. The entire amount of silver coinage since the foundation of the government is:—

Silver dollars	$341,533,888 00
Silver one-half dollars	122,822,414 50
Silver one-quarter dollars	38,831,202 25
Silver twenty-cent pieces	271,000 00
Silver dimes	21,704,516 10
Silver one-half dimes	4,880,219 40
Silver three-cent pieces	1,282,087 20
Total	$531,325,327 45

This does not include the trade dollar coinage.

There has been coined since 1878 $333,502,649 in standard silver dollars, $768,925.50 in half dollars, $1,184,-500.75 in quarter dollars, $271,000 in twenty-cent pieces, and $4,959,038.80 in dimes. Total subsidiary coin, $7,183,-465.05. Government statisticians ask us to believe that every silver dollar coined since 1878 still remains in this country. We are also asked to believe that all the subsidiary coin that has been minted since 1878, and $68,418,-371, a considerable portion of which was coined previous to the war, is still in use as currency. Senator Sherman declared that the entire silver circulation wears out and is renewed once in thirty years. The whole amount of subsidiary coin minted since 1793 is $189,791,439, and we are asked to believe that over forty per cent of this entire amount is still in use in this country. I deem it proper to make a liberal deduction from government estimates relative to silver currency.

PAPER CURRENCY.

The largest amount of legal tenders outstanding at any one time was $449,338,902, on June 30, 1864. From the date of their first issue, October, 1862, there has been issued and re-issued $2,253,997,808. The act of May 31, 1878, forbade their further destruction. At that time, according to the books of the Treasury, $346,681,016 was outstanding. Since that date the government has included this whole amount in its statement of the volume of currency. The largest issue of national bank currency was in December, 1873, when it amounted to $341,320,256. Since 1863, when the system went into operation, there have been $1,362,353,-706 issues and re-issues of this currency, and there was outstanding Sept. 30, 1889, $128,450,600. There is no data upon which to base an estimate of the loss by fire, wreck, flood or other accidents, including the lost and worn-out bills. The government in its statement makes no allowance for such contingencies. It is absurd, however, to assume there has been no loss on this account. Some idea may be formed of the loss in such cases by a comparison with the known statistics regarding fractional currency. Since 1863, when fractional currency was first issued, there has been issued and re-issued $368,720,079. The largest amount in circulation at any one time was $46,912,003.34, in 1874. The act of Jan. 14, 1875, provided for their retirement, since which time all of this kind of currency that has been presented has been redeemed. The amount outstanding June 30, 1880, was $15,589,888.37. By act of June 21, 1879, Congress declared that $8,375,934 had been lost or destroyed. Since then only $299,210.40 has been redeemed; and Senator Sherman, in a recent speech, declared that the remaining $6,915,743.97 is probably lost. Here, then, is proof that out of the $46,961,000 fractional currency issued, over $15,000,-000 remains unaccounted for, an absolute loss of thirty-three per cent in sixteen years.

The director of the Mint estimates $202,027,359 legal tenders and $244,703,508 silver certificates in circulation outside the Treasury and national banks. This shows about seventy-five cents more per capita of certificates than greenbacks among the people. If any one will take account of the paper currency received in the ordinary course of business, he will find $50 in certificates and treasury notes of 1890 for every $1 of original greenbacks. If this vast amount of greenbacks is circulating among the people, why is it not seen more frequently? Senator Stewart, in his speech on the free coinage of silver, said: "The greenbacks or treasury notes have been in circulation for twenty-eight years, and were used during the rebellion in the theatre of war.

A deduction of at least $50,000,000 ought to be made for loss of greenbacks."

Senators Daniel, Teller, Plumb, and others have declared that proper reductions should be made for such loss. Even Secretary Windom acknowledged before the Finance Committee that certain amounts should be taken from this statement, in order to show the true amount in circulation. Others have expressed similar opinions of equally as good authority.

CURRENCY HELD AS RESERVES.

In considering the amount of currency withheld from circulation by statute law, reference is made to the statistical abstract of 1889, page 28, table 26. "Amount of the cash reserve held by the national banks, also the whole amount required to be held by them: —

Oct. 5, 1887, cash held in banks . .	$245,026,709
Amount required to be held . . .	278,035,273
Oct. 4, 1888, cash held in banks	$268,152,277
Amount required to be held .	311,959,161
Sept. 30, 1889, cash held in banks .	$264,023,542
Amount required to be held . .	333,111,465

As this table comes from the Treasury Department, I will deduct $333,111,465 from the currency outstanding, as being held in reserve according to law, and as such out of circulation. The returns from 1,671 state banks, 1,324 private banks, and 969 savings banks and trust companies, Comptroller's Report, page 80, show $2,334,272,433 in deposits. The laws governing such institutions differ with different states. Some require more reserve than others, the range being from ten to twenty-five per cent of deposits. An estimate of ten per cent, therefore, would be very conservative, and give $233,427,242 as a reserve fund.

The amount held by the 3,647 banks not reporting can only be estimated. Placing it at $10,000 each, gives $36,-470,000, which is a very low estimate. This makes a total of $603,008,707. It has been urged that these reserves are really in circulation; that no distinction is made in the moneys paid out, and that they are part of the assets of the banks. The last two propositions are doubtless true; but the law demands that a certain per cent of the moneys deposited

shall be held as a reserve, and the banks that do not conform
to this law violate it at the risk of their charters. When the
farmer threshes his wheat, he calculates how much he will
want for seed and bread for his family; the remainder he can
sell. He does not remove the wheat for bread and seed from
the general bin, but when he has sold down to that amount
he stops selling. Just so with the banks. They keep all
their money together, but when they have loaned down to
their legal reserve they stop, or continue in violation of law.
Senator Plumb places this amount at $700,000,000; and
Senator Sherman, in a recent speech, said: "Can any one,
with a knowledge of the fact that we have in the course of
the year to disburse some $400,000,000, suppose that $10,-
000,000 as a working balance would be all sufficient? If
any bank should maintain on hand, for the redemption of
current deposits or any other form of liability coming in, at
least twenty-five per cent of the amount, even that would be
considered very close banking."

Perhaps the most convincing argument that can be adduced
is the position Secretary Windom and his predecessors have
taken in regard to the redemption of the greenbacks. One
hundred millions in gold have been and are now being held
to redeem $346,000,000 of legal tenders. This reserve of
twenty-eight and nine-tenths per cent is deemed necessary
for the safety of the public credit, and is, therefore, a guide
as to the amount required to keep private credit from being
doubted. If twenty-eight and nine-tenths per cent is
required by the government to protect the redemption of
these greenbacks, which the law of May 31, 1878, says shall
not be redeemed, surely an estimate of about fifteen per cent
is not too large for the protection of private or corporate
business. Either Senator Plumb is mistaken, or Senator
Sherman errs in judgment, and his predecessors have acted
unwisely in the administration of the Treasury, or my
figures must stand. It is difficult for me to determine how
a certain amount of currency held for a special purpose,
either by law or the dictate of business prudence, can be
considered as acting in a contradictory or opposite capacity.
When the reserve fund of a bank reaches the legal point,
discount, and consequently a further service to the people,
must cease. And no matter how often this sum may be
changed as regards denomination or kinds, the amount must

not go below a certain sum. I shall, therefore, contend that a reserve fund is so much of the amount outstanding that is located in the vaults of the banks, and as a consequence not in circulation.

CONCLUSIONS.

The whole amount held in United States Treasury is $712,416,883.36; from this should be deducted $375,272,-794, being the amount of gold and silver certificates outside the Treasury for which coin is held to redeem. This leaves $337,144,089.36 as the amount to be taken from the sum outstanding. During the fiscal year 1889 there was a net loss of gold and silver of $61,691,504. (See Mint Report, page 30.) As the amount of bullion remained the same, this was a loss to the circulation. It only remains now to deduct the $6,916,690 of fractional currency that is still counted in circulation, which has long since been destroyed, and the statement of deductions, that I consider fair and reasonable, will be complete, which is as follows: —

Amount outstanding as per treasurer's statement . $1,666,094,420 47
Amounts to be deducted:

Loss in gold coin . . .	$200,000,000 00	
Loss in silver coin . .	20,000,000 00	
Loss in paper currency .	50,000,000 00	
Loss in fractional currency .	6,916,690 00	
Held as reserves, total .	603,008,707 00	
Held in U. S. Treasury . .	337,144,089 36	
Coin sent abroad . . .	61,605,504 00	
Bullion counted as currency .	76,439,588 00	
		$1,355,204,578 36

In circulation . $310,889,842 11

The balance in circulation divided among 61,717,936 people, gives $4.97 per capita. While this small per capita may appear unreasonable or even absurd to many, I would suggest a careful revision of these figures item by item before hasty conclusions are made. The subject will bear a much closer investigation than at first seems probable; and since nearly every political economist declares that the volume of currency in circulation determines the level price of labor and its products, this article may be of some service in locating the difficulties which to-day surround every species of industry.

ALCOHOL IN ITS RELATION TO THE BIBLE.

A Reply to Alex. Gustafson's Criticism

BY HENRY A. HARTT, M. D.

ANOTHER champion has appeared in THE ARENA against me, who maintains that the wine sanctioned by Scripture was unfermented grape juice, and that this is the only kind of wine that Scripture ought to have sanctioned; and in relation to the Last Supper, he says: —

"Jesus claimed to be the Christ. If He were the Christ, He knew the nature of intoxicating wine, and could foresee what a terrible obstacle it would become in the path of His Kingdom upon earth. Could He, possessing such knowledge, have put that intoxicating cup to His disciples' lips? Could He have compared its poisoned contents to His own blood, shed for the remission of sins? Could He have constituted alcohol, that regal agent of damnation, as the most sacred symbol of salvation? Could He have wistfully looked forward to again supping with them in His Father's Kingdom, if the cup He used was intoxicating (poisoned)? It ought to be apparent from this to every sincere Christian, that to admit even the possibility of Jesus having used fermented wine, is to doubt His mission, and question His claims; and that to believe that He ever used the poisoned cup is to repudiate Him as Christ, hence proclaim Him the Antichrist."

I have never opposed the cause of Temperance when it was properly advocated. On the contrary, I have always admired its supporters for their courage and self-sacrificing benevolence, and have especially appreciated their successful efforts in dragging to light the enormous evil of drunkenness, and presenting it to mankind in all its magnitude and horrors. But when I see a champion come forth, arrayed in the armor of infidelity, and, in the name of Christ, presume to dictate to Him what He should or should not have done; and to declare authoritatively what the Scriptures should or should not have taught; and to charge that all

Christian men who differ from him, and who believe that unfermented grape juice is not wine, and that the wine of Scripture was alcoholic wine, are virtually guilty of doubting His mission, questioning His claims, repudiating Him as Christ, and hence proclaiming Him as Antichrist; — I challenge him as, practically, a foe both to the true interests of the cause of Temperance and of Christianity.

The philological argument to prove that the wine of Scripture was alcoholic wine, founded on the Hebrew word *yayin*, in the Old Testament, and on the corresponding Greek word *oinos*, in the New, is to me conclusive. The pretence that they are generic is, in my opinion, ridiculous. The hypothesis involves that the authors of the Bible employed for centuries two words, each representing two substances utterly dissimilar in their nature and effects. And now for nearly two thousand years the whole Christian world has accepted the definition which, for the first time, a small party in this country has suddenly found to be incredible and horrible.

The incidental remark of Jesus, in illustration of the new and old dispensations, that "Men do not put new wine into old bottles," furnishes indubitable evidence to the same effect; for what other explanation of it can be given than that new wine, which was still more or less in a state of fermentation, was put into new bottles (which were then made of wine-skins) because they only could resist the pressure produced thereby.

In my paper on "Alcohol in its Relation to the Bible," I referred to the passage in which Jesus is charged with being a winebibber, in order to show that He habitually used wine in accordance with the universal custom of the country; and so far from justifying the charge, I expressly ascribed it to the "benighted Pharisees." And yet my opponent, in commenting upon this point, says: "Surely His self-forgetting and self-sacrificing life, not to speak of His divinity, should have shielded Him from Christian indorsement of that libel!"

Such an amazing perverseness of criticism can only be excused on the ground of fanaticism.

In the famous rebuke of St. Paul to the Church of Corinth, my critic says that "the word translated 'drunken' is ambiguous; its original meaning is, merely filled with something, whether it be food or drink. It is plainly apparent that in this passage it has no reference to drink, but only to food. Satiety, not drunkenness, is the antithesis to hunger."

This criticism, in my judgment, affords no reason for changing the word "drunken," as given in the accepted version. It is not probable that the Apostle would have administered so severe a rebuke in that early age, if the irregularity of which he complained had been the observance of the sacred ordinance in connection with an ordinary repast, and if, in addition thereto, the only offence committed had been that some were hungry, and that others had taken too much solid food. Besides, the Apostle distinctly refers to drink when, in the conclusion of the admonition, he says; "What! have ye not houses to eat and to *drink* in? Or despise ye the Church of God, and shame them that have not? There is an obvious allusion to some sinful excess in the form of drunkenness, which could not have been produced by a super-abundance of unfermented grape juice, but must have been due to alcoholic wine, the *oinos* of the New Testament.

My critic admits that the only thing in the matter of drinking which the Bible condemns, is drunkenness, but adds: "Yet nowhere does the Bible define what is meant by drunkenness."

The Bible is not a dictionary. It takes for granted that its commandments and denunciations, the good things which it commends, and the evil things which it forbids, will be understood; and I am persuaded that it never entered into the imagination of prophet or evangelist, that there ever was or would be a man of sound mind upon the earth who did not or would not fully comprehend the meaning of the word, "drunkenness."

On the other hand, I doubt if prophet, evangelist, scientist, or philosopher ever heard or dreamed of the scientific vagaries set forth in the following statements : —

"The Bible's silence as to the meaning of drunkenness is the more remarkable and impressive in view of the fact that the most authoritative and latest data of science declare and demonstrate that drunkenness is neither a matter of amount of liquor or degree of intoxication, but solely of the kind of fluid taken. For science shows that the whole man — spirit, soul, and body — is palpably injured, and helpless descendants more so, by what is commonly termed moderate drinking. . . . Science, therefore, proves that there is no such

thing as harmless, moderate drinking ; that, indeed, moderate
drinking is simply moderate drunkenness."

The authority for this wonderful scientific discovery is not
given. It is utterly opposed to the teachings of physiological science and to the experience of mankind through all
the ages, and has obviously been wrought out in the laboratory of Prohibition.

Several paragraphs are devoted to the discussion of the
methods employed to preserve unfermented grape juice.

I have never denied that it is possible to accomplish
this feat, but have always understood that it is difficult.
Whether, however, it be easy or difficult, I marvel that they
who attach such infinite importance to this beverage have not
long since effected its manufacture on a gigantic scale, and
sought to bring about its substitution for that which they
deem the diabolical poison of alcohol.

The most startling objection of the article under review is
embodied in the following quotation : —

" The circumstances under which the Supper was held,
should alone preclude anybody — Christian or otherwise —
who understands them, from thinking that Jesus, in the Last
Supper, partook of intoxicating wine ; for He was a 'conform-
ing Jew,' His work to fulfill the law. The Supper took
place during Passover. According to Exodus xii. 15, whosoever used anything fermented during Passover, his soul
should be ' cut off from Israel.' Is it thinkable that, in His
Last Supper, Jesus should have made such a vital departure
from the law ? "

The Scripture referred to reads as follows : —

" Seven days shall ye eat unleavened bread ; even the first
day ye shall put leaven out of your houses ; for whosoever
eateth leavened bread, from the first day unto the seventh
day, that soul shall be ' cut off from Israel.' "

The commandment in this case is to eat unleavened bread ;
there is no allusion made to any drink, fermented or unfermented ; and unless some new rule has been dug out by
" higher criticism " from the literary caverns of the past,
whereby " ye shall eat unleavened bread " was construed so
as to include, " ye shall drink unfermented grape juice," the
charge against Christ of violating the law in selecting
veritable wine as an emblem of His blood in the Holy Com-
munion, like every other charge made against Him, before

the bar of Pilate or any other bar, must fall to the ground. This is a notable instance in which the reckless enthusiasts of these times, in order to establish an irrational or impracticable theory, substitute imaginations for facts, and even foist into an authoritative document, sacred or otherwise, language which is not there.

My opponent passes over entirely my solution of the problem of the prominence given to wine in the Bible. Unfermented grape juice has not, and cannot have, any spiritual significance more than any other ordinary article of food. But we find wine and two other substances — corn and oil — singled out from all others, and associated in the Mosaic ritual with all the offerings, festivals, and typical sacrifices of the Jews. Now, if we can discover three prominent, commanding, spiritual objects which these substances fitly represent, are we not warranted in believing that they were employed as the emblems of those objects? It is not necessary that they should have been understood in that relation either by Moses or any of his successors among the prophets and authors of the Old Testament. It is probable that they were not. Jesus said: "I am the bread of life which came down from Heaven, of which if any man eat, he shall never die." And at the Last Supper He selected bread as the representative of His body, saying: "This is my body broken for you." And on the same occasion He took the cup, and said: "This is my blood shed for you, and for many, for the remission of sins." In the parable of the ten virgins He revealed, for the first time in sacred history, the true significance of oil as a source of light and an emblem of His grace and spirit. This wonderful symbolism affords a striking evidence of the inspiration of the Pentateuch; an evidence which no criticism can invalidate and no ingenuity evade, but which, unfortunately, men otherwise distinguished for wisdom and piety entirely overlook in their zeal to establish a false theory.

An eminent clergyman of this city once said to me that when he was preparing a paper on the prevention and curability of drunkenness, to read before a famous Episcopal Church congress, he was struck with the prominence given to wine in the Bible, and that he was sure there was a reason for it which he had never met with in any of his theological studies, and that it had become a problem which he could not solve. But when I announced the following solution, he accepted it gladly.

Fermented grape juice alone is *bona fide* wine. Now one of its essential ingredients is alcohol, and from this ingredient it derives its stimulating and vitalizing force; and it is a remarkable fact that this substance cannot be produced without the destruction of food. To this, then, is wine indebted for its grand pre-eminence, for thereby it becomes a fit emblem of that infinite power of beneficence and love and source of spiritual and eternal life, the blood of a crucified Saviour, which could only be procured for the salvation of mankind by the sacrifice of His life.

In the light of this interpretation how stupendous was the miracle performed at the marriage feast in Cana of Galilee, in which water, that, as a necessary part of the food of man and beast, may justly be deemed an emblem of animal life, was, by this divine alchemy, transmuted into the emblem of the source of spiritual and eternal life. And thus in this incomparable achievement were symbolically set forth the two fundamental ideas of Christianity: the doctrine of the atonement, or the necessity of blood for the remission of sins, and the doctrine of regeneration, or the conversion of the animal into the spiritual, which was so fully and lucidly expounded by Christ to Nicodemus in His interview by night with that devout and intelligent Rabbi, " Verily, verily, I say unto thee, except a man be born again, he cannot see the Kingdom of God. . . . Verily, verily, I say unto thee, except a man be born of water and of the spirit, he cannot enter into the Kingdom of God. That which is born of the flesh, is flesh, and that which is born of the spirit, is spirit. Marvel not that I said unto thee, Ye must be born again."

Tolstoi, in his comments on this miracle in one of his works, says: —

" This occurrence, thus minutely described, is one of the most instructive passages in the Gospels — instructive as an example of the harm done by accepting literally the so-called canonical Gospels as something sacred. The occurrence in Cana of Galilee offers nothing interesting or instructive or noteworthy in any way. If it is a miracle it has no sense; if it is a juggler's trick, it is insulting; if it is a picture of manners or customs, it is unnecessary." But if the spiritual vision of this famous writer had been opened, and he could have understood as clearly and distinctly the divine lessons of the sacred Scriptures as he portrays and illustrates from day to day the beauties of literature and the wisdom and graciousness of a broad, humanitarian philosophy, he would not have fallen into this deplorable error with regard to the miracle at the marriage feast, but would have seen that it was a sublime act of supreme power which Jesus did to manifest His glory, and to present great doctrines and principles, in emblematic form, essential to the welfare of mankind throughout all generations. It shines forth as one of the brilliant stars in the resplendent galaxy, which the life of Christ, beaming with His miracles and parables, and all His glorious words and works, and His vicarious death and triumphant resurrection, has set up in the firmament of truth, and will continue, with its bright company, to shine and irradiate the heavens and the earth when the puny lights of science, falsely so-called, will be utterly extinguished and forgotten, or remembered only in the imperishable consciousness and repentant regrets of their deluded and unfortunate authors. Oh! what a pity it is that men of genius, instead of devoting their great abilities to the momentous task of unravelling the mysteries of science and religion, in order to show their true correspondence and unbroken harmony, should employ them in a malignant and diabolical effort to make obscurities still more obscure, and to darken counsel by words without knowledge.

But while we are disputing about the nature of biblical wine, there is a great practical evil regarding which there should be a perfect agreement. It prevailed extensively among the Jews and all the surrounding nations, and is to-day the chief curse of the civilized world. Whatever may be the character of biblical wine, wine used by the Jews in Jerusalem and throughout Judea was a source of unspeakable calamities, which called forth the cry: "Who have woe, who have sorrow, who have contentions, who have babbling, who have wounds without cause?" And the answer, "They that tarry long at the wine." And if now in this enlightened republic the same cry should be heard after the lapse of more than two thousand years, would there not come a similar response, with groanings that could not be uttered?

The question before us is, Can any way be found by which

all true citizens, of every name and party, may combine to crush this evil? It is admitted on all sides that prohibition is impracticable and could not be justified except as a matter of imperious necessity on the ground of public policy, after all the ordinary methods of civil and political restraint had been tried in vain. Now, there is a measure which is perfectly legitimate, which is successfully applied to analogous evils, and which undoubtedly would be effectual in this case. It is to me one of those insoluble problems, which we now and then meet with in human history, why this remedy has not been applied. Drunkenness throughout the Jewish and Christian dispensations has ever been thoroughly understood and clearly defined by the people, and held to be a sin against God and a crime against man. As a sin it is a ground of excommunication from the Church and exclusion from the Kingdom of Heaven. It is not only a crime, but a germinal crime, the prolific source-of two thirds of all the other crimes and of the pauperism which afflict society; but it has ever been treated, except in a certain class of cases under the Jewish polity, with marked indulgence and forbearance; and now in this country it has become the habit to sympathize with its perpetrators, and to cast the responsibility for their crime upon the shoulders of those who are engaged in the liquor traffic, making the latter the objects of unlimited vituperation and reproach, until, with all their intelligence and wealth, they may justly be styled a persecuted class, who require to expend millions of dollars annually to protect their business, which, when properly conducted, is as honorable and legitimate as any other in the field of commerce, from injurious legislation. It is time that we awoke from this hallucination, and abandoned this preposterous policy. The tide of fanaticism and folly is rushing on with the force of a cataract, and we know not where, in a few years, it will land us. In a recent able article in THE ARENA it was foretold that when women shall cease to be treated as children and an imbecile class, and shall take their true position in the field of politics, the sad lessons they have been taught by their sufferings would naturally array them in a united phalanx, without regard to their religions or general political views, on the side of prohibition against their common foe.

What, then, is the remedy? The enactment of a law in every state of this Union, making drunkenness a *bona fide* felony with an ignominious penalty, and similar in its provisions to every other law against felony. It will not be sufficient to make laws like the law of Vermont, which applies only to persons who are found intoxicated, and to those who create disorder in the streets, and which if applied to a respectable citizen in a state of inebriation would arouse popular indignation, and probably subject the prosecutor to summary political decapitation. The public mind requires to be educated on this subject, and I have long thought that the liquor dealers should be the leaders in this reform. They suffer more from drunkenness than any class except the immediate victims themselves. It is the only cause of the temperance agitation which has put them and their trade under a ban of disgrace as if they were condemned by the Almighty. They ought in self-defence to go forth as teachers of the people, and show them that it is grossly unjust to charge them with the results of the abuse of their traffic; that it would be just as reasonable to charge the bankers and money changers with all the results of the manifold abuses of gold and silver and bank notes; and to arraign the priesthood generally for all the terrible consequences of the abuse of the sacred rite of marriage; that the true principle is to punish the culprit, as set forth in the divine legislation and adopted in every other instance, in the jurisprudence of all the governments of the civilized world, and thus give to the traffic in alcoholic beverages the same protection which is everywhere given to the traffic in money.

Fellow-citizens of this Republic! "I speak as unto wise men; judge ye what I say."

DAWN: IN SAN DIEGO.

BY HEINE MILLER.

"TO THE UNKNOWN GOD."

I.

" 'Unto the unknown God,' you say?
Old man, as gray as San Miguel,
Sad, silent, and self-banished man,
You die, and die beneath the ban.
This is not well, this is not well:
My son, bend down your head and pray.

" You fled my flock, and sought this steep
And stony, star-lit, lonely, height
To hold strange thought with things of night
Long, long ago.   But now at last
Your life sinks surely to the past.
Lay hold, lay hold, the cross I bring
Where all God's goodly creatures cling,
And all the true and goodly keep.

" Yea!   You are good.   Dark-browed and low
Beneath your shaggy brows you look
On me, as you would read a book:
And darker still your dark brows grow
As I lift up the cross to pray,
And plead with you to walk its way.

" Aye, you are good!   There is not one,
From Tia Juana, to the reach
And bound of gray Pacific Beach,
From Coronado's palm-set isle
And palm-hung pathways, mile on mile,
But speaks old Sancho, good and true.
But, oh, my silent dying son
The cross alone can speak for you
When all is said and all is done.

" Come!   Turn your dim old eyes to me;
Have faith; and help me plant this cross

"Beyond where blackest billows toss,
 As you would plant some pleasant tree :
 Some fruitful orange tree, and know
 That it shall surely grow, and grow,
· As your own orange trees have grown,
 And be, as they, your very own.

"You smile at last, and pleasantly :
 You love your laden orange trees
 Set high above your silver seas
 With your own honest hand ; each tree
 A date, a day, a part, indeed,
 Of your own life, and walk, and creed.

"You love your steeps, your star-set blue ;
 You watch yon billows flash, and toss,
 And leap, and curve, in merry rout,
 You love to hear them laugh and shout —
 Men say you hear them talk to you ;
 Men say you sit and look and look,
 As one who reads some holy book —
 My son, wouldst look upon the cross ?

"Come, let me plant amid your trees
 My cross, that you may see and know
 'Twill surely grow, and grow, and grow,
 As grows some trusted little seed ;
 As grows some secret, small good deed ;
 The while you gaze upon your seas . . .
 Sweet Christ, now let it grow, and bear
 Fair fruit, as your own fruit is fair.

"Aye ! ever from the first I knew,
 And marked its flavor, freshness, hue,
 The gold of sunset and the gold
 Of morn, in each rich orange rolled.

"I mind me now, 'twas long since, friend,
 When first I climbed your path alone,
 A savage path of brush and stone ;
 And rattling serpents, without end.

"Yea, years ago, when blood and life
 Ran swift, and your sweet, faithful wife —
 What ! tears at last ; hot, piteous tears
 That through your bony fingers creep

" The while you bend your face, and weep
As if your very heart would break —
As if these tears were your heart's blood,
A pent-up, sudden, bursting flood —
Look on the cross, for Jesus' sake."

II.

'Twas night, and yet it was not night.
But far down in the cañon deep,
Where night had housed all day, to keep
Companion with the wolf, you might
Have hewn a statue out of night.

The shrill coyote loosed his tongue
Deep in the dark arroya's bed;
And bat and owl above his head
From out their gloomy caverns swung:
A swoop of wings, a catlike call;
A crackle of sharp chapparral!

Then sudden, fitful winds sprang out,
And swept the Mesa like a broom;
Wild, saucy winds, that sang of room!
They leapt the cañon with a shout
From dusty throats audaciously
And headlong, tore into the sea,
As tore the swine with lifted snout.

Some birds came, went, then came again
From out the hermit's wood-hung hill,
Came swift, and arrowlike, and still;
As you have seen birds, when the rain —
The great, big, high-born rain, leapt white
And sudden from a cloud, like night.

And then a dove, dear, nunlike, dove
With eyes all tenderness, with eyes
So loving, longing, full of love,
That when she reached her slender throat
And sang one low, sad, sweetest note,
Just one, so faint, so far, so near,
You could have wept with joy to hear.

The old man, as if he had slept,
Raised quick his head, then bowed, and wept

For joy, to hear once more her voice.
With childish joy he did rejoice
As one will joy, to surely learn
His dear, dead love is living still;
As one will joy, to know in turn
He too, is loved, with love to kill.

He put a hand forth, let it fall
And feebly close; and that was all.
And then he turned his tearful eyes
To meet the priest's, and spake this wise:
Now mind, I say, not one more word
That livelong night of nights was heard
By monk or man, from dusk till dawn;
And yet that man spake, on and on.

Why, know you not, soul speaks to soul?
I say the use of words shall pass.
Words are but fragments of the glass;
But silence is the perfect whole.
And thus the old man, bowed and wan,
And broken in his body, spake,
Spake youthful, ardent, on and on,
As dear love speaks for dear love's sake.

" You spoke of her, my wife; behold!
Behold my faithful, constant love.
Nay, nay, you shall not doubt my dove,
Perched there above your cross of gold!

" Yea, you have books, I know, to tell
Of far, fair heaven: but no hell
To her had been so terrible
As all sweet heaven, with its gold
And jasper gates, and great white throne,
Had she been banished hence alone.

" I say, not God himself could keep,
Beyond the stars, beneath the deep,
Or mid the stars, or mid the sea,
Her soul from my soul, one brief day,
But she would find some pretty way
To come and still companion me.

" And say, where bide your souls, good priest?
Lies heaven west, lies heaven east?

"Let us be frank, let us be fair.
Where is your heaven, good priest, where?

"Is there not room, is there not place
In all those boundless realms of space?
Is there not room in this sweet air,
Room mid my trees, room anywhere
For souls that love us thus so well
And love so well this beauteous world
But that they must be headlong hurled
Down, down, to undiscovered hell?

"Good priest, we questioned not one word
Of all the holy things we heard
Down in yon pleasant town of palms
Long, long ago, sweet chants, sweet psalms,
Sweet incense, and the solemn rite
Above the dear, believing dead.

"Nor do I question here to-night
One gentle word you may have said.
I would not doubt, for one brief hour,
Your word, your creed, your priestly power.
Let those who will, seek realms above
Remote from all that heart can love
In their ignoble dread of hell.
Give all, good priest, in charity;
Give heaven to all, if this may be,
And count it well, and very well.

"But I, I could not leave this spot
Where she is waiting by my side.
Forgive me, priest, it is not pride:
There is no God where she is not!

"You did not know her well. Her creed
Was yours; my faith it was the same.
My faith was fair, my lands were broad
Far down where yonder palm trees rise.
We two together worshipped God
From childhood. And we grew, indeed,
Devout in heart, as well as name,
And loved our palm-set paradise.

"We loved, we loved all things on earth,
However mean or miserable.

"We knew no thing that had not worth,
  And learned to know no need of hell.

"Indeed, good priest, so much indeed
  We found to do, we saw to love,
  We did not always look above
  As is commanded in your creed,
  But kept in heart one chiefest care,
  To make this fair world, still more fair.

"'Twas then that meek, pale Saxon came;
  With small, quick, greedy eyes of green,
  A snake's eyes, glittering and keen.
  And I, I could not fight, or fly
  His crafty wiles, at all; and I—
  Enough, enough! I signed my name.

"It was not loss of pleasure, place,
  Broad lands, or the serene delight
  Of doing good, that made dusk night
  O'er all the sunlight of her face.

"But there be little things that feed
  A woman's sweetness, day by day,
  That strong men miss not, do not need,
  But shorn of all, can go their way
  To battle, and but stronger grow,
  As grow great waves that gather so.

"She missed the music, missed the song,
  The pleasant speech of courteous men,
  Who came and went, a comely throng,
  Before her open window, when
  The sea sang with us, and we two
  Had heartfelt homage, warm and true.

"She missed the restfulness, the rest
  Of dulcet silence, the delight
  Of singing silence, when the town
  Put on its twilight robes of brown :
  When twilight wrapped herself with night
  And couched against the curtained west.

"But not one murmur, not one word
  From her sweet baby lips was heard.

" She only knew I could not bear
　To see sweet San Diego town,
　Her palm-set lanes, her pleasant square,
　Her people passing up and down,
　Without black hate, and deadly hate
　For him who housed within our gate.

" How pale she grew, how piteous pale
　The while I wrought, and ceaseless wrought
　To keep my soul from bitter thought,
　And build me high above the vale.
　Ah me, my selfish, Spanish pride!
　Enough of pride, enough of hate,
　Enough of her sad, piteous fate:
　She died: right here she sank and died.

" She died, and with her latest breath
　Did promise to return to me,
　As turns a dove unto her tree
　To find her mate at night, and rest:
　Died, clinging close unto my breast:
　Died, saying she would surely rise
　So soon as God had loosed her eyes
　From the strange wonderment of death.

" How beautiful is death! and how
　Surpassing good, and true, and fair!
　How just is death, how gently just
　To lay his sword against the thread
　Of life when life is surely dead
　And loose the sweet soul from the dust.
　Beneath that dove, that orange bough —
　How strange your cross should stand just there!

" And then I waited, hours and days:
　Those bitter days, they were as years.
　My soul groped through the darkest ways;
　I scarce could see God's face for tears.

" I clutched my knife, and I crept down
　A wolf, to San Diego town.
　On, on, mid my own palms once more,
　Keen knife in hand I crept that night.
　I passed the gate; then fled in fright;
　For black crape fluttered from the door.

"I climbed back here, with heart of stone:
I heard a low, soft, sweetest tone;
Looked up, and lo! there on that bough
She perched, as she sits perching now.

"I heard the bells peal from my height,
Peal pompously, peal piously;
Saw sable hearse, in plumes of night,
With not one thought of hate in me.
I watched the long train winding by,
A mournful, melancholy lie—;
A sable, solemn, mourning mile,
And only pitied him the while.
And she, she sang that whole day through;
Sad-voiced, as if she pitied too.

"They sang, 'His work is done, and well.'
They laid his body in his tomb
Of massive splendor. It lies there
In all its stolen pomp and gloom—
But list! his soul—his soul is where?
In hell! In hell! But where is hell?

"Hear me but this. Year after year
She trained my eye, she trained my ear;
No book to blind my eyes, or aught
To prate of hell, where hell is not,
I came to know at last, and well,
Such things as never book can tell.

"And where was that poor, dismal soul
Ye priests had sent to paradise?
I heard the long years roll, and roll,
As rolls the sea. My once dimmed eyes
Grew keen as long, sharp shafts of light.
With eager eyes and reaching face
I searched the stars, night after night:
That dismal soul was not in space!

"Meanwhile, my green trees grew and grew;
And, sad or glad, this much I knew,
It were no sin to make more fair
One spot on earth, to toil and share
With man, or beast, or bird; while she
Still sang her sad, sweet melody.

" One day, a perfumed day in white,
Such restful, fresh, and friendlike day —
Fair Mexico a mirage lay
High lifted in a sea of light —
Soft purple light, and far away;
I turned, yon pleasant pathway down,
And sauntered leisurely toward town.
I heard my dear love call and coo
And knew that she was happy too,
In her sad, sweet, and patient pain
Of waiting till I came again.

" Aye, I was glad, quite glad at last:
Not glad as I had been, when she
In that sweet, holy, palm-set past,
Walked with me by our palm-set sea,
But sadly and serenely glad:
As though 'twere twilight like, as though
You knew, and yet you did not know
That sadness, most supremely sad
Should lay upon you like a pall,
And would not, could not pass away
Till midnight, and God's perfect day
Dawns sudden on you, and the call
Of birds awakens you to morn —
A babe new-born; a soul new-born.

" Good priest, what are the birds for? Priest,
Build ye your heaven west or east?
Above, below, or anywhere?
I only ask, I only say
She sits there, waiting for the day,
The fair, full day, to guide me there.

" What, he? That creature? Ah, quite true
I wander much, I weary you:
I beg your pardon, gentle priest.
Returning up the stone-strewn steep,
Down in yon jungle, dank and deep,
Where toads and venomed reptiles creep,
There, there, I saw that hideous beast!

" Aye, there! right there, beside my road,
Close coiled behind a monstrous toad,
A huge flat-bellied reptile hid!
His tongue leapt red as flame, his eyes,

" His eyes were burning hells of lies,
 His head was like a coffin's lid :

" Saint George ! Saint George ! I gasped for breath.
 The beast tight coiled, all sudden, sprang
 High in the air, and rattling, sang
 His hateful, hissing song of death !

" My eyes met his. He shrank, he fell,
 Fell sullenly and slow. The swell
 Of braided, brassy neck forgot
 Its poise, and every venomed spot
 Lost lustre, and the coffin head
 Cowed level with the toad, and lay
 Low, quivering with hate and dread :
 The while I kept my upward way.

" What ! should have killed him ? Nay, good priest.
 I know not what, or where's your hell.
 But be it west or be it east
 His hell will answer very well.

" Nay, do not, do not question me ;
 I could not tell you why I know ;
 I only know that this is so,
 As sure as God is Equity.

" Good priest, forgive me, and good-by.
 The stars slow gather to their fold.
 I see God's garment's hem of gold
 Against the far, faint morning sky.

" Good priest, good priest, your God is where ?
 You come to me with book and creed,
 I cannot read your books, I read
 Yon boundless, open books of air.
 What time, or way, or place, I look
 I see God in His garden walk ;
 I hear Him through the thunders talk,
 As once He talked, with burning tongue,
 To Moses, when the world was young ;
 And, priest, what more is in your book ?

" Behold ! the holy grail is found,
 Found in each poppy's cup of gold ;
 And God walks with us as of old.

" Behold ! the burning bush still burns
 For man, whichever way he turns;
 And all God's earth is holy ground.

" And — and — good priest, bend low your head,
 The sands are crumbling where I tread,
 Beside the shoreless, soundless sea.
 Good priest, you came to pray, you said ;
 And now, what would you have of me?"

" Your blessing son, despite the ban."
  He fell before the dying man ;
 And when he raised his face from prayer,
 Sweet Dawn, and two sweet doves were there.

IN THE YEAR TEN THOUSAND.

BY WILLIAM HARBEN.

A. D. 10,000. An old man, more than six hundred years of age, was walking with a boy through a great museum. The people who were moving around them had beautiful forms, and faces which were indescribably refined and spiritual.

"Father," said the boy, "you promised to tell me to-day about the Dark Ages. I like to hear how men lived and thought long ago."

"It is no easy task to make you understand the past," was the reply. "It is hard to realize that man could have been so ignorant as he was eight thousand years ago, but come with me; I will show you something."

He led the boy to a cabinet containing a few time-worn books bound in solid gold.

"You have never seen a book," he said, taking out a large volume and carefully placing it on a silk cushion on a table. "There are only a few in the leading museums of the world. Time was when there were as many books on earth as inhabitants."

"I cannot understand," said the boy with a look of perplexity on his intellectual face. "I cannot see what people could have wanted with them; they are not attractive, they seem to be useless."

The old man smiled. "When I was your age, the subject was too deep for me; but as I grew older and made a close study of the history of the past, the use of books gradually became plain to me. We know that in the year 2000 they were read by the best minds. To make you understand this, I shall first have to explain that eight thousand years ago human beings communicated their thoughts to one another by making sounds with their tongues, and not by mind-reading, as you and I do. To understand me, you have simply to read my thoughts as well as your education will permit; but primitive man knew nothing about thought-intercourse, so he invented speech. Humanity then was divided up in various races, and each race had a separate language. As certain sounds conveyed definite ideas, so did signs and letters; and later, to facilitate the exchange of thought, writing and printing were invented. This book was printed."

The boy leaned forward and examined the pages closely; his young brow clouded. "I cannot understand," he said, "it seems so useless."

The old man put his delicate fingers on the page. "A line of these words may have conveyed a valuable thought to a reader long ago," he said, reflectively. "In fact, this book purports to be a history of the world up to the year 2000. Here are some pictures," he continued, turning the worn leaves carefully. "This is George Washington; this a pope of a church called the Roman Catholic; this is a man named Gladstone, who was a great political leader in England. Pictures then, as you see, were very crude. We have preserved some of the oil paintings made in those days. Art was in its cradle. In producing a painting of an object, the early artists mixed colored paints and spread them according to taste on stretched canvas or on the walls or windows of buildings. You know that our artists simply throw light and darkness into space in the necessary variations, and the effect is all that could be desired in the way of imitating nature. See that landscape in the alcove before you. The foliage of the trees, the grass, the flowers, the stretch of water, have every appearance of life because the light which produces them is alive."

The boy looked at the scene admiringly for a few minutes, then bent again over the book. Presently he recoiled from the pictures, a strange look of disgust struggling in his tender features.

"These men have awful faces," he said. "They are so unlike people living now. The man you call a pope looks like an animal. They all have huge mouths and frightfully heavy jaws. Surely men could not have looked like that."

"Yes," the old man replied, gently. "There is no doubt that human beings then bore a nearer resemblance to the lower animals than we now do. In the sculpture and portraits of all ages we can trace a gradual refinement in the appearances of men. The features of the human race to-day are more ideal. Thought has always given form and expression to faces. In those dark days the thoughts of men were not refined. Human beings died of starvation and lack of attention in cities where there were people so wealthy that they could not use their fortunes. And they were so nearly related to the lower animals that they believed in war. George Washington was for several centuries reverenced by millions of people as a great and good man; and yet under his leadership thousands of human beings lost their lives in battle."

The boy's susceptible face turned white.

"Do you mean that he encouraged men to kill one another?" he asked, bending more closely over the book.

"Yes, but we cannot blame him; he thought he was right. Millions of his countrymen applauded him. A greater warrior than he was a man named Napoleon Bonaparte. Washington fought under the belief that he was doing his country a service in defending it against enemies, but everything in history goes to prove that Bonaparte waged war to gratify a personal ambition to distinguish himself as a hero. Wild animals of the lowest orders were courageous, and would fight one another till they died; and yet the most refined of the human race, eight or nine thousand years ago, prided themselves on the same ferocity of nature. Women, the gentlest half of humanity, honored men more for bold achievements in shedding blood than for any other quality. But murder was not only committed in wars; men in private life killed one another; fathers and mothers were now and then so depraved as to put their own children to death; and the highest tribunals of the world executed murderers without dreaming that it was wrong, erroneously believing that to kill was the only way to prevent killing."

"Did no one in those days realize that it was horrible?" asked the youth.

"Yes," answered the father, "as far back as ten thousand years ago there was an humble man, it is said, who was called Jesus Christ. He went from place to place, telling every one he met that the world would be better if men would love one another as themselves."

"What kind of man was he?" asked the boy, with kindling eyes.

"He was a spiritual genius," was the earnest reply, "and the greatest that has ever lived."

"Did he prevent them from killing one another?" asked the youth, with a tender upward glance.

"No, for he himself was killed by men who were too barbarous to understand him. But long after his death his words were remembered. People were not civilized enough to put his teachings into practice, but they were able to see that he was right."

"After he was killed, did the people not do as he had told them?" asked the youth, after a pause of several minutes.

"It seems not," was the reply. "They said no human being could live as he had directed. And when he had been dead for several centuries, people began to say that he was the Son of God who had come to earth to show men how to live. Some even believed that he was God himself."

"Did they believe that he was a person like ourselves?"

The old man reflected for a few minutes, then, looking into the boy's eager face, he answered: "That subject will be hard for you to understand. I will try to make it plain. To the unformed minds of early humanity there could be nothing without a personal creator. As man could build a house with his own hands, and was superior to his work, so he argued that some unknown being, greater than all visible things, had made the universe. They called that being by different names according to the language they spoke. In English the word used was 'God.'"

"They believed that somebody had made the universe!" said the boy, "how very strange!"

"No, not somebody as you comprehend it," replied the father gently, "but some vague, infinite being who punished the evil and rewarded the good. Men could form no idea of a creator that did not in some way resemble themselves; and as they could subdue their enemies through fear and by the infliction of pain, so did they believe that God would punish those who did not please him. Some people long ago believed that God's punishment was inflicted after death for eternity. The numerous beliefs about the personality and laws of the creator caused more bloodshed in the gloomy days of the past than anything else. Religion was the foundation of many of the most horrible wars. People committed thousands of crimes in the name of the God of the universe. Men and women were burned alive because they would not believe certain creeds, and yet they adhered to convictions equally as preposterous; but you will learn all these things later in life. That picture before you was the last queen of England, called Victoria."

"I hoped that the women would not have such repulsive features as the men," said the boy, looking critically at the picture, "but this face makes me shudder. Why do they all look so coarse and brutal?"

"People living when this queen reigned had the most degrading habit that ever blackened the history of mankind."

"What was that?" asked the youth.

"The consumption of flesh. They believed that animals, fowls, and fish were created to be eaten."

"Is it possible?" The boy shuddered convulsively, and turned away from the book. "I understand now why their faces repel me so. I do not like to think that we have descended from such people."

"They knew no better," said the father. "As they gradually became more refined they learned to burn the meat over flames and to cook it in heated vessels to change its appearance. The places where animals were killed and sold were withdrawn to retired places. Mankind was slowly turning from the habit, but they did not know it. As early as 2050 learned men, calling themselves vegetarians, proved conclusively that the consumption of such food was cruel and barbarous, and that it retarded refine-

ment and mental growth. However, it was not till about 2300
that the vegetarian movement became of marked importance.
The most highly educated classes in all lands adopted vegeta-
rianism, and only the uneducated continued to kill and eat animals. The vegetarians tried for years to enact laws prohibiting
the consumption of flesh, but opposition was very strong. In
America in 2320 a colony was formed consisting of about three
hundred thousand vegetarians. They purchased large tracts of
land in what was known as the Indian Territory, and there made
their homes, determined to prove by example the efficacy of
their tenets. Within the first year the colony had doubled its
number: people joined it from all parts of the globe. In the
year 4000 it was a country of its own, and was the wonder of the
world. The brightest minds were born there. The greatest discoveries and inventions were made by its inhabitants. In 4030
Gillette discovered the process of manufacturing crystal. Up to
that time people had built their houses of natural stone, inflam-
mable wood, and metals; but the new material, being fireproof and
beautiful in its various colors, was used for all building purposes.
In 4050 Holloway found the submerged succession of mountain
chains across the Atlantic Ocean, and intended to construct a
bridge on their summits; but the vast improvement in air ships
rendered his plans impracticable.

"In 4051 John Saunders discovered and put into practice
thought-telegraphy. This discovery was the signal for the introduction in schools and colleges of the science of mind-reading,
and by the year 5000 so great had been the progress in that
branch of knowledge that words were spoken only among the
lowest of the uneducated. In no age of the world's history has
there been such an important discovery. It civilized the world.
Its early promoters did not dream of the vast good mind-reading
would accomplish. Slowly it killed evil. Societies for the prevention of evil thought were organized in all lands. Children
were born pure of mind and grew up in purity. Crime was
choked out of existence. If a man had an evil thought, it was
read in his heart, and he was not allowed to keep it. Men
at first shunned evil for fear of detection, and then grew to love
purity.

"In the year 6021 all countries of the world, having then a
common language, and being drawn together in brotherly love
by constant exchange of thought, agreed to call themselves a
union without ruler or rulers. It was the greatest event in the
history of the world. Certain sensitive mind students in Germany,
who had for years been trying to communicate with other planets
through the channel of thought, declared that, owing to the terrestrial unanimity of purpose in that direction, they had received

mental impressions from other worlds, and that thorough interplanetary intercourse was a future possibility.

"Important inventions were made as the mind of humanity grew more elevated. Thornton discovered the plan to heat the earth's surface from its internal fire, and this discovery made journeys to the wonderful ice-bound countries situated at the North and the South Poles easy of accomplishment. At the North Pole, in the extensive concave lands, was found a peculiar race of men. Their sun was the great perpetually boiling lake of lava which bubbled from the centre of the earth in the bottom of their bowl-shaped world. And a strange religion was theirs! They believed that the earth was a monster on whose hide they had to live for a mortal lifetime, and that to the good was given the power after death to walk over the icy waste to their god, whose starry eyes they could see twinkling in space, and that the evil were condemned to feed the fire in the stomach of the monster as long as it lived. They told beautiful stories about the creation of their world, and held that if they lived too near the hot, dazzling mouth of evil, they would become blinded to the soft, forgiving eyes of the god of space. Hence they suffered the extreme cold of the lands near the frozen seas, believing that the physical ordeal prepared them for the icy journey to immortal rest after death. But there were those who hungered after the balmy atmosphere and the wonderful fruits and flowers that grew in the lowlands, and they lived there in indolence and so-called sin."

The old man and his son left the museum and walked into a wonderful park. Flowers of the most beautiful kinds and of sweetest fragrance grew on all sides. They came to a tall tower, four thousand feet in height, built of manufactured crystal. Something, like a great white bird, a thousand feet long, flew across the sky and settled down on the tower's summit.

"This was one of the most wonderful inventions of the Seventieth century," said the old man. "The early inhabitants of the earth could not have dreamed that it would be possible to go around it in twenty-four hours. In fact, there was a time when they were not able to go around it at all. Scientists were astonished when a man called Malburn, a great inventor, announced that, at a height of four thousand feet, he could disconnect an air ship from the laws of gravitation, and cause it to stand still in space till the earth had turned over. Fancy what must have been that immortal genius' feelings when he stood in space and saw the earth for the first time whirling beneath him!"

They walked on for some distance across the park till they came to a great instrument made to magnify the music in light. Here they paused and seated themselves.

"It will soon be night," said the old man. "The tones are those of bleeding sunset. I came here last evening to listen to the musical struggle between the light of dying day and that of the coming stars. The sunlight had been playing a powerful solo; but the gentle chorus of the stars, led by the moon, was inexplicably touching. Light is the voice of immortality; it speaks in all things."

An hour passed. It was growing dark.

"Tell me what immortality is," said the boy. "What does life lead to?"

"We do not know," replied the old man. "If we knew we would be infinite. Immortality is increasing happiness for all time; it is" —

A meteor shot across the sky. There was a burst of musical laughter among the singing stars. The old man bent over the boy's face and kissed it. "Immortality," said he — "immortality must be love immortal."

A SCRAP OF COLLEGE LORE.

BY WILL ALLEN DROMGOOLE.

FROM the old homestead kitchen a voice rang out in song.
The dreamy, drawling pathos of the music betrayed the nationality, no less than the sex, of the singer.

> "Free grace an' dyen' love,
> Free grace an' dyen' love,
> Free grace an' dyen' love,
> Ter wash me white as snow."

Over and over again, in the cracked, crazy voice of an old
woman, a negress; but withal full of a strong, strange faith, that
seemed to fix itself upon something unseen but felt, and to cling
there, and hold.

The woman was busy preparing the early supper; for the sun
would soon drop behind the ragged old oaks that studded the
west lawn, and the master of the house would expect his beaten
biscuit whether he came at sunset or at midnight. And just as
like to come at one time as at the other, was the profligate young
master.

It would have been difficult to persuade old Tildy that he was
not the master of the house, although the *old* master's last will
and testament made it appear so. Handsome, reckless, and
dissipated to the last degree, he was, nevertheless, to the old
slave-mammy the same young master committed to her care by
the *real* master, in that same will which had seemingly cast him
off. That was five years before; it was *nine* years since the
mistress had committed the young master likewise to her love
and care. He was still young, and the only one of the seven
children born to the squire and his wife that had passed beyond
the years of early childhood. And *he* had broken their hearts;
had begun early upon the downward road, and kept steadily on
all those years. Thinking of those years, the biscuit beater made
a sudden stop, as if the years, those heavy weights, had snapped,
broken by their own heaviness.

The old woman leaned upon the wooden handle, and watched,
with her face to the kitchen window, the last rays of the sunset,
creeping across the bare, brown cotton-field, and tingeing the
gnarled oaks of the lawn with purple and red and dull amber.
An azure haze followed the sunlight, creeping up from the river
beyond the field, — Stone River, in the heart of Tennessee.

The face turned to the sunset was seamed and broken, but *such* a face. An artist, catching the fervor of devotion, the magnetic mingling of pain and pride, lightened by the finer lines of faith, the whole mellowed by that chastened patience which is born of love and sorrow, would have held his breath, lest fancy cheat him of an ideal, a *something* in bronze, that should puzzle the world for a name.

She was watching the azure shadows creeping across the cotton-field; the azure mist stirred sleeping memories, leading the slave-woman back where the smoke circled above a light-boat, plying somewhere along the Virginian waters. There was a prison, a slave-prison, and a market-place, and a woman, a strong, silent woman who held a little child by the hand. The woman was her mother, the child herself, a child of six years. She hid her face in the woman's dress while a shrill voice called for "a bid." A bid for a "likely nigger, going for a song."

"Ten dollars!" there came a bid. The hand clasping the child's grew cold, and the clasp grew closer.

Then a voice — she remembered that voice in her *dreams* sometimes, even yet — that voice sweeter than unknown music, that had said "fifty."

Fifty dollars for a baby! He had carried her home in his lap, before him on the saddle; and the heart of the strong old woman who had held the child's hand had gone with him also.

She had crept to his feet and begged leave to hug her baby, "just once, good marster," before she herself should be shipped to New Orleans.

"Don't beat her, marster!" — the slave's prayer still sobbed upon the wings of memory. "Don't beat her! she's only a nigger, but she's my baby! *don't* beat her!"

And the promise was given, and faithfully kept by the then young master. "Never a lick shall she have, so help me heaven."

The sunlight faded from the field, the amber and red left the oak trees, the shadows deepened. Before the slave's eye came the face of one fast in the agonies of death — a gentle face — a broken-hearted mother's face. It lay upon her arm.

"My boy," the white lips whispered. "My poor, poor boy! Mam-Tildy?"

"I'm here, mistiss."

Here! always here at the call of duty. She put her black face close to the gentle white one.

"As I have dealt with you, Mam-Tildy."

She understood, true old slave-heart.

"I'll foller him ter de grave, mistiss, an' hand him inter heaben ter yer, ef de good Lord spar's me."

Since then, when duty seemed too hard, and devotion reaped
only ingratitude, she heard again the soft voice calling: —

"Mam-Tildy?"

"Here I am, mistiss."

"As I have dealt with you, Mam-Tildy."

And waking, the old heart had renewed to itself the promise,
"I'll foller him ter de grave, an' hand him inter heaben ter his
mammy, ef de good Lord spa'rs me."

The old master slept beside the fair young mistress, in the
family burying-ground beyond the meadow, and in sight of the
gentle waters of Stone River. His proud old heart had broken
too. The tears rolled down the woman's dark cheek as she
recalled the last night on the old plantation, when it rained, and
rained, and the storm rattled at all the windows, and the river
burst its banks, flooding meadow and field until the cries of the
drowning things down in the low ground rang through the house
piteously.

Such a night! such a pitiless night, and black with despair!
An old man waited, that black night, with bowed head, for a step,
a boy's careless step; waiting and listening while the storm beat
furiously. O those footsteps of erring children! Note ye the
hell or heaven they carry! The gray dawn shivered at the window like a frozen foundling; and a song, a senseless, drunken
song, reached the strained ears of the master. A reeling figure
tottered up the strong old stairs: a shuffling, loathsome thing,
calling himself *his son*, and who, but for the will that day
executed, would have inherited those fair Tennessee lands, to be
squandered in drunken college revels.

The disappointment was too, *too* bitter. A shot rang out. The
old man could bear the burden of his son no longer.

The will left the plantation to the old nurse, the *baby* bought
at Richmond six and forty years before.

There Mam-Tildy's dreaming always ended. She came back
to her biscuit beating at this point, to protest, as usual.

"It orter be Marse Hal's house," she said to the dough, crisping
beneath the blows she laid upon it. "Ef I cud sell it I cud pay
his debts termorrer."

That was precisely what the old master meant she should *not*
do when he had tied the property against the young reprobate,
his son and lawful heir.

Mam-Tildy would take care of him, but he would not take care
of Mam-Tildy; and therefore the will had judiciously set the
property in the safer hands.

It was hers, Mam-Tildy's, "during her natural life."

"But it orter been Marse Hal's," she declared; "he needs it
mighty bad."

She spread the dough with the cedar rolling-pin, rolling it to a precise thickness, and keeping a kind of time to the song with which she had begun her task, —

> "Free grace an' dyen' love,
> Free grace an' dyen' love,
> Ter wash me white as snow.
> Way ober Jord'n, Lord " —

The song abruptly ended. Some one came up the gravelled walk; a quick, boyish step, a step she knew full well, although it did not stagger now, as was its wont. It *ran*, or the owner of it ran, straight across the piazza, into the kitchen; and although the hand placed on Mam-Tildy's arm shook, she knew the young master was not drunk.

"Hide me! Mam-Tildy, hide me!" he gasped. "I have killed a man, and they are after me!"

There was a boyish ring in the voice, despite the situation, that belonged wholly to Hal Gordon's character; a carelessness which had so annoyed the old squire, his father, who called it "dare-devilism," and which Mam-Tildy noticed even in the extremity of her distress.

She gave a hurried glance around the kitchen, then shoved her biscuit-board aside, and pointed to the large empty barrel upon which the board rested.

The next moment the board was in its place again, she was rolling her dough and singing, —

> "Free grace an' dyen' love,
> Ter wash me white as snow."

The sheriff's possee coming down the piazza had detected no break in the song, and the sheriff himself saw nothing odd in the fact that he had to call twice from the kitchen doorway before the busy old negress turned to hear his demand for Harry Gordon, the runaway from justice.

She dropped the rolling-pin with a great clatter: perhaps because she heard a defiant little laugh in the barrel; perhaps because she was, as the officers thought, so taken by surprise.

"Marsters," she begged, "don't tease a pore ole nigger dat er way. Ef Marse Hal hab done somefin, shore nuff, for de love ob God, don't stan' dar foolin', but tell ole Tildy an' let her go to him."

She had rubbed the dough from her hands and taken off her apron; the tears were raining down her cheeks when she reached for her sun bonnet hung upon a convenient peg.

The men were completely disarmed, touched to the quick by

her prompt response to the danger threatening the beloved
master.

"Go back, Aunt Tildy," said the sheriff. "He isn't worth your
affection. You can't go to him, for we have not yet found him.
Go back to your dough, and don't waste any more sleep on that
ungrateful scamp."

They left her, with her apron before her eyes, rocking to and
fro, and moaning.

"Ter de grave! ter de grave!" she sobbed. "I promised his
mammy. Yes, Lord, *good* Lord, ter de grave."

That night the fugitive received the coins, all Mam-Tildy's
ready money, which she poured into his hand, and stole away
under cover of darkness.

"Ef I cud jes' sell de place, little marster," she said at parting,
"de money ud fetch you out o' danger."

"Damn the place!" was the reply. "Only let me get well
away from it; it is getting too all-fired hot here to suit my fancy."

He drew his coat about his ears, a soft, fashionably made garment, for which the old negress had paid a fair sum, and started
toward the door. Twice he looked back. The old nurse sat in a
corner with her apron over her head, rocking and moaning.

She had sat thus, in that very corner, the night his mother
died. He went back, and laid his hand lightly upon her head.

"Mam-Tildy," he said, "I'll write you if I ever land beyond the
county jail, and you shall come to me. Hush! I swear it.
Good bye now. If I ever *should* get to heaven, Mam-Tildy,—
mind, I don't expect to, but *if* I should,— it will be your work."

He laughed softly, and, stooping, put his lips to the apron covering her head. She could not see that, despite the laugh, the boyish blue eyes held tears, nor did she understand that he knew
that never again would he set free foot upon the threshold of the
once proud old homestead.

She only knew that he passed out with a curse and a low
rippling laugh, and that her old heart was very desolate.

The next day news came: he had been taken. The man he
had shot lived a week, and in two months the murderer had received his sentence, life servitude in the state prison.

She rented the house, being unable to sell it, and followed him
to the loathsome den in the mountains which had been dignified
by the name of Branch Prison. Her little whitewashed cabin
stood upon a green rise between the stockade and the coal mine;
from either the door or the window she could see him at morning
and evening going to and coming from his work. At noon she
often went down where the men were eating their dinner, to carry
him something hot from her own kitchen. He laughed at her for

this, telling her it was as foolish as her old song of "Free grace and dying love."

One evening a squad of convicts coming in from the mine heard her singing, in that quaint, quavering treble, that same old hymn, and laughed, making many a joke of the song and singer. Odd, how those in its worst extremity make the lightest jest of life: solemn, serious old life with its burdens and heart-aches. He who laughs at life is apt to cry out against death. The convicts laughed at the old crone and her song; the convicts, blackened with evil, and with that deeper stain — sin. The one who laughed loudest was a young man of perhaps five and twenty years. Dissipation had been somewhat obliterated from the boyish face by five years' imprisonment and confinement in the underground workshops, — the mines.

The complexion was fair and delicate as a child's; and the hands, which Mam-Tildy kept carefully provided with gloves, were small and white, and delicately feminine. He had changed but little; in all but dissipation, so far as any one knew, he was the same Harry Gordon of five years before.

"Yer mammy's singing for ye, sonny," laughed one of the squad.

"I wonder where she got that queer song," said another. "There isn't so much in the words, yet somehow it makes a fellow want to go home to his mammy."

Again there was a laugh; life is *such* a jest.

"Because it's '*free*,' I reckon," said a third. "It's the only thing hereabouts that is."

"It is the first thing I remember to have ever heard," said Hal, who as a rule had but little to say to the men. "She trotted me on her knees and sang it. I think she sang it the day I was born, and I expect she will sing it at my funeral, if mine chances to get in ahead of hers."

Then the squad passed on up the hot, coal-sooted path to the stockade gate, and stood a moment to be counted. The old woman's song still reached their ears, faintly, —

> "*Free grace an' dyen' love,*
> *Ter wash me white as snow.*"

The chains rattled, the gate swung back, and the squad went in. There was no trace of emotion of any kind in any of their faces, except the face of Gordon; he was smiling.

A few minutes later he stood before his cell door, humming under his breath, —

> "*Free grace and dying love.*"

"What a funny old song," he said to himself. "I wonder

what it means anyhow. I shall ask Mam-Tildy next visit she makes to my *State* apartment."

He laughed again, in that half merry, half defiant, boyish way, and drew the little iron door open.

As it swung back he glanced up at a bit of dainty carving just above the entrance to his cell.

It was done in Latin, daintily, dexterously done, with his own pearl-handled pen-knife.

"Errare est humanum."

That was all of the college lore he had carried out into the world with him. All the use he had found for it was to make a motto for a felon's cell. His college course, like his life course, ended in a convict's cell. Ended, summed up, in that one sentence, *Errare est humanum.*

He laughed, as he divested himself of his mining clothes. The cleanly and careful were allowed a second suit; he was cleanly enough, and Mam-Tildy would have been more than satisfied if he had been half as careful with his soul as he was with the coarse prison uniform.

He was thinking of the motto; that little Latin device had wrought so many amusing incidents.

First, Mam-Tildy, when she came to bring the sweet cakes she had made for him, had asked what the inscription meant. How the old face had lighted up when he told her; and it had ever afterward been impossible to convince the old woman that it was a mere bit of handiwork, utterly without heart on the part of the convict.

The prison chaplain, too, had caught sight of the carving, and had straightway come into the cell, his mild eyes full of tears, and pressed the hand of the convict-student, and kneeling by the little iron prison bunk had prayed, *prayed,* with the beads upon his brow and agony in every feature, yet not once opening his lips for words. And Hal had stood by, that old boyish smile parting his daintily curved lips while the old chaplain prayed. He laughed aloud when later he had found the chaplain's card upon his little shelf. The bit of white pasteboard bore his own little motto in Latin, to which the pious man had added in pencil, *"condonare est divinum."*

That pleased Mam-Tildy mightily, when he told her about it; and she had teased him to add the preacher's "sign" to his own above the door, but he had laughingly refused.

The "sign" had amused him greatly; one morning, he remembered, a new gang had arrived at the Branch. Among the convicts was a young man convicted of murder in the second degree, and sentenced for ten years in the *pen.* In his native town he

was considered a dangerous and unreclaimable character, a boy
utterly without friends, since the time when his *college career* had
broken his mother's heart. Oh, these colleges! hot-beds of infidelity and generators of corruption.

Hal came upon the man the morning of his arrival at the
prison. He was standing in the corridor before young Gordon's
cell; he still wore his ball and chain, and he was manacled with
iron, just as the guard had left him. He was gazing at the Latin
inscription above the door.

"*To err is human.*" He had met only upbraidings, reproaches,
doubts, revilings. That little Latin device was the first touch of
forbearance that had ever come to him; the first whisper of con-
dolence or of condonation that had ever touched his wretched,
ill-spent life since he began his downward career. It came like
a breath from paradise. He forgot his chains, his handcuffs, the
long score of crime-blotted years. The sweet old boyhood time
came crowding back; he chased the ball across the college
campus; pored over his Greek and Latin under the sweet old
maple trees.

"*Errare est humanum.*" It was one of those mysterious messages that strike straight for the soul and batter its wall of rebellion down, and make for itself an abode there. The ten years'
term was commuted to five; the five by "good time made"
became four; and one morning the prison door swung back and
he passed out, a free man.

He had been very fond of young Gordon, fancying that to him
he was indebted for his reformation, and had wept upon his
shoulder at parting, and begged to be remembered sometimes.
Hal remembered that he had laughed and pushed him off; the
merry sparkle had still danced in his blue eyes when the two said
good bye, forever. They were totally unlike. Strange *he* should
have carved the inscription above *his* door: he, so light, so
shallow, so indifferent. Even Mam-Tildy had begged of him to
"try en be sober, en see things as they is."

"Sober!" he had replied. "It is bad enough to be here, Mam-
Tildy, but it is lucky I can laugh over it."

"Naw taint, little marster," she sobbed. "It am like slappin'
ob de good Lord in de face. Taint allus right ter laff; it am
better ter cry en ter laff sometimes, Marse Hal."

Yes, his scrap of college lore had stood him well. The lady
missionaries to the prison had been attracted by it; read a story
of high birth, strong temptation, and earnest repentance in the
simple words, and gave him special prayer. It was as if a dignified, refined sorrow hid in the old college exercise. All who saw
it conceived a tender interest in the fair-faced young convict. A
glamour of romance gathered about him. Young girls sought his

cell with flowers and gifts of jewels, and even the old ladies sent
in pretty bits of needle-work to decorate the cell of "the poor
student."

" *To err is human !* " What an appeal ; and to go up from that
black hole ; and from a soul cultivated, used to the higher walks.
Why, it was as if he said, " Careful, careful now how you judge —
the way is slippery, and to *err* is *human.* Your own feet "——

He was very peaceable and good-natured ; the guards and
wardens all liked him, although they still continued to wonder if
the lightness was genuine, or if the man truly had no feeling.
He seldom gave evidence of any, either of impatience or rebellion or of temper. He always did his work, just what was
required of him ; never a lick beyond or a blow below the requisite amount. The miners called him a " lazy bones " at first ; but
when they saw that always his work was faithfully and exactly
done, they gave that up, remembering how their own went
beyond the requirement to-day and to-morrow far below it. Nobody ever thought the trouble might have been a lack of ambition,
for nobody cared especially ; they only knew there *was* a peculiarity. His hands were always clean, conspicuously clean, down
the long prison dining-table where the hard-fisted coal diggers
were at their meals. He never held aloof from the others, yet
they seemed to feel, instinctively, that he *was* apart from and
above them. It was because of the Latin over his cell. His was
a life sentence ; he had no hope of reaching the outside world
again, and he seldom gave it a thought, except to laugh at Mam-
Tildy's foolish fancies that he would some day gain a pardon
by some great deed of heroism. There was a *hint* in these
foolish fancies, if he had but considered it. But he did *not* consider — considering meant melancholy, discontent. So he put
aside all unpleasant comparisons and unavailing longings ; he read
the books the old nurse brought him, played with the flowers sent
him, and munched the delicacies left every day at his door, much
in the same way that he ate the coarse prison fare, and in the
same way, of laughing indifference, that he had met his mother's
tears and his father's curse.

They tried to make a hero of him because of the Latin, but he
did not respond to the effort ; nothing in him responded to the
heroic in any sense. Only to poor old Mam-Tildy, in her tireless
devotion, her daily pilgrimage to his cell with clean sheets,
a white counterpane, fresh underclothing, never without some
offering — only to her was vouchsafed an abiding hope, a faith
that at last, at *last*, the little marster would " see things right."

One morning when, having received permission to do so, she
was scouring out his cell, and singing in the old familiar way, he
stopped on his way to join the mine gang, and said :——

"Mam-Tildy, that is a funny old song of yours. What does it mean anyhow, your 'free grace and dying love'?"

She paused in her work, and looked up at him from her knees, where she had crept in order to carry her scouring-cloth well under his bed. There was a perplexed, worried look in the faded old eyes. What did "free grace" mean? Free grace and dying love. Oh, for words, words; words that might *tell* him the true meaning of that grace, that love! *She* knew; her soul recognized the meaning long ago, but the poor old tongue had no cunning.

She shook her head — gray head it was, carefully bound in a white knotted handkerchief.

"You'll know some day, little marster," she said. "I can't tell yer, honey; ole Tildy aint got much sense; but you'll know what free grace am some day."

That noon, at the counting of the prisoners, he was absent. There is always a thrill follows the announcement that a convict is missing. Escaped? Dead? Pardoned? Gordon was neither; he was lying on an iron bunk in the hospital — still, unconscious, in a deadly stupor, and white and innocent-looking as a little child. A little child — he was like a child in many things; yet he had broken many hearts — his old father's, his poor mother's, and last of all Mam-Tildy's.

He had been hurt down in the mine; and before the news had fairly reached the stockade, the old negress was at the mouth of the pit, and would have gone on, right into that roar of nauseous gas and stifling sulphur, only that a guard prevented her.

"Stop, aunty," he said, "you can't pass there."

The old eyes filled.

"O marster, fur de love ob God, lemme go ter him!" she begged.

"No, come back; the tunnel is full of gas and smoke and falling slate. You can do him no earthly good. Come back, I tell you!"

"Marster, I promised his mammy ter foller him ter de grave itse'f."

She was moving right on, and weeping — not heeding, if indeed hearing, the command to "come back."

"I promised ole miss" — the smoke was stifling. Again the guard called to her, his gun levelled at the old gray head.

"*Will* you come back?"

"Naw, marster, I won't, I can't" — she was already in, beyond the black opening. "My feet wouldn't turn back ef I tried ter make 'em ter; lemme go!" Her voice came back to him from the tunnel, muffled and seeming afar off. "Fur de love ob God, lemme go ter him. I — promised — ole — miss"—

The words were a wail, a wail of agony and devotion.

They brought him out, however, by another tunnel, and the guard sent some one in to tell Mam-Tildy. When she came back they had carried him up to the prison hospital, and all the town knew of the "little student's" injury.

Feeble and old and heart-broken, she tottered to the stockade gate, the tears rolling down her wrinkled cheeks, her gray hair forgotten, its covering gone, and stopped to question the guard there.

"They say he will die," he told her, his heart full of a great pity.

But that was not what she wished to know.

"Marster," she said, "*how* wuz it?"

"The slate fell on him while he was eating his noon lunch — that was all."

All; she sighed and turned away, her last poor vain hope of heroism dead.

They refused her admittance at the hospital, but allowed her to crouch at the door of his prison cell, just under the old college text, and to nurse her grief near something that had been his. All the afternoon she sat there, moaning when no one was near, and praying always. She had prayed for so many years, poor old black mammy, and received for her faith — silence; silence, that maker of infidels and of blasphemers. Yet her faith held; she was ignorant, but it held, held; let the wise and the favored look to it. It held even while the white face of him who was the object of her prayers lay back upon the coarse prison pillow, waiting for death — for *death;* and still the old nurse's faith held.

It was a fair face, so touchingly childlike; the old smile still curved the delicate lips; the smile which had met the ills and failures of life, met death with the same boyish defiance — a foil to rob him of his terror.

The prison physician, together with the chaplain and the warden, had endeavored vainly to rouse him out of that deadly stupor. There was no response, not a quiver of the eyelids, to tell that he heard or lived.

"Is there nothing," said the chaplain, "that will arouse him, nothing that will touch him?"

"He has been here five years," said the warden, "and I have never known him show the slightest feeling except one morning when one of the men attempted to play a prank upon his old black nurse. He didn't really show any feeling then, for he laughed at the same time that he cracked the fellow's skull. It was hushed up; nobody held any ill-will against the boy, and the other had made himself obnoxious to the officials."

The physician, his hand still upon the pulse of the unconscious convict, turned suddenly to the warden.

"Go bring the old nurse," he commanded.

They had not far to send, and she came at once, tottering, the old body well-nigh spent. The surgeon was removing the electric battery with which he had been vainly endeavoring to recall life into the benumbed faculties, when the old negress entered. They moved aside to make room for her, for she was growing strangely feeble. Is it instinct that teaches those old black heroines those great, grand strokes upon the chords of the human heart? Is it instinct, like the brutes possess? Who dares insult Divinity with such a charge?

The old nurse tottered to the low prison bunk — her gray grizzled hair made a kind of setting for the dark face. Trouble in every wrinkle; grief, such as tender mothers know, in every motion of the trembling lips; but love, abiding devotion, burning in the fond, faded eyes resting upon the fragile form, bound in linen, upon which the blood stains showed glaringly. She bent over him, no tears in her eyes now.

"Marse Hal," she said, "does yer know me, honey? How is yer, little marster?"

O thou great electric king! Out upon thy puny power, that the whisper from a slave's lip can put thee to such shame! The delicate white hand moved slowly across the yellow sheet until it found the hand of the old nurse, and, clasping it, rested there. The prisoner sighed softly.

"Mam-Tildy?"

"Yes, my lam'."

"Take me home!"

It was the voice, the pleading prayer, of a homesick child. The nurse was the only one of the little group whose eyes were dry.

"Yes, honey," she replied, "Mam-Tildy gwine sen' yer home soon; she done promise ole miss."

She covered his small hand with both her own, and held it against her faithful old black breast, and sat there, with eyes closed, but with a kind of peace upon her tired face — as if, indeed, she had been transported back to the old innocent days upon the plantation.

"Mam-Tildy?"

"Yes, my lam'."

"Sing!"

She began to rock to and fro and to croon a hymn; but he stopped her with a movement of his head.

"No, no," he said; "sing your old — 'free grace' — you used to sing it — in the kitchen — at home."

Tremblingly, trustfully the old cracked voice began, and went bravely on to the end, —

> " Free grace an' dyen' love,
> Free grace an' dyen' love,
> Ter wash me white as snow."

When she finished he lay so still they believed him going indeed; but his lips moved faintly, and he murmured something about "the old college text" and "something" which he said "the chaplain added to it." Mam-Tildy's old song was running through his brain, confusing him absurdly; for he was mumbling something about "To err is human, free grace — divine," and smiling — knowing that he had tangled song and text. Mam-Tildy tried to help him.

"Free grace an' dyen' love, Marse Hal," she said.

"I know," he whispered; and suddenly, with strange strength, he lifted himself in bed and clasped his arm about the old mammy's neck, smiling the while — that old boyish smile she knew so well.

The surgeon took out his watch ; one, two, *five* minutes passed, then he placed his fingers upon the delicate, blue-veined wrist lying against Mam-Tildy's neck, and motioned a guard to drop the window curtain.

"Mam-Tildy," he said gently, "you may go now."

"Yes, marster," she replied, "I's ready. Old Tildy's work am done."

And unclasping his arm, she laid the dead boy back upon his pillow.

THE POET'S PRAYER.

BY GERALD MASSEY.

My Love in Heaven! love was not hid
By closing of a coffin-lid!

Dear Love in Heaven! true love survives
All separation in our lives!

O Love in Heaven, from you I win
Sure help without, and hope within!

My Love in Heaven, for me she waits
Like Morning golden at her Gates!

Dear Love in Heaven, let your sunrise
Make the dews lighter in mine eyes!

O Love in Heaven, for one wee while
Let me reflect your vanished smile!

My Love in Heaven, bid me rejoice
To hear once more love's earthly voice!

Dear Love in Heaven, your voice was low,
But the least whisper I should know!

O Love in Heaven, there is a way
To come back to me with your day!

My Love in Heaven can magnetize
And open wide mine inner eyes!

Dear Love in Heaven, as in a glass
Into another self we pass!

O Love in Heaven, shut out the night,
That I may see by spirit-light!

My Love in Heaven, give me the grace
To glimpse the glory in your face!

Dear Love in Heaven! Let me but see
You wear the crown of victory!

O Love in Heaven, from your dear eyes,
Two life-drops trembled crystal-wise,—

My Love in Heaven — those drops I stole
To anoint mine eyes with sight of soul!

Dear Love in Heaven, that precious dew
I took to gain *the sight of you!*

O Love in Heaven, reach down to me,
And lift my spirit up to see!

My Love in Heaven, the Euphrasy
Of sorrow purged mine eyes to see.

Dear Love in Heaven, with purity
Of life I wash my soul to see!

O Love in Heaven, unveil for me;
To God I give my soul to see!

SOME OF CIVILIZATION'S SILENT CURRENTS.

BY B. O. FLOWER.

THE present is so pre-eminently a transition period, a day of such striking contrasts and startling antitheses, that it is difficult for even the most sincere and conscientious thinker to grasp the true status of our civilization in all its bearings or gain anything like a just conception of the manifold agencies working seemingly at cross purposes and, from a superficial point of view, presenting an appearance dishearteningly chaotic. For on the one hand we see an arrogant plutocracy securing class privileges and special favors from incompetent or venial legislators; on the other, the aroused indignation of the wage-earning millions who appreciate that something is wrong, but whose mentality, dulled by grinding toil and canker-eating, anxious care, fails to grasp quickly the wise means of solution amid a babel of conflicting voices. On the one hand we see the tyranny of wealth, the heartless robbery of speculation and gambling, the revolting spectacle of criminal ostentation and the lavish expenditure of wealth in voluptuous enjoyment by thousands who neither toil nor spin. On the other hand, we hear, clearly ringing in trumpet tones, the voices of the prophets of the new day, denouncing present evils and demanding justice. Here in the daily journals one's eyes fall upon accounts of ten-thousand-dollar banquets, at which a few score of the *dilettante* sip champagne and further enervate their already shattered moral natures. In another column we read of mothers who, failing to secure work and finding starvation facing them, burn charcoal and thus kill themselves and children; or, perhaps, daughters who have struggled for life and virtue until the fight has become hopeless, and to save honor have sought death. At the present time, also, we behold floating palaces for millionnaires gliding up to wharves within gunshot of squalid dens where the starving are huddled in droves, daily sinking from man's holy estate to the level of animals, who exist in an atmosphere of filth, degradation, and moral death.

To the sincere and earnest inquirer who would be just to the present, and who furthermore desires to view conditions from the eagle's eyrie rather than from the vantage-ground of the valley, it is necessary to note the true significance of the deep currents which are making for civilization — not the voluble laudation of conservatism, which is the age-long, shallow cry of the worshipper of the past and the upholder of all conditions which bear the sanction of conventionalism, but rather those silent forces which escape the casual observer amid the prophetic warnings and the heart cries of the reformers' divinely fired souls on the one hand, and the brutal tyranny of corporate wealth, the heartless indifference of plutocracy, and the insufferable vulgarity of the parvenu element on the other — those silent agencies which without ostentation are doing so much toward stemming the tide of ignorance, crime, and degradation which are shedding abroad kindness and love as the sun sends forth life-giving heat; which are silently sowing the seeds of a better day, and reproducing in colors, visible even to the unschooled mind, the noblest ideals of a higher civilization which are floating before humanity's advancing columns.

Of the many organized agencies in philanthropy, in education, in practical business and social life, I will not now speak at length, because their worth is more or less appreciated even by the casual observer. The simple enumeration of a few of them will indicate how completely humanity is awaking along the whole line of human endeavor, and how strong is the higher current even in the disturbed waters of the present. The wonderful growth of the kindergarten schools; the even more marked progress of industrial education resulting in its introduction in a greater or less degree in various schools, and the establishment of industrial schools in the slums of almost all our great cities, and what is more, the steady growth of the idea, even in the circle of conventional education, that mere intellectual schooling is not only insufficient, but that it is a small part of a liberal education. Then, again, who can measure the influence already exerted by that marvellous movement which culminated in the organization of the working girls' clubs, or their almost incredible growth. The formation of various clubs by women in easier walks of life are also even now exerting an educating and stimulating influence upon thousands of our most thoughtful women. The Woman's Christian Temperance Union and its sister organization, the White Ribbon movement for social purity, are being felt more or less in millions of homes. The White Cross movement; societies for home culture and for ethical training; summer schools of philosophy, science and ethics; college extension; and Associated Charities, with all the encumbrances of conventionalism, are leavening society and doing far more than we realize to keep in check the baleful influences of the saloon, of the incoming tide of ignorant and vicious emigration, of the aggressive democracy of crime and vice now within our borders, and the vicious spirit of the business world, which to so large an extent worships gold and loses all finer thought in thought of self.

Beyond these organized agencies, whose power is more or less marked on every side, are unorganized and iconoclastic influences which, because they are silent and to a certain extent isolated, are overlooked by many social reformers. Into all our lives, at some time or another, have come the influence of other lives which has been elevating, stimulating, and ennobling, and we must remember that what is true in our personal experience is true of others. The influences of these uplifting waves are, in my judgment, the most subtle yet far-reaching power to-day making for a truer civilization. Few of us pause in the feverish race of life to take cognizance of the influence of these silent lives quietly toiling on every hand. Yet until their influence is placed in the scales, it is clearly impossible to strike a balance and determine the unmistakable trend of the times. To further emphasize this idea of the nature and extent of the influence for good of these sowers of civilization's seed, I wish to briefly touch on a few lives whose influence and whose inspiration have come into my own, either by their helpful words or by their teachings and personality, as in no other way can I so well illustrate the thought I wish to convey. These sowers of civilization's seeds, as I call them, always remind me of a story read to me when I was very young. It described a boy who wandered into an enchanted wood. Here a vision of marvellous beauty appeared to him saying, "If you succeed in finding my home, it will be ready for thee, and I will forever dwell with thee; but before you will find it, you must grow into my likeness." And the boy, haunted by the divine ideal, feverishly wandered the world over, seeking the wonderful face which embodied love, mercy, and knowledge; and as he journeyed he said to himself, "If I find her, I must be worthy of her." Hence he sought the sick and poor and needy wherever he travelled, soothed their sufferings, ministered to their wants; in short, became an angel of mercy and love. But this was not all; he said to himself, "I must gather the seeds of knowledge from all lands and climes through which I roam, that I may not appear a mental pauper in the presence of my loved one, for she bears the stamp of wisdom no less than love upon her high, splendid brow." And so he journeyed through life, and in its golden sunset, having left a trail of light wherever he had travelled, he laid him down to rest, and the angel touched his eyes, when lo! the scales fell, and he beheld his love. "At last!" he cried, extending his arms and falling on the earth. "I have been with thee always," returned the voice; "but not until thy spirit was worthy of a higher home was it best that thou should'st see me, for now no sense of inferiority will disturb thy soul during our progress

throughout eternity." I say the sight of these silent workers
for eternity always reminds me of this vision-haunted youth.
They have caught glimpses of nobler ideals; they cease to find
satisfaction in the selfish gratification; *they must help the world
onward; they must aid humanity.*

One of these chosen ones to whom I owe a debt through his
inspiring writings is Victor Hugo, that noble worker for a
better day; he who could not live for himself; who felt he must
give as bountiful nature gave; give as the sun and heaven give
their glory and their peace. Even when an exile on a barren
island, listening to the eternal swashing of the ocean on the rock-
bound shore, his pen was never idle. He seemed ever pursued by
the angel of utility, who, through his pen, sought to inspire other
lives. His great spirit voiced its inmost desire when he wrote
the following words of fire: —

Sacrifice to "the mob," O poet! Sacrifice to that unfortunate, disinherited, vanquished, vagabond, shoeless, famished, repudiated, despair-
ing mob; sacrifice to it, if it must be, and when it must be, thy repose,
thy fortune, thy joy, thy country, thy liberty, thy life. The mob is the
human race in misery. The mob is the mournful beginning of the
people. The mob is the great victim of darkness. Sacrifice to it thy
gold, and thy blood which is more than thy gold, and thy thought
which is more than thy blood, and thy love which is more than thy
thought; sacrifice to it everything except justice. Receive its com-
plaint; listen to it touching its faults and touching the faults of others;
hear its confession and its accusation. Give it thy ear, thy hand, thy
arm, thy heart. Do everything for it, excepting evil. Alas! it suffers
so much, and it knows nothing. Correct it, warn it, instruct it, guide it,
train it. Put it to the school of honesty. Make it spell truth, show it
the alphabet of reason, teach it to read virtue, probity, generosity,
mercy. Hold thy book wide open. Be there, attentive, vigilant, kind,
faithful, humble. Light up the brain, inflame the mind, extinguish
selfishness, and thyself give the example. For it is beautiful on this
sombre earth, during this dark life, brief passage to something beyond,
— it is beautiful that Force should have Right for a master, that Progress
should have Courage as a leader, that Intelligence should have Honor as
a sovereign, that Conscience should have Duty as a despot, that Civilization should have Liberty as a queen, and that the servant of Ignorance
should be the Light.

These lines express in a word the thought throbbing in the
soul, not only of the great teachers, but of every one who belongs
to that class who live for humanity and who so often shun all
prominence, scattering happiness in such a way that only the
recipients know what is being done. Some are writers and
workers, as was the great Frenchman; some are poets and
singers, as, for example, that rare and truly noble soul, that
typical son of true democracy, James G. Clark, who for years
has written songs of the human, songs of the dawn, songs of
justice; who has set them to music and then sung them into the
hearts of thousands, while he has taught the purest ethics, the

broadest charity, and an ideal altruism. Mr. Clark, while profoundly spiritual in nature, is as free in thought as Hugo. He is nothing if not liberal, and hates creeds, dogmas, and the narrow spirit of bigotry and persecution as much as did the great catholic spirit of the founder of Christianity. He, moreover, is as simple in his life and tastes as are his teachings fine and elevating. He is a prophet of the dawn; and the burden of his exalted faith is constantly finding expression in noble lines, as, for example, the following:—

> Swing inward, O gates of the future!
>   Swing outward, ye doors of the past,
> For the soul of the people is moving
>   And rising from slumber at last;
> The black forms of night are retreating,
>   The white peaks have signalled the day,
> And Freedom her long roll is beating,
>   And calling her sons to the fray.
>
> Swing inward, O gates! till the morning
>   Shall paint the brown mountains in gold,
> Till the life and the love of the New Time
>   Shall conquer the hate of the Old;
> Let the face and the hand of the Master
>   No longer be hidden from view,
> Nor the lands he prepared for the many
>   Be trampled and robbed by the few.
>
> The soil tells the same fruitful story,
>   The seasons their bounties display,
> And the flowers lift their faces in glory
>   To catch the warm kisses of day;
> While our fellows are treated as cattle
>   That are muzzled when treading the corn,
> And millions sink down in Life's battle
>   With a sigh for the day they were born.
>
> Swing inward, O gates of the future!
>   Swing outward, ye doors of the past.
> A giant is waking from slumber
>   And rending his fetters at last;
> From the dust where his proud tyrants found him,
>   Unhonored and scorned and betrayed,
> He shall rise with the sunlight around him,
>   And rule in the realm he has made.

Mr. Clark is not what would be called a popular poet, for, like men of his class, he has never sought fame or desired to press his claim on the attention of the world. To aid his fellow-men, to break the bonds of the enslaved, to secure justice for the oppressed, and to broaden the horizon and soften the hearts of all with whom he has come in contact — this has been the sole aim of this fine, true man.

Another noble nature to whom I, in common with thousands,

owe much, and whose personal influence and utterances by word
of mouth have been of inestimable value to me, is Professor
Joseph Rodes Buchanan, the many-sided man of genius, whose
"New Education" was the first work which gave the world a
glimpse of what an ideal education should be, and whose various
medical and scientific works have been of incalculable value to
those who are willing to find truth outside conventional high-
ways. As a teacher and editor, however, the influence of this
really great man will, I fancy, reach down the ages, exerting an
influence almost as potent as that of contributions to our educational and philosophical literature. During the past few years I
have received many letters from persons prominent in reform,
educational, and progressive work, who have voiced the following
sentiment, expressed by a well-known writer and worker for the
progress of the race: "It must have been a quarter of a century," writes this eminent gentleman, "since I had my thought
turned into broader paths by the same noble teaching and inspiring sentiments which I now find in THE ARENA. I received this
new inspiration from Professor Buchanan's 'Journal of Man,'
then published in Cincinnati." A congressman, who is one of the
bravest and most conscientious members of the House, said to
me last winter, "Years ago my interest in social, educational, and
reformative work was awakened and stimulated by Professor
Buchanan, who then lived in Cincinnati." Only a few days since
I received a letter from Mrs. Elizabeth Lyle Saxon, the noble-
souled lady who recently, by arousing the women of New
Orleans, succeeded in defeating an infamous ordinance which had
passed both branches of the city government, and, had it secured
the mayor's signature, would have licensed prostitution and
placed the Crescent City in this respect on the debased level of
Paris. In her letter Mrs. Saxon refers to the long and helpful
acquaintance she has enjoyed with Professor Buchanan, whom
she styles "The beloved friend of all womankind." I might continue almost indefinitely quoting from persons who are at the
present time moral levers in society, all referring in like manner
to the inspiration derived from this patient and profound worker
for humanity's weal. I have, however, cited these cases not
for the purpose of paying a well-merited tribute to the noble
master, to whom I owe a great debt for his inspiring thoughts
and helpful suggestions, but to illustrate the far-reaching influence of seed sown by him more than a quarter of a century ago.
Doubtless he little imagined the amount of good he was doing in
those long vanished years, when his thoughts were moulding
minds, and turning brains which might have drifted with the
world's gay and aimless current, into the stream of noble, human
endeavor. The life of Professor Buchanan affords a very strik-

ing illustration of the point I am seeking to impress: that these silent forces, so seldom taken into account by students of the social unrest of the present, are in fact one of the most powerful agencies operating for a higher civilization. Even the individuals who compose this leaven of a diviner civilization little realize what they are doing.

It is not alone among the writers, singers, orators, or teachers that we find these uncounted forces exerting an exalted influence; in the business and social worlds are many lives touched by the ideals of the higher civilization, and consecrated to all that is best in life. But their influence is least of all taken into account; for the world knows little of their benefactions when, as is usually the case with these natures, they strive to keep from the vulgar gaze of the world all knowledge of their deeds. As a shining example of this class I would mention the late Gideon F. T. Reed, largely through whose instrumentality and that of his noble wife, THE ARENA was founded.

Mr. Reed was one of the highest types of men I have ever known. He was a fine thinker, taking a deep pleasure in the best thought of our time. In the sphere of business he had few equals; rigidly just, thoroughly conscientious, and of untiring application, he succeeded along the high pathway of honorable business. During the closing years of his life paralysis rendered his lower limbs comparatively useless, but his mind remained clear and his heart warm; his thoughts seemed to ever go out from self to others; it was not his sufferings or his happiness which so much concerned him, as the burdens and happiness of those less blessed by wordly possessions. I never knew him to be other than cheerful, and I never knew him to express other than kind and charitable concern for the weak and erring. Instead of spending his honorably acquired wealth in vulgar ostentation or selfish gratification, he sought to spend it with the triple purpose in view of increasing the happiness of others, relieving sorrow and pain, and aiding the educational currents of the world. Where a parvenu would lavish hundreds of thousands on stables for fast horses, or steam launches, Mr. Reed supplied numbers of poor families with fuel and necessities during the long winter months. Instead of lavishing tens of thousands of dollars upon banquets, he munificently aided schools, libraries, hospitals, and other enterprises of an educational nature or philanthropic character; but in all his giving he sought to avoid any publicity. His chief desire was to make others happy and increase the volume of the world's knowledge. I never knew a sweeter or more lovable nature, or a mind which so constantly went out to those in distress. One afternoon, a short time before he passed from life, Mrs. Reed returned from a mission of charity, and almost the first words uttered by the invalid were, "How did you find them, and did they need anything?" He referred to an old man and woman; the former had many years before been in his employ. This was thoroughly characteristic of the man, whose ripe culture and warm heart were united to a spirit of wondrous gentleness; a man whose chief desire was to uplift his fellow-men, and who was willing that only they who enjoyed his beneficence should know what was done. In all his labors he was loyally seconded by his high-minded wife, who no less than Mr. Reed has untiringly sought to advance the noble works which marked the closing years of his life. Many men have succeeded in having their names trumpeted by the press of two continents as benefactors and philanthropists who have done far less than Mr. Reed. Few men have in a quiet way done so much to diffuse the light of knowledge and gladden oppressed, bruised, or burdened hearts as this splendid example of one of Nature's noblemen. And yet there are many, aye, very, very many who are silently following more or less success-fully this same path of noble endeavor. And thus in public life, among our writers, among our teachers, and in the realms of social and business life, there are thousands who are quietly but effectively helping humanity upward and onward.

These lives are typical; they stand for an influence little understood or appreciated; they are not among the organizations which, with slow movement, being more or less cumbered with conventionalism, are helping the world forward. None of the lives I have cited wore the label of any church or creed; they one and all were beyond the pale of dogma. Broad, noble, and illuminated by the divine light of love and wisdom, they have helped the world onward. And they are representative; they stand for a wonderful power which, like the undertow of the ocean, is carrying civilization with irresistible force toward a happier clime and a fairer land. It is my opinion to-day that the divine in man is stronger than ever before; but because I believe this, I would not for a moment relax our struggle for a better, grander, and nobler civilization. Wrongs are facing us on every side, which must be overthrown. Selfishness, avarice, lust, and dissipation are menacing civilization. Never were earnest reformers or moral soldiers more needed than now; and yet, in order that we may be wise and just, and that our hearts may be sustained by an unwavering faith in the triumph of good, let us not overlook or minify the splendid works of the sowers of civilization's seed, who are silently stimulating humanity to nobler endeavor, and brightening the hearts of millions.

THE ARENA.

EDITED BY B. O. FLOWER.

VOL. VI.

PUBLISHED BY
THE ARENA PUBLISHING CO.,
BOSTON, MASS.
1892.

The PINKHAM PRESS, 289 Congress Street, Boston.

CONTENTS.

CONTENTS.

ILLUSTRATIONS.

BOOKS OF THE DAY.

SULTAN TO SULTAN.*

"BIBLES and bullets," the laconic reply of the great German statesman to the query, "How will you conquer and civilize Africa," might
be used as an epigrammatic summary of the history of Christian civilization in its treatment of the heathen since the days of Columbus to the
present time. It is said that the cross and the sword were the weapons
of Spain during her conquests; but as some clever writer observes, the
Spaniards forgot the cross until the sword had laid low the poor savage.
The history of our Christian civilization in its treatment of savage and
heathen nations is such as may well bring the blush of shame to every
humane check. Spain, Portugal, France, Germany, England, and America have so frequently pursued a deliberate, cold-blooded policy, looking
toward the crushing of the weak, and based on heartlessness and injustice, that to the conquered nations Christianity means anything but a
religion of peace, good will, and universal brotherhood. To the rem-
nant of the red men who now behold themselves bereft of nature and
hemmed in on all sides by a merciless civilization, which year by year
encroaches more and more upon their already circumscribed territory,
Christian civilization is anything but the synonym of universal love or
fraternity. To the East Indian, crushed by the iron heel of England's
power and with mind stored with the story of British conquest, the
words "Christian civilization" call up in his heart a torrent of hate and
arouse all that is worst in his nature. To negroes who are being crushed
under the stern arm of Germany's advancing forces in Africa, Christian
civilization is no magic phrase, carrying to the mind thoughts of peace,
prosperity, or the ideas of human kindness or Divine love. To none of
these people, any more than to the races which have gone down before
the cohorts of our civilization in other ages, does Christianity carry the
idea of a religion of love. They who have marched to conquer have
claimed to be Christian peoples, and their God to the poor heathen is no
Prince of Peace. In the book which is before me, a woman, an American woman, who has accomplished a marvellous feat, hints at a more
excellent way than that pursued by men in conquering and civilizing in
the past. In the first place M. French-Sheldon has demonstrated that
it is not necessary for a traveller and explorer to leave behind a trail of

* "Sultan to Sultan." Adventures among the Masai and other tribes of East
Africa, by M. French-Sheldon. Illustrated by over three hundred and fifty photo-
gravures and text cuts. Red and gold cloth, pp. 432, price $5. Arena Publishing
Company, Boston.

blood; she has shown that kindness calls forth kindness; her progress
was beset by dangers, and she penetrated the land of many tribes
reputed to be very savage; yet of her caravan of one hundred and thirty-
seven only one died, and he was slain by a wild beast, while she was
everywhere treated with respect and loaded with presents. Our author
has very decided views about how we should proceed to civilize these
poor savages, which are anything but conventional. She does not believe in the bullet-Bible theory, and would send people to teach the African tribes the arts of peace; to show them how to read and cook, and how
to till the rich fields and convert nature's wealth into articles of food,
clothes, and the making of homes; and hand in hand with this practical,
industrial education she would teach them how to read and write, how
to develop the intellect, and in so teaching she would inculcate the
high ethical training without which there can be no ideal manhood or
womanhood.

The story of Mrs. Sheldon's travels is written in a bright, chatty
style. Occasionally her sentences are somewhat involved, but on the
whole her style is pleasing, and the reader is led from page to page, fas-
cinated with the subject-matter, which is more interesting than romance,
because it has the added interest of being a narration of facts which
increase the reader's store of knowledge. Of our author's style the
reader can form a fair idea from the description of her visits to the
Sultan of Zanzibar, which I give below. By way of introduction I
should say, Mrs. Sheldon, on arriving in East Africa, found the British
East Africa Company hostile to her project. They tried in many ways
to prevent the execution of her plans, and she found it impossible to
obtain the requisite number of porters and interpreters without the
influence of some one in authority. Our consul at Zanzibar interested
himself in her cause, and through him she obtained an audience with
the Sultan of Zanzibar. This audience and her subsequent visit to his
harem are given below.

Arriving at the palace, which is a most unpretentious structure, I was conducted up
a flight of long stairs, and was met by the Sultan on the landing. The few words
of salutation in Ki-Swahali I had mastered came tripping off my tongue in response
to the Sultan's *jambos*, obsequious smiles, and bows of welcome. After these cere-
monious preliminaries were over, one of the dragomen was commanded by the Sultan
to act as interpreter. The walls of the large, showy saloon were hung with red panels
embellished with quotations from the Koran in embossed gilt characters; great showy
crystal chandeliers hung from the ceiling; tables of beautiful inlaid workmanship
were ranged through the centre of the room, and tall-backed gilt chairs with crimson
satin cushions were arranged in a stilted fashion throughout the long saloon. The
floor had a crimson velvet carpet with such thick pile the tread of feet became
noiseless.

Once seated at one of the tables, feeling flushed by the curious scrutiny of all
the attendants who hovered about, I was gratified when the Sultan ordered a particularly staring oleaginous creature to serve coffee. This I drank with relish; but no
sooner was my cup partially empty than there was a quick succession of various sorts
of sherbets paraded for my refreshment; truly they were marvellous concoctions of all
colors, beginning with brown, closely followed by red, green, and white syrup-like

fluids in the daintiest glasses imaginable; but with suspicion, I avoided the strange, spicy, honeyed beverages, only touching the rim of each glass with my forefinger, then, out of courtesy, pressing my finger to my lips in sign of satiety, to excuse my declining such choice nectars.

Subsequent to these delicate civilities, the Sultan explained, with evident embarrassment, that it was not his custom to *ceremoniously* receive ladies; nevertheless he was quite desirous to be of service to me in every possible way. This was my chance to tell him of my proposed expedition to Kilimanjaro and Masai land. Pulling his *joho* (long loose embroidered coat) around him, exposing his bare feet encased in sandals, he expressed regret that I should desire to go to such a dangerous, wild section of Africa, and wished I might be dissuaded.

"Is not Zanzibar charming? Why not linger here as the friend of the Sultan?"

"No, not dissuaded," I firmly rejoined; "however, his Majesty could make it far easier and safer for me, if he felt inclined."

Again he wrapped his splendid gold-embroidered *joho* about him with a certain majesty and said imperiously, "Command us and it shall be done."

Explaining the difficulties my agent experienced in procuring porters, I urged that he would aid me by having all slaves volunteering speedily sworn in on the following Saturday; and when masters interfered with their slaves, or middlemen objected, to declare himself my friend, and command it otherwise.

"It shall be done."

He ordered his band to play some special pieces in my honor, which, as usual, wound up the performance by the national anthem, an explosive *pot pourri*. When I was on the point of leaving, after drenching me with otter of rose, he invited me, with great effusiveness, to return on the following Friday with a woman interpreter, to visit his harem; he also placed a carriage at my disposal during the entire time I remained in port, — I will not mar the lustre of his gallantry by describing the Sultan's vehicles and horses, — and he offered to take out his war ship Glasgow for my pleasure. This war ship, by the by, it is satirically said, was presented to the Sultan by a celebrated shipbuilder for the paltry sum of $200,000 (£40,000).

Friday's arrangements, owing to the difficulties of procuring a woman interpreter, either from the mission people or through my agents, seemed to be unavoidably cancelled, when I received a message from the Sultan summoning me to come, as he had himself secured the services of a woman interpreter. So I went, and received a most friendly reception. Through locked and barred doors I was conducted from one of the palaces — there are three in a row — to the other, and finally reaching a large saloon, the place where the interpreter was dismissed, that was in wild disorder, like the show-room of a barbaric merchant prince, — a dazzling variety and array of valuable gifts, curios, all sorts of purchasable splendors heaped incongruously one upon another upon tables, on the floor, and nothing showing to any advantage, the only impression given was of quantity and enormous value.

The Sultan's eldest daughter was brought in by a black woman slave, attended by two little black slave boys.

With a flash of pride the Sultan exclaimed, "See how a Sultan dresses his daughter! Look well, and tell to other Europeans how splendid are her jewels." The heavy gold anklets worn by this little child, but five years of age, impeded her moving with any freedom. Her crown, studded with jewels, must have pained her tender brow; and the gorgeous as well as curious necklaces suspended one upon another, to the number of a dozen, and numerous bracelets and finger rings, certainly must have been burdensome. The Sultan's lament is that he is unfortunate in having three daughters and no sons. He was curious to know if I had children; and when the negative response was conveyed to him, he asked boldly, "Has your husband many wives?" He smiled in a cynical way.

"Certainly not," I retorted with some contempt, vexed by his effrontery.

At this juncture a heavy embroidered portière was drawn aside by two Malay eunuchs, whose tongues were cut out to limit their power of disclosing secrets, and there appeared a haughty woman, gorgeously attired. Possessed with all the imperious disdain of an empress, she approached me, and rudely threw out her hand to me, at the same time ungraciously darting a glance of outraged feeling upon me. This, then, was the Sultana! Poor woman! did she presume I was another usurper of her legitimate place? Only a few moments expired when she was ushered out by two gross, horrid, greasy eunuchs, and the portière was drawn over the closing door. Within ten minutes after her Highness's exit, through another door entered in Indian file woman after woman of the Sultan's harem, to a number most amazing. Each one in turn approached me, extending her hand. To the first, who was a fine frank-looking creature, I arose to respond to her greeting, when the Sultan waved me down.

"Do not trouble yourself for them. There are too many, all alike, and not worth it."

Some of these poor, degraded concubines were sad-eyed and full of sorrow; others seemed defiant and triumphant, and yet others looked envious. Comparing the vast difference in the costliness and quantity of their jewels and dresses, it flashed across my mind that these distinctions were marks of favoritism. Each and every one of these royal concubines, at the command of the Sultan, bathed my right foot in rose-water; and in recognition of my superiority and evidence of their humility, each gave me one of her jewelled rings. The sum total was one hundred and forty-two.

The Sultan, after showing me about through the private rooms, as he professed he had never previously shown any one, queried what I thought of it all. With true American frankness, I declared it atrocious. He said he would gladly renounce his harem, "But I should lose my Arab constituency."

Most cautious man as this Sultan is respecting signing papers, always suspicious of some governmental policy that will involve him, he offered to visé my passport. This I declined, desirous that he should give me a special letter to any Arab caravans I might encounter on my trip up country. This he did. He also gave me his auto-graphed photograph; and I had the Sultan's word he would always be more than pleased to serve me in any possible way as his friend.

A feature of peculiar value and interest in this volume is the delightful description of the home life, the customs, habits, and modes of living of the various tribes. No former work on the Dark Continent has ever given anything like a full, intelligent, or real picture of the native negro races, for the reason that no traveller has ever before enjoyed such advantageous opportunities as Mrs. Sheldon. Then, again, a woman sees in domestic life what a man would never notice. The descriptions of the various tribes are very fascinating as well as highly instructive. I will give a glimpse of the tribes of the Taveta, one of the most interesting and intelligent of the natives, as given by Mrs. Sheldon. Space prevents my quoting more than a few paragraphs of this intensely interesting description. They will, however, prove sufficient to indicate the character of this feature of the work.

The English officers have placed a hand-mill within their boma for their own use, but generously accord to the natives the privilege of using it to grind their corn and banana flour; this relieves them of the tedious process of pounding the grain and dried fruit in a wooden or stone mortar with a heavy wooden pestle, an advantage they evidently seem to highly appreciate, for the mill is never idle all day long. Heretofore the women were allotted the task of pulverizing the corn and bananas to an impalpable flour, and with maternal solicitude strapped their babes upon their backs, afraid to put the little ones on the ground on account of the ravages of the white ants, and they would be quieted and rocked to sleep by the swaying motion of the mother's body as she monotonously wielded the heavy pestle.

Honey bees thrive, and the Wa-Taveta manufacture quantities of beehives out of logs. They are cylindrical in shape, three to four feet long, and a foot and a half in diameter, hollowed out and then closed at one end, with a puncture at the other to admit the ingress and egress of the bees.

The honey is rather dark in color, but most delicious in flavor and plentiful. It is put in hide boxes or calabashes. We several times came across dead hollow tree-trunks, branches lopped, standing erect, covered over with a removable piece of hide, punctured to admit the bees, which were used for hives. These primitives are utilitarians by nature.

Made hives are hung in the trees on the track of the bee ranges, where honey flowers are most abundant. A similar utensil to the made beehives is used in which to brew their *pombe*, a concoction of sugar-cane, bananas, or cocoanut, wimbe, and corn. When the mash is fresh the beverage tastes very much like unfermented mead or beer, but in the course of three days fermentation has reached a point when the brew becomes a subtle intoxicant; and as it is profusely brewed by almost every native of the tribe, they are during harvest time in a perpetual state of jollification, and all the unamiable qualities and propensities of their natures seem to be strangely affected by this intoxicant. It is a mistake to say that the Africans have been polluted in this respect by the invasion of white men, because they have always, as far as one can ascertain, used *pombe* and *tembo* or other native drinks.

The idea prevails that by the preservation of the skull the spirit of the departed is saved, and that the congregation in one place of the skulls of a family or tribe guarantees a future reunion.

Superstitions concerning death are decidedly obscure and extremely heterogeneous in East Africa, and yet there are little threads which have various origins, running through the tissues of what may be called their religion. They worship the moon and the sun, and revel in songs or chants addressed to the rain during planting seasons.

The Wa-Duruma near the coast beat drums, but they are the only tribe in the part of East Africa I visited where they use drums.

Strange native medical practices were revealed to me through the auspices of the Woman of Taveta. The old women are all skilled mid-wives. Mothers suffer very little during the period of gestation or in the throes of childbirth. A girl reaches puberty at the infantile age of ten. Youths are circumcised by their own election when they no longer wish to be children, but aspire to the station of *el-moran*, as early often as the age of twelve. The custom of circumcision must have maintained for many decades, for nature frequently simulates it, and the parents boast of an offspring so pre-eminently destined to be a warrior, and the favored boy is pointed out as one elect.

All the natives seem to possess a minor yet practical knowledge of the use of herbs and roots, and of imported medicaments. Sulphur, quinine, bluestone do they beseech the leaders of caravans for. They suffer from itch, ulcers, sore eyes, and fevers. The Woman of Taveta told me of bubbling hot-water *zorcis* (springs or pools) where those who were afflicted with various diseases, including smallpox and elephantiasis, made pilgrimages and were benefited, and of certain clays that the Wandorobo knew about and brought down country that possessed curative properties for coughs and stiff joints, a species of rheumatism, and sometimes progressive paralysis caused from excessive drinking and exposure to the elements. This paralysis, with marked and retributive selection, inflicts the sultans and important men of tribes, who are in position to command the largest harems, and indulge themselves like Sybarites.

Personal decoration attains a very great height at Taveta, especially among the young men, who are much given to dressing their hair in a very quaint fashion, drawing it in braided clumps, hanging down over the face, and divided in strands made over the back of the head, hanging over the shoulders, which they plaster with grease and red clay, to which they frequently add bead and metal pendants. These young fellows, who represent the Taveta snobs, smear their bodies with grease and tint themselves with red clay. They are very self-conscious and great posers, the very princes of dawdlers and slaves of fashion. They divide themselves up into little bevies, almost clubs, and they wear as an insignia or badge of fellowship or brotherhood little armlets made of a strip of cowhide, upon which are sewn beads in special devices and chosen colors, which seem to indicate their particular faction or club. They are great dancers and merrymakers. The young fellows gather in groups and dance as though in competition, one with the other; a daring aspirant will dash out from the circle apart from his companions, rush into the middle of a circumscribed space, and scream out, "Wow! wow!" another follows him and screams in the same way; and a third, and so on. These men will dance with their knees almost rigid, jumping into the air faster and faster, until they bound with amazing velocity, and their excitement becomes proportionately greater, and their energy waxes more and more spasmodic, leaving the ground frequently fully three feet as they spring into the air.

The women also engaged in dances, and especially as guests, during wedding festivities, bedecked with all their fine toggery, they separate themselves from the men and follow in a procession, one after another, with their hands upon each other's shoulders or hips, beating their feet in time, and singing a strange, monotonous plaint, now and then interspersed with shouts of laughter when they resume their measured processional steps, jingling all the bells they have about them with a peculiar jerk and fling of their hips and shoulders as they go round and round, threading their way through the forest, back again to the *boma* of the host of ceremony, drinking and carousing quite as much as the young fellows. A certain amount of dignity is put upon these gayeties by the presence of the elders; however, there seems no viciousness in any of their games and pleasures.

The children amuse themselves, as do other children, vying with each other shooting at a mark and at birds on wing with their bows and arrows, which they succeed in doing with great dexterity. They have some idea of forming companies and drilling, and accept a leader whom they are disposed to follow. Their education is a rudimentary one of imitation, and not of instruction. They are impressionable and observing. Their reasoning faculties naturally would be quickened and vivified by attrition and calling them into play, although at present they are, at times, somewhat slow to comprehend innovations to their old habits and customs. They are afraid of monkeys, and the lemur makes frequent nocturnal visitations to the settlements, to the distress of the people.

I came very near being betrayed into supposing that certain scars upon their bodies were the result of tattooing, but after close inspection found that they resulted from cupping, which they resort to for their headaches and stomach difficulties; in fact, no matter what malady afflicts them, they are great blood letters, and the simple methods they employ I adopted with great service during my caravan clinic. After excoriating the surface with a little knife or a piece of flint or a piece of wire, they place over it a gazelle horn, with the pointed end cut off, when they apply suction by holding the horn, first wet, firmly against the part to be cupped, and then drawing with their lips the blood; and if the malady is serious, they make several applications, on different places, drawing as much as an ounce and a half of blood from the sufferer.

Natives eat as a medicine, as a condiment, and as a stomachic great quantities of red peppers, which grow indigenously and abundantly. They are fond of raw plum tomatoes, which I discovered to be delicious, and identical in flavor to the cultivated tomato, perhaps a trifle more tart. Ears of corn or maize are spiked about their fireplaces, which consist of three stones canted inward so as to touch at the top, or placed upright, under which the fire is built, where they roast, bake, or boil the maize, which is most luscious. They also eat maize raw, and so did we before too ripe, when it is palatable and nutritious, full of sweet milky juice which slakes the thirst. When they cannot obtain pure salt, which they always crave, and is an appreciated article of barter, they use chunvi-stone, which has a brackish, alkaline flavor, and answers very well as a substitute. Salt is found in great abundance in some of these highland districts, according to good authority. Butter they churn by rolling across their *boma* grounds or by shaking large calabashes, or oblong wooden dug-out cylinders, like their honey boxes, filled with milk. Butter made of cow's milk is very white and waxy in appearance, strongly flavored with banana, for the cattle are fed during the rainy season on banana leaves and the fruit that is unfit to keep or exceeds the native's wants. The taste for this butter I fancy must be acquired by a foreigner. They also make goat's milk butter, called *gee*, oily, strongly flavored, and odoriferous as the goat itself. This product is used largely in the cookery of native gourmands, and adopted by caravans, but to my taste it was decidedly obnoxious.

Mutton obtained from sheep of the fat-tailed species is very strong, as is also that of the goats. The beef is more or less tough. The chickens, strangely enough called *ku-kus*, are very tiny and sinewy. Natives frequently sell a hen that is laying, with the proviso that the eggs laid for four days, or according to arrangement, should be theirs. It is a very quaint custom to string these chickens upon the pole carried by the cook's mate, with pots and pans, and a cloth pouch is kept fastened under the hen, so that if she lays on the march, the egg is preserved; and in order to make sure that the purchaser will not defraud the seller, the latter sends some boy of the tribe to follow the caravan three or four days, in order to take the product on the spot.

Africans all have a particular taste and decided preference for rotten eggs. It has been often cited that as a reward for some act of kindness on the part of white men to natives, that the women, under the guise of gratitude, have brought as thank-offerings, eggs — rotten eggs! Could they do more? Even their gratitude has been impugned by almost every explorer and traveller, simply because the native's expression of this sentiment is at variance with the white man's conception of what it should be. They gave what they valued most, yet this has been attributed to a mean trait of deception in their natures, which are judged as utterly devoid of gratitude. The civilized man is, after all, a thorough Procrustean, intolerant of the natural diversities of human nature, unjust and illiberal once he departs from the limitations of his own studied environments. He deliberately makes his reason impervious to new truths by a heterogeneous composite of principles and his own accepted ideals.

Polygamy exists. It seems almost as a necessity more than licentiousness, considering the environments. A man accumulates more land or more cattle than his first wife can attend; he purchases another wife, and so on. The wives are far from being jealous of each other; in truth, are delighted to welcome a new wife, and make great preparations for her. Each wife has her own hut, if indeed not her own *boma*. She has control of her own plantations, and has the supreme right to her children. Her moral standard is exactly the same as her husband's. A woman is only declassed when she holds *liaisons* with porters in a caravan or with the enemy of her husband. Marriage is by purchase; the wife is bought from her parents by cows, land, spears, etc.; then the marriage ceremony is consummated by capture. Her marital aspirant, with four or five of his comrades, pursues her, and after capture she is secluded four or five days; meanwhile the husband's friends have been permitted certain privileges before the husband claims her. This is simply atrocious. The wedding feast is held with great pomp and ceremony to every one but the bride, who is secluded and presumably undergoing a preparatory schooling in the hands of her husband's mother.

The established wives are full of merriment, and interchange many pleasantries with their lord and master, feeling that their daily toil will be lightened.

Frequently the Woman of Taveta would bring a man or woman to me and say, "This is my brother by my father, but not the same mother," and "This is my sister by the *el-moran* my mother lived with before she married," or "This is my brother by the same father and the same mother."

Childhood's limit is very brief with the African children; in good truth, it seemed to me there were no real children after six or eight years of age. That is, they engaged in the pursuits of, and mingled freely with, the adults, in so far as their physical strength and adolescence would admit. They seemed also to be perfectly acquainted with the existent relationships held by their seniors, even to the extent of passing comments upon certain customs, and avowing their future intentions to follow or abandon a similar course when they should have become *el-moran* (young man) or *en-aitto* (a marriageable young woman). This fact comes from the mediocre limitations of the native adult mind, hence the children's accession to the same is comparatively rapid, although I must disclaim that it evinces precocity. I heard a boy of about six say to a little girl no more than five years of age as he strode about, facing her, while he flourished his wooden spear, full of pride and impetuosity: "When I shall be *el-*

moran and thou *en-ditto*, I shall win and wear the bearded collar, and thou wilt be my wife, aye! Thou shalt have more beads than all of Endella's wives put together. I have spoken! Now walk with me and show to my fellows how a sultana should look." And the two midgets, with all the pomposity imaginable, made a circle round about the young people gathered in the market-place, to become the object of merriment and joke, but good-naturedly they gesticulated and returned the pleasantries of the different groups, and seemingly had their own little fun and glory by thus emphasizing their rosy prospects.

This bearded collar is worn by the Masai warrior who has twelve times "plunged to the heart of twelve foes his spear." Hence the ambitious, bellicose youngster proffered to his young Dulcinea no mean outlook, if his boast met with realization.

Throughout the section of East Africa I journeyed, I was in a constant state of wonderment over the happy, merry dispositions of the children, full of song and sport, like arboreal sprites. The region can well be called, as is Japan, the *Paradise of Children*. Archery clubs are formed among the youngsters and under the command of a leader, selected, or who asserts himself, because of his skill. They practice shooting at a mark, and vie with one another with a pardonable zest. They participate in games of running, become competitors in swimming, diving, and dancing. In imitation of adult blacksmiths, they make wooden spears, the precise counterfeits of the metal ones. They are venders of all sorts of produce at the markets, especially of chickens and eggs.

Another delightful feature of this work is the introduction of charming little incidents of life which illustrate so beautifully the fact that the human heart is the same in savage and civilized, and whether found under the skin blackened and burned for ages by the torrid sun, or under the delicate white of the northlier climes. Here, for example, is a charming little incident of this character.

One of the most touching incidents came under my personal observation whilst at Moschi, respecting a little native child, who had been captured by a slave-raider with other unfortunates, and freed by the German government. The missionaries are generally made custodians of the freed slaves, and receive from the government a pittance of not over five dollars (one pound), I believe, to take, educate, rear, clothe, and feed them. In this way it happened that the celebrated mission doctor, Wm. Baxter, who has spent the best part of his adult life in Africa, during a professional visit to the station where the little child, not over six years of age, had been placed, noticed him, and the child was immediately drawn by the doctor's kindliness and evinced love for children, and became deeply attached to him.

When the doctor had finished the duties of his professional visit, and returned to his own post, distant from the place where he met the child something like twelve or fifteen miles, and over a very difficult range of rugged steep foot-hills of Kilimanjaro, intersected by deep ravines, gullies, and water-courses, as well as being infested by wild animals, a day or so elapsed when one night he was aroused by his attendants, who brought a little native waif utterly worn out by fatigue and hunger. It was his little friend, who, unattended, had braved the terrors of night and prowling animals, and the hardships of a perilous journey, as he followed the tracks of the good doctor, guided only by his child's affection and innate instinct of trapper.

Touched as the doctor was by compassion for the devoted brave little soul, after the child had recuperated it was necessary that he should return him to his legitimate protectors. With much grief and disappointment to the child, and reluctance on the part of the doctor, this was done.

Before a fortnight had elapsed, again during the blackest hours of night the child put in an appearance at Moschi, the doctor's station, having eluded the vigilance of his warders, and ignoring the terrors he had encountered during his former escapade. Heroic little chap! The doctor could no longer resist his pleading words of love and desire to be his *m'toto* (little boy), and took measures to secure the right of guard-ianship.

When I saw this child he was trudging up a steep hill, bearing on his staff just like a little old man, his face radiant with a welcome for the doctor, who had been on a long journey. What will the future of this child be, I wonder!

The work also abounds in vivid description of personal adventure and incidents far more entertaining to the reader than they were to the traveller, as the following pen-picture of a visit from a large snake well illustrates:—

Observations made by me in East Africa at night were most unusual if not unique, and made me acquainted with certain peculiar revelations which nature seems to keep mysteriously concealed during the day. Creeping things, prowling animals, were ever on the alert just outside of the encampment, deterred from coming in by the numerous fires and the sentinels on watch. One night, experiencing great fatigue, I fell in a profound slumber lying in my palanquin within my tent, when suddenly I awoke with a shuddering apprehension of danger, and possessed by an instinctive feeling of the presence of some harmful thing. Involuntarily seizing my knife and pistol, I cried out, "Who is there!" No answer. Then I called out for the *askari* on guard, at the same time tried to penetrate the darkness surrounding me, when I became aware, through the atmospheric conditions, that a cold, clammy, moving object was above me, in truth almost touching me, on the top of my palanquin, the rattans of which were cracking as if under the pressure of a mangle. I was struggling to slide out of the palanquin without rising from my recumbent position, to avoid touching the thing, when the alarmed *askari* entered, carrying a lantern, to my abject horror revealing to me the object I had intuitively dreaded. My blood fairly seemed to congeal in my veins at the spectacle: it was an enormous python, about fifteen feet long, which had coiled around the top of the palanquin, and at that moment was ramping and thrusting its head out, searching for some attainable projection around which to coil its great, shiny, loathsome length of body. Seeing the python, the *askari* immediately yelled wildly out for help, and in a moment a dozen stalwart porters pitched in a merciless way with their knives upon the reptile, slashing and cutting its writhing body into inch bits. I am not ashamed to confess it was the supreme fear of my life, and almost paralyzed me. I came very near collapsing and relinquishing myself to the nervous shock; but there was no time for such an indulgence of weakness.

Physical appearances of a peculiar nature are also noted in an entertaining manner, as the following paragraph illustrates:—

In countries of such a climate the usual practice suggested by all good military tacticians, of surrounding a tent with a ditch, in case of rain, is a great mistake, excepting when absolutely necessary. Making personal observations on this point, in the hope of ameliorating my personal condition,—being a victim to chronic asthma,— I found that the newly upturned earth at night would emit a phosphorescent glow which would hang and hover about the little trench as if reluctant to part from its maternal source; and all sorts of crawling things would issue forth and revel in the unhealthy place. Another strange manifestation of these mists was evidenced in passing my hands through the thick, wavy veil and rubbing the palms together in a dark spot removed from the trench. They would glow with phosphorus as if I had dipped them in fire; and when one of the porters stepped out of these trenches he would leave his fiery footprint on the solid ground for some minutes after walking thereon. Such a miasmatic condition certainly cannot be conducive to the well-being of human creatures. I have also seen mists in Africa which were luminous and had certain powers of refracting the rays of the moon, which became iridescent and full of prismatic sheets and gleams. The effect was very much like a terrestrial aurora borealis, and the foliage would stand out bright, glistening, and green, as if the sunlight had fallen upon them after a rain. The appearance is very weird, and I inferred of common occurrence, as none of the men in the caravan noted it with any degree of surprise, which would indicate that they were accustomed to it.

These brief extracts from this volume, which in many respects is the most notable book of travel which has appeared in recent years, will, I think, give our readers a fair idea of the character of the work and its literary style. To appreciate the volume, however, one must see it as it is, sumptuously gotten up, containing nearly four hundred illustrations, many of which are full-page photogravures taken by Mrs. Sheldon; many also are faithful reproductions of ornaments, implements, and curios procured by the author from the various tribes. The illustrations aid greatly in understanding her description of the native customs, habits, dress, and articles of utility or ornament which prevail in this little-known region. The volume contains about five hundred pages, is printed in very large type on heavy plate paper, and is bound in African red and gold; one of the richest and most desirable holiday volumes of the year.   B. O. FLOWER.

THE ORIGIN, PURPOSE, AND DESTINY OF MAN.[*]

On taking up this work I was at first impressed with the sublime audacity of a writer who in the compass of one hundred pages sought to solve the three most profound problems which confront humanity. An examination of the work, however, proved that the author is a deep thinker, who possesses in a rare degree the power of condensing his thoughts. What most writers would extend over many hundred pages, are here given in five brief chapters. I know of no writer who states his propositions more concisely than Dr. Thornton; but this element necessitates close intellectual application on the part of the reader if he would follow the author, who rarely pauses to elucidate a proposition, and who presumes that his readers are philosophers as well as high thinkers. The work is divided into three major divisions: The Discussion of the Origin of Life; or, "The Philosophy of the Three Ethers"; "How to Make Medicine a Science," including a critical examination of the germ theory; "The Transmission Theory of Disease," and "Immortality," or the author's conception of the destiny of man.

In the introduction to his work Dr. Thornton thus states the basic principles upon which he builds his argument:—

That all things animate and inanimate, organic and inorganic, are made up of three states which I call the three ethers. Life I call the first ether, which is a continuous aggregate. The second ether I call a composition of the potentialities, heat, light, electricity, and magnetism, mechanical power being manifested during the activity of these potentialities. The third ether is a material nucleus which permits of the action of the other two ethers. All bodies manifesting the second and third ethers independently of the first, make up all inorganic bodies. Organized bodies require all three ethers. These two conditions constitute all things natural and supernatural. I com-

---

[*] "The Origin, Purpose, and Destiny of Man." By William Thornton. Cloth, pp. 100. Boston. Published by the author.

mence at the beginning, where life by divine impression enters the second ether, a composition of the potentialities. From thence it passes to the tangible substances, nature having prepared them for the inception of life. Finally man's state is reached by a process of evolution, that is in no way discordant or inharmonious with religion or the genesis of things. The progressive differentiation from the lowest forms of life to the highest known type, man, is presided over by the supernatural agencies, in which intelligence in the form of the Creator reigns supreme and the impression on the three ethers becomes evident.

In order to explain the relative positions occupied by the three ethers in forming the human body, and about which I am philosophizing, a single experiment will illustrate. If we evaporate a given quantity of water into steam inside of a globe of a given size, from which the air has been removed and to which a stopcock is adjusted, we shall find this vapor to fill the globe. If the same quantity of alcohol be evaporated in the same way in the same globe, we shall find the alcohol vapor to occupy the globe as if no steam were present. Now, by the same process if we evaporate the same quantity of ether in this globe, each one of these things will occupy the globe as if the other two were not present. We will suppose the globe to be a man. Take the water in the form of steam in the globe to represent the third ether from which all chemical compounds in nature are formed; the alcohol to represent the second ether, a composition of the imponderables or potentialities, heat, light, electricity, and magnetism; the evaporated ether to represent the continuous entity, life. These three vapors in the globe exist in the same relativity as the three ethers representing all organized beings.

Our author next advances his views more in detail.

Life, which is the first ether, enters into the potentialities of the second ether; from thence it passes to the third ether, which is the material tangible to us. The second ether permits the manifestation of heat, light, electricity, and magnetism, which are present in the form of a mechanical atmosphere of these agencies. Heat is drawn from this atmosphere by molecular agitation, more of which enters as the agitation is becoming intensified, and at a certain degree of this agitation light is attracted. Light is the visible expression of heat. Electricity is a modification of the same influence that produces light. . . . The imponderable or physical agencies of nature are the molecular groupings of the second ether. These agencies are pent up as potentialities in all the solids, liquids, and gases in the third ether; the disturbances of them give rise to the activities of atoms and molecules, and they may be called the directing influences for combination, in the production of different states of bodies. Material changes represent the disturbances of these potentialities. Electrical fixity is the cause of the relativity of the units in combination in solids, liquids, and gases, this fixity being the most feeble in gases. The unvarying inclination to combine is the cause of motion.

An example of the change of the state, which is evidence of divine impression, is seen when sulphur and iron combine chemically to form sulphate of iron, after which they manifest different properties from those that each manifested before uniting. Iron and sulphur are still present and have combined to form crystals. A molecular arrangement takes place which permits the passage of light through them. Iron and sulphur, both opaque before combining, are by the change rendered transparent in a measure, and are made to approach nearer to the state of the second ether by the presence in their bodies of more of the modified potentialities. Sulphuric acid added, containing more still of the potentialities, will in the presence of water place them still nearer to the second ether.

These brief extracts are given to enable the reader to obtain an idea of Dr. Thornton's position, which he sets forth in the first forty pages of his work. From the "Philosophy of the Three Ethers," he passes to the discussion of "How to Make Medicine a Science," an interesting subject in the present chaotic condition of thought in the medical world. According to Dr. Thornton's theory, each germ of life holds in image or impression all the units or cells of the body. "Here," he continues, "we have further evidence of the presence of the image of the Creator; for this image is without form till its development is complete through the material. . . . Life is that evidence of the supernatural endowment which originally entered nature during the formation of those units for the evolution of man. This being understood, the question naturally arises, What were the elements that nature first selected from the chemical world for man's formation? An analysis of his composition shows that she selected those elements which are the most abundant in nature: oxygen, hydrogen, nitrogen, carbon, sulphur, phosphorous, fluorine, chlorine, sodium, potassium, calcium, magnetism, silicium, iron, and many of the derivatives of these elements. If nature had been as successful in the selection of durable material in the formation of the more complex compounds essential to life, as she was in selecting the material to form the bony system, then her efforts would have been less abortive in what had the appearance of an attempt to perpetuate man's existence. This is evidenced by the bony system, which persists, preserving a comparatively unlimited identity, long after those complex compounds have passed away. . . . Man's foundation was of the most durable material, carefully selected from the most abundant compounds in nature, upon which she also relied in her foundation of the earth. Such being the case, it becomes an easy matter to see the glaring absurdity of trying to reproduce man's normal composition by those elements and compounds which are not at any time found in the body of man. The most powerful irritants and disturbers of the potentialities are to be found in those incompatibles prescribed by different members of the medical profession, —incompatibles that could not enter without violently disturbing the normal composition of the body by inharmonious action, and for this reason they should never be used."

After giving a list of over eighty drugs more or less popular with the medical profession which he holds should never be given, as they are never found in the human body, our author continues:—

Everything prescribed in the form of medicine should act more as a chemical food in building up the body by promoting organization; this could not be done by those means never found in the body at any time. The analyses of the different kinds of food taken into the body furnish us with an excellent guide in finding out, not only its normal composition, but also its matter of nutrition. This knowledge will enable us to replace any of the lacking elements, which give rise to malnutrition and diseases other than those of so-called miasmatic or contagious origin. The same method should be applied in formulating medicines as is expected will be the ultimate result obtained in the laboratory, in the formulation by chemical means of those complex compounds which are the essential principles of the human body. . . . If nature selected the most abundant things in nature from which to produce man's composition, is it not the highest absurdity to look for the least abundant things in nature to repair his condition when disease arises? From this fact, common sense as well as science shows distinctly why there is no science or system of medicine now practised or taught in any medical school throughout the world. . . . Anything, in fact, which arises and passes beyond a comparatively slight ailment and merges into a grave condition, medicine as practised to-day is unable to cope with, for the simple reason that common sense and science are not permitted to harmonize. . . Medicine can never become a science when wrong ideas in formulating prevail. When so many foreign ingredients, that are never found in the body at any time, are used as remedies for disease, we shall never obtain any but the most unsatisfactory results.

Again Dr. Thornton observes: —

Everything given in the form of medicine should promote organization, and prevent all those regressive changes going on in disease, by increasing the spermatic influence of cells.

Next, diseases of extraneous origin, and, lastly, decrepitude or old age are examined. But space prevents a further notice of this division of the work. I will dismiss it with a brief quotation : —

A complete system of medicine can be founded only on the following principle: From the animal, vegetable, and mineral kingdoms nothing must be selected but those elements which enter normally into the chemical composition of the body, everything else being incompatible with it; in short, nothing is to be introduced into the body in a diseased state but that which is formulated from the elements found in it in a healthy state. On this principle, every remedy used in disease would act invariably the same way under all circumstances. Then, and then only, should we have a complete system or science of medicine.

In his chapter on the germ theory of disease our author assails the popular and prevailing germ theory in a very able argument. He calls attention to the fact that these disease germs are " Microscopic units always present, either in or adjacent to the body, and ready to make an attack when an occasion presents itself. If this be the case, what is the condition necessary for them to manifest their pernicious influence? Incipient disorganization or decrepitude of the cells? If the condition for attack never arose, they would remain in their surroundings perfectly harmless as before, as we know they are present in myriads in both health and disease. More attention is given at the present time in the scientific world to the isolation of specific germs than to the prevention of their attack by elevating organization in devitalizing processes. Unless the condition arises, one cannot live upon another. What is this condition? It is this: That an environment must exist which is produced from a specific change in the composition of a part, rendering it susceptible to the support and growth of micro-organisms or " living" units. This condition evidences disorganizing processes. These parasites are present for the removal of all disorganized products, so that it is a wise provision in nature to furnish means, the absence of which would permit of the production of sufficient septic matter to annihilate whole colonies of subjects.

From the discussion of the germ theory, Dr. Thornton passes to an examination of the transmission theory, which he strongly upholds. The last ten pages of the work are given to a treatise on the problem of immortality. An idea of our author's views on this subject may be gleaned from the following lines : —

To the creative power of intuition we must look for a knowledge of the supernatural, and in this alone we have the evidence of infinity; to which inventive genius can testify, as intuition creates those things which have no material existence. The man who invents a machine can see the working of that machine before its construction as distinctly as though it were in working order before him, from which he creates his plans and drawings, the material furnishing merely the object or image of his mental creation. The same occurs when the painter creates his subject before it appears on the canvas. In fact, many instances could be adduced of the manifestation of this power of creative intuition. In the genesis of things where Moses says: " In his own image, male and female, created He them," he must have referred to the soul of man; for he could not mean that God was the image of both male and female-at the same time, but that the souls of male and female are equal. The image of God is manifested in the creative faculties of man, and not in his morphological figure. The difference between God and man seems clearly to be the following: The infinite power of God is to create a thing without previous existence, by command; and man brings into existence, through material, that which his intuition creates.

I cannot agree with Dr. Thornton in his views of eternal life as given in this work, as he seems to believe that the units of life, after their manifestations through matter on this planet, are allotted forever their future abiding-place in felicity or anguish; that death ends all opportunity for change; and to me this conception would make the Creator an inhuman monster, and creation a hideous tragedy of infinite dimensions. I believe that whatever lies beyond will come under the general law of progress, that seems so clearly to be one of the cardinal laws of life. I believe that when once the clogs which drag man sinward are cast aside, and the night of ignorance in which millions of souls grope and fall has been swallowed up in eternal light, the God essence of man's nature will climb Godward, feebly and lamely perchance at first, but nevertheless the trend will be upward. With one more quotation I close this interesting and thought-suggesting volume :—

Nature's process of evolution culminated in man. Is she to stop here, or is she by the same rate and manner going to produce a being still higher? I think, now that man's state has been reached, that a psychological differentiation may commence in continuation with the Darwinian morphological differentiation. Is there any evidence existing to-day which indicates anything like such an assertion of the spirit here in this world? This would require the gradational throwing off of this material concrete which we call man's body, until an ultimately developed spiritual state shall become the order of things. If the soul does not require feeding, such a state is possible. There are human beings who are so sensitively organized that they are impressionable to surrounding influences as though they were not manifesting anything but a spiritual state through a material body; a complete bundle of nerves and psychic influences. If such a state is to be possible, then death truly becomes swallowed up in victory. And there shall be no more deaths, neither shall there be any more disease contracted through the flesh. Corruption shall take on the incorruptible and dwell as an eternal entity, defying all material influences.

I have endeavored to give my readers as clear an idea of the work as the compass of a few pages would permit. It is a work which requires thoughtful reading; and whether or not one agrees with the author's conclusions, it will give the mind a healthy stimulus.

B. O. FLOWER.

SOME NOTABLE REFORMATIVE WORKS OF FICTION.*

During the past two years the energetic and wide-awake publishing house of F. J. Schulte & Co. of Chicago has eclipsed all other Western book-making firms in the number of works of fiction brought out and the general excellence which has characterized them. The novels published by this firm represent, as do the works of no other publishing house, the new literary movement in the West; a movement which is characteristic of the native soil and the temper of our times. They are realistic rather than idealistic, but in all instances clean and wholesome; and what is more, they are strongly reformative in their impulses. What the Lovells are doing for the fiction side of the new metaphysical movement which of late years has made such astonishing strides in the Western world, Schulte is doing for the great social and economic revolution which marks the present hour, and which in so many respects resembles the time immediately preceding the French Revolution, when the philosophers and pamphleteers flooded Paris with altruistic and socialistic literature, and when the common people were all reading and thinking, while the aristocracy were haughtily dancing and dissipating on wealth *acquired* rather than *earned*. Doubtless the most successful and widely read of the Schulte novels was "Cæsar's Column," by Ignatius Donnelly. This was one of the first books published by this firm, and scored an immense sale. I understand more than one hundred and fifty thousand copies have been sold, and the sale continues. In it Mr. Donnelly has pictured in a wonderfully truthful and realistic way the rapidly augmenting power of plutocracy, and has shown the legitimate results which are to follow, if there is no change, in a startling and dramatic manner. Another valuable work bearing upon social conditions which bears the imprint of this house is Mr. C. C. Post's "Driven from Sea to Sea," a thrilling romance of corporate crimes; a story which deals in a startling manner with a gigantic wrong suffered by the millions through the craft of unscrupulous promoters of monopolistic railways and the venality of lawmakers. Seldom if ever has the crime of organized power against the helpless industrial classes been advanced with such strength as in this story, which in my judgment is in many respects one of the strongest novels of modern times. It literally glows with vital thought. It should bring the blush of shame to the brow of every true American, and hasten the day when justice shall sit on the throne of power.

Scarcely less noteworthy is Robert H. Cowdrey's "A Tramp in Society," the great individualistic novel of our period of social unrest.

---

* "Cæsar's Column." By Ignatius Donnelly. "Driven from Sea to Sea." By C. C. Post. "Better Days." By Thomas and Anne Fitch. "A Tramp in Society." By Robert Cowdrey. "A Member of the Third House." By Hamlin Garland. "An Honest Lawyer." By A. M. Kerr. "The Price of the Ring." By Margaret Holmes. "A Man and a Woman." By Stanley Waterloo. Each volume cloth, except "The Price of the Ring," price, $1.25; "The Price of the Ring" is published only in paper. Published by F. J. Schulte & Co., 298 Dearborn Street, Chicago, Ill.

Few men understand the art of setting forth the injustice and the wrongs which are slowly but surely undermining our social fabric as does the gifted author of this story, which, considered apart from its reformative value, possesses as a story strong interest.

"Better Days; or, a Millionnaire of To-morrow," by Thomas and Anne Fitch, is another novel dealing with live social and economic problems such as are engrossing the public mind at the present time. It is a thoughtful presentation of social problems from a different point of view from Mr. Cowdrey's. Here again fiction, which is the most popular vehicle of the day for the teacher and reformer, is employed; and in this case, as with Messrs. Post and Cowdrey, the story has sufficient texture to be interesting from cover to cover. In "Better Days" one finds many helpful hints which will prove valuable in this moulding season of industrial and economic unrest.

Along a different line, but none the less reformative in its motive, is Hamlin Garland's "Member of the Third House," which is the most powerful unmasking of the intrigues and the corrupt practices of corporate power in our great eastern commonwealths which has ever been presented. This book John Wanamaker refused to sell over his counter. I cannot imagine the real reason which prompted this prohibition, as Mr. Garland did not have in mind the Keystone Bank or the corruption which has marked the city government of Philadelphia during recent years when he told his thrilling story. However, the work is one which all practical politicians who subscribe large funds to be disbursed during the closing hours of political campaigns would look upon with apprehension. "A Member of the Third House" is a powerful dramatic story which teaches a great truth. It is an alarm bell, rung late, it is true, but not yet too late to save the building.

Mr. Opie Read's works are also brought out by this firm; but as they were noticed by Mr. Garland in this department last month, I will not dwell upon them.

"An Honest Lawyer" is another noble novel recently issued by Mr. Schulte. It does not deal with economic conditions as much as types of our time. In it Mr. A. M. Kerr, the author, gives us a strong story closely knit. His picture of Silas Cornforth is vivid and true to life. Here we have a type of a numerous class, — the shrewd, avaricious, and ambitious man of the world. He is always careful not to go beyond the letter of the law, and is merciless toward those who do i. they chance to stand in his way. But he robs and ruins on all sides — always legally, but none the less remorselessly. This counterfeit coin which passes for respectable manhood is current in all communities to-day, but in the new era the test of true metal will be more severe. The ethical gauge will be lifted, and the Silas Cornforth will be branded as criminal no less than less pretentious violators of moral laws. Allen Farr, the hero of this work, is a pure, lovable creation, — an inspiration; he shows what a true man can be even in this age. "An

Honest Lawyer " is a book which fathers and mothers should read aloud at their fireside during the long winter evenings.

" The Price of the Ring," by Margaret Holmes, is a powerful novel which deals with the sex problem. At the head of the title of this volume we have this line which gives the key to the story, "Should there be one code of morals for men and another for women?" This story deals with the crime of infidelity to the marriage vows. A faithless husband and an erring wife figure in its pages. It is a strong plea for social purity, and is a fit companion for Helen Gardener's latest novel, " Pray You, Sir, Whose Daughter ? "

One of the poorest works from a literary point of view issued by this firm is Lewis Vital Bogy's novel, " In Office," a book which was so true to life that it cost its author his position in one of the government departments at Washington. I do not for a moment doubt that this book is history rather than fiction. It is not, however, in any sense a strong work. Quite the reverse is "Stanley Waterloo's realistic novel," "A Man and a Woman," a volume of far more than ordinary power, strong, frank, and keenly analytical. This work entitles the author to be recognized as one of the few really strong writers of fiction of our time. It is a story, however, which at times suggests Zola, but is not so repulsive in its shadows, and is far more attractive in its brighter pages.

Space forbids the mention of other excellent works of fiction along modern and reformative lines which have recently come from the press of this enterprising young firm. All the above mentioned volumes, except " In Office " and " The Price of the Ring," are richly bound in cloth with gilt top, and sell for $1.25 per volume. They would make an admirable set for a Christmas present for one desiring to supply a friend with choice reading along vital economic and reformative lines.

B. O. FLOWER.

AN ERRING WOMAN'S LOVE.

Ella Wheeler Wilcox's new book of poems is by far her strongest and noblest work. It gives me great pleasure to review this work, which throbs, as does no volume of poetry which has come to my notice in recent months, with the new life and vital thought which surcharges the moral atmosphere of the present. I quite shocked a staid, conventional friend a short time since by observing that, in my judgment, Ella Wheeler Wilcox was the prophet poetess of the dawning day. My friend observed that she had a very different opinion of the lady in question; a writer of sentimental and erotic verses, some of which she regarded quite questionable. " True," I replied, " our author is bold, frank, and unconventional, but her lines fairly glow with the noblest thought, a lofty morality pervades them; she writes to make the world better, and she is doing a noble work." In the volume before me Mrs. Wilcox

---

* " An Erring Woman's Love." By Ella Wheeler Wilcox. Cloth, pp. 157. Price. $2.50 and $1. Published by Lovell, Coryell & Co., New York.

appears at her best. No one can read this work without being made purer, gentler, and more considerate for others, or without having caught an inspiration which impels him upward. A lofty faith devoid of all bigotry; an unfaltering trust, which rests on conviction of eternal justice underlying creation; a sublime hope, which is neither circumscribed nor creed-bound, pervade the pages. The author enters fully into the new conception of life which is rapidly overcoming the old religious ideas as the rising sun overcomes the night. She has grasped the new ideal of God and man, life and duty, and this gives to her poems a vitality and worth which are entirely absent from the pages of those who write for the ease-loving, *dilettante* who clings to the old-time standard of "art for art's sake." The principal poem gives to this volume its title, "An Erring Woman's Love." It is a powerful sermon. It depicts a woman who has sinned for gold; who, rather than toil in rags, seeks ease through sin. Of this woman and her fatal choice our author, in her opening lines, observes:—

> Who looks beneath life's outer crust
> Is satisfied that God is just;
> Who looks not under, but about,
> Finds much to make him sad with doubt.
> For Virtue walks with feet worn bare,
> While Sin rides by with coach and pair:
> Men praise the modest heart and chaste,
> And yet they let it go to waste,
> And follow, fierce to have and hold,
> Some creature, wanton, selfish, bold.
>
> She saw but this, life's outer side,
> No higher faith was hers to guide;
> She worshipped gold and hated toil;
> And hence her youth with all its soil,
> With all its sins too dark to name,
> Of secret crimes and public shame,
> With all its trail of broken lives,
> Of ruined homes, neglected wives,
> And weeping mothers. Proud and gay
> She went her devastating way
> With untouched brow and fadeless grace.

At length into her life comes a man who fires in her soul for the first time the deep passion of a deathless love. He left her, but not until he had awakened in her heart that which until now had slumbered,— her real self. Then, leaping from the dungeon to which it had been driven, springs accusing Conscience. The past is unfolded.

> Accusing memories rose. She felt
> A loneliness that seemed to belt
> The universe in its embrace.
> It was as if from some high place
> A giant hand had reached and hurled
> To nothingness her petty world,
> And left her staring, awed, alone,
> Up into regions vast, unknown.

> There is no other loneliness
> That can so sadden and oppress,
> As when beside the burned-out fire
> Of sated passion and desire
> The wakening spirit, in a glance,
> Beholds its lost inheritance.

At length she falls upon her knees in an abandon of wretchedness. To her lips so unused to prayer come timidly, —

> " Lord, let me be a child again
> And grow up good." The strange prayer said,
> Like some o'er-weary child, her head
> She pillowed on her arm, and wept
> Low, shuddering sobs, until she slept
> And dreamed ; and in that dream she thought
> She sat within a vine-wreathed cot ;
> An infant slumbered on her breast ;
> She crooned a lullaby, and pressed
> Its waxen hand against her cheek ;
> While one too proud and fond to speak,
> The happy father of the child,
> Stood near, and gazing on them, smiled.

> She woke while still the lullaby
> Was on her lips — then such a cry,
> As souls in fabled realms below
> Might utter, voiced her awful woe.

> The mighty moral labor pain
> Of new-born conscience racked her brain
> And tore her soul. She understood
> The meaning now of womanhood
> And chastity, and o'er her came
> The full, dark sense of all her shame.

Vivid, and at times highly dramatic, are the lines which depict the hopelessness of the newly awakened soul as it pleads with the Infinite for the lost jewel of chastity. Then leaped forth a great truth, which is one of the most pertinent questions of the new day, and indicates that the hour is at hand when the vicious double standard must be abolished, when womanhood will demand a " white life for two." In these lines Mrs. Wilcox simply raised again the question which Helen Gardener puts with such terrible power in her great novel, " Is This Your Son, My Lord ? "

> Why, men have trod the burning track
> Of sin for years, and then gone back !
> And cannot I for sin atone,
> Or did Christ die for men alone?
> When God formed worlds, He failed to make
> A path for erring feet to take
> Back into light and peace again,
> Unless they were the feet of men.
> When woman errs, and then regrets,
> Her sun of hope forever sets.

The awful loneliness which comes to a heart which, through awakened

consciousness of a higher life, is stung with remorse, and yet who finds
in society so little of the divine spirit of altruism, especially in its
attitude toward erring woman, is hinted at in these lines, when the
subject of the poem prepares for self-destruction: —

> She seemed to stand upon a brink ;
> Behind her loomed the sinful past,
> Below her rocks, beyond her vast
> And awful darkness. Not one ray
> Of sun or star to show the way !
> She drew a long and shuddering breath.
> "There is no other path but death
> For me to tread," she sighed, " and so
> I will prepare my house and go."

Part second of this poem lifts the veil and gives us a glimpse of the
poet's conception of the beyond, a conception far more probable and
rational than that which came to the Calvinistic-moulded mind of
Milton. The soul of the dead is represented as awaking, but under the
delusion that the potion has failed and that she still dwells in the
mortal body. She, however, is enlightened by a voice by her side.
Looking up —

> She saw a weird and shadowy crowd
> With anguished lips, and shoulders bowed,

While a voice answered —

> With yonder shuddering, woeful throng
> Of suicides thy ways belong.
> Close to the earth a shadowy band,
> Unseen but seeing all, they stand
> Until their natural time to die,
> As God intended, shall draw nigh.
> On earth repentant, sick of sin,
> A ministering angel thou hadst been,
> Whose patient toil and deeds divine
> Had rescued souls as sad as thine.
> Each deed a firm ascending stair
> To lead beyond thy great despair.
> But now it is thy mournful fate
> To linger here and meditate.
>   When God shall send
> A second death to be thy friend,
> Thou need'st not fear a darker fate —
> Go forth with yonder throng and wait.

While this is the longest poem in the work, there are many others of
beauty and strength. The following, entitled "Two Women," is a
sermon in song, and reveals the author's strong love nature. In spirit
how like the action of Jesus with the woman taken in sin is this poem : —

> I know two women, and one is chaste
> And cold as the snows on a winter waste,
> Stainless ever in act and thought.
> (As a man, born dumb, in speech errs not.)
> But she has malice toward her kind,
> A cruel tongue and a jealous mind.

Void of pity and full of greed,
  She judges the world by her narrow creed
A brewer of quarrels, a breeder of hate,
  Yet she holds the key to " Society's " Gate.

The other woman, with heart of flame,
  Went mad for a love that marred her name ;
And out of the grave of her murdered faith
She rose like a soul that has passed through death.
Her aims are noble, her pity so broad,
It covers the world like the mercy of God.
A soother of discord, a healer of woes,
Peace follows her footsteps wherever she goes.
The worthier life of the two, no doubt,
And yet " **Society** " **locks her out.**

Here is another waif which contains the spirit of the **new day**: —

  Thoughts do not need the wings of words
    To fly to any goal.
  Like subtle lightnings, not like **birds,**
    They speed from soul to soul.

  Hide in your heart a bitter thought,
    Still it has power to blight.
  Think Love, although you speak it not,
    It gives the world **more light.**

A poem entitled " The Eternal Will " contains many noble thoughts.
I have space, however, for only one stanza: —

  There is no thing we cannot **overcome.**
    Say not thy evil instinct is inherited,
  Or that some trait inborn makes thy whole **life forlorn,**
    And calls down punishment that is not merited.
  Back of thy parents and grand-parents **lies**
    The Great Eternal Will. That, too, **is thine**
  Inheritance ; strong, beautiful, divine,
    Sure lever of success for one who tries.

I close this notice with a characteristic poem, illustrating far better
than any description the deep faith which characterizes those whose
brows are bathed in the light of the religion of the morrow; they who
have cast aside the shackles of creed and dogma, but who hold to all
that is vital, uplifting, or divine in pure religion.

  Luck is the tuning of our inmost thought
    To chord with God's great plan. That done, ah, know,
    Thy silent wishes to results shall grow,
  And day by day shall miracles be wrought.
  Once let thy being selflessly be brought
    To chime with universal good, and lo!
    What music from the spheres shall through thee flow !
  What benefits shall come to thee unsought!
  Shut out the noise of traffic! Rise above
    The body's clamor! With the soul's fine ear
    Attune thyself to harmonies divine.
  All, all are written in the key of Love ;
    Keep to the score, and thou hast naught to **fear,**
    Achievements yet undreamed of shall be thine.

"An Erring Woman's Love" is richly bound in colored cloth, stamped in gold and silver, with gilt edges. It is handsomely illustrated with numerous full-page illustrations printed on heavy plate paper. It is a superb gift volume. A cheaper edition, printed on smaller pages, bound plain and without illustrations, is also issued.

PSYCHOLOGY APPLIED TO THE ART OF TEACHING.*

"Psychology Applied to the Art of Teaching," by Professor Joseph Baldwin of the University of Texas, is one of the best short works on this absorbing theme now before the public. It belongs to Appleton's popular International Educational Series. All persons interested in psychology, psychical research, and kindred subjects should read this work. Few men possess, in as eminent degree as Professor Baldwin, the rare power of presenting his theme in a clear and concise manner. With a few sentences he brings before the reader's mind his thoughts in such a manner as to be retained. The idea seems to be so presented as to photograph itself upon the mind. The volume is divided in six parts, discussing the following branches of the subject: Education of the perceptive powers, education of the representative powers, education of the thought powers, education of the emotions, education of the will powers, and the art of teaching. I can cordially recommend this work, not only to teachers, although of course it is written especially for them, but to all persons interested in psychology.   B. O. FLOWER.

SUGGESTION.†

The attention of the reading world is now turned to psychological and psychical realms. Even science is beginning to appreciate the fact that patient study may result in far more than mere speculation. It is not strange that this general interest should be improved by novelists. Unfortunately, few persons capable of writing in an entertaining manner are sufficiently acquainted with the subject to write in an authoritative or scientific way, and, this being the case, readers are frequently led into misapprehension and exaggerated ideas which are unwarranted by the facts. This is always to be deplored; and from the information I have received from practical demonstrators in hypnotism, as well as my own investigations in this department of research, I am led to believe that Mabel Collins has fallen into this common error in her latest novel, "Suggestion." It is true a strong, magnetic person, who has never dissipated his powers by intemperance or excesses, might gain a powerful mesmeric control over even so bright and positive a lady as her heroine; but that a youth who had spent years in riotous living, who was wont to spend his nights in revels, and who had squandered a fortune in

---

* "Psychology Applied to the Art of Teaching." By Joseph Baldwin, A. M., LL. D. Cloth, pp. 381. D. Appleton & Co., New York.

† "Suggestion," a novel by Mabel Collins. Cloth, price $1.25. Published by Lovell, Gestefeld & Co., New York.

excesses and debauchery, could hold a strong, clean-souled, positive woman in the toils of his will, and compel her to do his bidding in defiance of her wishes, is improbable, if it is not absolutely impossible. This story reminds one of some of Mrs. Henry Woods' or Miss Braddon's novels, only the author is working in a new field. I cannot feel that the novel is worth the buying or the reading, unless a person desires simply to be absorbed in a story regardless of literary value or scientific accuracy. The book is handsomely printed and beautifully bound.

WHO PAYS YOUR TAXES?*

There is no greater misapprehension in economics than the idea that taxes are paid by persons upon whom they are directly assessed. It is this mistaken idea which works confusion in the farmer's mind and causes him to advocate a tax upon money and mortgages and other personal property. It is his belief that by more stringent laws of assessment, more inquisitorial codes of search, he can make the wealthy men of the cities pay their proper proportion of tax. Upon this basis, also, the workman computes his own escape from tax by advocating the rigid assessment of the great city store and warehouse.

If we were to suppose that the taxes upon personal property were properly assessed, that each merchant and manufacturer actually paid taxes on a true valuation of his goods, such as the law requires, the operation of the inexorable law of *incidence* would make it just that much harder for the mechanic, the small trader, and the farmer. The great business man would simply *shift just that much more to the consumer.*

Broadly, the matter may be stated thus: Every tax which makes trade and production difficult is added to the *expense* of production and trade, and is paid in the end by the consumer, and consequently by the many for the benefit of the few.

The farmer, by attempting to take the trade and manufacture of the city, finds himself paying the taxes in the extra cost of the cloth, machinery, and other articles he buys, or in the continued high cost when prices should fall with increase of production. This last consideration is most important. As production increases in effectiveness, prices of manufactured articles should fall in proportion, and wages should rise. It is the power of monopoly which comes in to prevent both of these desired results. It may be stated thus: Monopoly to-day pays the minimum of tax, while production and labor (by loss of wages) pays the maximum of tax, while the tax levied upon production and trade falls finally upon the consumer. All taxes being paid out of possible savings, it follows that the man who consumes the major part of his income in living pays the maximum of tax.

In other words, all taxes levied upon trade and production are shifted

*"Who Pays Your Taxes?" A consideration of taxation by David A. Wells, George H. Andrews, Thomas G. Shearman, etc. G. P. Putnam, New York.

from shoulder to shoulder till they rest at last on the man least able to bear them, who has no special privilege and who cannot shift his taxes by arbitrarily increasing the price of the product of his hands; that is, the farmer and the laborer.

All indirect taxation has this effect, and that is the central lesson of the little book edited by Butler Hall and published by Putnam of New York. The farmers should read the chapter by Thomas G. Shearman on the taxing of personal property as set forth in a study of facts in Ohio. It is complete in its showing of the failure of the present system, which lets the city off with the minimum of actual tax (so far as monopolies are concerned) and fosters a system of indirect taxation which is directly burdensome to the workingman and the farmer.

The system advocated is the exemption of personal property and improvements and the substitution of a direct tax upon all privileges in land. The more money we have, the cheaper interest will be ; the more houses we have, the cheaper rents will be ; the more unrestricted trade and production, the lower will be the cost of articles produced, and this without lowering wages ; for with the exemption of personal property and improvements from burdens, production will be enormously increased and demand for labor will give the laborer the power to demand higher wages instead of submitting to less ; and privilege, monopoly, will pay its taxes.

I wish this little book could be read by the farmers and the workers everywhere. It is full of just the sort of information needed to clear up false ideas about "Who Pays Your Taxes?"   HAMLIN GARLAND.

A TRUE SON OF LIBERTY.*

A story of the civil war written from a non-partisan point of view, by F. P. Williams. This story is not remarkable as a story. The author desires to show how easy it is for a sincere and honest lover of free thought and speech, a true lover of humanity, whose opinions run counter to the popular thought of the hour, especially when men's passions are aroused, to find himself ostracized by what is termed the "best element." In this story the hero, a minister, who is regarded in war times as a rebel, is tarred, feathered, and so brutally injured as to cause death on account of his opinions. His persecution reminds us of several similar but more atrocious outrages which have been perpetrated by the present administration; as, for example, the arrest and criminal prosecution, through the Postal Department, of Rev. J. B. Caldwell for publishing a plea for social purity, after he had criticised the Postal Department. The chief value of "A True Son of Liberty" lies in the fact that it will make men think and also take broader views of life. It will make men more tolerant, though by many it will be considered a very unpatriotic story.

---

*"A True Son of Liberty." By F. P. Williams. Cloth, pp. 190. Published for the author by E. Scott, 134 West 239th Street, New York.

A CLOSE SHAVE.*

Lovers of literature of the character of Jules Verne's "Around the World in Eighty Days" will enjoy Thomas W. Knox's story entitled "A Close Shave." It is a story of a voyage around the world in seventy days. In the preface the author observes:—

The object of the following is to show the possibility of making a journey around the world in seventy days from the time of starting, and to present the various aids to travel and communication which have appeared since Jules Verne published his famous volume entitled "Around the World in Eighty Days." Various scientific discoveries and inventions are thus brought to the reader's attention in their adaptation to the needs of the heroes of "A Close Shave." The geographical descriptions, routes, time-tables, monsoons, etc., may be relied upon as correct, and also the practices of pirates, boatmen, and other people encountered by the travellers in their adventurous journey.

The story is written, I should judge, for boys, and it abounds in adventures more or less probable. It is not a healthy work, as it is calculated to excite the roving spirit in youths; while the description of how the heroes slew the Chinese and Malay pirates is entirely out of keeping with the best thought of the hour. Then there is the presence of the melodramatic and mock-heroic which one expects in such works as "Around the World in Eighty Days" and "Mr. Barnes of New York," which, however strongly they appeal to immature tastes, nauseate a lover of literature. Like the conventional melodrama, the heroes are constantly facing death, but always escaping. The end, of course, is satisfactory to those in sympathy with the hero.

BOOKS RECEIVED.

"THE NEXT STEP FORWARD; OR, BETTER TIMES FOR US ALL," by Augustus Jacobson. Paper, pp. 76; price, 15 cents. Published by F. J. Schulte & Co., Chicago, Ill.

"BORN OF FLAME," by Margaret B. Peeke. Cloth, pp. 289. Published by J. B. Lippincott Co., Philadelphia, Penn.

"JACK'S FATHER," by W. E. Norris. Paper, pp. 180. Published by Lovell, Coryell & Co., New York.

"THE SOUL OF LILITH," by Marie Corelli. Paper, pp. 356; price, 50 cents. Published by Lovell, Coryell & Co.

"SQUIRE KATE; OR, COME, LIVE WITH ME, AND BE MY LOVE," by Robert Buchanan. Paper, pp. 323. Published by Lovell, Coryell & Co.

"ORIGIN, PURPOSE, AND DESTINY OF MAN," by William Thornton. Cloth, pp. 100. Published by the author.

"VANITAS," by Vernon Lee. Cloth, pp. 276. Published by Lovell, Coryell & Co., New York.

"SILVER THREADS OF THOUGHTS THAT LIVE," by Stella. Card-board covers, pp. 24; price, 35 cents. For sale 4353 Calumet Ave., Chicago.

---

* "A Close Shave." By Thomas W. Knox. Cloth, pp. 323. Published by the Price McGill Company, St. Paul, Minn.

"THE NEW RECTOR," by Stanley J. Weyman. Cloth, pp. 338; price, $1.25. Published by Lovell, Gestefeld & Co., New York.

"MORIAL THE MAHATMA; OR, THE BLACK MASTER OF TIBET," by Mabel Collins. Cloth, pp. 270; price, $1.25. Published by Lovell, Gestefeld & Co., New York.

"MARGERY OF QUETHER," by S. Baring-Gould. Cloth, pp. 286; price, $1.25. Published by Lovell, Gestefeld & Co., New York.

"TALES FROM TOWN TOPICS." Paper, pp. 223. Published by Town Topics Publishing Co., 21 West Twenty-third Street, New York.

"DORA DARLING," by Jane G. Austin. Paper, pp. 370; price, 50 cents. Published by Lee & Shepard, Boston.

"ARMY TALES," by John Strange Winter. Cloth, pp.   ; price, $1. Published by Lovell, Coryell & Co., New York.

"THE MAKING OF A MAN," by Rev. J. W. Lee, D. D. Cloth, pp. 372. Published by Cassell Publishing Co., New York.

"SUGGESTION," by Mabel Collins. Cloth, pp. 276; price, $1.25. Published by Lovell, Gestefeld & Co., 125 East Twenty-third Street, New York.

"AN ERRING WOMAN'S LOVE," by Ella Wheeler Wilcox. Cloth, pp. 157; price, $2.50. Published by Lovell, Coryell & Co., New York.

"A CLOSE SHAVE," by Thomas W. Knox. Cloth, pp. 323. Published by The Price-McGill Co., St. Paul, Minn.

"THE AMERICAN PEASANT," by T. H. Tibbles. Paper, pp. 145; price, 25 cents. Published by F. J. Schulte & Co., Chicago, Ill.

"THE SONG OF AMERICA AND COLUMBUS," by Kinahan Cornwallis. Cloth, pp. 278. Published at the office of the *Daily Investigator*, 66 Broadway, New York.

"THE OTHER HOUSE," by Kate Jordan. Cloth, pp. 183; price, $1.25. Published by Lovell, Coryell & Co., New York.

"L'EVANGELISTE," by Alphonse Daudet. Paper, pp. 304; price, 50 cents. Published by E. T. Neely, Chicago.

"MICHAEL AND THEODORA; A RUSSIAN STORY," by Amelia E. Barr. Cloth, pp. 168. Published by Bradley & Woodruff, Boston.

"THE PREACHER'S DAUGHTER; A DOMESTIC ROMANCE," by Amelia E. Barr. Cloth, pp. 298. Published by Bradley & Woodruff, Boston.

"OMOO; A NARRATIVE OF ADVENTURES IN THE SOUTH SEAS," by Herman Melville. Cloth, pp. 365; price, $1.50. Published by United States Book Co., New York.

"TYPEE; A REAL ROMANCE OF THE SOUTH SEAS." Cloth, pp. 389; price, $1.50. Published by United States Book Co., New York.

"THE INTERPRETER'S HOUSE," by B. Paul Neuman. Cloth, pp. 207. Published by T. Fisher Unwin, Paternoster Square, London.

NOTES AND ANNOUNCEMENTS.

Some Contributors during the Past Year.

THE following are a few of the eminent names which have appeared as contributors to THE ARENA during the past year: Camille Flammarion, Hon. David A. Wells, Rev. M. J. Savage, Edgar Fawcett, Rev. C. A. Bartol, Mary A. Livermore, Helen Campbell, Prof. T. Funck-Brentano of Paris, Dr. George Stuart, D. C. L., Hamlin Garland, Louise Chandler Moulton, Henry Wood, Dr. Richard Hodgson, LL. D., Prof. A. N. Jannaris of Athens, Greece, Hon. Walter Clark, LL. D., of the Supreme Court of North Carolina, Gen. J. B. Weaver of Iowa, Prof. Jos. Rodes Buchanan, M. D., W. D. McCrackan, A. M., Rabbi Solomon Schindler, Ella Wheeler Wilcox, May Wright Sewall, Emil Blum, Ph. D., Frances E. Willard, Sara A. Underwood, James A. Herne, Ibn Ishak, Prof. Willis Boughton of the Ohio State University, Mrs. Annie Jenness Miller, Frances M. Steele, Gail Hamilton, Rev. Thomas P. Hughes, D. D., Lady Harberton, Congressmen G. F. Williams, W. T. Ellis, Thomas E. Watson, Marriott Brosius, J. C. Burrows and William M. Springer, M. French-Sheldon, Prof. A. E. Dolbear of Tufts College, B. F. Underwood, Helen H. Gardener, Mrs. Gen. Lew Wallace, Will Allen Dromgoole, James H. Kyle, Joaquin Miller, and Prof. James T. Bixby, Ph. D. The above partial list of contributors for the past twelve months indicates how catholic in the range of thought is this magazine, and how thoroughly the truly progressive and reformative spirit of the age finds expression in the pages of THE ARENA. It has been our aim to make THE ARENA a busy man's library, essential to every earnest and progressive person. THE ARENA for 1893 will be even more brilliant than THE ARENA of the past.

The Bacon-Shakespeare Controversy.

In the December ARENA Rev. Dr. A. Nicholson, St. Albans, Warwickshire, Eng., will enter THE ARENA in defence of Shakespeare's claims. He will make a remarkably strong argument. Among the eminent thinkers who will be heard in this celebrated case either as attorneys, jurors, or specialists rendering opinions, are the following: The Marquis of Lorne, Edmund Gosse, Professor Donaldson, principal of St. Andrews University, Scotland, ex-President Rutherford B. Hayes, Gov. William E. Russell of Massachusetts, E. C. Stedman, Appleton Morgan, president of the New York Shakespeare Society, Col. Robert G. Ingersoll, Hon. Ignatius Donnelly, Prof. N. S. Shaler of Harvard, Prof. A. E. Dolbear of Tufts, Henry Irving, Joseph Jefferson, Luther R. Marsh, Mary A. Livermore, Henry W. Hilliard, Lewis O. Brastow, Dr. C. A. Bartol, Rev. M. J. Savage, George M. Towle, Gen. Marcus J. Wright, A. R. MacDonough, William E. Sheldon, Francis E. Abbott, Thomas G. Shearman, Henry George, Franklin H. Head, Hon. A. A. Adee, Mrs. Henry Pott, and Frances E. Willard.

Women Wage-Earners.

The first paper of Helen Campbell's notable series of papers on Women Wage-earners, their Past, Present, and Future, will be a feature of the December ARENA. No social reformer or person interested in the advancement of woman can afford to miss these remarkable papers.

Alfred Russel Wallace on Socialism.

Alfred Russel Wallace will contribute a notable paper to an early issue of THE ARENA on "The Next Step in Social Progress," giving his views as to the necessary remedy for the social inequalities of modern civilization. This paper will be one of a series on social wrongs and remedies.

Napoleon Ney on Occultism in Paris.

Among the notable papers which will appear in the December or January ARENA, will be an essay written by Napoleon Ney, the grandson of the great

Marshal of France. M. Ney discusses occultism in Paris in a manner which will be exceedingly interesting to our readers.

Suicides and our Civilization.

A careful and scholarly writer is now preparing for THE ARENA a paper on "Suicides and Civilization." It will contain statistics reaching back for a number of years, and comparative tables illustrating the ratio of suicides in various great American cities. Next it will discuss the leading causes and the remedies. It will be one of the most valuable papers of our series of present day problems, which will render THE ARENA for 1893 indispensable to thoughtful and wide-awake people.

Stories by Will Allen Dromgoole.

Among the many Southern writers who, during recent years, have acquired fame by their admirable work in character sketches and short stories, no one has risen more rapidly than Miss Will Allen Dromgoole. Many of her short stories, as, for example, "The Heart of Old Hickory," display a rare power of presenting human nature in fiction as only a genius can picture it. Some of her character sketches, as, for instance, "Fiddling his Way to Fame," are also superb. This month we give a strong story by this gifted young Southerner, and during 1893 THE ARENA will present the cream of her work in the line of short stories and character sketches.

Mr. Savage's Important Contribution to Psychical Science.

I desire to call special attention to the admirable paper of Mr. Savage in this issue of THE ARENA, because it is one of the most important papers of recent months on a subject which is rapidly growing in interest and importance. The preceding papers of Mr. Savage's series have been interesting and valuable as presenting many carefully verified psychical cases of a remarkable nature. In this paper the author makes many interesting and logical deductions. The real significance of these important problems will not be appreciated until men have grown great enough to rise above the arrogance of materialistic thought, which is a reaction from the all but universal credulity of the past and the shortsightedness of ecclesiasticism, which have hitherto so often opposed all honest investigation, owing to the fear that the establishment of new truths relating to the psychic realm would compel a revision of old-time creeds and dogmas.

The Poet of the Sierras.

In this issue we publish as a frontispiece a recent portrait of the unique figure in our literature, Joaquin Miller. This picture, which is as unconventional as is the poet himself, was taken for us and represents Mr. Miller on his own premises preparing for a little morning exercise. The poem, "Dawn in San Diego," which appears under his real name, "Heine," contains many lines of great beauty.

A Long Look Forward.

Mr. Will N. Harben, another Southern writer who has won an enviable place among the rising young authors of the New South, contributes an interesting conceit to this number of THE ARENA entitled "In the Year Ten Thousand." Mr. Harben's story "Almost Persuaded" has enjoyed a wide circulation, and, as I have before observed, must have accomplished much good, as it is one of the noblest sermons I have ever read. The Arena Publishing Company will at an early date publish a new story by Mr. Harben, which is by far his best and most finished work. It is entitled "A Romance of a Southern Town."

A Story for Our Times.

A really noble story, giving a woman's view of the broader life of woman, has just appeared from the press of Lovell, Gestefeld & Co. It is entitled "The Woman Who Dares," and is written by Ursula N. Gestefeld. It is a magnificent presentation of what expanding womanhood demands. I shall shortly review it at length. The price is $1.25, published only in cloth.

The Coal Trust and the Poor.

Notwithstanding the spasmodic protest of the press and the dismay of the public, the nineteenth century free-booters who live in palaces and bleed the nation that they may lavish millions on mistresses, race horses, banquets, summer villas, and yachts, continue to form great trusts which widen the gulf between the poor and the rich and prepare the field for revolution. I notice that the great coal trust has succeeded thus early in the season in raising the price of coal to six dollars a ton, which when retailed out by the basket, as it is to the very poor, doubtless means eight or nine dollars a ton; and these very poor are already on starvation's brink. Is it any wonder that crime increases, or that the dead sea of want and despair is broadening with each succeeding month? Have a care, gentlemen; you are sowing to the wind!

"The Dream Child."

Florence Huntley, the well-known editorial writer and newspaper correspondent, has written a most remarkable occult romance entitled "The Dream Child." It is the strongest and clearest presentation of Theosophy as taught by the best thinkers of India which we have ever read, and it is presented in the form of a most charming romance. All persons at the present time should be acquainted with the *leading or central thought* of Buddhism, whether or not they agree with this elaborate metaphysical philosophy. This story gives the higher aspects of the ancient religion in a most fascinating manner. "The Dream Child" is a noble work. Its ethical teaching is very exalted; its atmosphere very pure and inviting. The interest in the story is well sustained, and it will increase the spirit of tolerance, as well as enlarge the intellectual and moral vision of every reader. I hope to be able to review it at length in our next issue. The price in paper is 50 cents; cloth, $1. Published by The Arena Publishing Company.

Rev. Dr. Lyman Abbott.

Rev. Lyman Abbott will contribute a paper on a live theme to an early number of The Arena. He is one of our foremost ministers — a worthy successor to the Immortal Beecher.

Bacon or Shakespeare.

Among the eminent persons who have consented to serve as jurors in the Bacon-Shakespeare case since our last issue are the Marquis of Lorne, Edmund Gosse, Professor James Donaldson of St. Andrews University, Scotland, and Henry Irving. This case grows in interest, and will prove one of the most interesting literary discussions of the year.

Bishop J. L. Spalding.

Bishop J. L. Spalding will be heard in the pages of The Arena in an early issue. He is one of the clearest thinkers and most earnest workers among the eminent prelates of the Catholic Church. Next to Bishop Ireland he probably better represents the American impulses in the Roman Church than any other bishop.

Dr. Hughes on Afghan Question.

No man in America to-day is so well able to write authoritatively upon the Afghan question as Rev. Thomas P. Hughes, who this month furnishes our readers with many most interesting facts which he alone is able to properly present. This paper will, I feel confident, be read with keen interest by our readers.

A Roman Prelate on Sunday Opening of the Fair.

Bishop John Lansing Spalding of Peoria will contribute a paper to an early issue of The Arena on "The Sunday Opening of the World's Fair."

For the Comfort of Those Who Fear Cholera.

A friend forwards the following clipping from the *Cleveland World*. Thinking that our readers might be sufficiently interested in it to try the suggested preventive in case they happened in cholera infected regions, we publish it in full :—

During the terrible epidemics of '66 and '67 I tested, most fully, the efficacy of Dr. Constantine Hering's preventive of cholera, which is simple enough, being the flowers of sulphur, worn constantly in the socks. To quote from the eminent gentleman : " Put half a teaspoonful of the flowers of sulphur into each sock every morning during the epidemic, for cholera will never cross a line of sulphurated hydrogen." And he further said: " Among the many thousands who followed this, my advice, not a case of cholera occurred." And of the many hundreds of my friends in St. Louis and Memphis, whom I persuaded to use sulphur, none were attacked by the dread disease, though it was raging fiercely.

It is not at all unpleasant used externally, and after a few days' use — four or five — the system becomes charged with sulphurated hydrogen, as will appear from the discoloration of silver carried in the pocket, which, being death to the cholera germ, renders an attack impossible. Again Asiatic cholera has reached this country and begun its deadly work. I most earnestly urge that all my readers will use sulphur as above directed. Its fumes are now relied on as a disinfectant; and taken into the system through the pores of the feet, one becomes a veritable walking battery.

The dead physician to whom I refer was a very learned and very practical man.

Industrial Unrest in the Old World.

The London *Daily Chronicle* of September 8th contained an editorial of a column in length noticing approvingly our paper on the " Menace of Plutocracy." In closing the article the writer observes :—

The editor of THE ARENA believes with but too solid reason that this is a critical stage in the history of the Republic, and unless prompt measures are taken to prevent injustice on the part of capital, and amicably and peacefully to adjust the grievances between wealth and labor, the next decade will be marked by great social disturbances and terrible loss of life. The lesson has its application on this side of the Atlantic also.

Esoteric Teaching in the World's Great Religions.

A feature of THE ARENA for 1893 will be a series of papers on Esoteric Teaching in the World's Great Religions, one of the most interesting and important series of metaphysical papers of recent times. They are prepared by a well-known and scholarly writer, and will be read with great interest and profit by our readers.

Books and Children.

Few parents consider how much influence books exert, or might exert, on the minds of their children. Good books of an interesting character are the best of all Christmas, New Year, or birth-day presents, especially for the young. They enrich the mind while affording lasting pleasure of the highest and purest kind. If parents would set aside for good books the money usually spent on comparatively useless presents during the holiday season, they would be conferring a real benefit upon their loved ones: a benefit which in many cases would carry a helpful reflex influence on many other lives. Is not this a question for your thoughtful consideration at this season of the year?

A Moral Victory.

A notable moral victory has been won by the women of New Orleans, led by Mrs. Elizabeth Lyle Saxon. The Council of the Crescent City had passed a most infamous ordinance at the instigation of a young doctor and others who hoped to be immensely benefited by this class legislation. The ordinance proposed to license prostitution and place the inmates of houses of ill fame under the surveillance of the doctor in question and his aids. In other words, the system which has had such a debasing effect on morals in Paris was proposed for New Orleans, and but for the brave action of Mrs. Saxon, Mrs. Katharine Nobles, and other high-minded ladies of the Crescent City the measure would have become a law. All honor to the noble women of the Crescent City!

An Interesting Economic Paper.

In this issue will be found an interesting paper by N. A. Dunning on " The Volume of Currency." It is a thoughtful paper for the times, dealing with a problem which we predict will occupy the attention of our lawmakers more than any other national issue during the next four years.

Gone from Earth.

The loved wife and helpful companion of one of our valued contributors, Mr. P. Cameron of Toronto, Canada, has recently passed from the scenes of life. In his hour of deep grief my heart goes out to the invalid husband and the motherless children with feeling of deepest sympathy, and with pleasure I give place to a little memorial poem written in memory of the spirit which has passed into the splendors of a more perfect day.

KATE CAMERON.

DIED IN TORONTO, CANADA, AUG. 9, A. D. 1892.

And hast thou left us for a better land?
Borne on the white wings of an angel band,
Entering the portals of the land of rest
Where all is calm and peace, forever blest.

Thy work was done, thy fight well won,
Earth's exile o'er; nor moon nor sun
Shall beam on thee again. This shore
With noisy waves shall bear thy feet no more.

Loved wife and mother, whisper in our ear
Some wonted word to drive away the tear;
Shed on us something of the glorious light.
We think of thee, thy image crowds our sight.

We feel thee near us, yet no sound we hear
Of angel wings; nor dost thou say, I'm here.
Speak, spirit, speak! we wait, and yet we fear
That Death forbids the word our hearts to cheer.

The Spirit Answers.

Yes, it is true the icy hand of Death
Has sealed forever all of mortal breath.
My tongue would gladly tell the joy I know,
My arms would twine where often twined below,

But for the veil. That shuts out mortal view.
You shall ascend to me — I cannot come to you.
Deep as the love on earth to you I bore,
'T was but a fragment broken from this shore.

Think not, though silent to a mortal's ear,
That I, a spirit, cease to give you cheer
Or guard your journey from the rising sun
Till evening star proclaims your labor done.

I'm ever near you, hear your every sigh;
My wings you see not, yet believe me nigh;
I'm only waiting till my Master wills
To speak the word that o'er my spirit thrills.

That word is, Go and touch the mortal hand
Of those you loved once in the far-off land;
Tell them I bid them to come here
And join thee, wife and mother, in this sphere.

Lady Somerset and Frances E. Willard in The Arena.

Among papers of special interest which will early appear in THE ARENA are contributions from the pens of Lady Henry Somerset and Miss Frances E. Willard. The former discusses "The Genius of the New Temperance Movement in England," while Miss Willard will write upon "The Modern Temperance Movement in America."

The West in Literature.

A paper of more than ordinary interest in this number of THE ARENA is the clear, strong, and thoughtful paper by Hamlin Garland on "The West in Literature." It will be read with special interest by young authors, but I imagine all our readers will enjoy it. Mr. Garland bids fair to lead the new school of veritists or impressionists now becoming a real power in literature. "The West in Literature" is the opening paper of a series of contributions of special value to lovers of American literature and art. The second paper of this series will appear from the pen of the gifted sculptor, Wm. Ordway Parker, entitled "An American School of Sculpture."

An Important Contribution to Educational Literature.

We desire to call special attention to the brilliant and scholarly paper of Professor J. R. Buchanan on "The New Education and its Practical Application." It is one of those noble productions which belong to the literature of progress, and which carry thoughts and suggestions which will be brought into general use at an early date. We shall shortly publish another paper, no less interesting, from the pen of Professor Buchanan, dealing chiefly with industrial education.

The December Arena.

Among the good things which will appear in the December ARENA will be a paper by Bishop J. L. Spalding of Peoria, Ill., on "The Opening of the World's Fair on Sunday"; a paper by T. V. Powderly on "Government Ownership of

Railways"; a paper by W. P. McLaughlin on "Evictions in Tenement House Districts of New York City during the Past Year," in which many startling facts will be given, all taken from the official records. This will be the first paper of a series on our present social conditions, which will run through THE ARENA for 1893, making it absolutely indispensable to all persons interested in the social problems of the day. "The Occult in Paris," by Napoleon Ney, the first paper of our second series of psychical papers. M. Ney is a grandson of the great Marshal of France, and has made a careful study of occultism in the French metropolis, and discusses in a most interesting manner the widespread interest in all matters of a metaphysical and occult character. Dr. A. Nicholson, one of England's greatest Shakespearean scholars, will present a powerful paper in defence of the Shakespearean authorship of the plays ascribed to William Shakespeare. This paper will be a very notable contribution. Many other papers of special interest will appear in this number, which opens the seventh volume of THE ARENA.

A Spoil of Office.

The *Review of Reviews* for October contains the following concise review of "A Spoil of Office":—

"A Spoil of Office" is Mr. Hamlin Garland's best novel thus far. It deals with the new types of manhood and womanhood, and the new issues of life and motive in the northern Mississippi Valley. The hero is an Iowa boy, whom through his school days and early struggles on the prairie farm we follow to the halls of Congress. We have strong sidelights thrown upon the agrarian movements of the West and upon the low standards and actual corruptions that taint our American political life.

Of this remarkable novel of Western life, the *New York World* of September 17 has this to say:—

It is a criticism of American life from several points of view; a piece of fiction drawn from actual occurrences; a novel based on historical events; a wholesome sample of realistic writing; that is to say, it deals with real people who are important factors in the sociological advancement of the United States, and not at all with the exclusive class that represents nothing but leisure, money, and morbidity.

The writer after giving almost a column review to the work closes it in the following language:—

The denouement of the story is something like that of Dickens' "Great Expectations." We do not see Talcott and Miss Wilbur married, but that event is satisfactorily indicated. Garland is a strong and refreshing writer, and it is to be hoped that he will not permit success to conventionalize him. His picture of Bradley Talcott as "a spoil of office" is one admonitory to the farmer-boys.

This book is proving immensely popular among thoughtful American readers who appreciate pictures of real life as they are found to-day.

The Rise of the Swiss Republic.

The New York *Herald* for Sunday, October 9, has an exceedingly appreciative review of Mr. McCrackan's "The Rise of the Swiss Republic," a work which the reviewer claims is as "Good as gold; a work that should be treasured by the thoughtful student; a book to take the place of honor on the book shelf; to be read once, twice, thrice, and afterwards used for the purpose of reference as often as need be." This work is having a splendid sale and should be found in the library of every thoughtful American, as it is the most complete, comprehensive, and authoritative history of Switzerland ever written, and being written by an American and a great lover of the republic, it has many points of excellence which would not be found were Mr. McCrackan a European.

FUND FOR THE DESERVING POOR.

Last month we published an earnest appeal to our readers who wished to aid struggling humanity in the slums of Boston to contribute such an amount as they might feel able for this purpose. Below we give a statement of receipts and disbursements since our September statement. We can only add that winter is upon us; coal and food are higher. The infamous coal trust is adding greatly to the miseries of the very poor, who have to freeze when they have little money, so that the many time millionnaires who have monopolized God's great storehouses of heat, may add to their already overflowing coffers. Winter is here and the poor are starving and freezing. Those among our readers who feel that they can lighten hearts now bowed with crushing care, and sweeten homes now made very bitter by failure to obtain work at living prices, can accomplish this by forwarding whatever they feel they can afford to the editor of THE ARENA. We have, during the past year and a half, raised over $2,000, the most of which has already been disbursed for the relief or aid of those who were destitute and deserving.

ANNUAL REPORT.

Total receipts to date		$2,117 44
Total disbursements as per itemized reports published in ARENA up to the October number, including September reports		1,760 60
Disbursements as per report given below	$160 35	
		1,920 95
Balance from which reports have not been returned		$196 49

REPORT OF RECEIPTS.

Total receipts acknowledged up to October	$2,004 19	
Acknowledged in October ARENA	110 25	
Received from a friend, Stockton, Cal.	1 00	
C. L. H., Boston	2 00	
	$2,117 44	

EXPENDITURE OF ARENA POOR FUND FROM JULY 12 TO SEPTEMBER 12, 1892.

For groceries for destitute families	$7 25
For medicine	3 00
For nourishing food for the sick	1 40
Clothing for children	1 95
Repairs on fifty-three pairs of old boots and shoes donated	21 55
Aid in getting a situation for a man	2 50
Aid in paying rent	6 00
Temperance work and relief	3 45
Expenses in connection with summer outing for 765 children and mother from one to ten days each	67 75
For poor man with large family in great need	8 00
For two families in want	17 50
For clothes and rent for a poor woman kept from a situation owing to shabby clothes	20 00
	$160 35

RECAPITULATION.

Total receipts	$2,117 44
Total disbursements	1,920 95
Balance	196 49

A large proportion of this balance of $196 will have been spent before this report goes to press, and probably all will be exhausted before this line meets the reader's eye.

Rev. Walter J. Swaffield of the Bethel Mission, which is situated in the heart of the slums of the North End, presents his statement of disbursements made under his personal supervision, as follows: —

SUMMER OUTINGS FOR THE POOR.

No one who has spent an hour in the "social cellar" of Boston, and looked upon the sufferings and privations of the people, and breathed the impure and suffocating atmosphere in which men, women, and children linger through the livelong year, can fail to realize the great need for these kindred in distress having at least once a year a breath of fresh air and a sight of green fields and trees and smiling flowers. The readers of THE ARENA have made it possible, at a very small sacrifice on their part, for over seven hundred and sixty women and children to enjoy from one to twenty days at the seaside or in the country. If the contributors could only see the looks of surprise, and listen to the wild cries of delight, or spend an hour or more with the merry romping children from the slums, or greet those who have been sent away wasted and sick as they return with bounding step and glad report of feeling " so much better," and hear the hearty and sincere, "thank you," "thank you," they would feel that they were well repaid for all they had done, and only wish they had done more in the name of Him who went about doing good. Would you look in upon a few of the homes from which the children have been taken? Here are a few, only typical, however, of the many.

We were called to see a poor family on Hanover Street, who were reported as in great distress; found a poor sick woman, with an infant two weeks old. The mother, though weak and suffering, was bending over the wash-tub. No food in the house except a crust saved from the last evening meal for the dinner of a girl who just then came in from school with the faint but bitter cry, " O mother, I'm so hungry!" The crust is brought forth and devoured by the child, while mother and infant continue their fast from the evening before. (The husband went to sea six months ago, and has not been heard of since.) The wants of these poor ones were relieved, and mother and children sent into the country for three weeks. The poor woman has regained her strength, and the children are doing well.

On the same street a little cripple girl who was a great care to her mother, whose only way of making a living was by sewing, was sent into the country for the whole summer, and the mother for a few days, making her feel, as she said, as though " she could work all the time now."

We enter a dark alley, off one of the main streets, and in a wretched place find a poor man sick with rheumatism; his wife with a most painful felon on her finger, thus preventing her from doing what little work she could get for the support of the family — a little boy, sick with cholera infantum; two girls, whose white pinched faces were a sight to behold — they were all in a most desperate condition. Plain and proper nourishment was provided, and the whole family taken for several days to the seaside. Even this brief respite from such awful condition has seemed to give them new courage and health.

Such cases could be multiplied, but these are only fair samples of many others. One more must suffice. We had secured a place in the country for a poor old widow with two children dependent upon her, but she, being a Catholic, was forbidden by the priest to send them; she stoutly refused to obey him, telling him to his face that it was all well enough for him to sit in his gilded mansion and feast upon all the luxuries of the season, and to dictate to her who had but a crust to eat, and forbid her to accept the kindness of "true Christianity." She went with the children, and was very much improved on her return to the city, the priest notwithstanding. In behalf of the poor, and those who otherwise would have no earthly helpers, I desire to thank the readers of THE ARENA for their aid in this work.

Our kindergarten for these poor children has opened, and already the number in attendance is greater than one teacher can manage. Could not the expense of providing another teacher be borne by some friend of oppressed childhood?   WALTER J. SWAFFIELD.

SOME RECENT PRESS CRITICISMS.

An unrivalled favorite. — *Daily Post, Houston, Tex.*

Appeals strongly to thoughtful readers. — *Boston School Journal.*

No student's library is fully equipped without this magazine. — *Sentinel-Democrat, Alton, Ill.*

For variety and crispness of contents and breadth of view THE ARENA is the superior of all its rivals. — *Daily Free Press, Ottawa, Can.*

THE ARENA is one of the most vigorous of the literary magazines. It deals in history, science, ethics, economics, politics, education, fiction, and anything else that has to do with the life that now is. — *Ind. School Journal, Indianapolis, Ind.*

It is second in no department of popular literature to any periodical of its class on either side of the water. The September number is before us, crammed from cover to cover of its volume with good things. — *Daily Transcript, Lexington, Ky.*

THE ARENA gives far more space than any other leading magazine to the discussion of social, economic, religious, and educational problems. Its contributors also represent the flower of advanced thinkers and live reformers. The marked ability of its contributors and its absolute fearlessness explain largely the secret of its thus early taking a place at the head of the advanced column of review literature. — *The Daily American, Nashville, Tenn.*

This now national magazine, in its fairly earned reputation and solid influence, enters on its eighth volume with an array of distinguished writers and valuable matter not exceeded in like character and amount by any other periodical publication in the country. — *Daily Journal, Philipsburg, Penn.*

THE ARENA does not hang upon the heels of change, but advances with the latest thought, not stopping to heed the wails of the Philistines and the reproaches of the passive and proud element that always wants to be let alone, and would be content to stagnate rather than lose its repose long enough to glance outside of Sybaritic circles. — *Evening Standard, Troy, N. Y.*

THE ARENA may be said to occupy a field all its own. It stands among reviews the one great exponent of progressive thought, the one review whose writers are the dreamers of the time, who are trying to pierce the future and solve some of the problems which are keeping the human race from its highest development. — *The Enterprise, Ludlow, Vt.*

This interesting magazine will delight its thousands of readers. Its September table of contents presents a rich and varied assortment. The articles are vigorous and progressive. In so many excellent and thoughtful papers it is hard to distinguish; but we must confess that for ourselves we always turn with especial delight to the sayings of the editor. While we are not at all times in full agreement with Mr. Flower, his views on modern society and on whatever subject his pen handles are masterly and pregnant with sound judgment and timely advice. The editorials of THE ARENA rank it among the very first of our popular monthlies. Our progressive women will find in the September ARENA a symposium on dress reform which will interest them. — *Pittsburgh Catholic, Pittsburgh, Penn.*

Within the past two or three years THE ARENA has gained a wonderful hold on the reading public because of the excellence of the matter each number presents and of the wide range of subjects treated, as well as the high character of the contributors to its pages. —*Journal, Montgomery, Ala.*

THE ARENA.has long since forged its way into the very forefront of the great liberal and progressive reviews. Now it enters the field of literary criticism in such a way as to command the attention of America and Europe. The Bacon-Shakspeare controversy will elicit the attention of more eminent critics than any other purely literary discussion of the year. — *Daily Item, Lynn, Mass.*

THE ARENA is a magazine that should be as thoroughly read by newspaper men as the *North American Review*. It always contains exceptionally good papers on social, political, and religious problems, and all the advanced questions of the day. Its contributors are among the greatest thinkers and philosophers of our time, and their writings are liberal and logical.— *Weekly Journalist, Boston, Mass.*

Its list of regular contributors includes the most brilliant men of letters in this country and in Europe. It is circumscribed by no lines, dealing with subjects in every department of investigation, particularly those referring to humanity in its moral and social states. Its columns represent the consummate flower and fruitage of the best thought of the most advanced thinkers of the age. No school is excluded from its pages. In them a clear field is afforded for honest, manly criticism, the direction such criticism shall take being a secondary consideration. The broad-minded men and women of America have in THE ARENA a monthly collation of the best thought of the period, and it must be a source of gratification to them as well as to the publishers of the journal itself to find so full an appreciation of its pages. — *Daily Light, San Antonio, Texas.*

THE ARENA is one of the foremost representatives of progressive opinion. The October number is full of interesting and masterly inquiries. —*Penny Press, Middletown, Conn.*

IT affords us great pleasure to be able to announce that we have perfected arrangements for 1893 which enable us to promise our readers a number of special attractions which will, we believe, make THE ARENA *absolutely indispensable to every thinking man and woman* of our day who is in touch with the real vital thought of the hour. At the present time we will merely hint at a few of the important features which we believe will make THE ARENA for 1893 the most brilliant year in its history, and render it indispensable to all earnest, thoughtful persons.

THE WORLD'S PROGRESS DURING A QUARTER OF A CENTURY.

A series of papers by foremost thinkers among scientists, inventors, *litterateurs*, artists, social, economic and political reformers, educators and authoritative thinkers in religious and ethical circles. They will point out the progress which has marked research and attainment during the past quarter of a century in the special fields in which they are specialists. It is believed that these papers will in themselves be worth far more than the subscription price of THE ARENA.

SOCIAL CONDITIONS OF TO-DAY.

A series of papers, giving facts and figures, which will illustrate most vividly social conditions in city and country as they are found by the practical philanthropist as well as the compiler of statistics. This series will open in the December ARENA, and will deal with the subject of evictions of the poor in New York City as revealed in the court records by actual personal investigation. These papers will be valuable to social reformers and all persons interested in the moral revolution which is daily gaining momentum.

THE OUTLOOK, OR PRESENT DAY TENDENCIES.

Supplementing the papers on the world's progress during the past quarter of a century and the description of social conditions of to-day, will be a series of most thoughtful contributions on "The Outlook for the Future" along the various vital paths of thought and endeavor, prepared by master brains and close students of events. This series of papers must appeal with irresistible force to the thoughtful, earnest thousands, and go far toward satisfying the soul-cravings of the awakened millions of the present hour. Among the early contributions will be a paper by the eminent English scientist and social reformer Alfred Russel Wallace, entitled "The Next Step."

WOMEN WAGE-EARNERS OF AMERICA AND EUROPE.

Among the social and economic problems of the first magnitude to be authoritatively discussed in THE ARENA during the coming year, we will mention a series of papers, in many respects the most notable which has ever appeared, on "Women Wage-Earners in America, England, and France," by Helen Campbell, the author of "Darkness and Daylight in New York," "Prisoners of Poverty at Home," "Prisoners of Poverty Abroad," etc., etc. It will be remembered that Mrs. Campbell won the prize awarded the American Economic Association in 1891 for the finest monograph on Women Wage-Earners. These papers will embody the result of Mrs. Campbell's research at that time, as well as much of vital interest acquired by recent investigation relating to the condition of women bread-winners in America, England, and France. This series is merely one of many similar strong attractions for all persons interested in vital social problems.

WOMEN IN THE ARENA.

During the past year almost fifty contributions which have appeared in THE ARENA have come from the pens of women, among whom were Mary A. Livermore, Frances E. Willard, Helen H. Gardener, Louise Chandler Moulton, Helen Campbell, May Wright Sewall, Ella Wheeler Wilcox, Will Allen Dromgoole, Mrs. M. French-Sheldon, Gail Hamilton, and many other foremost writers and thinkers among the splendid coterie of thoughtful women of the new world. As we have before observed, no other review has ever shown anything like the hospitality to woman and her work as THE ARENA. During the ensuing year we will give a series of papers touching upon various aspects of woman's work and achievements in America. One of these papers will appear in an early issue of The Arena, in which the subject of women inventors will be discussed; another will notice women in journalism; other papers along the same lines will appear in early issues, while leading writers among the thoughtful women of America will continue to occupy a large portion of this review. Subjects also intimately connected with woman's progress will continue to be a feature of The Arena.

The series of psychical papers **PSYCHICAL SCIENCE,** by leading scientific investiga- **DISCUSSED BY** tors which has created so much **MASTER BRAINS.** interest, will be continued during the ensuing year. The Arena was the first great review of the world to attempt anything like a comprehensive presentation of little understood facts relating to psychical phenomena of our time. These papers, prepared by many of the most eminent thinkers of the day, have attracted general notice, as would naturally be the case when such persons as Alfred Russel Wallace, Camille Flammarion, Rev. M. J. Savage, and W. H. H. Myers present facts, and seriously discuss evidence pertaining to a realm of thought which, until a few years since, was regarded beyond the pale of critical scientific research. Through The Arena many of our most careful thinkers have been led to investigate psychical problems, and from every section we have received many communications relating to these interesting papers, which indicate a far-reaching interest. Our papers for 1893, like those of the past, will be from the pens of persons recognized as careful, conservative, and competent scientific investigators.

The broadening of religious thought and the crumbling of **THE** ancient creeds give peculiar **RELIGIOUS PROBLEMS** interest to religious discus- **OF THE** sions by eminent thinkers of **DAY.** ripe scholarship and undoubted sincerity and earnestness. The Arena for 1893 will contain many papers of special interest on live theological subjects, by such writers as Prof. James T. Bixby, Rabbi Solomon Schindler, Dr. Lyman Abbott, Rev. M. J. Savage, Rev. John W. Chadwick, Bishop J. L. Spalding, Rev. O.

P. Gifford, Prof. David Swing, and many other equally distinguished and representative thinkers. These papers will all be timely, thoughtful, and of interest to earnest people, whether or not they agree with the author's views.

EDUCATIONAL PAPERS. More depends upon the educational development of the rising generation than aught else, if civilization is to move uninterruptedly onward. But this education must be far different from the schooling of the past. The moral natures of children must be developed. Physical culture and industrial education also must keep pace with mental drill. Papers elucidating these ideas will be important features of the seventh and eighth volumes of THE ARENA; while all live problems in economics, ethics, and politics will find a place in our pages.

As our civilization so sorely needs ethical culture and moral development, a feature for 1893 will be papers along this line, with practical hints and suggestions for individuals, families, and circles of friends. **SELF-CULTURE PAPERS.**

LITERARY FEATURES.

THE BACON-SHAKESPEARE CASE. Great interest is being evinced in America and England in the Bacon-Shakespeare controversy, owing doubtless to the fact that here for the first time will be marshalled the best thought of the new and the old world in a full, fair, and impartial presentation of all sides of this interesting question. Edwin Reed's strong, concise, and thought-stimulating brief will be assailed by Prof. W. J. Rolfe, of Cambridge, Mass., and the two great English Shakespearean scholars, Dr. F. J. Furnivall and Rev. Dr. A. Nicholson; while the closing arguments for plaintiff and defendant will be by two brilliant Americans, whose names are for the present withheld. The jury will embrace many of the most eminent personages of the age. Among those who have already consented to act are the Marquis of Lorne, Rutherford B. Hayes, ex-President of the United States, Gov. Wm. E. Russell, of Massachusetts, Joseph Jefferson, Edmund C. Stedman, Edmund Gosse, Prof. N. S. Shaler, of Harvard, Prof. James Donaldson, University of St.

Andrews, Scotland, Prof. A. E. Dolbear, of Tufts College, Appleton Morgan, President of N. Y. Shakespeare Society, Rev. M. J. Savage, Dr. C. A. Bartol, Mary A. Livermore, Thomas G. Shearman, Luther R. Marsh, Henry George, A. R. McDonough, Frances E. Willard, Henry W. Hibbard, and many other eminent persons. The Bacon-Shakespeare case will be one of the most talked-of themes of the winter, and those who are not keeping abreast with the discussion will be *behind the times.*

Another very important   CRITICAL BIOGRAPHICAL
and valuable feature of   SKETCHES.
THE ARENA for 1893 will
be the regular publication of critical biographical sketches from the pens of persons eminently qualified to prepare helpful papers on the lives of eminent persons. Among the papers of this series now awaiting publication we mention the following: "Celsus," by Rev. Samuel J. Barrows, D. D., editor of the *Christian Register;* "Lao-Tsze," a Chinese mystic, by Prof. James T. Bixby, Ph. D.; "Benjamin Franklin" and "Thomas Paine," two brilliant papers by E. P. Powell, the well-known author of "Our Heredity from God," and "Charles Darwin," by the editor of THE ARENA. These studies in the lives of thought-moulders will be rich in suggestive lessons, as well as highly instructive.

                          Our short stories have proved one
SHORT STORIES,   of the most popular features of THE
PROSE ETCHINGS,   ARENA. During 1893 we will pub-
        AND   lish monthly a strong story from a
PEN PICTURES.   well-known writer. Our series for
                          next year will, taken together, make
an important contribution to the literature of the new world.

During the ensuing year we
will publish, regularly, portraits   PORTRAITS
of leading thinkers, and in cases   AND ILLUSTRATIONS.
where the text calls for illustra-
tions, choice engravings will be employed.

                          During 1892 THE ARENA, in addition to
THE BOOKS   its fifteen hundred and thirty-six pages of
      OF   reading matter, published almost two hun-
THE DAY.   dred pages of carefully prepared book re-
                  views and notices. Among the reviewers

were the editor of THE ARENA, Rabbi Solomon Schindler, Hamlin Garland, W. D. McCrackan, A. M., H. M. Starrett, and Neith Boyce. It has been the aim of the editor to have the reviews so written as to enable the reader to form a clear conception of the nature of the work and the author's style, thus enabling readers, not only to keep abreast with the book news of the day, but to judge intelligently of the merits of works before purchasing. The notices which have been set in fine type would of themselves, if set in the regular type of THE ARENA, make a volume of over five hundred pages. As this feature of THE ARENA has proved exceedingly popular, we have determined to continue it, and, in addition to the critics who have reviewed in the past, have made arrangements with Helen Campbell for occasional reviews of important works. This department is peculiar to THE ARENA, and is more than we promised our readers. It makes THE ARENA the largest review published, and adds very materially to its value. In 1893 we intend to make it a valuable bulletin of critical thought on the best books of the day.

CLOSING WORDS TO OUR READERS.

In the above we have only briefly outlined in a general way the attractions for 1893, hinting at a few of the good things we have in store for the great army of our subscribers. We believe we have in all cases in the past performed more than we have promised; and from arrangements now perfected, we feel justified in promising our readers that THE ARENA for 1893 will be abler, more brilliant, and more interesting than any previous year of its career.

In conclusion, we urge our friends who are in sympathy with our aims and objects, who believe in THE ARENA and who admire its spirit and courage, to show this review to their friends, and, when possible, induce them to give it a year's trial. We are determined to make THE ARENA for 1893 so strong, so vigorous, so brilliant, so virile, that no thoughtful man or woman can afford to be without it.

The month of driving, pelting rain and sleet; dangerous to the weak; trying even to the rugged.

To those who are weak, quick health fortification is at this time imperative. The system fortified with SCOTT'S EMULSION is well equipped to withstand the tax imposed by winter. Sudden Colds, Coughs, and Throat troubles yield promptly to its use --- equally important, it provides the system with an armor of flesh and strength that lessens chances of similar attacks later on.

SCOTT'S EMULSION

is Cod-Liver Oil made palatable and easy of assimilation. It is the essence of the life of all foods,—FAT. It checks Consumption and other forms of wasting diseases by building tissue anew—nothing mysterious—simply FOOD-LIFE going to SUSTAIN LIFE. The union of Hypophosphites of Lime and Soda adds to it a tonic effect wonderfully invigorating to brain and nerve.

PREPARED BY SCOTT & BOWNE, Chemists, New York.   SOLD BY ALL DRUGGISTS.

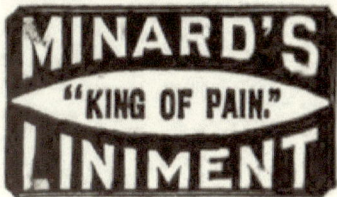

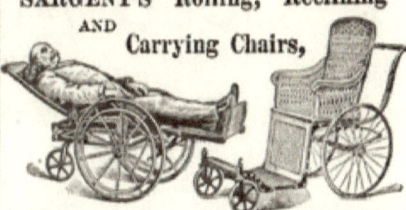

Are you dissatisfied

WITH THE STYLE AND APPEARANCE OF YOUR PRINTING?

If so

AND WISH SATISFACTORY WORK AT EQUITABLE PRICES

Correspond with the
Printers of this Magazine,

C. A. Pinkham & Co.,

289 Congress Street, Boston.

Telephone 1044.

Uptown office, 9 Milk Street.
Telephone 1081.

YES, MATTERS ARE BECOMING INTERESTING,

And in the Typewriting World to-day without doubt

The MOST interesting matter is

The New Yost Writing Machine!

And the NEXT most interesting is its

$5,000 Cash Columbian Fair Contest.

As to the Machine —

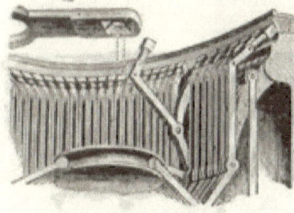

The Correct Way.

The NEW YOST, you will remember, is the champion of many new and wonderful ideas; Centre-Guide Alignment; non-wearing loose bearings; velocity touch; direct printing without ribbon; easy keyboard, etc. If you would understand its rapid march into popularity, and why it is head and shoulders above the patched-up models of other style machines, send for our handsome illustrated catalogue.

As to the Contest —

If you wish to advance the standard of typewriting, as the NEW YOST now for the first permits, by all means learn upon it, for you will at the same time master the other machines, and perhaps enrich your purse handsomely. **$5,000 in cash will positively be distributed by the judges at the World's Columbian Fair, as Follows:**

One Grand Prize of $1,000 — For the best exhibition of tabulated work, dictation, etc.

10 Prizes of $100 each — For the best original essays, subject "Typewriting as a Fine Art," etc.

20 Prizes of $50 each — For best speed on memorized sentence and dictation.

20 Prizes of $25 each — For the best transcripts of legal matter, fancy designs, etc.

50 Prizes of $10 each — (To pupils in typewriting schools only) for best essays, legal transcripts, fancy designs, business letters, etc.

10 Prizes of $100 each — **To proprietors of typewriting schools whose respective pupils obtain the largest number of above prizes.**

Write for full particulars and conditions.

Merchants Exchange National Bank, 257 Broadway, N. Y.
This is to certify that the Yost Writing Machine Co., 71 Broadway, New York, has made a special deposit with this bank of $5,000, subject to the draft of the Committee to be appointed by the Judges on Typewriters at the World's Columbian Fair at Chicago, Ill., in 1893, as described above.　　A. S. APGAR, CASHIER.
New York, June 20th, 1892.

**YOST
WRITING MACHINE CO.,
71 and 73 Broadway,
New York.**

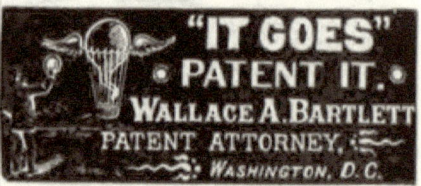

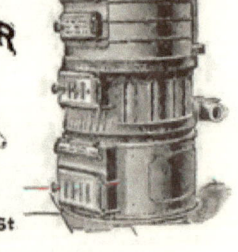

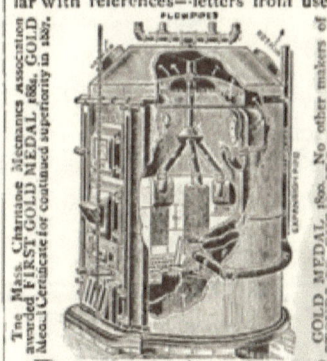

Baby's Bath of Beauty

For baby's skin, scalp and hair nothing in the whole world is so cleansing, so purifying and so beautifying as the celebrated **Cuticura Soap**, the most effective skin purifying and beautifying soap in the world, as well as purest and sweetest of toilet and nursery soaps. For irritating and scaly eruptions of the skin and scalp, with dry, thin and falling hair, red, rough hands with shapeless nails, and simple rashes and blemishes of infancy and childhood, it is absolutely incomparable. Thousands of grateful mothers pronounce it the only perfect baby soap.

CUTICURA SOAP

Is the only cure for pimples and blackheads, because the only preventive of inflammation and clogging of the pores—the cause of minor affections of the skin, scalp and hair. Sale greater than the combined sales of all other skin and complexion soaps.

How Babies Suffer when their tender skins are literally on fire with itching, scaly and blotchy skin and scalp diseases, none but mothers realize. A single application of the CUTICURA REMEDIES will afford immediate relief, permit rest and sleep, and point to a speedy and economical cure. Price: CUTICURA, the great Skin Cure, 50c.; CUTICURA SOAP, 25c.; CUTICURA RESOLVENT, the new Blood Purifier, $1.00. POTTER DRUG AND CHEMICAL CORPORATION, Boston. "ALL ABOUT THE SKIN, SCALP AND HAIR," mailed free.

c